D0090779

DEEP HARBOR

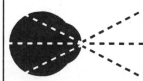

This Large Print Book carries the
Seal of Approval of N.A.V.H.

DEEP HARBOR

FERN MICHAELS

WHEELER PUBLISHING
A part of Gale, a Cengage Company

Farmington Hills, Mich • San Francisco • New York • Waterville, Maine
Meriden, Conn • Mason, Ohio • Chicago

Copyright © 2019 by Fern Michaels.
Fern Michaels is a registered trademark of KAP5, Inc.
Wheeler Publishing, a part of Gale, a Cengage Company.

ALL RIGHTS RESERVED
This book is a work of fiction. Names, characters, places, and incidents
either are the product of the author's imagination or are used
fictitiously. Any resemblance to actual events or locales or persons
living or dead is entirely coincidental.
Wheeler Publishing Large Print Hardcover.
The text of this Large Print edition is unabridged.
Other aspects of the book may vary from the original edition.
Set in 16 pt. Plantin.

LIBRARY OF CONGRESS CIP DATA ON FILE.
CATALOGUING IN PUBLICATION FOR THIS BOOK
IS AVAILABLE FROM THE LIBRARY OF CONGRESS

ISBN-13: 978-1-4328-5884-1 (hardcover)

Published in 2019 by arrangement with Kensington Books, an imprint
of Kensington Publishing Corp.

Printed in the United States of America
1 2 3 4 5 6 7 23 22 21 20 19

DEEP HARBOR

CHAPTER 1

Thirty-four-year-old Carol Anne Jansen — also known as CJ to her friends and colleagues — checked her running belt to make sure she had everything she needed for her jog along the Tidal Basin. One couldn't leave anything to chance with all the tourists, crazies, and government employees out for their daily run. Any and all manner of things could go wrong. Even in broad daylight. This was, after all, the nation's capital. And it was also an early spring break for most schools, which meant that there were twice as many tourists and crazies about.

She double-checked that she had her driver's license, which featured a picture of her round face, light brown hair that hung down to her shoulders, blue eyes — that sparkled in the sunlight, if not in the photograph — up-tilted eyebrows, narrow mouth, and tiny nose. She also had her government

ID that said she worked for Congressman Otto "Snapper" Lewis, the powerful chairman of the House Ways and Means committee, her lone credit card, and fifty dollars. She never carried more than fifty dollars for fear of having to hand it over to some thug. She was good to go. She zipped up the running belt, wrapped it around her waist, and slapped on her Fitbit.

CJ glanced over her shoulder to make sure her computer was in sleep mode. Check. Desk lamp off. Check. Desk drawers locked. Check.

The little digital clock on her desk said it was 5:10. It had been a light workday, which had allowed for the late-afternoon run. Congressman Lewis had told her she could leave even earlier, but she had declined to do so because she was conscientious to a fault. She thought about how insistent he'd been lately and wondered why, but in the end she shrugged it off as just another one of Snapper's quirks.

Satisfied that everything was in order, she opened the door to Snapper's office, and called out, "I'm leaving, boss. Unless you need me to do something." Not bothering to wait for a response, CJ rattled on. "Remember, you need to be on time this evening for that black-tie dinner at the Armory.

And I'm going to be late in the morning because I have an early appointment." CJ had an appointment with her therapist, whom she had been seeing ever since her brother, Kick, had died four years ago.

"Got it. Have a nice night, CJ."

He really doesn't sound right, CJ thought to herself. "Is something wrong, boss? You sound, I don't know, distracted? I know how you hate those dinners, but you can split after an hour. In fact, you should be leaving for the dinner now."

"I will, but I'm waiting for a phone call. Run along, CJ."

CJ chewed on her lower lip. He was waiting for a phone call? Snapper Lewis never waited for a phone call. He was the one who made the calls, and if you didn't pick up, you didn't get a second call. Weird.

"Okay, but be sure to log it in when it comes through. I don't need a ton of paperwork to chase down some dry cleaner calling to remind you to pick up your tux." It was all said in a joking manner in the hopes her boss would tell her who was calling. Nothing. It didn't work.

"Go already!" Congressman Lewis barked.

"Okay, okay, I'm gone. Be sure to turn

out all the lights and lock your desk and the door."

"Yes, Mother," he drawled, but CJ picked up the hint of anger in his voice. It was definitely time to leave.

Outside the office, CJ debated taking the elevator or the stairs. She was a health nut, so she opted for the stairs. She pulled at the heavy door and whizzed through it just as the elevator door opened. An unfamiliar scent wafted her way. *Wow,* she thought, *someone took a bath in some crappy cologne that must have come in gallon jugs.* She sniffed several times, hoping to get the abominable scent out of her nostrils.

Once she was in the parking garage, she headed to where she'd parked her ten-year-old Nissan Sentra and climbed in. The ride to the Tidal Basin wouldn't take that long; she'd run for forty minutes, then head home. The engine coughed and sputtered to life. She really needed to get a new car. Maybe a new used one. She put it on her to-do list and was about to shift from park to reverse when she remembered something that hit her like a whack to the side of her head. "Oh crap! Crap! Crap! Crap!" She had forgotten to leave the report the congressman was going to need for his 7:00 A.M. meeting. And he didn't have the keys to her desk. Banging her hands on the steering wheel, she knew she had to go back. "Hell! Well, maybe you'll start up when I get back!" she yelled at her lump of a junkmobile.

CJ hauled herself out of the car and ran back into the Rayburn House Office Building, in which she had toiled since the day she'd got out of college, twelve years ago. Twelve years. And all of them for Otto "Snapper" Lewis. There were people who said she was almost as powerful as Snapper, but she always pooh-poohed the idea. People were always trying to curry favor with the congressman and tried to get to him through her. It was a fruitless endeavor since she protected him against any and all such attempts. She was the proverbial brick wall against those he did not want to deal with. It was her job to both protect her boss and oversee the workings of his office. She wasn't sure, but she did think that she'd probably stop short of taking a bullet for him.

Because she was in good physical shape, she was able to take the stairs two at a time. When she arrived at the door that led to the hallway, her heart was pumping at the pace of a good workout. She frowned when she got a whiff of the same foul odor she'd

11

encountered earlier. Once she opened the door, the scent was so overwhelming that she gagged. The hallway smelled like a funeral home filled with too many flowers that had begun to rot.

CJ had her key in hand when she realized that the light was on in the congressman's office, which brought a frown to her face. Surely, his call must have come through by now. Rather than risk his wrath, pretended or otherwise, she walked around the corner to the second entrance to the suite and let herself into her own office, which was adjacent to his. If she was very quiet and didn't make any noise, she could be in and out, do what she had to do, and good old Snapper would never know she'd almost screwed up.

The moment she opened the door, however, she knew something was wrong. While she couldn't hear exactly what was being said, the tone of the loud voices was high-pitched and very ugly. She caught a word here and there. She stood still, uncertain what to do. Her inner self, which she relied on daily, told her to move her feet and get the hell out. Instead, she quietly advanced inside and walked over to her desk, which was in the middle of the room. Whatever was going on in the congressman's office was none of her business. It was after hours, so he was on his own. She kept trying to convince herself not to pay attention to what was transpiring in the other room.

CJ did what she had come to do. She opened her desk drawer and pulled out the bright yellow folder sitting on top. Snapper liked everything in yellow folders with bright green tabs. No other color. Just bright green tabs. It was another one of his many quirks. She centered it on her desk, relocked the drawer, and turned to leave. And that was when her leg hit the metal trash can next to her desk. She held back the desire to utter an expletive, and this time she paid attention to her inner self, which was warning her to hide.

Acting accordingly, she dropped down under her desk just as the door connecting her office to Congressman Lewis's opened. CJ sucked in her breath. The smell of cologne was so powerful, she thought she was going to gag, or even worse, sneeze.

"There's no one here. I told you my chief of staff left half an hour ago. I saw her leave. No one gets into the building after hours. Maybe you need to get your hearing checked, because I didn't hear anything. This is an old building; sounds carry through the vents. Maybe what you *think*

13

you heard is coming from the night cleaning crew. Can we just get this over with? I have a dinner I have to attend this evening. Well?" Snapper snarled as he marched back to his own office.

CJ waited, hardly daring to breathe. Would Mr. Crappy Cologne follow her boss's instructions or decide to investigate further? Ten seconds, twenty seconds. Then footsteps. But the door connecting the offices still did not close. And now she could hear them more clearly.

CJ strained to hear what the two men were saying. Whatever it was, they were not friends — of that she was absolutely certain. Snapper always treated people with respect, even those he wasn't fond of. Not this man. She could hear the hate in his voice.

"You know what you have to do. I hope I don't have to come back here again," Mr. Crappy Cologne said in a menacing tone of voice.

CJ continued to listen, hearing things that made no sense. What did make sense to her was that Mr. Crappy Cologne was threatening her boss. She heard words like "Robotron" and "getting it done pronto!" What exactly was Robotron? The name sounded familiar. She knew she'd heard it recently but could not recall where and in exactly what context. What was it?

"Just get the hell out of my office. Now!"

CJ almost jumped out of her skin when she heard the next sound. She didn't have to see the action to know that her boss had just gotten kicked in the groin. "Don't you ever make the mistake of telling me what to do again. Tell me you understand what I just said. And then tell me you're sorry," Mr. Crappy Cologne growled, demanding that Snapper demean himself with an apology.

CJ waited, hardly daring to breathe. "I understand. I'm . . . I'm sss . . . sorry," Snapper finally responded, gasping for air. CJ could hardly believe her ears. One of the most powerful men on Capitol Hill, in the country, apologizing to the man who had just pounded him to the floor. She moved slightly, so she could peek out of her hidey-hole. Directly in her line of vision she could see her boss writhing on the floor in the fetal position as he struggled to catch his breath.

After the man who had assaulted the congressman left, CJ wanted to go to her boss's aid, but her inner-self voice warned her against making such a move. Better to wait it out. In all twelve years of working for Snapper Lewis in the Rayburn House Office Building, first as a low-level aide and now as his chief of staff, this was the first time she felt as if she were swimming in deep, uncharted waters. So she leaned back and waited until she could leave without being noticed.

Finally, sounds coming from the outer office told her that Snapper was off the floor and tidying up his desk, all the time making low, groaning sounds with every move he made. She could hear him shuffling about as he packed up his briefcase. Her instincts and common sense told her he wasn't going to make the black-tie dinner that would be starting within the hour.

Finally, the lights went out, and the door to the hallway opened, then closed. CJ literally exploded from under her desk and ran into Snapper's office. It looked just the way it always looked, but it smelled terrible.

What to do? Go home of course. Take the stairs. Go slow. Make sure Snapper had left the entire area before she went back into the parking garage and hit the highway. It was lucky that his spot in the garage was nowhere near hers, so he would not see that her car was still there. She forced herself to wait ten more minutes before she exited through her own office door. Then she used up another ten minutes taking the stairs to the garage in the basement. She cursed under her breath because now she was right in the middle of rush-hour traffic.

Climbing back into her car, she hissed, "You better start up right now or off to the junkyard you go!" As if the car understood her threat, it turned over immediately. *Huh. I should try that trick every time I get into this thing.* At least something was finally going right.

Forty minutes later, the Nissan Sentra made a right turn onto the street where she lived. The traffic had been brutal. She pushed the button to open the security gate, pulled into the driveway, and stopped for a few minutes before she popped the garage door open. Every day that she lived in this house, she did the exact same thing. The deed said it was her house but she had never felt like it was hers. It had belonged to her older brother, Kick, and his life partner, Colin Kelly.

This particular house was one of the biggest, most prestigious custom-built houses in all of Kalorama, matching the elegance and historic themes of the neighborhood. She had interesting neighbors, including some of the country's highest-profile politicians and their offspring. But that merely made her feel more isolated. Not that she cared a twit about her neighbors, the house's architecture, or its furnishings, as opulent as they were. She'd give it all up in a heartbeat to have her brother Kick back in her life, so she wouldn't feel like an orphan.

When CJ was ten years old, she had been on an overnight Girl Scout camping trip when their parents died in a fiery car wreck on the way home from a yachting regatta. Kick had blamed himself because he had been racing that day. Why had he insisted that they come for the festivities? He had been racing for several years and was finally confident enough in his skills to have his family on hand. After the accident, he was guilt-ridden and took over parenting his sister. Kick had raised her, and she, in turn, had loved and adored him.

Kick was whip-smart, and by the time he, too, had been taken from her in a boat-related accident, he and Colin Kelly owned a string of sixty-four restaurants. The chain was called KC's Hatchery.

"How bizarre," she would often think. Her parents were killed coming home from a boating party and her brother was killed in a boating accident almost twenty years to the day later. She wasn't sure if she could go near the water ever again. Even jogging along the Tidal Basin gave her the willies at times.

When their parents died, it had become local gossip that the Jansens had no money. The high life of social galas, together with conspicuous overspending, had taken its toll on the family finances. The Jansens should have downsized years before they died, but CJ's mother was all about "what people thought," and the embarrassment would have killed her.

At the time of their parents' death, Kick had already graduated from the Culinary Institute of America in Hyde Park, New York, and had just gotten his MBA from Wharton. He was the "it" boy of up-and-coming restaurateurs in the DC area when his parents were killed. A life insurance policy was all that remained of their estate; their impersonation of the upper-middle-class wealthy had left them with virtually nothing else. Even their house was mortgaged to the hilt. Kick was able to use the insurance money to support CJ — at least until he could get more backing for his restaurant enterprise. One of the first people to pony up investment money was Colin Kelly, who became Kick's partner in KC's Hatchery and, eventually, his life partner.

CJ had inherited everything except for one

piece of property that Colin kept — a cabin near Salisbury on the eastern shore of Maryland. Colin and Kick would spend weekends there when they wanted to get away from all the glitz and social climbers. The Wallet Sniffers. People who always had their hand out, looking for a loan or presenting a new business proposition that needed financing. Colin and Kick were great partners, in life and business. Kick knew how to run a restaurant, and Colin knew the business side. Investing was second nature to Colin, and his skill at dealing with people was equally impressive.

After Kick's death, when the property had been settled and the will read, CJ saw — for the first time — the brokerage accounts that were now hers. They were so robust that she almost got dizzy just looking at the bottom line. She had wanted Colin to take all of Kick's estate, but he absolutely refused. He didn't want the house or Kick's half of KC's Hatchery; he didn't want the Italian sports cars in the garage. He didn't want the Aspen ski chalet or the estate in Hawaii that Kick had purchased from his share of the profits. The cabin was the only thing that gave Colin the very personal and intimate connection with Kick that he wished to maintain even after Kick's death.

In spite of all the restaurants, it was the cabin that Colin and Kick had been the most proud of, a place to which they could retreat away from the prying eyes of the public. It was something they had literally built — together. Each weekend for years, they would go to Home Depot and load up their supersized pickup truck and head out.

With Kick's death, other than the cabin, CJ owned all the property, including half of KC's Hatchery, which made her a very rich woman indeed. She could have retired at age thirty and lived a life of leisure. But she wasn't comfortable with any of it and had never given a moment's thought to retiring. She remembered hearing her parents arguing in the dark of night about money, and how much self-control it took for her father not to lose his temper over her mother's self-indulgence.

CJ sighed. Someday, she was going to figure out why she tortured herself like this every day. She didn't have to live here. She could live anywhere she wanted in Washington or the suburbs of Maryland or Virginia. After Kick had died, she somehow convinced herself that he wanted her here. Otherwise, she concluded, he wouldn't have left the ten-thousand-square-foot house to her, along with all the rest of his worldly possessions. He would have left them to Colin.

Colin had explained to her in great detail how he and Kick had made wills and how their property was to be distributed if either one of them died. Colin would get the cabin if Kick died, just as Kick would have gotten it if Colin had died. She couldn't argue with him after that discussion. He was very clear. And totally sincere. So, she had no option other than to accept Kick's wishes as expressed in his will. Nonetheless, she had never touched the money in the estate or the cars in the garage. She'd never visited the vacation spots, either. Yes, she did live in the house — that was her one concession. She used the large guest bedroom suite on the first floor. It had a luxurious adjoining bath, a small sitting room, and sliding doors that opened onto a patio surrounded by impeccable landscaping. Down the hall was the monster kitchen in which she cooked on rare occasion. Her "cooking" amounted to using a microwave to heat up a prepared dish, or perhaps leftover Chinese food she had brought home. More often than not, because of her late hours, she ate out, ordered in, or picked up something on the way home. Clearly, she was no chef like her brother.

Shaking her head over the memories of the past and the bizarre circumstance of the afternoon, she finally punched the code for the garage door, drove in, parked, and turned off the engine.

Except for her old junkmobile, the garage looked like a European sports car showroom with three Italian beauties in it: a red Maserati, an electric-blue Lamborghini, and a canary-yellow Alfa Romeo. They were all spectacular sports cars. In his leisure hours, if Kick wasn't sailing, he'd be motoring on long journeys in one of his "babies." It was his only real indulgence. The vacation homes were mostly used for cooking classes for teens who showed promise in the kitchen. There would be regional competitions, and Kick would select a handful of young adults, both men and women, who would spend several days under his tutelage. It was a superb opportunity for the young chefs.

Snapping out of her deep thoughts, CJ frowned and looked at the contrast between her heap and the shining exteriors of the Italian sports cars, exteriors whose gloss she maintained by having her local mechanic's son come every other month to keep them in top-notch condition, wiping, polishing, and taking them for a spin in the neighborhood so that they remained in fine shape.

She did a quick jog to the door leading to the kitchen but first she had to wait for the retina scanner and thumbprint scanner to recognize her, after which she had to type in a code that changed every three days, a reminder of the new code kept in her cell phone.

In plain English, it was a pain in the ass, but she was safe here in Kick and Colin's fortress. Today, she was thankful for the security. That encounter with Snapper and Mr. Crappy Cologne left her more than slightly at sea.

There was nothing particularly welcoming about the state-of-the-art kitchen because CJ had never taken the time to do anything with it. There were no green plants, no colorful place mats, no knickknacks, no magnets on the Sub-Zero refrigerator. Nothing was color coordinated. It was just a kitchen. Everything in it was high-tech, functional, and totally sterile.

CJ kicked off her sneakers, marched barefoot to the wine cooler, and pulled out a bottle of Caymus Cabernet. This was going to be both her main course *and* her dessert. She needed to think. She absentmindedly opened the bottle with the wall-mounted BOJ corkscrew and poured the

24

wine into a Baccarat goblet. She curled up on the window seat and gazed out at the backyard. It was still a little light out, so she could see the flowering shrubs along the borders and the Bloodgood Japanese maple in the center of the lawn. She downed the first glass in two gulps and poured another.

Snapper was in trouble, of that there was no doubt. Whether it was of his own making or not, she had no way of knowing. And it had something to do with Robotron, whatever that was. And the guy with the awful-smelling cologne that he apparently bathed in? She wondered how Snapper could know someone like that, someone who had kicked Snapper to the ground, then forced him to apologize, no less. It didn't make any sense. Kick had always said that when something didn't make sense, it was probably because someone was doing something that was just plain stupid.

CJ was about to pour her third glass of wine when she thought about her early appointment with her therapist. She quickly sent off a text to the shrink's after-hours phone. No way was she going to keep that appointment tomorrow, not with what was going on at the office. She was going to go in early and see how Snapper had documented the phantom phone call that had probably never happened, and she would check the log book to see how he recorded Mr. Crappy Cologne's visit. She was virtually certain that there would be no entry for a phone call or a visit. She could mention the phone call but not the visit. To do so would alert Snapper that she had been in the office after she had left for the day.

Maybe she needed to eat something. Crackers, maybe, but she didn't have any. She looked in the Sub-Zero, but the only thing in there was a wedge of cheese and some leftover Chinese food, with hair growing on it. After she tossed the Chinese, she ripped the wrapper off the cheese and bit down. Extra sharp cheddar. With a real tang. It made her eyes water. She spit it out and went back to her goblet to rinse her mouth. "How about that for spending money wisely," she quipped, "a sixty-five-dollar bottle of mouthwash!" Being wasteful wasn't her style. But a good bottle of wine was about the only extravagance she allowed herself.

CHAPTER 2

Congressman Lewis fumbled with his key fob at the door of his Watergate condo. His hand was shaking so badly, it took three tries before he managed to get the door unlocked. He pushed the door open and galloped into the condo as though hounds were on his heels. He loved hearing the sound of the door closing, knowing it would lock automatically. He dropped his heavy briefcase in the middle of the foyer and made a beeline for the bar on the wall of the long, spacious living room. The room was his favorite place in the whole twenty-five-hundred-square-foot condominium. From that room, he had a spectacular view of the city. He thought about making his special martini — five ounces of gin, one-half ounce of vermouth, a twist of lemon, and some Angostura bitters — but decided he needed a pure hit of the twenty-five-year-old Glenlivet scotch he kept for special occasions. Not that this was the kind of occasion he had been thinking of. Hand shaking, he upended the bottle and guzzled until his eyes started to water. Then he poured two ounces into a squat tumbler and headed for the black leather sofa in the middle of the room.

"Son of a bitch!" he bellowed to the emptiness around him. "Son of a bitch!" he roared a second time. He gulped at the amber liquid in the tumbler, then set it down on the glass coffee table with a thump. Why was he so upset? He had known this day might come. Knew it in every pore of his body. He had lived in fear of it, and now that it was here, he wasn't prepared.

How weird that he could handle world affairs, raise money out the wazoo, schmooze on both sides of the aisle, and yet he couldn't take care of his own goddamn business.

Snapper leaned back into the soft, luxurious, leather sofa and closed his eyes. Life as he'd come to know it was never going to be the same. He mourned the loss as his mind raced. But did he deserve to go down in flames for trying to help a family member? Didn't his thirty years in the House of Representatives count, the last six of which as the chairman of the Ways and Means committee after being the ranking member for two years before that? But he knew that he would be remembered — if he was remembered at all — for what was about to happen, and it made him feel sick to his stomach. Too much whiskey with no food. Not a good plan.

He struggled out of the depths of the sofa and shuffled into the kitchen, where he made a pot of coffee and headed to the master bedroom. He stripped down and pulled on a set of ancient sweats from his college years, which still fit his six-foot-two, two-hundred-twenty-pound frame. They were like old friends, and he would never give them up, not for anything. They defined him was how he thought of it. He was never an "out-with-the-old-and-in-with-the-new" kind of guy. He padded back to the kitchen to make himself a sandwich.

Snapper's twice-a-week day-housekeeper always made sure the refrigerator was full. Snapper wondered who ate the food because he rarely ate at home even though he was an excellent cook. But cooking took time, one of the few things he did not have. He finally came to the conclusion the she ate the food herself or took it home to her family. And could he begrudge her that? Not at all. She was a woman of modest means, and since he hated to see anything go to waste, he never said a word, glad that he could help.

Snapper sliced thick pieces from an Applewood Farms ham. Adding lettuce, tomatoes, and Duke's Mayonnaise, he had it all. The sandwich was so thick, he had to press down with the palms of his hands or he wouldn't be able to bite into it. He forced himself to eat and drank two cups of black coffee. Eyeing the Glenlivet bottle he'd carried into the kitchen, he shook his head. He had had enough for one day. He needed his wits about him from here on in.

Jesus, Mary, and Joseph! He'd forgotten all about the black-tie dinner at the Armory. Damn it to . . . He looked at the clock. By now, the waitstaff would be serving dessert and coffee. There was no way he could make it at this point. He consoled himself with the fact that Dick Franz, the congressman from Delaware, had told him in the middle of the afternoon that he was going home because of a stomach bug that had hit the House Office Building. As far as excuses went, it would have to do. Not that he usually cared one way or another about missing a dinner. And right now, he certainly didn't care. Tomorrow, when he had to explain to CJ why he didn't attend, would be a different story. But the stomach excuse would suffice.

Carol Anne Jansen, with the winsome smile, shoulder-length light brown hair, and sparkling blue eyes. If he had a daughter, he would want her to be just like CJ. He was so fond of her that he had put her in his will. Although, her being much wealthier than he could hope to be, she would never need anything from him, but it was a gesture on his part to show how much he valued her as a person. He appreciated and loved her loyalty to him and her job. Little did she know he had a complete dossier on her filed away in the condo directly underneath where he was standing. He'd taken a page out of J. Edgar Hoover's playbook and kept dossiers on every single member of the House of Representatives and the Senate. He had years' and years' worth of files. One just never knew what to expect in Washington, so it was "cover your ass" no matter how low you were or how high you rose. And he had done just that.

Only on a very rare occasion was he required to use any of the information he'd compiled to get a bill passed. But now it looked like he was going to have to use some of it when the Medical Advancement financing bill came up for a vote in three days.

What mattered was Robotron, not necessarily the good of the people. But then again, rarely was legislation altruistic, more often being a matter of which special interests stood to gain from any piece of legislation and how that would affect one's chances of reelection.

Snapper tidied up the kitchen and cleaned the coffeepot before he headed to the stairway that would take him down to the condo he'd bought directly underneath this one. He owned the lower condo but didn't live in it. It was basically a "safe house," except that rather than a place of safety for people, it was a repository of information. The condo had only the bare essentials in the way of furnishings, which kept the maintenance down to a minimum. Still, the dusty remnants of his best friend Billy Sykes remained.

Billy and Snapper had been friends for years, from even before Snapper had first been elected to the House. Billy was also his accountant and financial advisor. Billy, in fact, was someone he trusted with his life. The trust from which the bills for Snapper's brother's care were paid was in a fictitious name that Billy had arranged. It had taken a lot of maneuvering, but Billy was magician-like when it came to moving money. He had even managed to transfer the proceeds from the sale of the Lewis family horse farm in Colts Neck into that special account. A little less than one and a half million dollars. Seemed like a lot of money at the time, but with the facility charging twenty-five thousand a month for George's care, he had known that even with a 5 percent return on the principal and the one million from the insurance company it would barely last ten years, and they were now going into year thirteen at Sun Valley Institute . . . long past George's life expectancy.

When George was thirty-five, he had suffered a brain aneurism. The medical term was subarachnoid hemorrhage. Similar to a stroke. It had left George debilitated to the extent he could not speak and lost all movement on the entire left side of his body. He needed round-the-clock care. He was given a very grave prognosis. Maybe two, three years to live. By that time, Snapper, at age forty-seven, was beginning his ninth term in Congress. But as the years passed, George remained in a comatose state. The EEG showed some brain activity, but there was no physical movement of any kind. He was not technically brain-dead, so the artificial care continued. Snapper recalled the Karen

Ann Quinlan case, in which she did not die until nine years after her family obtained a court order to remove her from the "extraordinary means" of a ventilator, but Snapper was not about to unplug his brother.

Growing up, there wasn't much sibling rivalry between them. In fact, there wasn't a whole lot of interaction of any kind. George had been a "surprise" to his parents, so by the time George was five, Snapper was about to graduate from high school and head off to college. To George, he had always been the distant big brother.

With their parents gone, and no other family, it became incumbent on Snapper to see to George's well-being. He knew he couldn't care for George at home, so he decided to find a quiet place for George to live out whatever life he still had left to him.

Insurance only covered the costs up to a certain point, and Snapper had to make some hard decisions. But no one ever thought George would have remained alive for this amount of time. Nope. The two and a half million hadn't lasted nearly long enough, and five years ago, Snapper had started to become desperate about how he would be able to continue to provide for George.

He supposed that his need to care for his

brother was one of the reasons he was so particularly fond of CJ. Her brother had cared for her when the family was in crisis. Another was that he had no other family to speak of. Yes, other than George, CJ was about as close to family he had.

Billy Sykes had now been off the grid for over five years. Otto "Snapper" Lewis still didn't quite understand how Billy had managed to set up the trust so Snapper could access it without question from the financial institutions and the convalescent center where George lived . . . if one could call what George had a life. But Billy arranged for all transactions to come from the trust fund although the original funds in it had been depleted over time. In this way, it was possible to keep George's condition a secret, allowing Snapper to avoid the inevitable media attention knowledge of George and Snapper's relationship would bring. The media loved horror stories, and Snapper wasn't going to allow him and his brother to become an act in a media circus.

Standing by the door to the stairway, Snapper thought back to one of the strangest and saddest days of his life.

He and Billy would often meet for a getaway in the Everglades. Snapper loved to take photos of the mangroves and the gators. One Friday afternoon, he got a call at the office from Billy, who said, "We gotta meet, Snapper. I'll be at the fishing hut in the Everglades tomorrow afternoon. Be there. It's urgent."

Snapper couldn't recall a time in the past when Billy had pressured him to meet him anywhere. Billy's voice was tense, almost panicked. Snapper got off the phone and booked a flight on the next plane from DC National to Miami. He'd have a car rental waiting, then make the hour-long drive to the airboat marina where he and Billy would load up their gear and head out for fishing and shooting photos.

Snapper was trying to quell the tension. A few shots of whiskey on the plane had helped calm his nerves. He could not imagine what the emergency was, but it had to be bad if Billy needed to see him. And see him in a very remote location.

It was about six o'clock when Snapper maneuvered the light craft through the canals, skimming the surface of the water. He had mastered this unique vessel years before, allowing him to enjoy the quiet and solitude of the Everglades. It was the contrast with the fiery debates, long, drawn-out arguments, and seemingly unending committee meetings that made his time in the Everglades so alluring.

The sun was setting, and the sky was a panorama of pink, purple, and puffy orange clouds. In the summer, the thunderheads coming off the Everglades water would create havoc, with downpours and horrific lightning. One needed to be prepared for such an occasion although most of the trips Snapper and Billy took were in the early spring. Snapper marveled at the sight of the colors in the sky.

As he rounded the last mangrove before the campsite, he saw Billy, dressed in a sweat suit and wearing hip boots, building a small fire, which Snapper assumed would be used to cook their dinner. Whatever they caught, they cooked. Alligators, of course, were off-limits as far as hunting was concerned. Photos of those reptilian creatures were all one was allowed.

Snapper skimmed the marsh and shut down the propeller. He gave his sports bag a heave and tossed it over the side of the boat. "Billy! What the hell is going on? Everything okay?"

"Snap. Things are really heating up. We gotta, or at least I gotta, pull out of this. I've been hearing they are getting into bank accounts and trusts to try to follow terrorist money."

"What are you talking about? They? Who?"

"FBI, I heard. Listen, you're okay, and the transfers will remain intact. I made all the arrangements for you, but I have to disappear."

"Billy, what the hell are you talking about?" Snapper repeated his original question, but he was a little more aggressive this time.

"Snapper. There has been a lot of chatter about the source of the money for these terrorist cells."

"But isn't that confidential? I do work for the US government. I think I have a grasp of the law!" Snapper was getting impatient.

"Yeah. Well, there is a lot of crap going down. While they were looking for the money chains for terrorists, they came across a lot of stuff that had nothing to do with what they were originally searching for. A lot. Not just transfers of money but insider trading as well. The FBI is under a lot of pressure lately to prove they know what the hell they're doing. Ever since nine/ eleven, people have been asking questions, and not many of them have been answered. It's causing a lot of trouble in the Bureau. I'm sure I don't need to tell you! Anyway, the NSA started audio surveillance on major players, and when they got some intel about money transfers, they brought in the FBI. Then the FBI discovered some large deposits in the accounts of high-ranking government officials. There is a lot of trouble brewing, and I have to become invisible. Real soon. Like now."

Snapper was stupefied. "Okay. Slow down. Let's take this one piece at a time. I knew the NSA was investigating some people, and yes, I know it's an invasion of privacy, but with the Homeland Security Act, they can pretty much look up anyone's ass if they want. So you're saying that they caught some chatter about large wire transfers?"

"Yeah. Pretty much. And with me being a broker and handling those kinds of transfers, they're looking at everything I touch. So I created a dummy account that cannot be traced back to me that you will be able to access and still do what you need to do for George. Here." Billy handed Snapper a thick envelope. "It's all in here. The passwords, the account numbers. And the deed to my condo. It's yours. I have got no family, so use it for the 'George Project.' It can be your secret office."

Snapper could not believe what he was hearing. "This is giving me the creeps, Billy. What are you going to do?"

"I have places in Belize and in Costa Rica. I'm a small enough operator that I doubt they'll waste time and effort to make a case and come after me. They're looking for bigger fish . . . no pun intended. But if I stay, I might get caught up in some sting operation they initiate so they can get people higher on the food chain."

"But wait. What about this insider-trading thing? Do you think we've been exposed in some way?" Beads of sweat were forming on Snapper's forehead, and it wasn't from the humidity.

"I've got you set up so you can move the funds in small increments, which won't set off any bells. It's all in there." Billy pointed to the pouch. "Trust me."

"I always have, Billy. How will I contact you?"

"You won't. This is it, *mi amigo.* I love you like a brother, but if you know where I am, it could ultimately end up bad for both of us. The less you know, the better. In fact, the only things you need to know are in that folder. Save yourself, Snap." Billy moved closer to Snapper and threw his arms around him. "Be well and take care of George."

"Billy, aren't you going to stay and have some supper?" Snapper could see that he'd already caught, cleaned, and spitted some fish.

"Sorry, Snap, I'm out of here. My plane is leaving tonight, and I intend to be on it." And with that, Billy jumped into the airboat he had rented earlier and took off, leaving Snapper standing alone with a most bewildered expression on his face.

That was the last time Snapper ever saw Billy, and he never heard from him again. Nor did anyone ever ask any questions after Billy "moved out." Not one. The man had no family and no friends, just business acquaintances and Snapper. And anyone who was acquainted with Billy just assumed he had moved to Costa Rica, something he had spoken of doing a number of times. As far as the world in which Billy had moved was concerned, it was as if the man had never existed.

Snapper knew Billy would have covered all the bases and secured the folder in a waterproof cooler. He wasn't up for any dense reading that night, and he wouldn't feel safe going through that kind of paperwork in a swamp anyway. No, reading what Billy had given him would have to wait until he returned to DC the next day.

On the flight back, Snapper wondered how someone like Billy Sykes managed not to leave a footprint. But Billy was stealthy and clever, which was another reason Snapper had trusted him as much as he did.

Still standing by the door, Snapper returned his thoughts to the task at hand. The door had a stainless steel Bio-Mastic Fingerprint Deadbolt. Snapper pressed his finger on the lock and opened the door to the stairway that led down to Billy's — make that Snapper's second — condo. He turned on the lights and checked everything — the appliances, the door locks, the windows. He turned the air-conditioning unit higher to get rid of the musty smell. Even though he visited the condo once a week, it still held an empty, no-one-lives-here feel to it.

Snapper headed straight for the spare room Billy had used for his office. He hadn't changed a thing except Billy's password, which was now "Gator." He hated the word but knew he needed to use something he would *never* forget. And what had happened that day in the Everglades would be something he would never forget.

He turned on the computer and waited for it to boot. He moved the mouse to the icon that would bring up the brokerage account that Billy had arranged. He e-mailed the broker, bought a few stocks, and then, as an afterthought, sent a personal e-mail to the broker, asking him what he thought of Robotron. The broker replied that it had been a solid company with an excellent business model, but its stock had been steadily declining. It had been at one hundred dollars a share in January, but had slipped to sixty over the past several months. Its earnings report had been disappointing. Snapper instructed him to place an order for five thousand shares with a limit of thirty dollars per share. There were no questions from Billy's broker because Snapper made sure he never deviated from Billy's trading practices and instructions.

Three days later, the news of a Robotron recall hit the media like a tornado. Thousands of robotic operating devices, it seemed, were going to be recalled. The stock tumbled and lost 50 percent of its value within a week — hitting that magical number of thirty dollars per share. The recall was the tipping point for Robotron.

This was going to be the last one. The last bit of financial sleight of hand. Billy had been right those five years ago. He had seen it coming. There was a growing speculation in the capital about inside information being used to make killings in the market, but using the information he had on how to make a bundle was too much to resist, especially considering the twenty-five thousand dollars he had to pay out each month for George. Shortly after Billy's departure, President Obama signed STOCK, the Stop Trading on Congressional Knowledge Act. The heat was on. Yes. This last trade would be the end of it. It had to be.

The following week, when the vote on the Medical Advancement financing bill came to the floor of the House, as agreed, Snapper voted yes. Yes to increased spending on medical research. Research in robotics.

Within days of the bill's passing, a press conference was held, and a spokesperson from Robotron made a startling announcement. *There was going to be no recall.* The report of such a recall had been part of the "fake news" tidal wave. The spokesperson went on to say, "Unfortunately, our entire computer system was hacked. We have called in the NSA to assist in finding and apprehending the criminals who so boldly breached our system. We regret any and all loss of value for our shareholders, but we can reassure everyone that we will make this right by continuing to provide the best and most advanced technology in robotic medical technology."

Shareholders who sold off their stock when it was in freefall were furious, but those who bought the shares after they fell were ecstatic.

With the passage of the Medical Advancement financing bill, Robotron executives immediately sought out the new government funding. They were wise not to take company jets — as those idiots from the auto industry had done back in 2008, a piece of idiocy that had allowed the media to have a field day criticizing government bailouts even though, as things turned out, the taxpayers actually saw a substantial return on the government investment. In any event, it took very little to convince the overseers of the money that some of it should be used to help Robotron advance the field of robotic surgery. The news of the financial infusion gave Robotron stock the kick in the ass Snapper and his cohorts had been counting on. The stock raced up to seventy dollars per share. The market went wild over the stock — just like Abracadabra when they went for their IPO. Snapper was relieved and dismayed at the same time. He knew that what he had done was wrong. It was illegal and immoral, but he saw no other way to help keep his brother in a good health-care facility.

Snapper reviewed the last two weeks to himself. *Time to get out of this game. I have about four more years' worth of money for George socked away in that account, and it just keeps getting riskier — especially with that weasel Leonard Franklin. Cripes, does he have to take a bath in that cheap cologne? This has to end. That pharmaceutical distribution bill is coming up, and I don't want to be any part of fueling the opioid epidemic. Even with all the PR and antidrug ads, it would be years before two million addicts got clean. If ever. No. I don't care who else is involved. Let* them *make the money. I'm done. It's over.*

CHAPTER 3

CJ had noticed that Snapper had been very edgy over the last two weeks. When she tried to talk to him, he would blow her off. She realized she hadn't asked him about the black-tie dinner for fear she would slip up and mention the guy with the stinky cologne, but then thought it would be odd if she never asked him.

"Hey, boss, I meant to ask, how was that black-tie dinner at the Armory week before last?"

"Huh? What? Black-tie . . . oh yeah . . . must have been some kind of bug; my stomach was upset, so I decided not to go. Eating a rubber chicken would have just made it worse."

Considering the wallop he took from Mr. Crappy Cologne, CJ wasn't surprised that he had not gone, but she wasn't going to push any further. Something was amiss, and her inner self was nagging the hell out of her.

"Boss, I'm going to get some lunch. Want me to bring you anything?" A typical, normal, everyday kind of question.

"What? No." That was becoming an automatic response to almost everything she asked.

"You okay? You seem a little stressed. Is there anything I can do? Schedule a massage?"

"I'm fine. I just need to clear my head. Go. Get some lunch. I'm fine. Really."

CJ was not convinced he was fine, but she grabbed her jacket and headed out for a stroll and a salad. She, too, needed to clear her head. *What is going on with Snapper? He is certainly beginning to behave like his nickname.* She shrugged, took the stairs, and strolled past the security guard's station.

"Getting a bite. Want me to pick up a cup of java on my way back?"

"I'm good, but thanks." Marcus, the security guard, gave CJ a two-finger salute.

Suddenly, she noticed a familiar smell. That god-awful cologne again!

"Hey, Marcus," she said, turning back to the guard, "did someone just come through stinking like a French whorehouse?"

"French whorehouse? What have you been

doing with your free time, Ms. Jansen? How would you know what a French whorehouse smells like?"

"No, seriously. There's a guy who's been in the building who wears this absolutely abominable cologne. More like takes a bath in it." She screwed up her face as if she just smelled horse manure.

"I thought I smelled something, but I thought it was the cleaning people trying out some new kind of disinfectant, but can't say I saw anybody with a cloud hanging around them . . . you know, like that kid in the *Peanuts* cartoon?"

CJ smiled at the thought of Pig Pen. "No, I think Pig Pen probably smells better! See you in a bit."

That smell. She could not get it out of her nose. And she knew it was the same stench that had wafted from Snapper's office that horrible night.

When CJ returned with her salad, the smell was still pervasive. "Marcus, are you sure you didn't *smell* anyone come through? The odor is still in the air!"

"I took a quick break a few minutes ago. Maybe. But let me check with Carl." Marcus picked up his walkie-talkie. "Yo, Carl, you have anyone come through smelling like a French whore?" He winked at CJ. "No.

Everything is cool here. Just got a noseful of something and was wondering." The voice on the other end of the walkie-talkie signed off, saying, "You got too much free time on your hands, brother."

CJ, still not convinced, headed toward her office with lunch in hand only to find that Snapper had left. And without leaving a note. Nothing. Except that smell again! His coat was gone and so was his briefcase. She checked both calendars: his and her own. Nothing on either one. No committee meetings, no appointments. This was really out of character for Snapper. He was diligent about always letting her know his whereabouts in case there were any emergencies, calls, or meetings that were arranged at the last minute.

She ran toward the elevator and anxiously pushed the button for the lobby. *Cripes, I should have taken the stairs. Freaking elevators. They're as old as this town!*

When she reached the ground floor, she started toward Marcus but thought better of it. He would think she was losing her mind. It had taken her a while to get over her brother's death, and she knew that some folks thought she was still a little shaky even after four years. Looking for a mysterious man who smelled like cheap cologne would certainly add to everyone's concern that she wasn't fully recovered from the trauma of his death.

She breezed past the security desk, trying to pick up the scent again. *Add bloodhound to my résumé,* she mockingly chided herself. Several corridors down, the smell was getting stronger again when she heard voices coming from inside Congressman Dillard's office. Loud voices. And familiar. She had heard that voice before — and not just Dillard's — as surely as she had smelled that horrible stench before. She tried to lean closer to the door, but too many people were coming back from lunch to do so unobtrusively, and she was beginning to feel self-conscious.

Maybe I'm being paranoid, she tried to tell herself. No. The fine hairs on the back of her neck definitely said otherwise. And her nose agreed wholeheartedly. Something was fishy, and it was something more than the smell. Suddenly, she heard one of the voices announce in a tone that indicated that the speaker was fed up, "I said I'll take care of it!" On that note, one of the doors to the hallway opened, and she immediately turned to walk in the opposite direction. Oh, that smell! It's him all right! She tried to get a good look at his face, but he clearly knew to keep his head down and was well aware of the placement of the security cameras. Her palms were starting to sweat. She needed to move fast but not too fast. She was already feeling conspicuous.

CJ took the stairs back to her office to see if she had overlooked anything, any clue that Snapper might have left as to why he had disappeared in such an unusual way. Again, nothing.

Having nothing to go on to understand Snapper's behavior, she tried to busy herself with answering the pile of e-mails she had printed out, watching the mini digital clock slowly mark the afternoon hours. She finally picked up her cell and dialed Colin.

"Hey, Col, you going to the cemetery on Saturday?"

"Don't I always?" Colin sighed. "I know I'm just torturing myself."

"I hear ya."

"Why? You have something in mind?"

"Can we have lunch afterward? I need to pick your brain."

"Ha. You mean what's left of it. Tell me, what's going on, CJ? Everything okay?"

"I'm not really sure, and I don't want to sound crackers. See you at eleven?"

"You got it."

CJ was relieved that she was going to see

Colin on Saturday. She missed the dinners her brother would prepare for the three of them. Colin had a really good head on his shoulders and was very savvy when it came to all sorts of investments, including stocks. She was going to ask him about Robotron.

Finally, when the LED changed from 4:29 to 4:30, she grabbed her coat and headed down the stairs. When she got to the garage, she noticed that Snapper's car was still in its spot. She wondered if Snapper had taken a car service. But that seemed unlikely since she would have been the one to make the reservation. *I'm not liking any of this.*

CJ walked to her own car, got in, and patted the dashboard as if it were her pet. "You're going to start up just fine for me, aren't you? I've already had enough excitement for one day."

She made the sign of the cross and laughed. She wasn't Catholic, but she had seen that gesture so often, she thought it couldn't hurt. She turned the key, and the car started without a hitch. At last! Something was working right. She really needed to get a new car. Though she had several in her garage, they were all much too expensive to her taste. Maybe she should trade one of them in and get another. She could get two others for as much as one of those cars cost.

Actually, she could probably get several cars. She knew so little about high-end cars that she could barely distinguish one make of Italian sports car from another. Maybe it was time to be practical instead of fearful. Ever since her parents' death, the memories of their angry voices, late at night, arguing about money had led CJ to resolve never to live anywhere near beyond her means. And to her, that meant budgeting in accordance with the money she earned from working as Snapper Lewis's chief of staff. Given that she was a multimillionaire with an income from her half of the business that dwarfed her government salary, she knew she was being ridiculous. In addition, she could easily afford to buy a new car on her salary alone, for heaven's sake.

Yeah, maybe this week. It's time. It was past time for her to get over her mourning and begin to enjoy what her brother had left her. "Kick would want you to," Colin would constantly nag at her. She resigned herself to getting it done. But nothing ostentatious. She and Colin would go look for cars together. Everyone knew that male customers were much more likely to get a good deal from a car salesman than female customers.

When she turned onto her street, after

unlocking the security gate, entering the garage, and waiting to go through the hoops necessary to enter the house proper, she took a deep breath and contemplated whether she should open the Brunello or the Nebbiolo. Both were warm and rich and looked beautiful in the wine goblet. "Damn it. I forgot to pick up cheese." She got back in her car, backed out of the garage, and made a quick trip to her favorite gourmet market.

That was another thing Kick had taught her — wine pairings. The only big question was which bottle was she going to open? She'd get an assortment of cheeses and figure that out when she was finally ready to sit down and ponder the recent odd happenings.

When she was back home and in the house, she decided on the Nebbiolo, poured the wine into a goblet, and made a nice cheese board for herself. Realizing that she had been sitting for over an hour reminiscing about her days with Kick and Colin, she snapped back to the task at hand. She also realized that she had made a good dent in the bottle.

What to do? Open another? No, that would just make her groggy, and she needed to think. Think! What, she asked herself, was going on with Snapper? He seemed so edgy. And that guy, the one who stunk so bad? Who was he?

The sudden sound of the phone made her jump out of her seat! Who the hell was calling at this hour, she wondered? It was late. Looking at her phone, it said, "Boss." With a sigh of relief she answered the phone and blurted, "Finally! Where are you? What is going on? Is everything okay? Why didn't you leave me a note when you left?" The words were tumbling out of her mouth before she could hear an answer.

"Hello. Is this Carol Anne Jansen?" a strange voice came through the line.

"Speaking. Who is this? And why are you calling from my boss's phone?" CJ was uneasy.

"This is Detective Daniel Harris. Your name and number was in Congressman Lewis's phone, listed under 'In Case of Emergency.' "

"What emergency?"

"I'm afraid I have some bad news, Ms. Jansen. Can you come down to the precinct?"

After the events of the past couple of weeks, CJ wasn't sure that the person on the other end of the line was really a police detective and not some impostor.

"What precinct? What are you talking about?" CJ was getting more agitated.

"First District Substation. Or would you prefer we have someone pick you up?"

Well, that wasn't going to happen. She had no idea who this guy was. It could be Mr. Crappy Cologne for all she knew.

"No. I'll come down. Where should I go? Whom should I ask for? What is this all about? Can't you tell me anything?" CJ was trying not to panic.

Getting no good answers to her questions other than that she should ask for Detective Daniel Harris, she thought that perhaps she should call Colin and ask him to go to the station with her. But it would take too long for him to get here. She'd have to take her little junkmobile out one more time. But then, realizing that her very-much-used auto was never reliable, she thought once more, *Cripes, I need a new car. That's all I need is that hunk of junk to break down while I'm doing the same!* So, she tapped the Uber app on her phone. *Stay calm,* she kept telling herself.

Instead of calling, she sent a text to Colin: **Something happened to Snapper. Going to police station. Will call when I know more**. She realized that Colin probably wouldn't see her text until the morning, but she wanted him to be on call then if she needed him.

Within a few minutes, an Uber arrived, and she hopped in. "First District Substation at Capitol Hill." The driver nodded. *He looks like he's twelve,* she thought to herself. "You know how to get there?"

"Yes, ma'am," he said, as he pushed the gas pedal to the floor, throwing CJ back into the seat. *No wonder they're trying to regulate these guys,* she thought to herself as she shook her head. More regulations. Swell. More work for me. But in this case, maybe not such a bad idea.

CHAPTER 4

After a hair-raising ride to the precinct, CJ threw two twenty-dollar bills at the driver. "Here. Keep the change. And buy a map, for heaven's sake!"

Bouncing from the Uber as quickly as she could, CJ noticed she was almost out of breath. She hadn't run anywhere, but the anxiety arising from the disturbing phone call was making her sweat. She ran up the front steps of the police station, bumping into people as she took two steps at a time. "Sorry . . . excuse me . . . sorry . . ."

"Hey, lady. Slow down. Nobody's in no hurry to get into a police station. . . ." one onlooker grumbled at her.

"Sorry . . . so sorry . . ." Breathless and shaking, she walked over to the front desk. "Is there a Detective Harris here? Daniel Harris, I think is his name."

"Okay. Take it easy, miss. Yes, there is a Detective Harris here. Whom shall I say is inquiring?" The red-haired cadet with green eyes and a pleasant-looking face smiled reassuringly.

"I'm . . . I'm CJ, uh . . . Carol Anne Jansen. He called me about Congressman Lewis."

Suddenly, the expression on the cadet's face became somber. "One minute, please. I'll get him." He picked up the phone and pushed a button. "Detective Harris? There's a Miss Jansen here. She said you called her? Right. Will do." As he clicked the phone he looked up at CJ. This time the sympathy showed very clearly. "He'll be right with you."

Within two minutes, a tall man, over six feet, around fifty years old, thin and fit, with a full head of salt-and-pepper hair, came into the lobby. When he opened his mouth to greet her, the caps on his front teeth shone in the light from the overhead illumination. "Miss Jansen? I'm Daniel Harris. Won't you come into my office?"

"Yes, of course. What is this all about?" CJ was trying to maintain her composure, but her inner self was telling her to scream.

Harris offered her a chair. "Please sit down."

"I can't until you tell me what's going on," she responded, her voice rising. "Where is

Snapper? I mean Congressman Lewis? What is going on? Why am I here?" She took a deep breath and steadied herself by leaning her hand on the back of the chair in front of her.

As soon as the words "I am sorry to inform you . . ." came out of the detective's mouth, CJ thought she would faint but readied herself for the rest of the sentence. ". . . Congressman Lewis's body was found in his car earlier this evening. It was an apparent suicide."

CJ thought she heard an oncoming train rush through her mind. "What? What did you just say?"

"Unfortunately, Congressman Lewis took his own life."

"But how? Why? That's just not possible! He would *never* do such a thing!" CJ protested as if her words would make it not be true.

"Carbon-monoxide poisoning."

"Carbon-monoxide poisoning?" she parroted.

"Yes. Apparently, he connected a hose from the exhaust pipe of his car, attached the hose to the front window of his car using duct tape, and pumped the gas into the car."

"I just can't believe this. I cannot believe

this is happening. Happened. Where?" She was shaking, her voice shrill.

"In the garage at the Rayburn Building. Security found him around eight this evening."

"The garage at the Rayburn Building? This is not making any sense. He left the office early, but his car was still in its place when I left. But he wasn't in the car. I thought he had taken a car service even though I had not booked one. I cannot believe this. Where is he now?"

"They took him to the county morgue. Do you know of any family members we should contact?"

"I think he has a brother somewhere, but he never talked about any family. Never. Ever. Some people are like that. They have no one." Suddenly, it hit CJ that she had suffered yet another loss, and she burst into tears. "I'm sorry. It's just . . . I mean . . . I can't believe this. Any of it." She wiped her eyes on her sleeve. "Did he leave a note? Anything?"

"I'm sorry to say he did not. Actually, about two-thirds of suicides do not leave a note. I guess they figure people would know; or they are in such a state of despair, they don't think about it. It's the act itself they focus on. Or so I've been told."

Trying to hold it together, she gave him a quizzical look. *How would you know what they focus on if they're already dead?*

As if he read her mind, Harris continued. "There have been thousands of unsuccessful suicides, and when/if the person is in therapy, they usually tell their therapist about what they were thinking when they attempted to commit suicide. Of course, we don't know any personal information about the patients, but the mental-health community has been gathering statistics for the past two decades."

Heaving a big sigh, as if trying to clear her head, CJ asked about the car and its contents. "Was his briefcase in the car? Did he leave any kind of clue? Are you absolutely certain it's him?" She was begging for a different outcome.

Harris understood the shock. He had seen it many times before. Sometimes the person whom you least expect takes his or her own life.

"Yes, we have his fingerprints and are waiting on the dental records. But the fingerprints match." Harris lifted the folder from his desk. "Do you think you want to take a look at his photo? We took it from the morgue's closed-circuit camera. Maybe that will give you some closure."

"I . . . I suppose so," CJ stuttered, and took a deep breath as Harris handed her the photo of what appeared to be the dead congressman. It only took a brief glance to see it was Snapper. CJ was starting to shake uncontrollably.

"Can I get you a glass of water?"

"No. I'm . . . I'm fine. What about his car?" CJ was trying to keep her composure as her mind was racing.

"The car was towed to the police lot and there are a few personal items. Forensics is done, so we can release them. Do you want to get them? I can walk you over."

"Thank you. I'd appreciate that." She stood as tall as she could, shoulders back, head up, hoping her legs would not give out on her.

As Detective Harris ushered CJ through the precinct, he asked her casual questions. How long have you known the congressman? How long have you worked for him? Was he easy to get along with? Did he have much of a social life with all the hours he put in?

It all seemed innocuous, but CJ felt that there was an underlying agenda behind the banal questions, and she answered them in the same manner they were delivered. Matter-of-factly. Twelve years. Twelve years.

Yes. Grouchy sometimes but generally kind. The only social life he had were those boring black-tie events where he would have to make "a cameo appearance." That's how he referred to his attendance.

When they reached the car, the detective opened the front passenger side. "It's totally clear now . . . the air quality, I mean."

As CJ poked her head in to open the glove compartment, she gasped at the smell. But it wasn't the smell of any kind of gas. It was the smell of god-awful cologne.

Whipping her head from out of the car, she barked, "Detective, did anyone look at the security surveillance tapes? Did anyone look at it at the time he was supposed to have killed himself?"

"Most cameras are primarily focused on the entrance and exits. We just don't have the man . . . I mean people-power to cover every square inch of every building in this city. Parking garages are secure enough since you need a series of pass codes to get in and out. We keep the footage for thirty days; otherwise, it would take up too much data space."

"Do you mind if I take a look at it for the time Congressman Lewis was in his car? It's sickening to think someone could have been monitoring the cameras and could have stopped this from happening." CJ was finally beginning to think rationally. And this situation required all the rational thinking she could summon.

"If you think you want to put yourself through this . . . but I have to tell you that when we went back to check the footage, the camera was at an odd angle, so we couldn't see the actual events occur. The camera was positioned so we could only get a glimpse of the rear passenger side. At first, it looked like the congressman was checking for something under the car, but we couldn't see exactly what he was looking for."

"But did you see his face? Was it recognizable?" CJ was starting to sound like a detective at this point.

"Well . . . no." Harris hesitated. "But he was wearing the same Burberry raincoat we found him in."

"So you really didn't see who attached the hose to the exhaust pipe? Is that what you're telling me?"

"Ms. Jansen. I know this is a great shock to you, but it does happen. People get depressed and despondent, and from what you said, he has no family. Maybe the stress of working in this pressure-cooker town finally got the better of him."

"No. I do not, will not accept that. He was a workaholic. He loved what he did. Hell, he answered his own phone! And to be quite frank, I don't think he'd know how to hook up a hose to an exhaust pipe!" CJ was unconvinced. "I really think this needs more investigating. It's just not right." CJ's gut was churning at this point. "So, if you can get me clearance to look at the tapes, I want to go through them."

Harris sighed. "Okay, but again, if you really feel it's necessary. I can call security as soon as we get back to my office, and we can arrange for you to come in tomorrow morning to look through the footage."

They walked back in silence, CJ's mind turning with questions, doubts, and suspicions. *Snapper would never do this,* she kept repeating to herself. *Never.*

CHAPTER 5

When Colin had first met Kick, twenty-four years ago, Kick had his hands full with raising his ten-year-old sister and trying to start a business. Kick had just graduated from Wharton and was spending the summer racing his sailboat off the eastern shore of Maryland when his parents were killed returning from a regatta. Kick was bereft. They had finally accepted Kick's coming out and went to support him in a race among his boating friends who were also gay. The only saving grace was that his little sister had been away at camp. That was when Kick first discovered there was no money in the family coffers. His family had been living a lie. The only money in the estate was a small insurance policy, and that was going to have to cover CJ. Relatives were aghast, but Kick had his suspicions about why his parents were, essentially, broke. His mother had begun to drink heavily and she and his dad were fighting all the time. At first he thought the arguments were about him, but after several tear-filled phone calls from CJ, he knew there was a serious problem even if he did not know exactly what it was. After the accident, CJ told him that the fights were about money, and he realized that he had to give his sister a secure environment in which to grow up. Despite the urgings of his relatives not to take on the burden of raising a ten-year-old girl, he took charge of her upbringing.

When Kick felt comfortable enough with Colin to tell him about his responsibility for his sibling, Colin immediately began to come up with a way for Kick to start his restaurant business and meet his responsibility for raising his sister.

Colin had always been a "mathlete." He had begun to grasp numbers when he first started playing with baby blocks. Much to his parents' surprise and concern, he learned his numbers very quickly. They knew he was different, but exactly how different was yet to be seen. By the third grade he was learning algebra and was moved into the fifth-grade math class, where he got perfect scores on every test. Finally, when he was eleven years old, his parents sought to enroll him at Hargrave Military Academy's summer camp. Though he was one year under the required age for the camp, his math scores and letters of recommendation from his teachers led the school to waive the age requirement in his case. Since he was a mathematical genius, he was able to get financial assistance to attend.

Though his teachers urged him to think about a career as a scientist, Colin had very different ideas. He wanted to put his talent to use as a way to make money. Being a member of a low-income family, Colin was very aware of his family's financial struggles. His dad worked two jobs, and his mom spent her days in the cafeteria at a local school. Growing up, he wore his older brother's hand-me-downs, which his mother would mend so that they looked almost like new, certainly as good as one could buy at a local used clothing store. To be sure, there was always a hot meal on the table, but Colin knew that providing even the essentials was no easy task. Solving the problems scientists dealt with, interesting as that might be, was not what he was going to do with his life. He was determined to use his talent at mathematics to make money, so his family could live a better life, so his mom could go to the beauty parlor more than twice a year.

When he was thirteen, Colin started reading the *Wall Street Journal* and making mock stock acquisitions. He would take his imaginary earnings and reinvest in other equities. By his senior year in high school, if Colin's stock portfolio was real, he would already have been a millionaire! He used an account of his "mock-stock" trading as part of his entrance application to the University of Pennsylvania and was awarded a full scholarship. While he was in college, he realized that he had little interest in dating or getting married and having a family. Women weren't as important to him as they were to his classmates.

He had a full head of thick black hair, a long, thin face with a roman nose, piercing green eyes, and an incongruously wide mouth for a face shaped as his was. Though he was six foot two, with broad shoulders and a narrow waist, giving him the look of an athlete, he actually had no interest in sports at all. He did enjoy being outdoors, so he usually had a summerlike tan all year.

During one of his visits at Thanksgiving, his mom asked him, "Colin, honey, do you have a girlfriend?"

Colin squirmed in his seat, not knowing how to respond. He considered himself more asexual at that point, not showing any definite preference one way or the other.

"Mom, I am so busy with school that I don't have time to date. I'm trying to graduate in three years, so I can start working for real."

"But, sweetheart, you need to make time for some fun. After all, college should be a life experience, not just homework."

"Yeah, I know. But I really love my classes, and I'm learning so much. I'm telling you, you will be able to quit the hash slinging as soon as I graduate and get a job!" With this pronouncement, Colin maneuvered the conversation to something else.

"Son, you know I enjoy my job. I don't know what I would do if I didn't have one!" Colin's mother never wanted her children to feel she was suffering or pushing herself on their behalf.

"Please, Mother. You could volunteer at the hospital, join the garden club, all sorts of things you would *want* to do, rather than *have* to do!"

"You're such a good boy, Colin. And I so much appreciate your dedication to your schooling, and of course to us. But we're just fine." His mother was always playing June Cleaver.

As planned, Colin graduated in three years, began applying for jobs in finance, and landed a spot in a small investment firm in Washington, DC. He could still be close to his family and live in one of the most interesting and exciting cities in the world.

By the time he was twenty-eight, Colin was worth several million dollars. He had an instinct for spotting stocks that were about to enter a significant uptrend, buying them just as they began to break out, and selling them at or near the peak. He was especially adept at investing in technology stocks, and since some of the greatest winners were in technology, Colin made a lot of money for himself and his clients.

As promised, he bought his parents a lovely but modest house in Virginia and provided an income so that his father was able to retire and his mom could join the garden club and get her hair done once a week.

Colin was proud of his accomplishments but began to feel a pang of loneliness and an absence of purpose. "Okay, pal. So you can make money. Now what?" He looked into the mirror one evening and decided to become involved in local charities. But which one? He had heard about a no-kill animal shelter that was celebrating its twenty-fifth anniversary. It seemed funny that very few people seemed to know about it, but after a little research he discovered they had a 97 percent adoption rate and needed funding for a new dog run. The fund-raiser was going to feature several of the most talented nuevo cuisine chefs. It would be a contest that would be decided by a vote of the guests. Sounded like a good use of his time, and a lot of great food.

The event took place at the National Union Building, and that was where he first saw his future life partner: Kendall "Kick" Carlson Jansen. Kick was intense, focusing on every detail of the grilled lamb lollipops with cilantro lime sauce, and the presentation to every guest that waited in line for this extraordinary delight. After walking around the large main ballroom on the second floor of the building, Colin was intoxicated by the aroma coming from the small grill plate on one chef's table and decided he would wait the twenty or so minutes before he could savor the dish.

"Would you hold my place in line?" Colin begged the person behind him. "I think I need to quench my thirst, and it looks like we're going to be here awhile."

A beautiful Asian woman, with piercing green eyes, black hair, and a generous mouth, wearing a pencil skirt and a sheer blouse from Bergdorf Goodman, looked him squarely in the face and smiled. "Of course," she said in a flirtatious manner, "provided you bring me a cosmopolitan!"

Colin nodded and headed toward the bar. One of his colleagues was also attending the event and elbowed him. "Nice work with Lily Tam!"

"What are you talking about?" Colin was genuinely puzzled.

"I saw the two of you standing together, and now you're getting her a drink. She is one hot-looking woman. Attaboy!"

Colin smiled and stammered a bit. "Oh, she was just standing in line behind me, and I offered to get her a drink if she held my place."

"Yeah. Whatever it takes, bro. Good luck."

Colin had been with one woman one time in college and had not been all that impressed with the experience. He was confounded that he had had no emotional response to the encounter whatsoever. Odd. Every once in a while, he would ask himself, *What is wrong with me?* This would happen from time to time, especially after he and some business associates would go out for drinks, and they would flirt with every woman in the bar.

When he returned to the line and handed Lily Tam her cosmopolitan, she tried to start a conversation with him. When that did not work, she decided to try the food from a different chef. By the time she left, there were only a few people ahead of him, and when Kick looked up from serving the next guest, their eyes locked. Something went through Colin like a lightning bolt, and it scared the crap out of him.

When it was his turn to reap the reward of waiting in line, he thought he would drop the plate. Kick looked up again and smiled. "Hope you like them. I've been working on this recipe for weeks!"

Colin could barely speak. "I'm not much of a lamb-chop guy, but the mob seems to be favoring your dish. I waited in line for twenty minutes! I mean, I'm not complaining. I'm impressed! At myself!" Colin finally gave a chortle. "I'm not a wait-in-line kind of guy either! These must be pretty special!"

Kick also seemed a little nervous, but he attributed it to the stress of the event and the contest. Even though there was no monetary prize, the exposure to Washington's elite could raise his visibility. And perhaps that would lead to his getting some funding for his restaurant dream.

"Well, I hope you enjoy them!" Kick smiled as Colin took his first bite, juice running down the corner of his mouth.

"Oh my God! These are incredible! And boy am I a sloppy eater!" Colin went to grab a handful of napkins when Kick reached over and handed him one of his clean bar towels.

"You may need this. I have two more on the grill for you!" Kick flashed that winning smile again, making Colin very self-conscious.

"I don't know if the people behind me would appreciate me glomming up your lamby-pops! We don't want to incite a riot!" Colin took a quick look over his shoulder and noticed frowns and hurry-up gestures.

"Well, this *is* Washington, DC. Riots are a part of life!" Kick was easy with his humor. "Let me get through this mob and I'll fix up some extra for you. Go have another drink. By the looks of it, I should be able to serve you seconds in about another fifteen minutes."

"That sounds like an excellent plan, Chef . . ." Colin leaned in a little closer to check Kick's name tag. "Chef Kick! You can tell me how you got that name when I come back. See you in a few."

For the first time in his life, Colin was feeling an attraction to another human being, a handsome younger man, thin, about six feet tall, with receding light brown hair, a smallish nose, full mouth, and eyes the color of cornstalks in the middle of summer. And he was absolutely comfortable with it! He felt as if he had had an epiphany. Suddenly, it hit him. *I found a total stranger — a man at that — attractive, and I got a vibe he was feeling the same way! What the hell do I do now?* He took a deep breath, slowed his pace, and continued to think. *You will go back to that handsome, talented man and wolf down those luscious lamb chops he's preparing for you. That's what you will do!*

Having decided on a course of action, Colin marched himself to the bar and ordered a double martini. A big shot of courage. This was a whole new world for him, and he needed to steady his nerves. Funny thing . . . he never got nervous about big trades. But this? This was different.

Throwing back the martini, Colin regained his composure and strutted across the polished hardwood floor in the direction of Kick's station. The crowd had thinned and he was bracing himself for . . . for what? *Lamb chops, idiot,* he told himself.

Trying not to act nervous or jumpy, Colin made his way to the front of the line again. "I wasn't sure if second helpings were gauche."

Kick looked up again from his grill. "Not

with that suit." Kick was admiring how impeccably dressed his new gourmand was. "Italian?"

Colin blushed a bit. "Is there any other? Oh, I don't mean to sound like a snob, but the Italians know how to dress a man . . . and a woman! And the shoes! The leather!" Suddenly, Colin felt very much at ease. Someone who could cook like that and recognize an Italian-made suit could become a very good friend indeed!

Kick chuckled. "Not snobby at all! I admire a man who appreciates fine workmanship."

"Well, I certainly appreciate yours! You have quite a knack for cooking!"

With the tension between them broken, each of them discovered that he had met a kindred spirit.

"I could try to impress you with other fabulous dishes . . . that is, if you are not otherwise involved. I mean, I don't want to sound forward, but . . ."

Colin quickly interrupted. "No . . . I mean yes. 'Yes' to another dish, and 'no' to involved!"

"Splendid!" Kick was beginning to relax after all the stress of competing for the approval of the guests. The evening was finally winding down.

"Let me give you my card, and when you feel like whipping up something scrumptious, give me a call." Colin reached into his breast pocket, pulled out a Ferragamo wallet, and handed his business card to Kick.

Kick wiped his hands on his bar towel and slightly grazed Colin's hand as he reached for the card. "Investments?" Kick was curious. That's exactly what he needed, but he didn't want Colin to think he was only interested in his business venture.

"Yes. Investing is mostly math. I was a crackerjack at math in grammar school, and I started following the market and making mock stock trades as a hobby."

"How do you start investments as a hobby?" Kick was becoming more curious.

"Long story. What do you say we discuss our personal histories over that fabulous dinner you're going to prepare?"

"Sounds like a plan. How is your kitchen?" Kick queried. "If it's okay with you, I can bring the supplies, or you can come over to my place and dig your way to the dining-room table. I have boxes of tools I still haven't unpacked!"

"Actually, I have a state-of-the-art kitchen that hasn't seen a frying pan since I moved in. Guess I'm not a chef like you. Mostly eat out or order in."

"I hear that a lot. So, is there any particular night that's good for you?"

Colin pulled out his pocket date minder and pointed to Thursday.

"Thursday it is! Time?"

"I guess that will depend on how much time you need to prepare dinner." Colin smiled back.

"I like to plan about two hours. Prep. Observe. Cook. I do sip a glass of wine in between!"

"Any particular vintage?" Colin was getting very excited about this new friend and new experience.

"I'll leave it to you. I usually suggest one red and one white — not necessarily only one bottle of each, but that will give me some flexibility in the mcnu."

"Well, then, I'll be sure to have plenty of both!" Colin took out his Montblanc pen, retrieved his card from Kick's hand, and wrote his home address on the back. "Did we settle on a time?"

Kick laughed. "No, I was waiting for you to tell me when you would like dinner served. I'll work backward."

"Eight o'clock?"

"At eight o'clock, dinner will be served. I shall arrive at six to begin preparations."

"Fantastic! I'll look forward to seeing you

then! Good luck with the contest. I'm sure you'll be the winner!"

As Colin had predicted, Kick took first place in the competition, and a story about him appeared in the *Washington Post*'s Arts and Entertainment section. For the first time in months, Kick began to feel as if the bumpy road of his life was about to smooth out a bit.

When Thursday rolled around, Kick was busy shopping at his favorite specialty stores, picking up fresh figs, kiwi, and pomegranate. Then off to the Cheese Cave for some luscious Humboldt Fog, a triple-cream Brie, and Manchego. That's where dinner would start. He had already wowed Colin with his lamb lollipops, so he considered roasted halibut. No. Not everyone liked fish. Veal? Could be a PC issue. Chicken? Boring. Beef? Beef was always a safe bet. But did he want to be safe? Too bad he hadn't thought about the braised short-rib recipe he had been working on sooner. Six hours of marinade and two and a half hours of cooking time. He glanced at his watch. If he hustled, he could prepare the short ribs at home and bring them over. They could sit in the gravy while he worked on the rest of the meal.

The cheese and fruit would be desert.

Nothing too sweet after a big meal. They would start with a burrata and heirloom tomatoes in a lightly drizzled pesto, followed by a roasted beet and pistachio salad in a citrus dressing, then the short ribs served over mashed potatoes and roasted vegetables. Was that going over the top? Maybe, but Kick was psyched.

After running to the butcher, he hightailed it back to his own kitchen and began the marinade for the short ribs. It was only eleven in the morning so he still had time — even if he had to finish cooking the ribs at Colin's, it wouldn't be a problem.

Kick arrived at six o'clock sharp, arms loaded with baskets, bags, and a crock-pot.

"You look like you robbed the gourmet market!" Colin laughed as he opened the door. "And what is it that smells so yummy?"

"Our entrée. I decided to make something that would take a little more time than I had planned, so I started it at home."

Colin grabbed some of the packages and led Kick through the stark apartment to the promised state-of-the-art kitchen.

"Great setup!" Kick was relieved that there was actually room to move around and prepare the meal. Too often "state of the art" meant high-end appliances but not necessarily a lot of work space. "Impressive! I could have a field day in here!"

That had been the beginning of a wonderful romance that lasted over twenty years. Had it not been for that fifteen-year-old drunk teenager, Kick would still be alive today.

Kick had gone to their vacation spot near Salisbury, Maryland, to get his boat ready for the annual regatta. That evening, when he was checking the GPS, the roar of a Jet Ski boomed through, the air followed by a horrific crash seconds later. Both vessels exploded in flames, leaving Kick burned over 80 percent of his body. By the time Colin made it to the hospital, Kick was almost dead. His final words were mumbled, but Colin clearly heard him say, "Keep an eye on CJ for me."

Colin remembered when Kick had introduced him to his sister. She was lanky, like her brother, and a bit of a spitfire. But what preteen girl wasn't? She was very bright and had a keen sense of humor. Yes, you could tell they were brother and sister. As CJ went through all her pubescent stages, Colin and Kick managed to chart that unfamiliar territory together, and the three of them became a very close-knit family.

Kick had wanted to start a restaurant

chain that would serve wholesome food. Not just fried, dried, and thrown into a bag. After that first dinner he had prepared for Colin, Colin set out to make Kick's dream reality by seeing to the financing. The company grew into a major chain and was worth millions by the time Kick had died. Colin continued to run the business, and CJ moved into Kick's house. It was actually hers under the terms of Kick's will, but she never really wanted the material things Kick had left her, including the house, so she lived modestly in only one area. Colin thought it was odd, but he thought he understood. They both missed him and wanted to be as close to him as they could. Even if it was just sitting in the kitchen.

During the four years since Kick's death, Colin and CJ had become even closer. They were each other's confidants and shelter from the emotional storm. So when CJ called and left him a message, he could tell that something must be bothering her. Something other than still grieving over the loss of her brother. He was worried about her. Something about the way she sounded on the phone did not seem right.

CHAPTER 6

It was the crack of dawn when Colin finally got through to CJ. "What the hell happened?"

"Snapper is dead." CJ could barely get the words out. "They say it was a suicide."

"What? That's impossible!" Colin knew the congressman well and echoed CJ's sentiments.

"Yeah. Something is seriously wrong. They said he killed himself in his car, using carbon monoxide. I don't think he would even know how. I'm heading to the police station in a couple of hours to look at the footage of the surveillance tapes."

"Do you want me to go with you?" Colin was growing tense over this new tragedy facing CJ. She was just getting over the death of her brother, and now this.

"Let me go see what the hell is going on, and I'll let you know. Don't go anywhere."

"Sweetie, I'll be wherever you need me to be."

CJ gave her wreck of a car a mean look before she attempted to start the engine. Much to her surprise, the junk-mobile once again cooperated. Still, she knew she needed to trade it in for something more reliable. She punched in the code to the garage door and headed to the station house, where Detective Harris had arranged for her to use a small media room in which to look through the security footage.

CJ stared at the video for hours, her eyes growing weary. She spotted Snapper walking from the stairwell to his car. Harris was right. It was hard to see the driver's seat given the angle of the camera. It was a full three minutes later she saw a man dressed in a Burberry trench coat with his head bent down, away from direct sight of the camera. That head tilt! The same slant, as if avoiding a camera. She remembered Mr. Crappy Cologne's body language as he was walking down the hallway. Damn it! She tried to increase the image, but doing so only made it grainier. Damn it! Damn it! Her palms were starting to sweat, and once again her inner self was screaming inside her. *It's him! I just know it! But how can I prove it?* It was going to be a big challenge. She knew instinctively that what had happened had something to do with the night of Snapper's and Mr. Crappy Cologne's confrontation, and that company, Robotron.

After staring at the footage for several hours, she decided to call it quits and sent a text to Colin: **CU at house? 6:00?** A quick ping back: **K.**

Before Colin arrived, CJ pulled out a bottle of Joseph Phelps, removed the cork, and poured the contents into a decanter to open the body and nuances of the wine. How she missed those wine tastings with Kick. This was one of his favorite California Cabernets.

Pacing back and forth, CJ was trying to be patient with the wine and waiting for Colin. Finally, the doorbell rang, and the wine was ready to drink.

"Hey! Are you okay?" Colin asked, warmth mixed with worry. "What's going on? That's just crazy news about Snapper. Why do you think he did it?"

Tears started rolling down CJ's face. "Suicide? I don't believe it for one second." Her voice started to increase in volume and her tone turned acid.

"I know this is a big shock, CJ, but people do it. And sometimes without any warning. It's baffling, but maybe if you think back over the past few weeks, you'll see some kind of pattern. A change in his behavior?"

"He had been crankier than usual. And distracted. But nothing, and I mean nothing I hadn't seen when he'd been under a lot of pressure. It makes no sense." CJ was settling down as best she could and sat down at the edge of the sofa.

"Sorry, kiddo, I know this has got to be rough." Words were not coming easily to Colin.

"Well, he's definitely dead. But the 'how' is what I'm not buying." CJ tried to maintain her composure. It was going to take a lot to get through another loss in her life, and the idea that she hadn't seen it coming was very disturbing to her.

"Okay. Let's start at the beginning. Is this what you wanted to see me about on Saturday? But wait. Snapper was still okay when you called."

"Exactly!" CJ jumped from her perch. "I know you're going to think I'm totally bonkers, but something big, and I mean big, is going down in the House of Representatives."

Colin, trying to keep the conversation light, replied, "If *only* something were going on . . . but nothing seems to be getting done in Congress! Even if the House passes legislation, it ends up dying in the Senate."

"Stop. I'm serious. I hate to use the word 'nefarious,' but that is as close as I can come right now."

"Okay. Okay. No more joking around. Like I said, let's start at the beginning. When you called, what did you want to talk about?"

CJ recounted the events of the evening when she was leaving early to go for a run. Snapper had a black-tie event and said he was waiting for a phone call. She took the stairs to the garage, but as she entered the stairwell, the elevator doors opened and the smell of a horrible cologne wafted out. When she got to her car, she remembered she had forgotten to leave a folder on her desk, so she returned to the office. As she was entering the hallway to her office, she was hit with the same stench she had encountered earlier.

"Cheap cologne? What does that have to do with anything?" Colin was trying to be patient.

"More like crap cologne. The odor was barreling through the hall like a jet stream. I heard voices in Snapper's office, and since I did not want him to know about my goof, I used the side door to enter my own office. When I opened the door, the smell got stronger, and I could hear Snapper arguing with this guy. Something about Robotron. And then Mr. Crappy Cologne kicked Snapper in the groin!"

"Where were you all this time?" Colin looked horrified.

"I ducked under my desk after I had clumsily knocked into the trash can." Her eyes were rolling, and she was shaking her head.

"Who do you think you are, Nancy Drew?"

"It was such a heated argument that I wanted to get out of there as quickly as possible and without being seen. It was strange. Weird. I never, *ever* saw Snapper allow himself to be bullied. So I got out of Dodge as soon as I could."

"Okay. But what does that have to do with Snapper's suicide?"

"You mean 'apparent suicide.' That's just it. I could hear a few words, something about Robotron and a vote. Do you remember a couple of weeks ago, when there was an announcement about a recall of defective robotic surgical equipment from hundreds of hospitals?"

"Yeah, that was some kind of debacle. Fake news. Stocks dropped before the company realized no recall was necessary, that they had been hacked. How does that garbage happen anyway?"

"That's my point, Colin. How *does* that garbage happen? Obviously, someone manipulated the phony recall and the leak about it. It was manipulated, just like pretty much everything else is."

"So what are you going to do about this? Who can you talk to?"

"That's the problem. Who would believe me? But get this — the alleged suicide occurred the same day I had gotten another whiff of the guy with the awful cologne in the lobby."

"Again, Nancy Drew, where was Mr. Crappy Cologne at the time you sniffed him out?"

"I had left Snapper in his office. I was running out to grab a salad. When I got to the lobby, I asked Marcus, the security guard, if he had noticed anyone reeking like a French whorehouse, but he said no. So I went to the café and picked up a salad and headed back to the office. When I got back to my desk, Snapper was gone. He had no outside appointments and hadn't left me a note. When I stepped into his office to check for his briefcase, I smelled that disgusting stench again, so I made a beeline back to the lobby to see if Marcus had an update on Mr. Crappy Cologne. That's when I got a whiff and followed it down the hallway."

"Okay, missy. Now you're making me nervous with your sleuthing." Colin was on the border of "Is she delusional because of grief?" and "This doesn't sound right to me, either."

"Colin. I'm not nuts. I followed the scent to Congressman Dillard's office, and I could hear him arguing with someone. One of them said, 'It's being taken care of, but you need to take care of me, as in *now.*' The other guy, who I assumed was Dillard, said for the guy to calm down and come back later. I flattened myself against the wall as Pepé Le Pew came out. I tried to get a look at his face, but he had tilted his head in a way that indicated he knew exactly where the security cameras were and intended to avoid them. I'm telling you, Colin, something big is going on and Snapper's suicide, murder, whatever, has something to do with this."

"Are you saying that you think Snapper was murdered by Mr. Crappy Cologne? And that there was some kind of conspiracy that involved Snapper, this other congressman, and the guy with the smelly cologne?" Colin was beginning to think CJ's imagination was running a bit wild.

"Well, let's look at the facts." CJ pulled out a yellow pad and pen. "Snapper has an argument with Mr. Crappy Cologne over a company, Robotron. Then came the recall, dropping the stock. Whoops. Bad info. 'Never mind,' " she added, mimicking Gilda Radner's Emily Litella.

"Meanwhile, Congress passes a bill pouring research money into medical-supply initiatives, and guess who was one of the big beneficiaries of that influx of cash? You got it — Robotron. And guess whose stock skyrocketed? Again, Robotron. A couple of weeks later, Snapper is dead. Coincidence? I don't *think* so." CJ tossed the pad on the floor, crossed her arms, and glared at Colin, daring him to contradict her.

"Okay, I understand why you think all of this is suspicious, but they did find him in his car after a hose was connected to the exhaust pipe."

"Well, they couldn't just murder him outright, could they? *That* would have been suspicious."

"So you think they faked his suicide? To cover something up?" Colin was trying to put the pieces together himself.

"Yeah. And yeah. It has something to do with Robotron stock. I can feel it in my gut." CJ was finally coming to grips with the events and appeared to have a renewed strength.

"So what do you propose, Miss Drew?"

"Please stop calling me that. I am serious. This is something that needs to be investigated further."

"Okay, but how are you going to convince the police to open an investigation into a possible murder when they are convinced that no crime occurred?"

"I think a toxicology report has to be run on Snapper. They may have drugged him before arranging that his death appear to be a suicide. When I was taken to the car and leaned in, guess what I smelled? Horrible cologne."

"Yes, but how did they get his body into the car without being seen by the security cameras?"

"Maybe he was already in his car. Maybe he was supposed to meet Mr. Crappy Cologne in his car and he injected Snapper with something to knock him out. It's possible, don't you think?"

"Oh boy. You've been watching too much *Dateline* or *Forensic Files*. That's quite a stretch."

"You have any other ideas, Mr. Logical Thinker?"

CJ's sarcasm was not lost on Colin. "We

could go to Snapper's apartment and check it out."

"Isn't that trespassing?" Colin looked leery.

"Not if one has a key."

"Okay, Miss Marple, but let's wait until tomorrow morning. You need to get some rest, and maybe this will look a little different in the light of day. Do you want me to stay here tonight?"

"Yeah, that would be great. Thanks, Colin. You've always been such a good pal. I'm going to get into my pj's and try to sleep."

"I'm just a shout away if you need anything."

CHAPTER 7

After a night of tossing and turning, CJ started her morning ritual making coffee in the French press.

"Good morning, sunshine. You feeling any better today?" Colin asked.

"As if. I don't think I slept a wink. Here, have a cup and let's get moving."

CJ handed Colin a mug and went to her room to get dressed. "I'll be ready in a half hour."

When CJ returned, Colin had been thinking about the Italian sports cars sitting in the garage and the vast difference between them and CJ's junk heap. It was with a pang of nostalgia that he remembered the long drives he and Kick would take. "Are you ever going to do something with the sports cars in the garage? Or at least your piece of junk?"

"Funny you should say that. I was thinking it was time to trade in the two-hundred-fifty-thousand-mile tin can for something more reliable. In fact, I was going to ask you to go with me. You know cars have never been my thing."

"Of course I will. You just say when."

"Well, let's get this Snapper thing unraveled first, and then we can talk cars."

"Absolutely. And let's take my car if you don't mind," Colin replied.

CJ grabbed her jacket and purse as they headed out the front door instead of the garage door since Colin's car was in the driveway.

Colin ushered CJ toward his Alpha Romeo. "The Watergate, correct?"

"Correct."

CJ buckled herself into the lush passenger seat. The smell of the Italian leather was almost heady. They say the sense of smell is the fastest line to your memory. Maybe that's why she didn't want to get rid of the cars. She gave Colin's arm a squeeze as he clicked to open the security gate, drove the car out onto the streets of Washington, DC, heading to the famous, infamous building.

CJ stopped at the checkpoint in the lobby and showed her ID to the security guard, who nodded in acknowledgment. She and Colin stood silently as the elevator in Snapper's building reached his floor.

"It's just down the hall." CJ pointed with a nod of her head.

"Huh. Watergate. Ironic, don't you think?" Colin was still not convinced anything untoward had taken place, thinking the suicide was just the sad story of a lonely, overworked man who could no longer take the strain. "The hallmark of political espionage."

"Will you please stop the sarcasm? This is tough enough to deal with." CJ gave him her sideways look of "stop messing with me."

"Okay. Sorry. But it does seem . . ."

"Will you please shut the hell up until we have more to go on?" CJ keyed the door open and they entered the eerily quiet condo.

"What are we looking for?" Colin asked in a hushed voice.

"I have no idea, but I don't think we need to whisper. Snapper was a very meticulous man. Everything was always in order. You take the bedroom, and I'll start in his den."

"But, I repeat, what are we looking for?" Colin was trying to humor CJ. He was very uncomfortable going through a dead man's personal belongings.

"Check his closet for anything that doesn't look organized or is in a state of disarray.

99

You know, just in case someone else was here snooping around. Or if he might have left some kind of clue."

"I dunno. This is creeping me out a little."

"You're a big boy, Colin. A captain of industry. My hero. Don't be such a wuss. Go. Look." She turned him around and gave him a shove.

"All right! All right! Stop being so bossy." Colin was heading toward the bedroom when he passed a door with hardware somewhat similar to Kick's house: a Sargent and Greenleaf biometric fingerprint lock. "CJ! Check this out! A fingerprint lock. Do you know the pin for this, or does it have your print?"

"What? I have no idea. Crap. We need his fingerprint. There's got to be a way to get this open. Maybe what's behind this door will give us what we're looking for."

"And what exactly *are* we looking for again?"

"*Something!*" CJ tried to control her voice. "We'll know it when we find it. I can't help believing that there is something much bigger going on."

"Okay, but how do you propose that we get past this safety device?" Colin was stabbing his finger on the keypad, illustrating

100

the lack of response he was getting from the lock.

"Wait! Maybe we can get a fingerprint from one of Snapper's bottles or glasses," she said, eyeing the bar.

"Oh my God. Do you really think that kind of stuff works in the real world?"

"Yes. I think it's called latent prints or something like that." CJ went to the kitchen and rifled through a drawer, looking for Scotch Tape, as Colin threw himself on the black-leather sofa and buried his head in his hands.

"Look. I have a very good friend at the FBI. Maybe he can help us out without our becoming criminals." Colin was trying to think logically about how to proceed with this madcap scheme.

"What are you going to tell him? I'm on a mission of paranoia?"

"No. I'll tell him you're trying to get the congressman's estate in order and that while you were here, you came across this lock that you do not know how to open since there was no key for it. The fact that you are already legitimately in the condo means that he should not have any suspicion about what you are doing. Let me give him a call and see what advice he can give us."

CJ looked at him warily but consented.

"Okay, but make it convincing about my getting his affairs in order. And that I'm *not* playing amateur sleuth. Besides, I really *am* trying to get his affairs in order."

Colin pulled out his phone and hit the speed dial for his friend Matt. "Matt? Colin. Yeah, I heard they announced Congressman Lewis's suicide earlier today. CJ? She's pretty upset. That's one reason I'm calling. She has keys to his condo and needs to get paperwork and some other personal things, but there's a lock that requires a fingerprint . . . yes, a Sargent and Greenleaf. Uh-huh. Okay." Colin was gesturing for CJ to come closer. "Sure. An hour? Yes. The Watergate. Great. Thanks, I'll let her know."

"What? What did he say?" She was pulling on his shirtsleeve like a kid begging for attention.

"He's going to meet you here in an hour. Try to act like you're just doing your job. Your *real* job."

"But what if what's behind the door is something awful? We don't necessarily want him to find out what's there."

"He doesn't have a warrant, so he has no legal grounds to be looking for anything. He's just coming by as a favor to give you advice as to how to get the lock open. Just stay cool until he gets here and we have a better idea how to proceed."

"I don't like any of this, but we have to get to the other side of that door."

An hour later, Matt showed his badge to the security guard at the checkpoint in the lobby and was directed to the correct elevator. When CJ got the call from the lobby that Agent Mullan was on his way up, she went to stand in the doorway and wait, trying to seem casual.

She offered her hand. "Hey, Matt, thanks for stopping by. I have to get a bunch of files and paperwork, and I don't have the combo to this one door. Please come in."

"Colin. I wasn't expecting to see you here." Agent Matthew Mullan looked quizzically at Colin, then at CJ.

"He's here for moral support. It's been very upsetting. When I realized I couldn't get past that lock, I called Colin, and he suggested calling you since you're *the* super G-man!" Trying to mask her nerves with a compliment, CJ smiled and moved aside so that Matt could enter.

"Yes, I can see where it would be a very disturbing situation." As he entered, Mullan instinctively followed his training and did a thorough scan of the room. "You would never have thought Congressman Lewis would come to such a tragic end."

Taking a very deep breath, CJ tried to hide all of her emotions. "To be honest, I find it very hard to believe." Then she realized that her mouth was in danger of becoming a runaway train, so she stopped herself from continuing to voice her suspicions about Snapper's demise.

"So let's take a look at the security lock and see whom I can recommend." Mullan was still checking out the surroundings. Snapper had been a very organized man, both at home and his office. Not a thing was out of place.

CJ motioned to the mysterious door. Her nerves were on edge. Her inner self was nagging at her again. *Why would he have something like that when this building is like Fort Knox?* it seemed to be asking.

"Looks like the standard S and G high-security lock, but we have someone on staff who can manage to open this." Scrutinizing the room once again, Mullan continued, "I'm sure we can get some prints off his personal belongings."

"See! I told you they can do that kind of thing." CJ was feeling rather vindicated as she gave Colin her "I told you so" look. Turning to face Matt, she asked, "How soon could they get here?"

"Let me give him a call. I suppose we can

consider this official business since he was a member of Congress."

CJ was getting nervous. What if there was something incriminating behind the door? It had to be pretty serious for Snapper to have installed that kind of lock. She was beginning to regret having had Colin make the call.

"Uh, does it have to be *official* business? I mean, what if it's something very personal that he wouldn't want people to know about? It seems pretty obvious he didn't want easy access to it. I'm really not sure what to do."

Mullan took a deep breath. "I understand your wanting to maintain his privacy. And since it was a suicide, there is no reason for the authorities to get involved. This would just be a courtesy out of respect for Congressman Lewis and his family."

CJ was still uneasy about having someone from the government intruding into business that Snapper clearly wanted no one to know about. "Matt, I mean Agent Mullan" — CJ was vacillating between casual frenzy and professional respect — "I'm not sure about this. I know Colin called you as a friend, but I'd rather just hire a locksmith to work on that thing. I really only wanted to find out if there was an easy way to open it. We . . . I have something similar where I live — my brother had it installed. Maybe I should get in touch with them. I'm sorry for inconveniencing you. I should never have asked Colin to bother you with this. I guess I just wasn't thinking straight." Her mouth was moving faster than she wanted.

Mullan looked over at Colin, who gave him the "it's okay" look, which was not lost on CJ. "Oh. Wait. You two?" she said.

"You two, what?" Suddenly realizing his relationship with Mullan was about to be exposed, Colin's face turned red, and both men became a little uneasy. Colin had wanted to tell CJ that he had met someone but wasn't sure if CJ was ready. It had been four years since Kick had died, and the loneliness had only added to his depression.

Matthew Mullan and Colin had met at a Gay Pride gala in Truro on Cape Cod several years before Kick died. After Kick's death, Matt had reached out to offer his condolences, and they started an innocent friendship. Matt was not out of the closet since being gay was not something that helped one's career in the Bureau. Since making friends wasn't easy for Colin, he appreciated a sympathetic ear. After almost four years of hanging out as friends, it looked like their relationship was about to enter into a more serious phase.

"So, how long have the two of you known each other?" CJ was pulling out her detective hat again.

"We actually first met a number of years ago, when Kick sponsored that fund-raiser in Truro. After Kick died, Matt and I started hanging out. It was a rough time for all of us, and I appreciated his company."

"And I appreciated his discretion," Mullan added, trying to get past this rather awkward moment.

CJ looked at Mullan, then at Colin. "Hey, guys, I think it's great that you found one another, but jeez, Colin, you could have told me." CJ was beginning to soften again.

Both men heaved a big sigh of relief. "This is why I wasn't concerned about asking Matt to come over. He knows how to be circumspect."

"Okay, so let's get this show on the road. What do we need to do to get through this barricade?" CJ was becoming more and more relaxed over the bizarre situation.

"Let me call my guy in the office." Agent Mullan pulled out his cell and pulled up his contacts list. "Gus? It's Matt. Matt Mullan. Yeah. Hey. Listen, I am at Congressman Lewis's residence. Yes, he did. I know. Sad. I'm with his chief of staff, Carol Anne Jansen. She's here trying to get his personal affairs in order, but there's a door with a Sargent and Greenleaf lock. Yeah, fingerprint. Can you get over to the Watergate and give her a hand?" Mullan turned toward CJ, and asked, "How long will you be here?"

"As long as I have to be."

"She said she'll be here as long as necessary," Mullan continued on the phone. "How soon could you get here? An hour?" Looking at CJ at the same time, she gave a thumbs-up. "Okay great. Don't worry about the paperwork. I'll take care of it. Sure thing. Thanks."

"Great. Thank you so much." Relief was pouring from CJ. Knowing that Mullan was an ally took away a lot of the trepidation she had been feeling. "Will you wait?"

"Sure. I don't have to be back until two. Some kind of big meeting with the department heads." Mullan was much more casual now.

An hour later, the phone rang to announce the locksmith's arrival. Mullan answered the door and ushered him toward the offending door lock.

"Yeah. Seen a lot of these lately. I guess in this town, no one feels safe." The locksmith was wearing a very official FBI jumpsuit and carrying a very official-looking case. Addressing CJ, he asked, "Ma'am, do I have your permission to open this lock? Sorry, but it's standard procedure to ask."

The question did seem rather foolish, but it was the government after all. "Oh, for goodness sake. Of course." CJ was beginning to feel that sense of foreboding again, knowing something unseemly could be lurking behind that mysterious door.

It took less than a few minutes for the locksmith to peel some prints off a bottle on the bar and transfer them onto another piece of glass, then he used some kind of algorithm to unlock the door.

As the door swung open they peered inside to find a staircase leading to the floor below.

"What in the hell is *this*?" CJ's mind was racing.

CHAPTER 8

Everyone had a shocked and questioning expression at the discovery. CJ peered into the stairwell, not sure whether she should be the first one to descend or if she should slam the door shut and turn everyone away. *What can be down there?*

Agent Mullan took charge and offered to check. "Would you like me to proceed?"

Not sure of what they would find, CJ gave Colin a begging look. "Let me go. I don't think there will be anything dangerous. It's probably just another part of Snapper's condo." With trepidation, Colin took the first few steps, CJ following close behind.

"Agent Mullan, would you mind waiting at the top of the stairs? I think we'll be okay. We'll yell if we need you." CJ was much more concerned about finding something incriminating rather than someone with a weapon or some sort of *Raiders of the Lost Ark* booby traps.

"Roger that," Mullan announced as he waved off the locksmith. "Send the paperwork to my attention. And thanks for coming.

"You sure you guys are going to be okay down there? I do have a gun." Mullan was trying to be reassuring.

"We'll be fine." CJ's voice began to turn into a whisper. "What in the hell? This looks like a completely different condo. He never mentioned any of this to me."

"It's a little stuffy," Colin said, sniffing the air. "And there's no odor of cologne, crappy or otherwise. Almost like no one lives here, but everything seems to be in place. You don't think Snapper was hiding something down here, do you?"

"Like what?" CJ still could not wrap her head around this mysterious place. Clearly, it was a condo. But whose?

"I don't know. Obviously, he was hiding something down here. Why else would he have a high-security lock on the door? Check out the front door and see if it's bolted." Colin was the one giving orders now.

CJ cautiously walked toward the front entrance and could see it was double-bolted from the inside. "Well, no one was getting in from this door either."

The apartment was austere, the furnishings an absolute minimum. It felt as if no one had lived there for a while. Years. There was some dust but no signs of life in the kitchen or the bathroom. It was almost as if it was a model apartment — something to show to renters or prospective owners. Colin had been looking through the closets. "Nothing here. No clothes, no toothbrushes. *Nada.*"

It was very odd, and CJ was becoming very uneasy. She made her way toward the desk. "Huh. Look at this. A computer. I'm sure it's password protected, too." CJ tried typing in the few passwords Snapper had entrusted her with. "Son of a bitch. What could he have been working on?" she said absentmindedly.

"Robotron?" Colin came up with the most logical answer. "Check the drawers. Maybe there'll be a clue for the password."

CJ opened the first drawer and found pencils, some paper clips, a pad, and rubber bands. When she tried to open the file drawer, she realized that it, too, was locked. "Ugh!"

"You guys okay down there?" Mullan had been waiting patiently at the top of the stairs.

"Yeah." Colin turned to CJ. "Maybe we

should have him come down and give us a hand."

"But what if we find something illegal? Wouldn't he be bound to call it in or something?"

"I'll be right back. Don't touch anything." Colin ran up the stairs to talk to Matt. "CJ's concerned about your position. What if we find something that's not quite on the up-and-up?"

"Like what?"

"I have no idea. This is like a treasure hunt, or something. Maybe not so much a treasure? Anyway, what do you think? Are you required by law to confiscate anything?"

"That's a bizarre question, but given the circumstances, nothing seems too bizarre at the moment."

Colin lowered his voice. "Listen. CJ thinks Snapper was murdered."

"Seriously?" Mullan clearly hadn't contemplated anything like that.

"Yes. That's really why we're here. She thinks someone killed him and made it look like a suicide. She was afraid to tell the police for fear they'd think she was just going through another state of grief and shock."

"I can understand that for sure. All of it. But why does she think he was murdered?"

"She overheard him arguing with someone in his office one night when she wasn't supposed to be there. Something about Robotron, and the guy Snapper was arguing with smelled like a French whorehouse, or at least that's how she described the odor to the security guy at the Rayburn House Office Building."

"Hold on a minute. Robotron and a whorehouse?" Mullan seemed more confused by the minute.

"Yeah. Maybe I should have her explain it to you. Wait here for a few minutes. Let me go check on her."

When Colin returned, he found CJ sitting at the desk, the lock jimmied with a screwdriver she had found under the kitchen sink. She was staring at a pile of folders, particularly the one with her name on it.

"Well, breaking and entering can now be added to your résumé," Colin tried to joke.

"Try dossier. Snapper had a file on me." CJ was crestfallen. She had no idea why he would have it, or why he would have kept it. She had been a loyal employee for twelve years.

"A what? Dossier? Why on earth would he have that?" Colin came up behind her and looked over her shoulder. "It doesn't look very incriminating. Maybe he kept files on everyone. He was in the business of politics, and you know it's hard to find people you can trust in this town."

"Exactly. Didn't he trust me?"

"I'm sure he did. You said he let you keep copies of his calendar, and you do have some of his passwords. Did you figure out the one for the computer?"

"Not yet. But there was also this photo of him and some guy in the drawer. It looks like they're on an airboat, somewhere in a swamp."

"Didn't he used to go to the Everglades once in a while to fish or whatever they do there? Catch alligators or something?"

"Yeah. He used to go, but it's probably been five years. He'd meet up with a friend, and they'd go 'gator hunting,' but they only took photos. Snapper wasn't into killing anything. In fact, that's how he got the nickname 'Snapper.' He was always snapping photographs. But everyone thought it was because he would snap at people he disagreed with, and he had no incentive to disabuse anyone of that notion."

Suddenly, a thought struck her. "Gator." She typed that into the keyboard, and a screen popped up. There was an odd icon that she double-clicked.

"Holy smoke! What in the world is this?"

CJ found herself staring at what looked like the big board on Wall Street.

"That's a trading site. It's for people who want to place trades with their brokers, but it's anonymous. It's like Snapchat. The message disappears after you send it. No copies of anything. No server. Nothing. It's the 'dark Web' of finances. That's how people move money to foreign accounts or accounts where they don't want a direct trail back to them."

"This is all very confusing. I've never heard of this." CJ wasn't sure if she should touch any of it, not knowing what it was or what it could reveal.

She moved the mouse over to a folder with the label "George" on it and clicked. There were subfolders with names like "doctors," "nursing staff," "hospitals," "medical equipment," "Sun Valley Institute." Each folder contained invoices that at first glance totaled tens of thousands of dollars. Hundreds of thousands. But each invoice also said "George Lewis."

"Colin. This must be Snapper's brother. I knew he had one, but he never spoke of him. I figured it was some kind of family thing."

"It would appear that George had some serious health issues. Click on 'Sun Valley

Institute.' "

CJ double-clicked and saw dozens more subfolders, each one designating a year. As she clicked through the invoices she realized that it was costing over twenty-five thousand dollars a month for George's upkeep. "Oh my God. How in the hell was he able to afford this?"

"Maybe we should take a look at that trading site. Scoot over. I've done this before. And don't give me that look. It was all legitimate. It just happened to be after hours, and I rarely used it." Colin bent over the monitor and made a few passes with the mouse. *Robotron.*

They both snapped their heads toward each other. "Robotron! See, I told you something was up with that company!" CJ felt slightly vindicated, but their discovery only revealed yet another mystery. "But what? What was this all about?"

"I hate to tell you, but it looks like Snapper was trading, and maybe not so legitimately."

"But why? Unless it was to support George. That would have to be the only reason Snapper would make illegal trades. And that would certainly explain a few things. Like Mr. Crappy Cologne." CJ sat back in the chair. "Yep. Mr. Crappy Cologne has something to do with this."

"Maybe I should get Matt down here."

"No! If Snapper was doing something illegal, then Matt would have to report it. We need to sort this out before we bring anyone else into it. You're the only one I can trust about this, Col."

His face scrunched up as he thought about how complex this situation was becoming. "Okay. But where do we take it from here? We need some kind of professional help if you think you're onto something dangerous. I mean it. This is not a Miss Marple mystery. Maybe I can talk to Matt off the record. As in speaking hypothetically."

CJ's nerves were shot. She was so used to being in control of her life since she graduated from college that the loss of control was frightening. Now her brother was gone, and so was her boss, which meant so was her job.

"I dunno, Colin. We need time to piece some of this together before we open another can of worms. And my brain is way overloaded. Let's leave everything alone for now, go back to the house, and try to make some sense of it. I can't take another shock today, and who knows what else we'll find if we keep looking. Besides, I need a glass of wine. I don't care if it's not happy hour yet. We'll grab some lunch to bring back to the house." CJ grabbed the dossier Snapper had compiled on her and shoved it under her sweater.

"Good idea. We can come back tomorrow and see what else we can unravel. This was a lot to absorb." Pulling CJ up by the arm, Colin added, "We'll get to the bottom of this. I promise."

They shut the lights and turned off the computer, leaving everything the way they had found it. Except for the broken lock on the file drawer, no one would know that anyone had been there. And who else was there who would even know about this place? Another question that had no answer. Yet.

When they reached the top of the stairs, Matt, seeing their weary faces, tried to make light of the day's events. "So, was it a dungeon?"

"No, just a smaller version of this condo. It may have been for guests. Constituents visiting, maybe." CJ tried to hide her concern and confusion. "But I did find a bunch of files I need to go through with a new set of eyes. The ones I have right now are bleary."

"We're heading back to CJ's. Want to join

us?" Colin was trying to be casual.

"Thanks, but I have to get back to the office. There's a big meeting this afternoon with the head honchos. Rain check?"

"Absolutely." Colin smiled. "Thanks very much for doing this."

"You take care, CJ. If you need anything, just give a holler."

"Yes. Thanks so much for your help. I have a lot of sorting to do, so I may take you up on that offer!" She poked Colin with her elbow as if to say she'd make something up if she had to, but by the look of things, she had plenty of ammo for an Agatha Christie novel.

CHAPTER 9

CJ and Colin headed toward the elevator in silence. They were both trying to make sense of what they had just discovered, but neither of them wanted to speak for fear of someone's overhearing their being caught on camera. This was the Watergate, after all. The biggest political scandal of the twentieth century had started in this very building.

Once they reached Colin's car and were confident they were not in earshot of anyone, they looked at each other and in unison said, "Holy mackerel! What the hell was that?" Finally, the tension was broken, and they laughed out loud.

"Wow. And I bet you thought I was nutters!" CJ tried to catch her breath. The fresh air and just being outside was refreshing.

"Yeah. Wow. And yes, I did think you were going off the deep end, but that secret hideaway with those files? Holy mackerel is right! Okay, let's pick up some sandwiches and get back to the house. We have some serious sleuthing ahead of us."

"May I call you one of the Hardy Boys now?" CJ teased. "Are you convinced that a toxicology report is called for?"

"Yes I am. We just need to figure out how we can get it done." Colin was thinking that maybe Matt could order the report, but his doing so would lead to a lot of questions that neither one of them wanted to answer since it appeared that Snapper had been engaged in something that was probably illegal, however well motivated it might have been.

"I think the next of kin could request something like that, no? But it would appear that George is the only next of kin, and it doesn't seem that he would be capable of asking. Oh my God. George!" It suddenly occurred to CJ that someone needed to notify his caregivers.

"What about George?"

"Shouldn't we let him know? Let them know?" CJ's mind was racing to the next conundrum. *How are we supposed to notify his caregivers if we weren't supposed to know about them and George?* "Col, we have to tell them."

"I think we need to follow the money, as

they say." Colin was attempting to put a logical plan together. "When we go back tomorrow, we'll have to see what other accounts there are and whether or not they're tied together somehow. He had to have a way to transfer the money to Sun Valley."

"Maybe we should go back. Do a little more intel gathering."

"That won't be necessary." Colin pulled out a flash drive from his pocket. "I copied the files. We can't get into the net, but maybe we can do our own forensic accounting with what's on here."

"What the . . . How did you?" CJ was baffled.

"When you were engrossed in reading your dossier, my pretty." Colin winked and handed her the Samsung 32GB USB 3.0 flash drive that he always carried with him.

"Do you always carry one of these with you? Or was it just a hunch that we might need it today?"

"Ever since Kick forgot his laptop for a big presentation. I would back up his files and keep the drive on my key chain."

"Huh." CJ was wondering what other secrets Colin might be hiding from her.

"Let's stop at Brennan's Deli. I think I need some red meat in my sandwich."

They pulled into the gourmet deli's parking lot, and Colin got out and went inside. CJ waited in the car and looked at the dossier again. "Why would he have this?" she muttered to herself. "Too many things are happening. And I'm not sure I like any of them."

Colin returned a few minutes later with a bag of sandwiches and some kettle chips.

"I think this should hold us for the rest of the afternoon. Maybe into the evening. Got you roast beef with melted cheddar, lettuce, tomato, and a dash of horseradish. Oh, and a grilled brie with apples to wash it down!"

"Well, I *was* in training for the marathon, but it appears that investigating this Snapper situation is going to have to replace that training for now. Thanks! Two of my favorites."

They pulled into "the fortress," as CJ sometimes referred to it, went through the security checkpoint, and entered the house through the kitchen.

Colin unpacked their lunch and arranged a beautiful presentation on an Arte Italica platter, accompanied by two Baccarat wine goblets.

CJ looked over as Colin prepared the place settings for their lunch, remembering how picky Kick was about how food was served. He would often say, "Just because it's a chain of restaurants, it doesn't have to serve food the way other chains do. People should feel special when they are dining out — no matter where they are. Unless they're in their car. In that case, they can drool all over themselves for all I care."

Looking at Colin, CJ said, "I'm really glad you're here. We don't spend enough time together anymore. It's just too bad it took this crazy mess to make it happen."

"You know you're like a sister to me. And, you're right. We should spend more time together, and it looks like that's going to be happening. By the way, I'm sorry I didn't mention Matt to you sooner. As I said, we had been friends, then one night one thing —"

CJ stopped him in his tracks. "I don't need all the details, thank you very much." But smiling back at him, she continued, "I know how much you loved Kick. But I also know how lonely life can be, especially after losing someone. It's a double-edged sword. You want to be with the person you loved, but that's no longer possible, so you take solace in the company of others. Besides, Matt seems like a pretty nice guy. Too bad I had to meet him under these circumstances."

"He is a good guy. I hope I can keep

everything in balance. We are going to need his help, you know."

"Yeah, I know. But we need to make a to-do list. I guess the first thing is to notify George. I can tell them a half-truth. I was Snapper's assistant. I *could* have known about George. The part that's tricky is how did the money get to the facility? We'll have to figure that out."

"Maybe there'll be something on the flash drive. If not, I can surf the computer when we go back tomorrow."

Colin had set up the place mats on the large square coffee table in the living room and set down the tray of sandwiches and chips. "What are we drinking? White or red?"

CJ eyed the butler pantry in the distance. "Hmmmm . . . maybe a Pinot Noir? I think there's a 2006 Scott Paul Audrey in there. Did you know that he named it after Audrey Hepburn?"

"My, haven't we grown into quite the sommelier?" Colin chuckled and headed toward the wine cooler.

"Yeah, I guess everyone needs a hobby."

Colin opened the wine and poured. CJ took a big gulp. "That's not how one is supposed to drink fine wine," Colin teased.

"I would have gone for a shot of good

Kentucky bourbon, but it's not five o'clock yet," CJ said in defense of her eagerness to calm down. "I'll slow down as soon as it hits my bloodstream. But you're right. This stuff needs more respect." She lifted the glass and peered into its ruby color. "Mmmmm . . . it certainly warms the palate, not to mention soothes my one last nerve."

"I'll grab the laptop in the den, and we can start to comb through the files." Colin was about to get up when CJ stopped him.

"No. Wait. Let's just enjoy our lunch and the wine. It's been a while since I shared a meal with good company."

Colin sat back down on the floor. "You're right. But see? You've gotten me all wound up about this murder-and-mayhem theory. So, speaking of theories, what do you think is going on?"

"Well, first of all, we know that Mr. El Stinko is involved somehow; George is part of the equation; and there is a secret hideaway and secret bank account. Robotron is also in the picture. I wonder who else is involved. I suspect one of the other players is Congressman Dillard. It seems like we have at least two different scenarios running in tandem." CJ was using her talent at analyzing situations as she had for Snapper.

"Right. So El Stinko is on the Robotron side of the story and George the other? Is that what you're thinking?"

"It would seem that way, and somehow, they intersect. I just wonder how long this has been going on. And that condo. I had no idea it existed." CJ poured more wine into her glass and refilled Colin's.

"Did you notice any mail? That might lead to some answers."

"No, but I wasn't looking. Honestly, that computer, the dossier, and the photo were enough to boggle my mind. Thinking about the whole secret-condo thing makes me dizzy."

"We should probably check the tax records and see who's listed as the owner. That's part of the public record, so it shouldn't be hard to get." Colin started writing notes on the yellow pad that had been lying on the floor from the night before.

"Do you think it could be under someone else's name?"

"I have no idea, but it's something we can cross off the list. I suppose that with all the secrecy, it could very well be under someone else's name." Colin scribbled on the pad: "Check Property Tax." "Would it be the New Hampshire address or Virginia?"

"It's Twenty-Seven Hundred Virginia

Avenue," CJ replied absentmindedly.

"Okay. Let's make two lists: One is Mr. Crappy Cologne and Robotron, the other George and the secret condo. I'll go down to the tax assessor's office tomorrow."

"Can you pull up the invoices for George from Sun Valley? Maybe there's something there that can tell us how they were being paid every month. If I'm supposed to be so close to the congressman, then I know that. Right? I mean, I'll be the one notifying Sun Valley, so there will be lots of questions about who is going to continue paying the bills."

"Let's see what we have." Colin retrieved the laptop and opened the folder labeled "Sun Valley Institute." "Payment received. Payment received. Payment received. Every month it looks like the same amount, twenty-five thousand dollars, but there's no indication where the payments came from."

"Crap. Is there a bank ledger somewhere on that drive? Anything that would resemble a record? Or payments?"

Colin searched the folder labels. "Here's one called 'slush.' Let's try that one." He clicked on the folder and several subfolders appeared. One of them was labeled "George." Drilling down, Colin let out a low whistle. "Good Lord. There are PDFs of bank statements."

"From where?" CJ was getting excited over this new clue.

"Sackville Bank. Cayman Islands." Colin was furiously typing now.

"Cayman Islands? I always heard about that place, and how people used its banks to hide money and avoid paying taxes, but it never occurred to me that it would figure in to any situation I would be involved with." CJ was beginning to discover how naive she had been. "Wow. Twelve years I worked for that guy, and never did I suspect anything like this was going on."

"Don't feel so bad. He was a mover and shaker, and for a very long time. He knew how to work around people. It was his job."

"I can't help but feel a little betrayed. That dossier, and now this." CJ finished her wine. "Here. I think this needs to be fixed." She handed her empty goblet to Colin.

He smiled, grabbed his own empty goblet, and went to open another bottle. "Same vintage?" he called from the pantry.

"Whatever you like, Columbo," CJ retorted, returning the tease.

"Aw, c'mon. I'm not disheveled. And you know I hate cigars. How about that cute guy from *Law and Order*? Chris Noth? I can't remember his character's name."

"Mike Logan," CJ responded casually.

"Ha! So you're a crime drama queen?"

"I am not a drama queen. I am a crime drama goddess. Get that straight!" CJ was displaying more of her wry sense of humor as she called upon her analytical powers.

"Thank you for correcting me. Drama goddess."

"Excuse me, but that's '*crime* drama goddess' to you!"

Finally, they were both beginning to relax. The wine had taken off the edge, and they were secure, sitting on the floor in the space that held such wonderful memories.

"Col?" CJ was about to pry into the newly discovered relationship between Colin and Matt. Her voice lilted, signaling that she was about to get inquisitive.

"Yes?" Colin answered, mimicking her tone of voice.

"Tell me more about you and Matt. He does seem very nice."

"I told you. We knew each other. He reached out. We started hanging out. He's good company." Colin was matter-of-fact, ticking off the items on the list.

"I know you told me all that. But how do you feel about him?"

Colin wasn't comfortable entering into this uncharted territory with CJ.

"I'm not really sure."

"Oh, major blow-off! Please don't BS me."

Colin couldn't tell whether or not she was getting angry or just pretending to. It had been a very emotional two days.

"Seriously. I can take it. I get it. You need company. Twenty years with someone, then suddenly, nothing. It's tough." CJ suddenly realized that she really had no idea what it was like to lose a lover. Parents? Yes. Brother? Definitely. Lover? Nope. Only if you counted the few failed relationships she'd had, and she could barely remember them, they were so unmemorable and short-lived.

"Okay, so maybe I don't know what it's like, but I can imagine. I miss him tons, so it must kill you. Sorry. Too many death references."

"Yeah, there seems to be an epidemic of them. But to answer your question, and I mean 'seriously,' " stressing her word, "Matt is good company. Are we an item? I don't think I know what that means. Do we see other people? I know I don't, and, honestly, we've never had that conversation. We haven't done 'it' yet, if you get my drift. So is it a relationship? Kinda. I guess you could say it's still in the developmental stages." Colin sounded as if he was actually formulating his opinion as the words were coming out of his mouth.

"Wait. What? You haven't slept together?" CJ was genuinely surprised.

"I didn't say we hadn't *slept* together. We just cuddled. Oh jeez, I cannot believe I'm actually telling you all this." Colin was ready and eager to get back to cybersleuthing.

"Huh. That actually makes a lot of sense. People are in such a rush to jump into bed. And then, before they know it, they're in a relationship with an asshole."

CJ was pondering the history of her love life, which had been nonexistent ever since Kick's death.

"Who are you calling an asshole?"

"No one. Just thinking about my track record with relationships. And now that I am thinking about it, I have a laundry list of assholes, none of whose exit from my life caused any emotional waves."

They both broke out in laughter as they polished off the second bottle of wine.

"So what's next on our agenda, Drama Goddess?"

"How many times do I have to tell you, it's *Crime* Drama Goddess. I think that tomorrow, we need to, as in *you* need to, review the bank-transfer documents. Then we have to plan a trip to Sun Valley Institute.

Sun Valley? Isn't that somewhere in Utah?"

"Yes, it is, but this place is in California." Colin tossed the pad on the table.

"What time is it? It's still daylight. Why do I feel like it's midnight?" CJ began to yawn.

"Maybe because you haven't slept in two days, have been on an emotional roller coaster, discovered disturbing and mysterious information, and washed it down with an entire bottle of wine."

"But it was fine wine." CJ rested her head against the sofa as her heavy eyelids closed and she slipped into a long-overdue nap.

Colin took the glass from her hand, propped a pillow behind her head, and returned to his search of the files downloaded from the thumb drive.

Two hours later, CJ awoke with a start. "Whoa! Did you get the license plate from that truck that hit me?"

Colin smiled over at her. "You finally hit the wall, sister. You feeling okay?"

"Mmmm . . . just a little shaky. Like I need about fifteen more hours of sleep."

"No surprise. I'll whip up a little dinner. Go put on your pj's. After we eat something, I will show you what I found while you were napping."

"You found something?"

"Yes. Relax. Nothing earth shattering. Just part of the money trail."

"Show me now!"

"Okay. But first, go wash your face and put on your pajamas, please."

"What am I, twelve?" CJ thought back to when she was actually twelve and Kick said those same words to her.

"For now, yes. Now scoot!"

CJ dragged herself to her feet and marched into her room. A shower, she decided, would be better. "I'm going to clean up my act. Give me a few minutes," she yelled down the hallway.

Colin rummaged through the refrigerator, finding only cheese and grapes. He had forgotten how lax CJ was about grocery shopping. But then he remembered that Kick always had quiche in the freezer in the butler pantry. How bad could it be, if there was still some in there? Four years? Could be nasty. Still, it was worth a try. Sure enough, there were several. One of the KC's Hatchery's specialties was quiche. But they were not called quiche. They were called Kick's Egg Pies in an attempt to make them more palatable to the masses. And they were. Kick's Egg Pies came in several flavors and sizes. Kick had created his own version of quiche lorraine. It was made of the same basic ingredients: eggs, cream, and a buttery crust, but Kick put a "kick" to one, using pepperoni instead of ham. Turned out it was one of the biggest sellers. He also had healthier versions, with vegetables, egg substitutes, and light cream. He wanted the food to be delicious and hot but not so bad as to clog one's arteries.

Colin pulled out a roasted-vegetable pie, brushed off the worst of the frost, and gave it a sniff. Smelled okay. Worst case, he would throw it away, and they'd eat cheese for dinner. They could order in instead, but that would take a while. Lunch had been hours before, and a brie sandwich wouldn't be enough. They both needed to resupply.

"Yum . . . what's that I smell?" CJ was returning in a fresh pair of pajamas and drying her hair with a towel. "You found something to cook?"

"Frozen quiche — or 'egg pie' as our advertising and promotion department would have it. It was in the other freezer. Granted, it's a little old, like at least four years old, but we can always toss it if it sucks."

"Wish I had known. I would have gladly traded all that moo shoo pork for one of those!"

"It's ironic." Colin began to tick off a list

with his fingers. "First of all, you consider yourself a 'health nut'? Salad and Chinese food. Takeout no less! Second, your brother was a chef and half owner of a chain of restaurants, which you now own half of. You should be embarrassed. You have the absolute worst palate of anyone I know!" He was definitely teasing her. It wasn't the first time he had commented on her lousy food choices.

"Ah, but I do have a good palate for wine." She winked and pulled two new bottles from the cooler. "White?"

"Sancerre or Sauvignon Blanc?"

"Take your pick." She held up both.

"Let's start with the one on the left."

CJ opened the designated bottle, grabbed two white wine goblets from the Baccarat collection, and settled down on the floor. Colin joined her after serving the warm pie.

"You go first." CJ was pointing her fork at his slice. "If it tastes like crap, let me know."

"Oh thanks. I think you should go first since I was the one who found this bounty!"

"My point exactly. You found it. You heated it. You try it!" But she was only kidding. Before he had a chance to respond, she was digging in. "Oh my God! This is as good as the day it was made! Jeez, I wish I had known they were in there! Wonder what else has been preserved on ice?"

"Looked like there were a couple of pot pies, but I didn't investigate further. I was skeptically optimistic." Colin, too, was enjoying the dish.

"Skeptically optimistic? Isn't that an oxymoron?" CJ wiped her mouth and took another huge forkful.

"Not any more than 'cautiously optimistic.' Which brings me to my initial findings. I think we'll be able to discover the entire money trail, but it will still require some serious effort." Colin pulled open a folder of papers he had printed from the flash drive. "It appears that there is a trust fund in the name of George Lewis, who resides at Sun Valley Institute in Southern California. Each month an automatic transfer of twenty-five thousand dollars is made from the trust fund to the facility. He's been there for almost thirteen years."

"But what's wrong with him?" CJ's eyes had widened in half disbelief.

"CJ, I'm not exactly sure, but it appears he needs a lot of medical equipment: breathing apparatus and several monitors. Tons of stuff."

"Wow." CJ was trying to imagine such a horrible existence. "I wonder why Snapper never mentioned it."

"Who knows? Maybe he didn't want the media all over it. But one thing is certain — the fund started with about one and a half million thirteen years ago."

"What? One and a half million?" CJ dropped her fork and almost choked on her wine.

"Yeah. Apparently the Lewis family had a small horse farm in Colts Neck, New Jersey, and Snapper sold it and put all of the proceeds into the trust."

"Holy cow." CJ could hardly believe the words coming out of Colin's mouth.

"Indeed. But get this. Over the past four years, there have been additional transfers into the trust from an unknown source. That's where I need to dig some more."

"What do you mean?" CJ could barely stand this influx of information.

"One and a half mil doesn't last very long if you're spending twenty-five thousand a month. The trust was down to less than five hundred thousand when the additional funds started to be deposited."

"Okay. I'm confused. Start again." CJ was pouring another glass from the bottle that was chilling in the ice bucket.

Colin began. "The trust started with one and a half million with transfers of twenty-five thousand every month. After a few months, there was a deposit to the trust of a little over one million from an insurance company. When the fund got below five hundred thousand, five years ago, more money started flowing into the account. Sometimes as much as two hundred fifty thousand, but usually fifty thousand every couple of months. Looks like Snapper was trying to maintain enough to pay for at least a year's worth of care in the trust."

"But where was all that other money coming from?" CJ looked bewildered.

"As I said, one million came from an insurance company, but that was almost thirteen years ago. I assume that it was some kind of settlement, but I'm not sure."

"Okay, wait. Leaving the insurance money aside, when did the additional deposits start?"

"Looks like they began about five years ago."

"But where were they coming from?" CJ was trying not to sound demanding, but her frustration and confusion were rising.

"That's what I cannot figure out." Colin tossed the folder on the floor and poured himself another glass. "I would need access to the Web again."

"You mean the dark Web?" CJ asked, emphasizing "dark."

"Yes, ma'am. And I can't do it from here. Snapper had his system rigged so it could only be accessed from his computer."

"Cripes. Now we have two mysteries to solve." CJ was staring blankly at the fireplace.

"Uh, I think we need to focus on one issue at a time. First, we need to notify the family. Whatever is left of it. Which brings me to my next item. Pack your bags because we are going to LA tomorrow morning to visit George."

"What? I can't leave now! I have too much to do at the office! Until they can find a replacement for Snapper, there is a pile of garbage I have to deal with." CJ was not about to get on a plane.

"Tomorrow is Friday. Take one day off. We'll be back on Sunday. We've gotta do this, CJ. We have to go to that facility. Maybe there are other family members you don't know about. But we have to start there."

CJ gave a big sigh. "I know you're right, but this is just way too much for me to absorb."

"There's a Virgin Atlantic flight that leaves National airport at nine in the morning. We'll be there before one with the time change, and, if we're lucky, we'll be at Sun

141

Valley by two."

"Don't you think we need to call them ahead of time and let them know we're coming?"

"Actually, no. With all this drama going on, I think a surprise visit is called for. If there is anything hinky going on, we don't want to give them the opportunity to cover it up." Colin was resolute about the need to do it his way.

"I suppose you're right. All this financial obscurity, Snapper's 'apparent' suicide, the mysterious condo below his. I am stupefied. So where do we begin?"

"LA. George. Sun Valley Institute. We'll just have to work backward. Once we can confirm there *is* a George, we can try to figure out where that additional money came from and what the hell really happened to Snapper."

CJ let out a huge "UGH!" and poured another glass for both of them.

"Just when I thought my only problem was a crappy car . . ."

CHAPTER 10

Colin and CJ were up at dawn and drove out to Reagan National Airport in silence. Both were trying to make sense of the past few days of confusion. Snapper, suicide? Never. A secret condo? Why? A very secret and very private financial connection to a health-care facility. George. But why the mystery? And the latest deposits into a trust fund. Where was that money coming from? It all had to be connected. But why? And how? And who else was involved? *Mr. Crappy Cologne for sure.* CJ knew that much deep in her gut. Maybe once they were at Sun Valley Institute, some of this would become clear.

Colin parked in the short-term lot, and they grabbed their carry-on bags. "Gate twenty-three. Flight boards in an hour. Let's get through security and find a bar. I think a couple of Bloody Marys are in order. It's five o'clock somewhere," Colin said, repeating one of CJ's favorite lines when it came to consuming alcohol beverages.

"And a Xanax," CJ joked.

"Funny girl. Since when did you get involved with antianxiety meds?" Colin asked, evidently surprised at what she had said.

"Interesting you should say that. About a year ago, there was some chatter on the Hill about loosening the regulations on prescribing antidepressants, antianxiety meds, and analgesics. Snapper was involved in the talks."

Suddenly a frown appeared on her face. "Colin, you don't suppose Snapper was involved in some sort of backroom dealings?"

"Well, something was going on. He didn't make enough money to be depositing the amounts he did into the trust fund, so the money had to be coming from somewhere. And it's hard to see how that money could have been legally obtained."

"I just cannot imagine Snapper doing anything illegal, or immoral for that matter."

"People do very strange things when they're desperate." Colin was matter-of-fact. "If he was running out of funds for George, maybe doing something illegal and immoral was his only course of action."

"I hate to think Snapper would resort to unseemly measures. It's just not like him."

"You mean it wasn't like him," Colin said, correcting her use of the present tense to past tense.

"I still can't believe he's gone."

"My point exactly. You would never have thought he would commit suicide, either. So maybe whatever he was involved in got the better of him, and he couldn't look himself in the mirror anymore." Colin was beginning to suggest what seemed to be a very logical conclusion as to the cause of Snapper's death.

"I suppose that could be true, but I'm still not willing to believe he killed himself." CJ was not going to give up her own theory, regardless of how logical alternate theories of the case were. "And his involvement in something illegal with Mr. Crappy Cologne could be the reason why he might have been murdered instead. Nope. I'm not buying the suicide thing. At least not right now."

Colin took a deep breath. He knew he was in for a wild ride with CJ and her strong will.

The flight was uneventful, and they landed on time. Colin had arranged for a rental and they punched the address into the GPS.

"Should take us about forty-five minutes to get there."

CJ settled into the passenger seat and started fiddling with the radio stations. "Jeez, is hip-hop the only thing they play on the radio these days?" She was frantically pushing buttons.

"You need to find a classic rock station . . . if any still exist."

Grumbling to herself, CJ went through every number on the dial until she found "Life in the Fast Lane" by the Eagles. "I was hoping California wouldn't forget its native sons!"

"Don Henley is from Texas, love."

"Yeah, but they were the ones who came up with that California style of rock."

"Oh, but let's not forget the Beach Boys. They put California on the music map," Colin reminded her.

"Beach Boys? Are they like Boyz II Men?" CJ asked mockingly.

"Cute. You're just too young to know good music. The stuff they're cranking out now kinda sucks. Okay, maybe a few good artists, but with all the electronics that are available, anyone can be made to sound good. Even you!" Colin got in a jab, knowing CJ had no musical sense whatsoever.

"Ha. Ha. So I'm no Adele, but I'm no

Tiny Tim either. See . . . I do have some knowledge of music history."

"Tiny Tim wasn't music. History, yes, but his appearance on the scene was the demise of popular music as we knew it. In fact, I blame him for ruining our culture!"

"Tiny Tim? How did he do that?" CJ was truly puzzled.

"Okay, maybe not him per se. But someone put an extremely ugly dude with unwashed hair carrying a ukulele on television. And let's throw in that he had no talent. It was all downhill after that. The main event in entertainment was a circus sideshow of extremes."

"Huh. You have quite an opinion, Mr. Virtuoso." CJ laughed for the first time in eight hours.

"No, seriously. Everything has turned to garbage. Music. Film, TV? They create networks just to have a place to throw crap and hike up cable bills. Then there's politics. I don't need to tell you how crappy *that* business is."

CJ sighed. "On that, you're not kidding. I've been so naive. I really thought that by taking a job in Washington, I could do something worthwhile. So much for all my classes in political science."

"Don't be so hard on yourself. You had

good intentions, and I am sure Snapper did, too, when he first started out in politics. But I think that's part of the whole problem. Politicians create the rules to suit their own agendas. Maybe it was always like that, but it sure seems a lot more corrupt now than ever before. And nothing gets done for the people."

"Colin! I've never heard you on this particular soapbox before. Where is all this coming from? I know Washington is in a state of turmoil, but you always were pretty closemouthed about your politics." CJ was seeing a side of Colin she had not known existed.

"Yeah, I know. And that's part of the problem. People like me. People who are sufficiently affluent and could have a little influence have been keeping their noses to the grindstone, making money, paying taxes, and moving forward every day. When we finally looked up to see what was happening to the country, it was shocking. Shame on me. I should have been more involved. It's our fault."

"Well, it's not too late. Snapper always answered the questions his constituents raised and tried to deal with their issues in a timely fashion." CJ knew this for a fact because was she in charge of seeing that

148

such matters were dealt with. She was the one who prioritized them for her boss.

"Yeah, but Snapper is from a different brand of politics. He actually cared about his constituents. I doubt many of them do. They just want to keep their untouchable jobs, their benefits, and their perks. It's a career, for sure. The day of the citizen legislator, who takes time out from his or her real life to serve the country, then returns to private life, is over. And the country is a lot worse off for that."

CJ was trying not to slip into a dark mood. "Snapper was a special man indeed. He was almost a father figure to me, you know."

"Yes, sweetie, I do know. And that's why I'm on this cockamamie journey with you. I want to get to the bottom of whatever it is because I know you'll never rest until you get some resolution." Colin was thinking back to Kick's dying breath, when he said, "Keep an eye on CJ for me." Neither of them had had any idea they would be involved in political and financial espionage. Colin thought it would be limited to her love life, her health, and her job. But this? This was way more than he had bargained for, but he loved Kick. And he truly loved CJ. He wasn't going to let her travel down this rabbit hole alone.

"Almost there." Colin saw the final turn according to the GPS coming up on the right. As they made the turn, they were surprised to find a very small, modest building with a simple sign: SUN VALLEY INSTITUTE. It was a beautifully landscaped property, and the building had only two stories.

"I don't know what I was expecting." CJ turned to Colin. "I guess it's not the Betty Ford, eh?"

"Maybe they don't get a lot of long-term residents here. And it is pretty pricey." Colin pulled into a spot that said VISITOR PARKING.

"I'm a little nervous. You?" CJ mouthed in Colin's direction.

"Yeah. Kinda. This isn't exactly what we normally do on a Friday afternoon. C'mon. Let's get this show on the road."

CJ slowly unbuckled her seat belt and opened the door, but then hesitated. "I hope we're doing the right thing."

"We just flew three thousand miles to notify what we think is Snapper's next of kin. We are here with good intentions. Remember that." Colin was trying to be reassuring.

"Yeah. Good intentions with a hidden agenda."

"All right. Pull up your big-girl pants, and let's do this. Now!"

As they walked slowly toward the entrance, CJ's hands started to shake.

Colin took her by the elbow and led her into the small lobby.

"Hello," Colin said to the blue-eyed blonde sitting behind a desk with a sign on it that said RECEPTION AREA. PLEASE SIGN IN. "My name is Colin Kelly. This is Carol Anne Jansen. Carol worked for Congressman Otto Lewis. I believe that his brother George is a resident here."

CJ squeezed Colin's hand so tight, he thought she might break it off.

The receptionist gave them a suspicious once-over. "How do you do. May I ask what this is about?"

"We have some very unfortunate news about Congressman Lewis, and we wanted to deliver it to his brother, George, in person. George Lewis? He *is* a resident here, is he not?"

"Just a moment." The receptionist stood in her highly starched uniform and disappeared into a back room. Colin and CJ looked at each other and shrugged.

A few minutes later, a short, fairly portly, gray-haired man about the same age as Colin came out. "Good afternoon. I'm Ste-

151

phen Monahan. I am the day manager at the institute. What can I do for you?"

After Colin repeated what he had just told the receptionist, Monahan inquired, "What kind of unfortunate news?"

Colin was losing his patience. "Is George Lewis a resident here or not? And if he is not, can someone tell me why Congressman Lewis has been paying this facility twenty-five thousand dollars a month for the past thirteen years?"

"My apologies. We try to exercise discretion to protect the privacy of our residents as best we can. Please follow me."

Monahan led them to a small, austere office, with a desk, filing cabinet, and two chairs for visitors. There was a computer sitting on the desk. "Please. Sit. How can I be of assistance?"

CJ was about to lose her cool when Colin spoke a few decibels louder than before. "Look. We're here to speak to George. We have news about his brother."

"What kind of news?"

"Do you not watch television?" CJ could no longer control her angst and anger. "Congressman Lewis was found dead in his car earlier this week. They said it was a suicide, but —" Colin cut her off before she could continue further.

"But, we were not certain who his next of kin was until we came across George Lewis's name and the name of your facility. So is he here or not?" Now Colin's face was turning red.

"Well, yes. George is a resident here. But he is not in any condition to have visitors," Monahan answered in a monotone.

"So what do you suggest?" Colin regained his composure.

"He's paralyzed. In a comatose state. I am not able to share any information with you as it is covered by patient-doctor privilege."

CJ's hands flew to her face to hide her shock. Colin steadied himself and repeated his last sentence again. "What do you suggest?"

"Perhaps if you come back tomorrow?" The way Monahan made the suggestion, it seemed as if he were reading from a script.

"Do you mean in case he comes out of his coma overnight?" CJ made no attempt to hide the sarcasm inherent in her question. "No. We have flown across the country to inform Congressman Lewis's next of kin of his brother's death. And we intend to tell him now. Today. So, we'll just wait." CJ slammed her body into the chair and folded her arms over her chest as if daring Monahan and anyone else he might choose to involve to remove her forcibly from the premises.

Monahan gave the ceiling a "why does this have to happen when I'm on duty?" look.

"Ms. Jansen is the executor of Congressman Lewis's estate. Therefore, if you choose to have the institute continue to provide George with the care he has been receiving, whatever that amounts to, you will presumably want the institute to continue to receive payment for its services. I suggest you figure it out, as in now, not tomorrow or the next day or the next week. So, as Ms. Jansen, indicated, we'll wait."

"This is highly irregular. I need to consult my superiors. It may be a while." Monahan shoved his chair back, stood, and, muttering something under his breath, marched out of the room as if the Furies were chasing him.

"What the — ?" CJ looked at Colin. "Seriously? What kind of place is this? A prison?"

"Well, if he's paralyzed and on life support, there could be a problem."

"What if he's not here? What if he's also dead, and this place has been taking Snapper's money all this time? I don't remember Snapper's ever making a trip out here. And I think I would know if he had."

Colin cringed. Another theory about evil

154

people doing bad things.

"Oh jeez, CJ. How many conspiracies do you think were swirling around Snapper?"

"Occam's razor, the simplest explanation. Corruption. All over the place."

"Okay, girl, now you're being paranoid. And we just might want to curb our conversation." Colin made a gesture, pointing to his ear as if someone might be listening.

"Yeah. Whatever."

About fifteen minutes later, Monahan returned, and said to CJ, "George has been on life support for years. He would not know if anyone was in the room. If you can show me documentation that you are, in fact, the executor of the estate, we can bring you up to his room, but I feel obliged to warn you, you will find being there very disturbing."

CJ jumped out of the chair and slammed her hands on his desk. "We are going to see George *today*! Unless he's not here, and you've been taking Congressman Lewis's money all this time for nothing!"

Colin stood, put his hand on her shoulder, and gave Monahan a stern look. "This situation is becoming rather suspicious. I can understand wanting to preserve the privacy of your residents, but this is a serious situation. George's brother is dead, which means there is no one who can fund his care."

Monahan's swarthy face turned pale. "Mr. Kelly, Ms. Jansen, please try to understand my position. Do you have any documentation?"

CJ was fuming.

Colin jumped in before CJ could put her hands around Monahan's throat.

"We need to verify George's condition so we can assess how to move forward." Colin was keeping his wits about him because he knew CJ was about to explode. Understanding the roadblocks of the HIPAA law — the Health Insurance Portability and Accountability Act, which was passed to protect patient privacy — Colin had had the presence of mind to make a copy of the document, which was not Snapper's will, interestingly enough, naming CJ executor. Colin had deliberately looked for it when he was perusing the files on the thumb drive. He knew that it would become necessary to have it for a multitude of reasons. He pulled it from his pocket and handed it to Monahan. "This should suffice."

Monahan took the envelope gingerly as CJ looked on with ill-concealed amazement, having assumed that Colin was bluffing to get access to George.

Monahan shuffled through the papers. "I

see. Please give me a few minutes."

Colin was beginning to wonder if it was a good idea to choke the crap out of this weasel. Monahan walked out of the office once again, returning a few minutes later.

Sighing deeply, Monahan said, "Okay. Follow me then. But I warn you. It's not a pretty sight, and George won't understand anything you try to tell him."

"Yeah, we get it." By this time, CJ was thoroughly exasperated and did not care who knew it.

Both of them stood and began to follow the pudgy little manager down the hall to an elevator. He pushed the button and the extra wide doors opened. He held the door as Colin and CJ entered the cavernous, hospital-style elevator.

CJ was squeezing Colin's arm and trying to stay calm. Colin himself was more agitated than CJ could remember.

Monahan stepped out first and led the way down the hall. The institute was basically a nursing home with hospice care. There were about ten units on the floor — each door open to reveal very sick and disabled people. Some were on life support. Some looked as if they were already dead. Being there was totally creepy, and CJ thought she might pass out.

As they approached the last door on the right, Monahan repeated his words from before but this time with a little more annoyance. "Be prepared. I told you that it's not pretty."

Colin and CJ quietly peered around the doorjamb and slowly approached the bed. Monahan was right. George was not a pretty sight. One side of his body was flaccid, and the side of his face drooped like it was made out of Jell-O. As if he sensed that someone had entered the room, he let out an eerie groan. "Yes, George, you have company." Monahan was matter-of-fact, as if he and George carried on perfectly normal conversations. "These people are friends of your brother Otto."

"Does he understand what you're saying?" CJ whispered.

"The brain scans don't show much electrical activity. We do our best." Despite his bureaucratic manner, it was obvious that Monahan was proud of the care provided by the institute.

"Yeah. I'm sure you do. You certainly get paid enough." CJ was still on edge.

Monahan gave her a dirty look. "Please, Ms. Jansen, let's not have this discussion in front of the patient."

"Oh. Right," CJ replied with some sarcasm. "Let's not disturb George and have this conversation elsewhere."

Colin took the reins from CJ, trying to keep confrontation to a minimum. "George? Can you hear me?"

Monahan, seeming not to care about avoiding a confrontation, rolled his eyes.

A thud-like grunt emanated from George, causing everyone to take a step back.

Colin repeated the question, "George? Can you hear me?" But this time, there was no response.

"See. I told you." Monahan was beginning to sound like a five-year-old telling his parents something they had not wanted to believe.

CJ took in a big breath to steady herself and put her hand on his right arm. "George? My name is CJ. I worked for your brother in Washington."

"What is she doing?" Monahan said, almost as if whispering.

"She's trying to communicate, you idiot." At this point, Colin had given up on avoiding a confrontation and no longer cared if he insulted the smarmy manager.

CJ continued, "I know your brother has been helping these people to take care of you."

No response. She continued, "I'm sorry

to have to tell you this, but something happened to Otto. He passed away a few days ago." An almost inaudible sound came from George.

CJ's head snapped around and looked sternly into Monahan's face.

"It seems as if George understood exactly what I said."

"Uh. Well, that could just be a reflex response to audible stimuli." Monahan's palms were beginning to sweat. He had never seen this before with George. Never.

"Is there a doctor on duty we can speak with?" Colin, who was stunned but composed, asked.

"She makes her rounds in about an hour." Monahan was turning pale. "I can assure you this has never happened before."

"Yeah. I bet." CJ looked back at George and continued, "Don't worry. Someone will still take care of you. Try to rest now." She grabbed Colin's sleeve to steady herself and pulled him toward the door. At the same time, she gave Monahan a strong head gesture to follow her.

Once they were in the hallway, she hissed at Monahan, "George is not the vegetable you implied he was!"

Monahan put up his hands as if to fend off any blows that CJ might land on his puffy face. "Okay. Okay. Let me page the doctor, and we can discuss this." He was really sweating now, and he wiped his brow with one hand.

CJ's head was reeling. Clearly, George needed the kind of care the institute provided, but it was still shocking to see him and to think he had been this way for over a decade. Snapper had carried this burden so secretively all these years. It was mind-boggling. But it also helped to explain why Snapper was the advocate of affordable health care that he was. He had a personal interest in the matter based on personal experience. He and all his colleagues had their insured rear ends covered by the loyal taxpayers of the country. Now CJ could understand his passionate concern about the financial crisis families with very sick members were dealing with. She shook her head as if she were shaking out a hill of ants.

She pulled Colin aside. "We need to figure out a lot of stuff here. But where do we begin?"

"Let's see what the doctor has to say. But I don't think there's any option but to keep him here. At least for now. We can't disrupt his life."

"Yeah. Some life," CJ interrupted. "And we'll also want to see the books. Or at least what other money they may be receiving. I don't suppose there is another income stream, but I want to be sure Snapper wasn't getting ripped off."

"You have a lot of mysteries to solve, Nancy Drew. Let's start with gathering the facts." Colin took her by the elbow and led her back to the elevator, where Monahan was leaning up against the wall. He looked like he was about to need nursing care himself.

The ride to the main floor was quick, and Monahan was squirming. "We have a lounge area down the hall from my office. There is coffee, tea, and some vending machines." He was hoping he could dump them. At least until the doctor arrived. He needed reinforcement. Who knew what these people were up to?

Sure, Sun Valley Institute was making money off George, but they were also taking care of him. Better than most would or could. Monahan was trying to calm down. His job was easy. He sat in an office all day reviewing intake reports, sending letters, and, too frequently, death certificates to families. But he rarely had to deal with family members face-to-face. This was a very odd situation. No one from George's family had ever visited. And Monahan had had no idea that George was related to the congressman who had committed suicide. The money for George's care came from a trust. *I'm just the day manager,* he thought to himself. *Someone at the top will have to deal with this. It's way above my pay grade. A congressman, for heaven's sake!*

Colin and CJ took Monahan up on his suggestion and headed toward the room from which the aroma of coffee being brewed issued. The room was decorated in cheerful colors, orange and yellow, and had a sunset mural on one wall. A small sofa sat under the mural, flanked by two side tables and club chairs. On one wall were four vending machines offering the usual packaged sugar, salt, and fat-making items, while another had natural protein drinks. On the adjoining wall was a countertop that held a large Keurig machine and a basket filled with a variety of coffees, teas, and other hot beverages.

CJ headed straight toward the sofa and practically threw herself down on it.

"Colin? What the hell is going on? This has been one insane week!" She thought she might cry if she had the energy.

"One thing at a time. We need to sort this out. As I said, George seems to be well taken care of. We just need to sort out the money situation. I think there was at least another three hundred fifty thousand left in the trust. That will buy us another year." Then he lowered his voice. "If he makes it for another year. Wow. He looks like he is on the edge."

"I know. This is all too much. I wonder if Snapper had any idea how bad off he was. He must have, no?" CJ was ruminating out loud.

"You'd know better than I. You kept track of every move the congressman made."

"Yeah. Pretty much. The only time he ever traveled was for official business or to go on those photo retreats in the Everglades that I mentioned. I don't remember his ever going anywhere else other than on congressional business." CJ was wracking her brain to remember any odd trips to California.

"They probably have a visitor's log we can check." Colin was as curious as CJ.

"They may say it's an invasion of the privacy of the other residents," CJ replied, putting on her constitutional hat.

"We can ask."

Monahan appeared in the doorway with a fiftysomething, tired-looking woman wearing a white coat over a tailored pantsuit. "Hello. I'm Dr. Briggs. I understand you were visiting George Lewis. What can I help

164

you with?" She sounded cordial.

Colin extended his hand. "I'm Colin Kelly, and this is Carol Anne Jansen. She was Congressman Otto Lewis's chief of staff."

Dr. Briggs shook his hand and turned to CJ.

"I'm CJ. Yes, I was Congressman Lewis's chief of staff. You probably heard about his passing this week?"

"Yes. My condolences. I understand he had a fine reputation. Unusual for DC these days." Dr. Briggs was trying to cut through the tension in the room.

If she only knew. CJ's mind was whirling. It was as if Colin could read her mind when he jumped in with, "Indeed. Is there a place we can sit and chat in private?" He noticed that other people had entered the lounge to grab coffee or a candy bar.

"Yes. In my office. Follow me." Dr. Briggs turned and headed toward the other end of the hall, past the entry foyer.

"Are you both from Washington?" Dr. Briggs continued trying to cut the tension with small talk.

"Just outside the city," Colin offered. Nothing more.

As they entered the doctor's austere office, she gestured toward the two chairs in front of her desk as she took hers. "Please sit down. Now, what can I do for you?" She smiled at CJ, knowing that she was the loose cannon in the room.

"You can tell us why George seemed to respond to me when Mr. Monahan indicated that he was in a vegetative state." CJ crossed her arms in front of her chest as if to say, "Impress me."

"Are you his legal guardian?" Dr. Briggs pulled out the patient-confidentiality card up front.

"Well, no. But I was his brother's chief of staff and I am the executor of his estate."

"Then I'm sorry, but I cannot discuss George's condition with you." Dr. Briggs emphasized the name of the patient.

"We flew across the country to assure ourselves that George's care was sufficient so that financing it at this facility would continue." Colin was offering a new window on their relationship to George's care — money.

Dr. Briggs sat up in her chair, realizing what Colin was implying.

"Isn't there a will?" With that question, Briggs's confidence seemed to return.

CJ and Colin shot each other a horrified stare. Neither had gotten that far. CJ had been obsessed with the suicide declaration, and Colin was engrossed in following the money trail. It would have come up eventually — there obviously had to be a will since there was a legal document naming CJ executor, but they had both been distracted by all the confusion, and in their haste to find Sun Valley Institute, they had ignored a crucial piece of the puzzle as far as financing George's medical care was concerned — the will!

Colin took the lead again, switching to CEO mode. "Of course there's a will, and to reiterate, Ms. Jansen is the executor of said will. And we wanted to be sure there was no lapse in transferring funds or other support for George." CJ was impressed with Colin's demeanor. "Hence our immediate trip out here. We needed to inform the next of kin, who would be George."

The challenge wasn't lost on the doctor. She didn't want them transferring George to another facility, but she could not legally discuss his condition.

"How was he when you went to his room?" Dr. Briggs was being coy. Monahan had obviously filled her in before she went into the lounge.

"Didn't Mr. Monahan tell you? I got a response from George." CJ was abrupt.

"Sometimes patients involuntarily respond

to external stimuli. It doesn't mean they are actually processing the information in a cognitive way," Dr. Briggs continued in her sterile fashion.

"But I felt that he heard me." CJ was relying on what her inner voice was telling her.

"Yes, that too isn't unusual. Visitors think they have reached the patient in an extraordinary way. That, too, can be attributed to a different set of external stimuli."

"Oh, cut the medical monologue, will you." CJ was on the verge of losing the last bit of cool she could muster, but she took Colin's cue. "How would he respond to a different environment? I mean, if we were to move him to say, someplace closer to us?"

Back to the concern of losing the revenue, Dr. Briggs softened a bit. "It could be detrimental to his health. Moving him so great a distance. That's a very long ambulance ride."

"Certainly there are air-travel options for people like George." CJ was sure of it, though she did not really want to consider moving George, by air or any other way, as an option. She was simply trying to get information out of the annoying woman in the white coat.

"Well, yes, of course. But it is still a very long journey, and as you saw for yourself, he needs constant oxygen and is hooked up to a number of monitors." Dr. Briggs was beginning to sound anxious.

"Okay. So let's do this. You can keep George's physical health confidential, but we want to look at the invoices and all the payments." Colin sounded very much like the boardroom chairman he was.

"I . . . I don't know if that too is a violation." The doctor was beginning to stutter.

"Cut the crap, Doc. We know Snapper, I mean Congressman Lewis, had been transferring twenty-five thousand dollars a month, not counting any extras." CJ was done playing nice. "As executor of his estate, I can legally demand copies of nonmedical information. If you want that money train to keep on running, we have to compare notes."

Realizing she had little choice, Dr. Briggs stood up and smoothed her stiff white jacket. "Come with me. I'll take you to our accounting office."

CJ and Colin shot each other thumbs-up glances.

The doctor led them to another small but utilitarian office a few doors down, in which a young, red-haired woman with fingernails like claws sat in front of a computer. "Fiona, please pull up all the records you have for

George Lewis for the past two" — she looked at CJ and Colin quizzically, and Colin showed her three fingers — "make that three years. All financial transactions for his account, please."

Fiona started to click away. "Do you want a printout, or shall I put it on a flash drive?"

"Both, if that won't be too much trouble." Colin was delighted he had the option. It would make it much easier to scrutinize the transactions when they got back to DC.

"Nah. Do it all the time." Fiona turned her back to the computer and continued to tap dance on the keyboard. In a few minutes, the printer began to cough out pages of information. CJ could hardly contain herself. Finally! Something. Anything, at this point, was a step in the right direction, whatever direction that actually turned out to be. They'd figure it out. Eventually.

Shortly, all thirty-six pages were assembled with a binder clip and handed over to Colin with a wink. He always got a kick out of it when women tried to flirt with him. His amusement wasn't lost on CJ either. She gave him a subtle nudge with her elbow.

At first glance, everything looked on the up-and-up, so with that they both expressed their appreciation. Colin said, "As soon as we get the rest of Congressman Lewis's affairs in order we will be in touch. Meanwhile, you will continue to get the monthly payments."

The color came back to Dr. Briggs's face, and she extended her hand. "Thank you for your confidence in our care." She turned to CJ, who she knew was the harder to please of the two. "If you have any questions about anything . . ."

"Except his health," CJ interrupted.

"Yes, of course. Please feel free to call me. Here is my card, with my cell-phone number."

She handed a card to each of them.

"We will also send you information as to George's legal guardian when we return to Washington." With that, Colin ended the conversation, and he and CJ left the building.

"Oh. My. God. That was such an ordeal. I don't know what I need more, a nap or a drink!" CJ got into the car and buckled her seat belt.

"Let's start with a drink. It's easier than trying to drink while you're napping."

CJ let out the first grunt of laughter and relief. "Onward! I hear a Tito's martini calling my name."

CHAPTER 11

There was a lot of information to process. Snapper's death, for one. CJ was not settling for suicide and planned on pursuing the truth behind that once she recovered from jet lag and the harrowing trip to Sun Valley Institute. *Poor George. He's lived like that for years. What goes on in his mind?* Now his situation, for sure, was mind-boggling.

She was going to let Colin handle the matter of providing financing for George's care. She had a different matter to handle.

On the Monday after they got back, CJ went to her office to finish her work and start clearing out her desk. She had sixty days, there was a boatload of correspondence to complete, and all the other members of Snapper's staff had departed to seek other jobs in Congress. The governor would request a special election to fill out the remaining twenty months of Snapper's

172

term. It all seemed surreal, everything seeming to happen all at once while she was standing still, unable to match the speed at which things around her were happening.

She had to focus on what was left of her job, but she was also distracted by the alleged suicide. CJ was determined to get to the bottom of it, but there were too many other tasks that needed to be done at the moment and too few hands to do them.

She phoned Detective Harris to let him know that she was still doubtful that Snapper had committed suicide and that she would like to view the security footage one more time.

"Of course, CJ. I totally understand; I am more than happy to accommodate you. However, the sooner you can get here, the better. I'm working on a lot of cases, and I don't know how much time I'll be able to give you."

"Oh." CJ thought she would have open access since it was a member of the House of Representatives who had died. "I apologize. I didn't realize that his death was being treated like any other case. He *was* a congressman, after all." She was trying not to whine, but she was mentally and physically exhausted. She couldn't even think about jogging at this point.

"True. But the coroner has ruled it a suicide, so we are closing the case." Harris was trying to be helpful, but he knew that CJ was not inclined to drop the matter.

"But . . . how . . . I mean . . . it's just too strange." CJ's discontent left her sputtering.

"I know how difficult this must be for you. . . ."

"Do you? Do you really know? Do you know how many people whom I've loved have died on me?" She was on the verge of hysteria.

"I'm sorry. No, actually, I don't."

"Well, let's just say too many! Just tell me when to be there," she said, her voice shrill.

"How about tomorrow afternoon? Say four thirty? We should be winding down by then, and you can have the room for a couple of hours. How does that sound?" Harris was trying his best to be kind and accommodating.

"Fine. I'll see you at four thirty." She slammed the phone down, buried her face in her hands, and began to sob. When the phone on her desk rang, she was immediately forced to regain her composure.

"Hey." It was Colin. "I have some good news. I found Snapper's will on the flash drive. He left everything to George, so that should cover some of his expenses. The two condos should bring in a reasonable amount of money."

"Yeah. If we don't find any other surprises. And I have some news, too. The coroner has ruled that Snapper committed suicide, so the police have closed the investigation of his death."

Ignoring for the moment what CJ has said, Colin continued, "I also found the deed for both, and they look pretty clean; there are no mortgages on either one. At least, none I could find. Probably can get at least one point two million on each one." Colin sounded relieved that at least one issue, continued care of George, could be easily resolved.

"Well, that, at least, is some *good* news." CJ started to relax. "When can Dr. Winslow go there and evaluate him?"

Earlier that morning, before CJ went to work, Colin and CJ had sought out the best neurologist in the city, who had agreed to fly to California and run a series of tests on George.

"Probably won't be for another three to four weeks. And we have to get 'Dr. Stiff' to let him in." Colin was referring to Dr. Briggs, George's physician at the facility.

CJ let out a guffaw for the first time in almost two weeks. "Find out anything else,

Mr. Hardy?"

"As a matter of fact I did. He left his pocket watch to you. Odd thing, no?"

CJ smiled. "He always said my timing was as accurate as his watch. It was one of his prized possessions. It had been his grandfather's. Wow. That was kind of sweet." She heaved a big sigh. "Huh. So anything else to report?"

"Easy, girl. There's a lot to sift through. I still cannot figure out the origin of the money that has been going into the trust. That will take some extra sleuthing, Miss Drew." Colin was beginning to enjoy their Nancy Drew/Hardy Boys references.

"Yeah. Me too. I'm going down to the police station tomorrow afternoon to look at the security footage again." CJ's mood darkened.

"Listen. Are you sure you want to go down this road? I mean, the coroner said it was a suicide and the police have closed the investigation. They have plenty of evidence that supports the coroner's ruling." Colin was trying to get CJ to stop thinking that Snapper had been murdered.

"I don't care what the coroner said. I know that Snapper would not have killed himself. Period." CJ was unwavering.

"Okay. Do you want to meet me afterward, and we can compare notes?"

"Of course. I just don't know how long I'll be there."

Colin knew that since the case had been closed, Detective Harris was merely humoring CJ by letting her view the tape a second time. "Let's say seven thirty. If you're running late just text me; otherwise, I'll see you at the house. Okay?"

"Yes. Colin, I want you to know how much I appreciate your helping me with all of this. I don't know what I would do without you. You've been my rock."

"And you, mine." Colin was happy to do whatever he could to rally around CJ. He had made a promise to Kick. And besides, he was very fond of her. They had leaned on each other for comfort over the past four years.

"Okay. Gotta get back to answering all the constituents' e-mails and letters. I only have sixty more days before I am out of a job."

"Really?" Colin sounded surprised. "If only they were that efficient with everything else."

"Yeah. Right. Okay. Gotta go. See you tomorrow." CJ hung up, feeling a little better knowing that Snapper had made provisions for George in his will. And the watch. It was very special. Then she realized it had not been among his personal effects. A troubled look came over her face. *What would he have done with it?*

She flew out of her chair and began rifling through Snapper's desk. In the left-side drawer was a brown envelope with her name on it. Her hands started to shake as she gingerly opened it. Inside was a note repeating the words she had said only a few minutes before:

CJ — You're the only person whose timing is as good as this watch. — Snapper

She almost dropped the package. The likelihood that he had committed suicide was becoming stronger since it seemed that he knew he would die. Still, she could not let go of the nagging feeling that all was not as it seemed. Maybe a jog would clear her head. She looked at the timepiece, which read 3:30. Yes. She would go for a run.

An hour later, CJ went through her ritual. Computer in sleep mode. Check. Desk lamp off. Check. Desk drawers locked. Check. Driver's license, ID, some cash.

Slipping into her sweats, she headed down the stairs to the lobby. Immediately, she was hit by the putrid smell of god-awful cologne!

Mr. Crappy Cologne! He was in the building.

CJ headed toward the corridor where she had spotted him before. As she rounded the corner, she ran smack-dab into him, practically knocking both of them over. This time she got a good look at his face. *Butt ugly* was her first thought, followed by *creepy.* She was rattled as she blurted, "Excuse me!"

"No problem," came his husky and recognizable voice. Mr. Crappy Cologne straightened up and gave her a menacing look as if he knew who she was.

CJ quickly turned on her heels and headed out the door. *What was he doing here? Had he seen Congressman Dillard again? There is something going on. I can* feel *it.*

She headed toward the lobby and hurried over to Marcus. "Marcus, remember when I asked you about a guy who smelled like a French whorehouse?"

Marcus let out a big laugh. "Sure do! Not too many people come up with that question. Why?"

"Because he was in the building again." CJ was trying not to sound neurotic.

"Sorry, CJ, but I didn't see, or should I say 'smell' anyone who fits that description."

"Huh. Okay. Well, if you do, text me, okay?"

"Sure thing." Marcus noticed she was wearing her jogging clothes. "Have a good run!"

CJ left the lobby thinking that maybe Mr. Crappy Cologne had some other way of entering the building. That would take a lot of clearance, but then again, congressmen had lots of strings they could pull.

Her head was swimming with questions. *Who was that guy? What was he up to? What was Snapper up to? Why was he also going to Dillard's office? And why does he have to wear such awful cologne?* That last thought actually amused her.

She ran on her usual route. First, a strong sprint until she got winded, then she slowed down — even though her mind was racing the entire time. As soon as she got back to the house, she was going to look at that list she and Colin had started the first time they were together after Snapper's death.

When she got back to the parking garage, she gave her dilapidated car a stern look, and warned, "Don't even think of screwing around with me today. I am *not* in the mood."

She got into the jalopy and shoved the key into the ignition; and much to her surprise, it started right away. *Hmmm . . . maybe talking to inanimate objects really does work.*

Strapping herself in, she headed to the house.

After opening the security gate, pulling into the driveway, and entering the garage, CJ went through the required rigmarole to get into the house. Once inside, she began to feel a little calmer. The endorphins from her run had certainly helped.

She threw the keys on the pink marble console table that Kick had imported from Italy and headed toward the wine cooler. Tonight called for the 2007 Alta Vista Malbec from Argentina. This time, she had remembered to stop at the Charcuterie to pick up some smoky cured beef and a good stinky Italian Robiola cheese. Plus one of their crusty baguettes. She uncorked the wine and let it breathe for a few minutes as she fixed her plate. CJ couldn't remember the last time she had had an appetite. Seeing Mr. Crappy Cologne in the building had renewed her spirit. She was going to get to the bottom of what that son of a bitch was up to and, hopefully, figure out what had really happened to Snapper.

Before she settled on the floor in front of the coffee table she sent Colin a text: Ran into Mr. Crappy Cologne today. Literally. Got a glimpse of his face.

Ug-lee. CU tomorrow. XOCJ

CHAPTER 12

When CJ rolled out of bed after a long night of reading the notes she and Colin had put together, she was a little weary. She probably should have stopped after the third glass of wine, but boy was it good. Especially with the cheese. She cursed herself for drinking too much but relented almost immediately. It was time to get going. She was going to finish up a lot of correspondence, then head to the police station, where she would review the security tapes once again. Afterward, she and Colin were planning to confer at the house.

Arriving at the Rayburn Building, she stifled a yawn as she entered the lobby and saw Marcus at the security checkpoint. "Any signs of Pepé Le Pew?" she joked.

"No, ma'am. But if I sniff him out, I'll let you know immediately!" Marcus was enjoying the banter. He knew she wasn't going to be working there much longer. That is, unless whoever got elected chose to keep her on. It wouldn't be a bad idea. New congressmen barely had a chance to figure out what they were doing before they had to run for reelection. Stupid system.

Snapper had not wanted any type of viewing or funeral. He had indicated that he be cremated. She would plan a memorial service for him, but it would take place only after she had finished carrying out her official duties. So, at least that was one thing she would not have to deal with immediately.

CJ headed to the office and groaned at the pile of papers still sitting on her desk. "I guess you aren't going to answer yourselves, are you?" Thinking about how her car had responded to her comments, she grinned. *Wouldn't it be wonderful if letters* could *answer themselves?* she thought. *Except then, no one would ever write letters, would they? Oh well, time to get to work.*

The day went by rather quickly, and when she looked at the clock, she was surprised to find that it was already four o'clock. She had to hustle to make her appointment at four thirty. And the traffic was going to be horrendous.

She hustled down to the garage and glared at her car, reminding herself that she really,

really needed to get a new one. Maybe tomorrow.

As she backed out of her parking space, she thanked God her car had started without a hitch. She took the quickest route, and, as she approached an amber light, she pumped the brakes lightly. Nothing. She pumped again, harder this time. Still nothing. She pumped harder and harder. She reached for the emergency brake and tried to pull it. Nothing. The car would not stop. She braced herself for the inevitable collision with the Mazda directly in front of her that had stopped for the light, which was now red. When the crash came, CJ hit her head on the steering wheel just before the air bags deployed. She could feel blood trickling down her face.

The driver of the unfortunate Mazda exited his car, looked at the damage to the rear end, and started to scream at CJ. "What the hell is wrong with you? Texting? You asshole!" He was livid.

CJ could only moan. She pushed the air bags out of her way and pulled herself from the car. "I . . . I . . . don't know what . . ." were the only words she could utter before she collapsed to the road.

Several minutes later, an ambulance appeared and an EMT gave her oxygen, treated her head wound, and checked her vitals. "Miss? How are you feeling?" The kind voice of the EMT sounded fuzzy.

"I'm . . . I'm okay. What happened?" CJ was still dizzy.

"You slammed into the car in front of you," said a police officer, who was standing in front of her with a notepad.

"I tried to stop, but the brakes . . . they were soft . . . they didn't work. I kept pumping, but nothing. And the emergency brake didn't work, either." She was starting to come around. "I was trying to stop the car. It wouldn't stop." Her voice was still weak.

"Okay, Ms. Jansen. You do realize I am going to have to issue you a citation for reckless driving."

"But I wasn't being reckless. Honest. The brakes . . . they failed. It's an old car." CJ's voice was soft; she was still confused.

"Well, it's going to have to be towed. You really creamed the front end." The police officer tore the ticket from his book. "We called a truck. Should be here shortly. We have enough traffic problems without people clogging up the intersections." He handed over the ticket. "You can dispute this in court if you want."

CJ's hands were trembling. *Court. Police station.* She remembered she had an appointment with Detective Harris. "Officer" — she peered at his name tag — "Walters, could you contact Detective Harris at the substation? I had an appointment with him at four thirty. Please?" she begged.

The cop pulled his walkie-talkie out of his shoulder holster. Crackling sounds could be heard, then voices as he muttered into the mouthpiece. "Roger that." He turned back to her. "If you're okay, I'll give you a lift." Suddenly, he was being very accommodating.

"Sure. Thanks. Yes, I'm okay. Just a little shaken." CJ continued to press the ice pack to her head. "Can you let me know where they're taking my car?"

"If I were you, I'd have them take it to the junkyard." The officer was trying to make light of the situation.

"Huh. Maybe later. First, I want my mechanic to take a look at the brakes, so when I do go to court, I'll have some evidence supporting my account of what happened."

"If you say so. Got a particular shop you want the tow to take it to?"

"My mechanic's place is near where I live." She wrote down the name and address with her trembling hand. The police officer made a whistling sound, and said, "That's

186

some fancy neighborhood. You got a different car you drive when you're there?"

"I will now."

CJ fumbled for her phone and sent a text
to Colin: In car accident. On my way to police
station. See you later. Need new car.

He quickly responded: U sure Ur okay?
Want me to come down there?

CJ pinged back: Probably a good idea. TY.

CJ continued to hold the ice pack on her
forehead as the patrol car zigzagged through
the traffic. "I noticed you have a government security pass in your handbag. Sorry.
We had to look for ID."

"Yes, I'm . . . I was Congressman Lewis's
chief of staff." CJ tried to sound coherent.

"You mean the one who smoked himself
in the garage?" The officer had no couth.

"Yes. That one." CJ didn't bother to
continue this conversation. She wasn't in
the mood for idle chatter, especially about
Snapper and his death.

"You feeling okay?" The officer looked at
her through the rearview mirror.

"I'm fine. Still a little shaken up. That's
all." *Bullshit,* she told herself. *Things couldn't
get much worse.*

As they arrived at the police station, the
officer helped her out of the car and up the
stairs. *Chivalry is not dead. Maybe just uncon-*

scious, she thought to herself.

"Ms. Jansen here to see Detective Harris." The officer was putting on his best official demeanor.

"I'm okay. You can leave me here," CJ said, offering to allow Walters to return to his duties.

"No. Not until I get you settled."

Wow. When under the scrutiny of superior officers, this guy can pull out all the stops. CJ was losing her patience but remained steady on her feet.

The desk officer called Detective Harris, who appeared shortly.

"CJ. Are you okay? I heard you were in a bit of a fender-bender." Harris held his hand out and took her arm. She looked frazzled.

"Yes. I'm fine. Please, I need everyone to stop fussing. I appreciate it, but I am sure Officer Walters has to get back to work." *And outta my hair,* she thought to herself. "Thank you, Officer, for the lift and for your assistance."

"It's my pleasure to serve," Walters replied smoothly.

Yeah, and Bob's your uncle. Another sarcastic thought flew through her mind.

Detective Harris led CJ to the media room. "Are you sure you want to do this today? We can reschedule for tomorrow."

"No. It's okay. I know you're busy, and I have a lot to deal with, including getting a new car. But thanks." CJ was firm. She knew the clock was ticking if she wanted to make a case for murder.

As they entered the room, CJ noticed how much colder it was than in the outer offices, and a chill went down her spine.

"Are you sure you're okay?" Harris pressed.

"I'm fine. Really. I just didn't remember the room's being this cold the last time."

"It's because of all the equipment. But you also had a shock. Sit down. I'll get you some water."

CJ took a seat and marveled at all the monitors, computers, and keyboards.

I'm sure I'll find something, she told herself. *Just look at all of this.*

Harris returned with two bottles of cold water and handed one to CJ. "Sorry. We don't have any glasses. We used to, but people kept leaving them all over. You know how guys are."

CJ grunted a slight laugh. "I suppose." She actually didn't. It dawned on her that she had no clue when it came to the opposite sex. They truly were from Mars.

Harris set up the video and began to run

189

the footage. Just like the first time, the congressman was walking from the stairwell to his car. Then a full three minutes later, a man dressed in a Burberry trench coat appeared with his head bent down, keeping out of direct sight of the camera. And again, like the first time, she was jolted by the head tilt!

"That's him!" CJ was certain. This time she was sure that it was Mr. Crappy Cologne because she had bumped into him just the day before.

"That's who?" Harris was clearly confused.

"The guy who was in Snapper's office fighting with him a couple of weeks ago. He smells like a French whorehouse. He and Snapper got into some kind of argument, and he assaulted the congressman. Then I saw him in Congressman Dillard's office the same week, reeking of that abominable-smelling cologne. That's how I was able to recognize him as I had not seen his face the time that he kicked Congressman Lewis in the groin." CJ was talking so fast, Detective Harris put his hands up.

"Slow down, CJ. You said he was in Snapper's office? And then you saw him in Congressman Dillard's office?" Harris was trying to follow CJ's runaway train of

190

thought.

"Yes. I had to go back to my office and overheard them. I didn't see his face until a couple days later. Well, no, actually I didn't see his face that time. I smelled his cologne. You cannot miss it. It is unforgettable."

"You smelled his cologne." Harris repeated her words.

"Yes. I smelled *him*. He takes a bath in this disgusting cologne."

"So did you actually see his face?" Harris pressed her.

"Not until yesterday. I was leaving the building to go for a run, I got a whiff of him again, and I followed the cloud down the hallway. When I turned the corner, I ran smack into him. That's when I saw his face for the first and only time." She was starting to slow down so she wouldn't sound like a nutcase.

"So you actually saw this man's face? In the lobby?"

"No, in a hallway." CJ was trying not to get cranked up again. "I smelled him twice, then a third time, and that time I actually saw his face. Get it?"

"Got it." Harris was actually writing it all down. "Do you remember overhearing anything? Like when he was in Congressman Lewis's office?"

"Yes, something about Robotron. But I really didn't hear more than that, which was when he kicked Snapper. But then I overheard another loud conversation with him and Dillard a few days later."

"But you hadn't seen his face yet. Is that correct?" It almost sounded like Harris was interrogating her.

"Correct. No face. Just smell and loud voices." CJ folded her arms across her chest.

"Did you hear anything they said in Dillard's office?" Harris pressed on.

" 'I said I'll take care of it!' " CJ parroted what she remembered.

"Take care of what?" Harris was getting confused.

"That's what someone said — 'I said I'll take care of it,' " CJ clarified, and continued, "But I'm not sure which of them said it, Mr. Crappy Cologne or Congressman Dillard."

"And then what happened?"

"Mr. Crappy Cologne stomped out of the office. I leaned against the wall, so he wouldn't see me. I noticed he dodged the security camera by keeping his head tilted the same way the man in the Burberry trench coat does in the security tape."

"All this is very interesting, CJ. Have you told anyone else?"

"Only Colin. My brother's partner."

"Okay. Let's run the footage one more time." Harris was either starting to believe her or simply humoring her.

The image was still grainy. She couldn't get a good look at the man's face. She knew it would be almost impossible to prove that Mr. Crappy Cologne was involved. Tears ran down her face. What a hell of a day. Week. Month. She needed to go home and take a long hot bath. And have a few glasses of wine. Colin would be arriving shortly, and he could drive her home.

"CJ, I want you to know that I'm not taking this lightly. But as you know, we don't have a lot to go on. I'll ask forensics to take another look at his car to see if there was anything suspicious. It's still in the lot as far as I know."

"It should be because I didn't sign any release papers for it." CJ knew that much at least.

A few minutes later, there was a slight knock on the door, and Harris let Colin in.

He took one look at her and thought she had been hit by a bus. "CJ! Good heavens! What the hell happened? You look terrible!"

"Oh thanks. I feel like I look. Something went wrong with my brakes, and I slammed into the car in front of me. Thank God we were at a traffic light instead of on the Belt-way."

"You okay?" Colin peered closely.

"Yes. Just a hot mess."

"I guess this means you're going to finally get a new car?" Colin was trying to lighten the mood.

CJ gave him her sideways *"no shit, Sher-lock"* glance. "Yes. New car." She was begin-ning to feel better, the shock of the crash and her discovery beginning to wane.

"Okay, sister. Let's get you home. Okay with you, Detective?" Every once in a while Colin would refer to CJ as "sister," espe-cially if he was being playful.

"Fine with me. CJ, do you think you could come back in a few days and give me a statement about what you saw and heard?"

"Really?" CJ was pleasantly surprised. Harris was finally starting to believe her? "Of course. Just let me know when." She gave Colin the thumbs-up when Harris wasn't looking. Colin responded with an eye roll.

"Will do. Meanwhile, go get some rest." Harris walked them to the waiting area and said good night.

On the way to the house, CJ was starting to rally. "Wow. I think he actually believed me. Although I'm not sure why." She frowned.

"That's a good thing, no?" Colin glanced at her from the driver's seat. "Isn't that what you wanted?"

"Yes, but something still doesn't feel right."

"Uh boy. Here we go . . ."

"Seriously, Colin. I think he has a different agenda."

"Like what?"

"I dunno, but my gut is telling me that there's something else going on."

"Nancy Drew, you're going to have to keep your imagination at bay. Just go back, give him your statement, then see where it leads. You're not the detective, may I remind you. You only play one in your pretend life."

"Very funny. Well, we'll see about that." And after she said that, she rested her head against the window and dozed off.

Chapter 13

Once they arrived at the house, CJ took a hot bath while Colin prepared a light dinner for them. Another egg pie, but this time he had picked a fresh one up at the closest Hatchery. They polished off a bottle of Whispering Angel Rosé and decided that reviewing all the information was not in the cards that evening. CJ had been tossed around physically and mentally, and they called it a night.

The next morning, Wednesday, CJ was feeling a little unsteady but good enough to go to the office and slog through the balance of the correspondence. She was always amazed at the amount of written letters that still came through the mailroom. Remarkable, actually, in this day and age of digital communications.

During the lunch hour, she took an Uber to the car-rental agency so she could have some wheels until she found a new car. She still wasn't about to drive any of those Italian jewels in the garage. Maybe one day, but not today.

Thankfully, it was a quiet day, and she placed a few phone calls about her wrecked car and made some appointments to test-drive a couple of SUVs. She wanted to be visible to everyone else who was driving what she referred to as an "urban assault vehicle." She lined up a Jeep, a Ford Escape, and a Hyundai. She wasn't about to go overboard with something pricey. A good utility vehicle was all she needed.

The phone rang around two thirty. It was her auto mechanic with the report about her brakes.

"Ms. Jansen? Ernie here. Somethin' funny about them brake lines. Both for the regular brakes and the emergency brake." Ernie had a bit of a southern drawl.

"What do you mean?" CJ sat up in her chair as if the Sunday school teacher were about to enter the room.

"Well, I'm seeing a few little holes. Teeny puncture marks. Can't say how that coulda happened. Not regula' wear 'n' tear."

"Huh? What are you saying?" CJ's forehead crinkled.

"I'm saying that I ain't seen nothin' like this before, Ms. Jansen. It looks like some-

197

one or somethin' took an awl to the lines."

"An awl?"

"Yeah, one of them things you use to punch holes. Looks like a screwdriver, but it's pointy on the end. Kinda like an ice pick."

"What? Are you saying someone tampered with my brakes?" CJ bolted upright and was now standing.

"Yes, ma'am. That ain't all, Ms. Jansen. If the brakes hadn't failed, it woulda only been a matter o' time before the steering went, too." Ernie might not have sounded like an expert, but he was a crackerjack mechanic.

"Wait. What are you saying?" CJ was getting impatient — something that was starting to become the norm.

"I'm sayin' that the steering fluid was almost down to a trickle. If you hadn't crashed into that car in fron' o' you when you did, you wouldn'ta been able to steer it, either. That woulda happened within a few blocks from where the accident happened. I don't want to scare the bejesus outta ya, but puttin' two 'n' two together, I'm thinkin' someone messed with your car and tried to kill you."

CJ's hand flew to her mouth. *Why would someone do this?* That was the first thought that came to her mind. Her second sent a

chill down her spine — *Mr. Crappy Cologne.*
But why?

"Ms. Jansen? You still there?" Ernie had kept on talking, but CJ had stopped paying attention at "someone messed with your car and tried to kill you."

"Oh yes, Ernie. Sorry. I'm just a little stunned. Can you take some photos for me? Maybe write something up? This is a little unnerving." CJ was remaining as calm as she could given the news Ernie had just delivered. Her adrenal glands were working overtime. She needed to call someone. Who? Colin? Harris? Matt? She didn't even have his number.

"Ya darn tootin'. Would set my one last nerve on edge, too." Ernie was prattling away. "And fer sure I can snap a few pictures. I got me one of them smartphones. Sometimes I think it's smarter than me! It's got so many gizmos on it, I don't know what to make of them."

"Yes, I know the feeling. I prefer something simple, but that's not the way of the world now. I'll be over later today if that works for you." CJ's mind was racing. *What to do first?*

"Sure thing, Miss Jansen. I'll be here all day. Working on one of them fancy Porsche sports cars. Them things take a lot of time, and it still ain't easy gettin' parts."

CJ was mimicking a wheel with her finger to try to telepathically get Ernie to speed it up and get off the phone.

"Thanks, Ernie. I'll see you in a bit." She hung up without waiting for him to say good-bye and put the phone down.

After drumming her fingers on her desk for a few minutes, she started making a list of the incidents of the past few weeks: Snapper has altercation with Mr. Crappy Cologne. Mr. Crappy Cologne is in Dillard's office. Snapper allegedly commits suicide. She smells the odor of stinky cologne in Snapper's car. She and Colin discover that Snapper has a secret condo, secret files, and a secret bank account. Throw in a secret brother. Mr. Crappy Cologne is back at the Rayburn Building. He sees her face when they collide. Her brakes don't work because her car had been tampered with.

That ought to get someone's attention. But whose? Who would be most likely to believe me? She punched in Colin's number on speed dial.

"Yo, CJ. What's up?" Colin sounded cheerful.

"A lot is what's up."

Colin cringed on the other end of the call. "Uh-oh, Nancy Drew."

"No. This is a lot more serious than playing detective." And she sounded like it was. CJ wasn't about to fall apart now. Her voice was steady. "Remember I said that I thought something was wrong with my brakes? Well, there was. Plenty. As a matter of fact, someone tried to kill me by tampering with them. . . ." After waiting a beat for Colin to digest what she had said, she added, "And whoever messed with the brakes rigged the power steering. Unless, of course, there are two people trying to kill me." Another beat. "Colin? Are you listening?"

"Did Ernie call you?"

"Of course he called me. I wasn't about to crawl under my car." Now annoyance was in the tone of her voice. "Colin, this is serious. And I think I know who's behind it."

"That stink-o dude from the office?" Colin was wary of drawing conclusions but attentive.

"Yes. Mr. Crappy Cologne. I made a list of the series of events — the way we did at home. But this time I added the tampering with my car and the accident. We need to tell someone."

"Jeez. Okay. Take it easy." Colin was the one who was getting rattled now.

"I *am* taking it easy. I want to roast that son of a bitch. Whom should we talk to?

Maybe Matt? I'd go to Harris, but the investigation into Snapper's death is officially closed, and he's got other things to work on. Not that Matt doesn't, but at least you know him and trust him, right? You do trust him?" CJ wanted to be absolutely certain before she moved forward and disclosed what they knew.

"Of course I trust him. He helped us at Snapper's, didn't he?" Colin was trying not to be defensive.

"And that's why I think we should go to him first. At least he'd be able to tell us what to do next. Can you call him? Please?"

"Of course. Let me give him a buzz now, and I'll call you right back." Colin hung up, immediately dialed Matt's number, and made arrangements for all of them to meet at CJ's later that evening.

He called CJ back right away. "Okay. He's going to meet us at the house around seven. You okay to drive?"

"I'm fine. I'm on a mission now. See you later." Just as she was about to click off the phone, she added in a much softer voice, "Thanks, pal. I don't know what I'd do without you."

"Get yourself into a lot more trouble, I imagine!"

CJ glanced at the digital clock on her

desk. It read 3:30. She still had at least an hour of work left, so she dug into the pile on her desk. When she looked up again, it was almost six. She jumped out of her chair and tidied up her desk. Lights off. Door locked. Crappy cologne smell. "What the hell?" CJ peered out the side door to see if that creep was lurking in the hall. For someone who was very sneaky, he certainly left a trail of stench. She shook her head at the thought. Then she saw a shadow move in the distance. Quietly, she closed her door and sat back in her chair. How was she going to get out of her office without being seen? That is, assuming he was waiting for her and intending to finish what he had begun. She picked up the house phone and called the night security desk.

"Yes, Ms. Jansen? How can I help you?" came a comforting voice on the other end.

"Hi. I had a slight car accident yesterday, and I'm a little stiff and have some boxes to carry. Would you be able to send someone up here to give me a hand?"

"Sure. Do you need a hand truck or something?"

"No. Nothing heavy-duty. Just another pair of hands would be helpful. I'd really appreciate it."

"No problem, Ms. Jansen. I'll have someone come up shortly." The guard hung up the phone. CJ looked around the office to see what she could put in the banker's box to support her faked call for assistance. She spotted some heavy bookends and an almanac. That ought to do it. Then she thought she should put something in front of the main door. Trash can. It wouldn't stop him, but at least she'd know when she came back if someone had been in the office. The cleaning people wouldn't bother coming in since there would be a major sweep once a new member of the House arrived.

Satisfied she could continue her ruse, she packed up the rest of her personal items and waited for her escort.

A few minutes later, there was a knock on her door that made her leap from her seat. Easy girl.

"Yes?"

"Ms. Jansen? It's me, Larry. I'm here to help you with your stuff."

CJ heaved a big sigh of relief, opened the door, and pointed to the box.

"Thank you so much. I'm sorry to be a nuisance, but I totaled my car, and I'm a little sore."

"No problem. Just show me where to go." Larry picked up the box as if it weighed no more than a feather and followed her out.

The stench of Mr. Crappy Cologne had evaporated somewhat, so he must have left the floor. CJ hadn't realized how tense and sore she really was until she got into her rental, sat comfortably in the seat, and headed home. On the way, she stopped at Ernie's to pick up the photos and the report. Thankfully, he wasn't there and had just left everything in a brown envelope with her name on it. She simply wasn't in the mood for small talk. She would have to save all her wind for later, when she would walk through the events with Matt.

Colin was already at the house when she arrived, and he had opened a bottle of wine and poured himself a glass.

"You're *the* best!" She gave him a peck on the cheek and took the goblet he was holding from his hand.

"Hey! That was mine. I can pour one for you," Colin chided her in a teasing way.

"No time." CJ took a huge swig of the wine.

"Take it easy. We have a heavy-duty night ahead."

"No kidding." CJ walked over to the sofa and practically threw herself on it.

"Wow. Wow. Wow. Just when I thought things could not get more bizarre. Maybe this is all a dream, like in *Dallas,* when what's her name woke up from a dream. That was pretty lame, by the way . . . and then she woke up. Seriously? The entire season turned out to be a dream? I hate when writers cop out like that."

"Aren't you a little young to be talking about shows from the eighties?" Colin eyed her from the kitchen.

"Ah, but I watched *Dallas: The Next Generation.* That was *really* lame if you ask me."

"Well, now I know where you get your cynicism from. Kick hated those shows, too." Colin remembered the times when he and Kick would have one of those rare relaxing evenings and wrestle over the remote.

"Yeah. He tortured me with PBS. Wanted me to be sophisticated." CJ swirled the wine in her glass, avoiding the real subject at hand.

"Okay, sister." Colin eyed the brown envelope, which contained a flash drive and a sheet of paper. "The envelope, please."

CJ nudged it with her foot as if it were something she wanted to scrape off the bottom of her shoe.

Colin opened the envelope and read the brief report:

Damage to brake lines, regular and

emergency. Appear to have several punc-
tures.

Seal on power steering pump also dam-
aged.

Damages do not appear to be normal
wear and tear in spite of mileage, make,
and model.

He reread the last line out loud in a soft
voice, concern mounting on his face and in
his stance.

"Nice, eh? Now someone is trying to kill
me, too!" CJ pulled one of the toss pillows
and hugged it to her chest. "Why, Colin,
why? I don't understand. What the hell is
going on here?" She held back the tears that
were welling up.

"I wish I knew. Maybe you're really onto
something about Snapper's death. Maybe
someone really did kill him. Cripes. Well,
Matt should be here shortly. Let's see what
he has to offer and what steps we need to
take."

He poured them each another glass of
wine and sat down next to CJ. She rested
her head on his shoulder and sighed might-
ily. "And you guys thought I was bonkers.
But ya know something? My inner self kept
nagging at me, and it's never been wrong.
Not a single time."

"I know, sweetie. We'll sort this out." Colin put his arm around her and gave her a hug.

A few moments later, the sound of the intercom buzzer alongside the security gate broke the silence. Colin got up to answer the in-house phone. "Hello?"

"It's Matt."

Colin released the security gate, and Matt pulled into the driveway. He parked his car and headed to the front door, where Colin was waiting for him.

"Thanks for coming over."

"No problem. Nice place." Matt was taking in the enormity of the house and its fine furnishings.

"Yeah. Kick had a knack for decorating. Big surprise. Although I don't want to sound like I'm stereotyping!" Colin was being as upbeat as he could in light of the situation.

"He certainly had good taste." Matt kept admiring the statues and artwork as he followed Colin to the great room off the kitchen, where CJ was half slumped on the sofa.

She rallied and stood, almost spilling the wine in her glass. "Sorry. I'm a little shaky."

"So I've heard. And for good reason I am sure." Matt was calm and even tempered. One had to be in his line of work. Logic.

Reasoning. Patience. Yes, patience. That was always the tough one, especially when they were trying to crack a case.

"Please sit. Can I get you something to drink?" Colin was being the polite host to his friend.

"Since I'm off duty, and this is not official business, I would love a vodka on the rocks."

"Tito's? Chopin? Ketel One? Belvedere?" Colin rattled off the various spirits.

"Tito's, please. It's gluten free!" Matt chuckled.

"Coming right up!" Colin moved toward the marble-topped bar and pulled the bottle out from the freezer drawer.

"Tell me, do you really have a freezer just for vodka?" Matt was impressed.

"It's better that way," CJ chimed in. "When I really need a stiff drink, I throw a nipple on one!" She was trying to elevate her mood with her wit.

"I doubt that. You don't look like the type." Matt was still trying to keep the mood more upbeat. He knew this was going to be a difficult conversation.

"No, I'm more the type that someone wants dead." CJ's comment cut through the room like the ice pick or awl that had punctured her brake lines.

Matt pulled out a pad and pen. "Let's

start at the beginning. Try to remember as many details as possible. Maybe we can put some of the pieces of this puzzle together."

CJ, with Colin's help, recounted all the peculiar circumstances, starting with the night of Snapper's and Mr. Crappy Cologne's quarrel. When it came to discovering the computer and the financial transactions, she hesitated.

When she looked at Colin, he nodded for her to continue. "When we were at Snapper's, and you helped us with the lock, we came across . . . this is off the record, right?" She needed reassurance.

"I'm here as a friend. Look. Evidence." Matt held up his glass of vodka. "I'm imbibing an alcoholic beverage. That definitely makes this off the record."

"Okay. Well, we found a computer that had a lot of financial information on it. There is a trust fund that Snapper was using to pay for his brother George's expenses. Colin knows more about the transactions, but Snapper has — had — a brother who is in an institution owing to a massive stroke suffered, get this, thirteen years ago. Money was being transferred every month to a place called Sun Valley Institute, in California. Colin and I went out there Friday to check it out and notify George. He's in really bad shape — a vegetative state. But they say there is still some brain activity. Very sad. Anyway, there was a lot of money transferred over the past thirteen years. I know some of it came from selling the family estate and some from insurance, but there's a whole lot of money that we can't figure out where it came from. Some kind of dark Web thing. As I said, Colin can fill you in on that."

Matt was writing as fast as he could. "How much money was being transferred every month?"

"Twenty-five thousand for housing, but sometimes there were other expenses for equipment, et cetera. It looks like Snapper spent well over three million in the past thirteen years."

"That *is* a lot of money," Matt concurred. "But you mentioned the dark Web? What's that all about?"

Colin glanced at CJ this time, looking for approval. She nodded.

"We found a lot of transactions for a fund that releases monthly automatic payments to a health facility. But I am having trouble finding the source of the funds. And it appears that the trading has been done on the dark Web."

"Most people have never even heard of

the dark Web," Matt said. "It's the back room of the Internet. From buying drugs, guns, to hiding money, human trafficking. Throw in gathering the personal details of millions of unsuspecting people. Everything is off the grid. People have no idea how massive this underworld trading is. We have established an entire division dedicated to finding and tracking illegal sites. It's hard to fight enemies if you don't even know they exist." Matt kept writing.

"That's how I found the initial trust and the transfers. But I could not find the source of the money. But that's not what concerns us now. At least not as far as the latest developments." Colin continued the time line. "When CJ went to get Snapper's personal effects from his car, she noticed the same rancid smell of cologne. She's spotted him and smelled him in the halls of the Rayburn House Office Building. And Monday, she actually ran into him. Literally."

Matt turned to CJ. "Then what happened?"

"I got a look at his face. Ugly dude. The next day, I was driving to the police station to take another look at the security-tape footage when my brakes would not work, and I hit the car in front of me at an intersection. My mechanic said someone had tampered with the brake lines *and* the seal on the power steering pump."

The room went quiet for a moment as Matt digested this new information.

"Here." CJ handed the brown envelope to Matt. "My mechanic's report and a flash drive with photos. I think someone was trying to kill me. Ernie, he's my mechanic, says that if I had not run into that car at the intersection, the steering would have gone within a few blocks. And, all along I've been saying that Snapper's death was not a suicide. I think he was murdered." There. Done. She'd put it all out there for the FBI agent. "And I am positive that the crap cologne guy is the one who killed him and tried to kill me."

"Considering everything you've told me, it does sound logical." Matt was still writing vigorously. "Do you think you could describe him to one of our sketch artists?" His voice was steady.

"Sketch artist?" CJ was stunned that he seemed to believe her enough to suggest using a sketch artist.

"We could also try reviewing the footage from the lobby security cameras, but they tend to tape over them pretty quickly. I can look into that as well," Matt said.

"But wait. Didn't you say this was not official business?" Suddenly, her inner self was getting worried.

"Of course. But this does sound rather serious. If we can identify the man you refer to, he might have a rap sheet."

"Yeah, but . . . I . . . I thought this was between us. I mean, I am absolutely certain Snapper did not kill himself, but —"

"But nothing, CJ. This is what you wanted. Someone to believe your theory." Colin was firm but kind.

"Yes. Okay, but how does all of this play out?" CJ knew that if she was right, she was stepping into a big pile of bullpucky.

Matt took the lead. "You'll come down to our office and meet with one of our sketch artists. We'll run it through the computer. If we get a match, I'll get in touch with DC police. We have a very good working relationship. Well, at least some of us do."

"So unless you get a match, all this stays with us?" CJ was pumping Matt for reassurance.

"Yes. It has to. I've had two drinks!" Matt was giving her what she needed: someone who would listen to her allegations and someone who had the authority to do something about it.

"Come down to my office tomorrow after

you're finished with work. Say five o'clock? I'll make sure there's someone available to sit with you." Looking at his watch, Matt got up. "I'd better get going. Thanks for the libations, and thanks for the information. CJ, we will get to the bottom of this. I promise."

As Colin walked Matt to the door, he lowered his voice.

"I really appreciate this, Matt. In the beginning, I thought CJ's imagination was running wild. But with the events of the past few weeks, and her car incident yesterday, I am now sure that something is going on. What it is, unfortunately, I have no idea. But definitely something."

Matt squeezed Colin's bicep. "Not to worry. We'll take good care of her."

As Colin shut the door, it occurred to him that Matt had said, "*We'll* take good care of her." *What did Matt mean when he said that? And who's the 'we'?* He shook off his apprehension, thinking he was getting a little more paranoid, too.

CJ sat up as Colin came back into the room. "So?"

"So what?" Colin shot back.

"So did you make your next date with him?"

"What? No. We didn't discuss that. Why?"

"Because you said you liked him and you had spent time with him. Just wonderin' . . . one of us has to have some kind of love interest. It's been too long for both of us." CJ sat back in the luxurious sofa and plopped her feet on the marble-and-stainless-steel coffee table. Nuevo Italian decor. Kick had loved everything Italian. Funny that he hadn't opened an Italian restaurant. CJ would often tease him about it. As she glanced around the room, she added: "Col, I know Kick would want you to be happy. It's been four years. I think it's okay if you want to like someone. It doesn't take anything away from what you had with Kick. It just enhances your life further."

"My, aren't we being the contemplative one tonight?" Colin had rarely heard CJ wax philosophical. She was funny and thoughtful, not rarely in a deep, reflective mood.

"Seriously, Colin. Just look at everything that's happened lately. Snapper. George. My car. And let's not forget the mysterious common denominator, the Smellenator. Life is crazy and unpredictable. Then, if we peel back another layer, there's Kick. Who would have thought we'd lose him so soon? Go back another layer to my parents. It's just all too obvious that time is fleeting, and the only time we really have is the present."

"Wow. What have you been reading lately?" Colin was taken aback by the seriousness of her reflections.

"I don't have to read to figure out what the hell is going on around me. At least realize that maybe I *don't* know what the hell is going on around me, and maybe I'm, we, are supposed to take each day as it comes and try to squeeze some joy out of it."

"You've got a very good point. But right now, I think we need to concentrate on what happened to you and make sure you're protected until we can sort this out."

"They don't offer protective custody unless a crime has been committed," CJ reminded him.

"Okay, whatever; we'll go down and have you meet with a sketch artist. Once that's done, then perhaps Matt will be able to take this to the next level. Whatever that might be. See? I'm trying to think the way you just said. Take the day as it comes."

"Right. But I still think it's okay to like someone, Col. Really. You deserve to be happy."

"As do you."

CHAPTER 14

Thursday morning, CJ decided to go for a run before work. It wasn't her usual routine, but after that heart-to-heart talk with Colin about living more in the present, she decided it was time to walk the walk, so to speak.

As she exited through the garage, she glanced over at her rental and remembered that she had an appointment to test-drive an SUV that afternoon. Selecting a new car would have to wait another day. She was getting weary of all the daily surprises and secrecy.

She checked her watch and decided she had time for about a twenty-minute jaunt. That ought to get her lungs open and the blood pumping. She headed down the driveway and punched the security release button. The gates opened and she jogged toward the road. About forty feet into her run, she heard the bellow of a motorcycle behind her. Just as she glanced over her shoulder, it dawned on her that the bike was aiming for her. She leaped into the well-manicured boxwood of the house next door, and screamed, *"Asshole!"*

With a few more cuts and scrapes added to her tally of injuries, she headed back to the house.

"What the hell happened to you now?" Colin demanded, noticing more scratches on her face and a few leaves in her hair.

"I had a run-in with some landscaping. Some asshole on a bike almost hit me."

"What kind of bike?"

"The big, loud, obnoxious kind."

"Are you okay? Did he stop to help you up?" Colin's concern was rising.

"Yeah. I'm okay, but no, he didn't stop. I swear it looked like the guy was coming right at me." CJ was struck by what she had just said, and they looked at each other in horror.

"Oh my God. Whoever it is, he knows where I live." CJ slumped down on a stool in front of the large island prep counter in the middle of the kitchen.

"Okay. Maybe we should go straight to Matt's this morning," Colin said, taking control.

"No. I have a ton of work to finish, and I

219

am sure he has a lot going on today. Let's just keep our appointment."

"What if I go with you to work?"

"What, you're my bodyguard now?" CJ was exhausted, and it wasn't quite eight in the morning. She was thinking about the day ahead.

"Very funny. Okay, how about this — I'll drive you to work and pick you up. That way, you won't be alone at any point outside the Rayburn Building."

"That sounds like a fine plan. Let me go change into something less athletic, and we can head out." She got up and went to her room to put on her work outfit.

They left through the front door since Colin's car was still parked in the driveway. Colin pressed the button for the gate to open and pulled through. He stopped the car and waited for the gates to close behind him. "What are you doing?" CJ looked puzzled.

Not wanting to alarm CJ further, he didn't say that he wanted to be sure no one snuck through the gate while it was closing behind them. His concern for CJ's safety had grown exponentially. "Huh? Nothing. Just going through my mental checklist."

Once Colin was sure CJ had entered the Rayburn Building, he knew she would be okay since security there was tight enough. Even though that stink-o guy was able to get into the building, Colin felt pretty sure that he wouldn't try to pull a stunt inside.

For the rest of the morning, CJ muddled through the paperwork and the e-mails. Instead of her normal walk to get a bite for lunch, she opted for the cafeteria in the building. She didn't want to take any chances on the streets of Washington. And she knew she wasn't being paranoid. It struck her as odd, though, that she was maintaining her calm through all of this. Maybe she was just going through the motions while being in shock. No. She was sure she had her head on straight. Her inner self echoed her conscious thoughts, telling her that she had to think. Clearly.

On her way to lunch, she stopped in the restroom and got a glimpse of herself in the mirror. "Boy, do you look like death warmed over." Getting closer to the mirror, she pulled at her fine features. CJ was a pretty woman; at least she had been until now. Physically fit. Again, at least up until now. Collarbone-length light brown hair. As she peered further, she noticed a few gray hairs scattered among the brown. *Oh swell. I really do look like something the dog dragged in . . . if I had one. And if I did, he probably wouldn't want anything to do with me. Ugh.*

CJ splashed some cold water on her face and continued to admonish herself. Looking back into the mirror, she had a sudden change of tone. "Okay. That's enough of a pity party." She continued to speak to herself in the mirror. "You are going to call a salon and get that hair into shape, get a facial, and maybe a makeover. You are not going to let some slimeball stench-o-meter get to you." With that pronouncement, she stood straight and reminded herself of a famous writer's words: "Head up, boobs out, ass in place!"

She marched into her office and found Christophe's phone number and dialed. The receptionist with an accent sounded appropriately snooty for such a high-end salon. "Good afternoon. I would like to make an appointment for a cut, color, and makeup," CJ barked back.

"Ven voud yew like to come in?" The receptionist sounded bored.

"How soon can you get me in?" CJ was impatiently tapping a pen on her desk.

"Ven voud yew like to come in?" the receptionist repeated with more snark.

CJ knew she wasn't going to get anywhere unless she was specific. "How about tomorrow?"

"Vell, vee usually need two veeks."

CJ was going to push Snottypants's buttons. "I am so glad to hear that. How about tomorrow?"

This generated an annoyed sigh on the other end. "Led me check," Snottypants said, and put CJ on hold — or "ignore" as CJ would often refer to the waiting time.

CJ smirked at her verbal volleyball game with the hostess without the mostest.

"Vee can fit yew in tomorrow afternoon at three o'clock. Name please." She was losing her accent. CJ's smirk turned into a big smile. "Carol Anne Jansen. Tank yew," she replied, deliberately imitating the receptionist.

What seemed to be a short time later, her cell phone rang. It was Colin, letting her know he was waiting for her on the street outside.

"Be down in a few." CJ went through her usual checklist routine before she left. Computer sleep mode. Check. Desk lamp off. Check. Desk drawers locked. Check.

As she was getting into the car, she exploded with excitement. "Col . . . you'll never guess what I did today!"

He cringed at the thought of what she might have done now. God only knew what she could get into in less than a day.

"Are you sure that I want to hear it?"

She slapped him on the arm, and announced, "I'm getting a makeover tomorrow at a snooty salon!"

That was not what he had expected to hear. "You what? With everything that's going on, you're having a spa day?"

"Yes. I. Am. Besides, it's not a spa day. It's a makeover day. Remember what we were talking about last night? Living in the present? Well, I think it's time for this girl to live. Period. Enough grieving and living in fear."

Colin turned sideways so he could take in this new attitude. "What the hell have you been reading?" He repeated the question he had asked the night before.

"I'm serious. Yes, we have a lot to uncover and resolve, but there's no reason why I should look downtrodden or frumpy."

"Frumpy? You? Granted, you're no fashionista, but I'd never describe you as frumpy." Colin was trying to be kind as he proceeded to unravel the mystery of this new version of Carol Anne Jansen, the woman he had known since she was a child of ten.

"Come on. I'm a plain Jane. I need to give myself a little umph. Lift my spirits."

"If you say so about needing a little umph.

But you're not a plain Jane. You never were." Colin was being reassuring. "So what exactly are you unfrumping?"

"Hair for one. Can you believe I found some gray? Yikes! And a little makeover!" CJ sounded excited about something for the first time in a very long while.

"Huh." Colin was pleased at her new attitude but also a little confused. "Well, I am happy to hear you so cheerful. It will do you good, I am sure." That said, he put the car in gear and headed to the J. Edgar Hoover Building and her appointment with a sketch artist.

"I'm a little nervous. And excited." CJ was in a genuinely good mood.

Colin peeked in her direction. "Are you okay?"

"Yes! I'm a little nervous. And excited," CJ repeated, wondering if she was going to have to repeat everything to everyone. "Why?"

"Well, you've been through a lot. Snapper. The condo. Both of them. Trip to LA. Car crash. Motorcycle altercation. Just sayin'. It's a lot for one person to go through in less than a month. And let's not forget where we're headed today! Sketch artist for Monsieur Le Pew." Colin wasn't sure if he believed CJ's mood. Was she delirious?

"I *know*! And all that is exactly why I'm trying to look at things in a different light. With a new hairdo to boot!" CJ sat back in her seat, folded her arms in an "and that's the way it is" sort of way.

"Okay, cookie. You're the boss!" Colin smiled at her and patted her on the knee.

Once they were through the security checkpoint, Matt greeted them and showed CJ to a small, windowless room. "Can I get you something to drink?" Matt asked cordially.

"Um, just water. Room temp if that's okay."

"Coming right up." Matt nodded for Colin to follow him. "We'll be right back."

Walking to the kitchen area, Matt spoke softly. "We are really serious about this."

Colin responded with, "Who are the 'we'? Am I missing something here?"

"I'm not at liberty to discuss details, but let's just say we are investigating a few incidents involving some high-ranking people in the government. This guy CJ saw could be an important link."

Colin was taken aback. "High-ranking people?"

"I've already said too much, but I want you to know that we'll make sure all of this is kept confidential." Matt was annoyed with himself for having divulged any information, but he knew he had to give up something to keep CJ and Colin in the mix.

"Okay, fine. But what about some protection for her? The car? The motorcycle dude I mentioned earlier today on the phone? She's in danger for sure." Colin needed reassurance.

"If we can match the sketch with someone in our files, we'll at least have someone we can tail."

"I don't give a shit about him. I'm worried about her!" Colin wasn't liking the nonchalant air from Matt and raised his voice a bit.

"I totally understand. I'll get someone on it. But as you should know, we can't offer official protection unless a crime has been committed and we know who the perpetrator is. . . ."

"Hold on! She needs protection. Period. I'm not going to have her go through all this only to have someone push her in front of a bus! From what I can glean, she's offering you some valuable information. The least you can do in return is to keep her safe." Colin was trying very hard to rein in his anger.

"I said 'official protection.' We do have ways. Please, don't ask me any more questions. I promise we will look after her once we get a match."

"And what if you don't get a match? You're going to let her be a sitting duck?"

"Colin, please, let's not take this any further. Especially here." Matt gestured with a nod and an eye roll, as if to say, *Remember where we are. The headquarters of the FBI.*

"Right. Got it." Colin wasn't sure if he really got it, whatever it was, but he knew that arguing wasn't going to get him any further.

"Come on. Drew — yes the artist's name is Drew — will be here shortly." Matt smiled, and Colin returned the grin.

They carried a few bottles of water into the room in which CJ was waiting patiently. A few minutes later, the artist arrived.

"CJ, this is Drew. Drew, this is Carol Anne Jansen."

CJ could hardly keep from laughing. "Nice to meet you, Drew."

"Yeah, I know. Drew drew. But can he really draw? I get it all the time."

The artist was a diminutive man in his early sixties. With a matter-of-fact tone, he continued, "Shall we get started?"

CJ sat next to him at the large conference table as Colin and Matt exited the room. They didn't want to interfere with her concentration.

It took less than an hour for CJ to give Drew a very detailed description. "Too bad you can't do a scratch and sniff."

Drew gave her a confused look, and she explained, "The guy wears the worst cologne. And lots of it. You can smell him a mile away."

The artist smiled politely and handed her the sketch pad. "Look familiar?"

CJ was surprised at how well Drew had rendered the composite drawing.

Drew opened the door and peered out into the hall, looking for Matt. He spotted him down the hall, leaning against a wall and talking to Colin. "Agent Mullan?"

Matt and Colin immediately walked over. "Looks like we have something. Ms. Jansen says that she is sure this is what he looks like, but hoped it could be a 'scratch and sniff.' Drew was finally showing that he had a sense of humor, which broke the ice among all of them.

"Thanks, Drew." Matt took the drawing from him. "Okay. I'll run this down and see what we come up with. It may take a while."

"What's 'a while'?" CJ asked.

"Could be twenty-four hours. Could be less. But we'll let you know as soon as we have something. Obviously, we won't be able to give you any details as to who he is, but —"

"But what?" CJ interrupted, showing her frustration and confusion. "This guy tried to kill me and probably killed Snapper, too!"

Colin put his arm around her. "Matt has this covered. Let's get a bite to eat." He turned her in the direction of the elevator.

"But . . . but . . ." CJ tried to protest, but Colin gave her a brotherly shove.

"It's been a long day. We are outta here. There is nothing left for you to do today except have some food and a nice glass of wine. Besides, you have another big day tomorrow . . . at the spa."

Remembering her new motto, CJ took a deep breath and said, "Indeed." Turning back to Matt, and in a more conciliatory voice, she offered her gratitude. "Thanks very much for believing me. When all of this is over, please have dinner with us. Colin knows how to use a microwave like a pro!"

"I'd like that. And thanks for being so brave." Matt shook her hand and briefly made eye contact with Colin before he headed in the opposite direction.

CHAPTER 15

After the meeting with the sketch artist, Colin and CJ decided to head for CJ's. It had been a very trying day. They ordered Thai and picked it up on the way to the house. CJ hit the sheets early, and Colin continued to go through the folders on the jump drive, trying to make sense of Snapper's financial dealings. At some point, he decided, he would have to go back to Snapper's secret condo and spend time digging through the transactions on the dark Web. If he could figure out how to do so.

Friday morning, smelling the deep aromatic coffee Colin had put through the French press, CJ bounded into the kitchen. "Hmmmm . . . I think the smell of coffee is intoxicating." She had a dreamy look on her face.

"My, aren't we in another kind of mood today." Colin poured her a cup and handed it over with the carafe of cream.

"Yes. I. Am. I told you, I'm trying to be more Zen." Colin gave her a sideways look. "What, you don't believe me?"

"Whatever's come over you, I think I like it. Zen or not."

"What was wrong with me before?" Her tone of voice sounded a little defensive.

"Nothing, sweetie. I'm just finding this new attitude refreshing. You've been through a helluva lot. It's good to see you upbeat, smiling, and excited. Even if it's only about a haircut."

"It's a makeover, Mr. Kelly, sir. I am making myself over inside and out!" CJ sounded almost like a child who had just won a trip to Disney World when she said it.

"So what time is your big appointment?"

"Oh, Ms. Fake Accent gave me a three o'clock. Why is everyone in this town so phony?" She hopped on the stool, propped her elbows on the counter, and rested her chin in both hands.

"It's a requirement. Hell, you should know. You've been in the thick of it for years."

"Yeah, but Snapper was different. He was down-to-earth. No bullpucky. 'Do what the people sent you here to do,' was his motto. He would get so pissed when the party demanded he spend time on the phone soliciting campaign contributions. 'That's not what I'm here for,' he'd bellow, and hang up on whoever was bugging him. Damn it. I miss him."

"I know you do. But let's not get maudlin. You have a big day ahead. Remember, it's the new you!"

"Indeed. Got any breakfast food for me?"

"Ha. You? Ms. Protein-bar?"

"It's the new me, remember? How about whipping up some eggs? Toast?"

Colin smiled at this enlightened version of CJ. "I think I can whip something up. Go get dressed."

CJ headed to her suite and pondered what she should wear for her makeover. Does it matter? Today it did. She had never gone to a fancy-dancy salon for her haircuts. It was always the Clip Shop. In and out. Thirty-five bucks. This was a new experience, and she had to admit she was a little intimidated. How odd. She could run a congressman's office, handle all sorts of political types, Masters of the Universe, complaining constituents, and all the nonsense at work, but walking into a high-end salon made her nervous. Simply put, she was not accustomed to anything fancy or frivolous. Dealing with the assholes of Washington was something she had become proficient at.

Getting glamorized was completely different.

She pulled on her best pantsuit, charcoal gray. The one she would usually wear to a luncheon. Not too fancy but upscale enough to say she was important. She toyed with the idea of her Tiffany silver-braid necklace — the one Kick had given her for her twenty-first birthday — but decided it was too much. Taking a deep breath, she looked closely in the mirror. "Okay, girlfriend. Say good-bye to the old, dowdy CJ. The new and improved version will be here soon."

Colin once again insisted on driving her to work, and he said he would pick her up to take her to her hair appointment. He was not comfortable with her meandering alone while some maniac was yet to be identified and incarcerated.

CJ was getting out of the car when she reminded Colin to pick her up at two thirty. "My appointment is at three o'clock. It's only three miles from here, but you know how traffic can be. I don't want Ms. Fake Accent getting her panties in a knot."

"You got it. See you later."

"Call me if you hear anything from Matt," CJ said, and turned to enter the Rayburn House Office Building.

"You'll be the first," Colin replied, not

sure whether or not CJ had heard him.

"Hey, CJ!" It was Marcus the security guard calling her over to him. "Remember the dude you asked me about? Mr. French Whorehouse?"

"I sure do. What about him?"

"I think I smelled him here when I got in."

"Really?" She was at full attention. So, Mr. Crappy Cologne was back on the scene. The taste of bile crawled up her throat.

"Yes, ma'am. And I think he was headed down the corridor. I didn't see nothin', but I sure smelled somethin' goin' in that direction. Thought you'd like to know."

"Thank you, Marcus." CJ wasn't sure if she should pursue this latest sighting. Make that sniffing. She stood for a moment and decided to walk toward Dillard's office to see if the smell continued. It did. Voices. Again.

"What do you mean you're not going to try again? You were supposed to handle this one, too! Hell, Franklin. You get a nice piece of the action. You need to earn it." Whoever was speaking sounded angry and frustrated. Suddenly, an inner door slammed, and CJ could no longer hear what was going on. But she had a name. Franklin. Was that a first name or a last name? No matter. It was a lead.

She crept away from the door, fearing she would have another run-in with the rancid-smelling Franklin, and headed to her office. She scrolled through her phone trying to find Matt's number until she realized it was Colin who had made all the contacts. "Damn." She dialed Colin's number, but when the call went straight to voice mail, she remembered that he had a board meeting and would be unreachable for a couple of hours. "Hell." She left him a short message. "Call me. Mr. Crappy Cologne is on the premises, and I don't have Matt's number."

She pulled out the directory for all the agencies of the government, dialed the number for the FBI, and got the usual recording. "If you know your party's extension, please dial it now."

"Cripes. If I knew my party's extension, I wouldn't be calling you!" CJ yelled into the phone. "Whatever happened to human contact?" she asked herself out loud. Finally, after pressing 0 a dozen times, a living, breathing person answered. CJ was almost out of breath. "Agent Matthew Mullan, please."

After what seemed like the longest three

minutes of her life, Matt finally got on the line. "This is Agent Mullan. How can I help you?"

"Matt. It's CJ. I have a name for you."

"A name? What do you mean?"

"Mr. Crappy Cologne was here . . . in the building. I overheard him arguing with someone in Dillard's office — I assume it was Dillard — and Dillard called him Franklin."

"Franklin? Is that a first name or a last name?" Matt pushed.

"I have no way of knowing, but I heard the name just a few minutes ago. What should I do?"

Matt stiffened. "Do absolutely nothing. Stay in your office. Lock the door."

CJ was trembling. "Uh . . . okay. Are you coming here?"

"Yes. I'll be there within the half hour. Sit tight."

She hung up the phone and left another message for Colin. "I spoke to Matt. He's on the way. I've locked the door of my office. Call me as soon as you get this."

CJ was shaking by now. She tried to use logic on herself. *No one would pull a stunt here. The building is surrounded by security. It's going to be okay.*

A sudden knock on the door sent her flying out of her seat. She didn't know if she should answer it or not.

"Ms. Jansen?" It was Marcus. "You okay?"

"Yes. I'm fine." She moved closer to the door. "Are you alone?"

"Yes. Nobody in the hall, either."

CJ unlocked the door and let him in. "Sorry. Just a little jumpy. A lot's happened."

"I can only imagine. I just wanted to let you know that the smelly dude left. Man, were you right about him. What's up with that?"

CJ began to relax a bit. "Maybe he has really bad BO."

They both broke into a guffaw. "Is there anything I can do for you, Ms. Jansen?"

"No. I'm fine. But thanks for checking on me."

"No problem. I'll keep you posted if we have any more stinky aromas in the building."

About a half hour later, another knock on her door made her bounce from her chair again. "CJ? It's Matt Mullan."

She opened the door and let Matt and another man — someone she didn't recognize — in. She gave Matt a suspicious look.

"CJ, this is Agent Blomberg. He's working on a case that may have something to do

238

with all of this."

"All of what? I don't know what the 'this' is!" CJ was trying to keep her cool.

"I'm not at liberty to give you any details at the moment, but we did get a match from your sketch. The guy's name is Leonard Franklin. Yes. You heard it right."

CJ's hand flew to her mouth. "But . . . who is he? And why is he after me?"

"We don't know for sure if he's the one who tampered with your car or tried to run you down, but he does have a rap sheet a few miles long."

"Who else would be after me?" CJ was practically pleading.

"We are going to assume he's part of it, but we need you to make a positive ID."

"How? Are you going to arrest him?"

"We are going to bring him in for questioning. You don't need to concern yourself as to why or how. We just need you to confirm that it was he whom you saw in this building."

"When is all this going to happen?" Suddenly CJ was concerned about her spa appointment.

"Probably sometime tomorrow. I can't give you any more details about it. At least for now. I spoke with Colin, and he'll be keeping an eye on you until we can sort this out." Mullan spoke very matter-of-factly.

"Wait. You and Colin decided who was going to be my babysitter?" CJ didn't know if she should be pissed or relieved.

"CJ, I know this has been a very trying time, but you're going to have to trust me. Tomorrow, if you make the ID, we'll get the ball rolling for protection. Okay? Meanwhile, Colin isn't going to be alone in this. I'll be hanging around, too. I have the evening off, so maybe he can show me how adept he is at using a microwave." Matt smiled at her, trying desperately to cut through the tension and put her at ease.

CJ heaved a big sigh. Her head was spinning. It was all too much.

The rest of the day blew by quickly. There were still piles of condolence cards to respond to, letters, and e-mails. She wasn't sure how she was going to get through all of it, but she was certain she wasn't going to let it bury her in worry.

At two thirty, her phone rang, and it was Colin, letting her know he was outside. Computer in sleep mode. Check. Desk drawers locked. Check. Lamp off. Check. Ass in place. Check.

On the ride to the salon, CJ and Colin were trying to come up with some ideas about what to serve for dinner. "No offense to Kick, but I don't think I can look at another egg pie this week," CJ whined.

"Well, there's always chicken! Might as well keep the dinner in the family. We'll stop at a Hatchery and get a few dinners. Here, call them. How long do you think your thing will be?" Colin handed the phone to CJ.

"Not sure. I'm thinking two hours, maybe."

"Okay, so tell them we'll pick the food up around six."

She placed the order for three full dinners: roasted chicken, several sides, biscuits, and apple pie for dessert.

"Three dinners? You on some kind of binge eating?"

"Matt is going to be very impressed with your culinary skills! Open door. Place food on microwave plate. Shut door. Press high, medium, or low button. And one button for the timer. *Ding!*"

Colin looked at her as if she had gone around the bend. "What in God's name are you talking about?"

"Matt said he would be interested to see your microwave cooking skills in action. He's coming by tonight to help you babysit me."

"Oh, is that the plan?"

"It is." CJ sunk deeply into the buttery

soft seat as Colin continued the drive to the salon.

CJ looked over her shoulder as she was exiting the car, and asked, "Are you coming in?"

"I guess I should. Being on duty and all." Colin gave her a funny grin.

"Good. This way I won't feel like a total alien in that place."

The salon was modern and posh, and everyone had some bizarre haircut or color. CJ almost turned and walked out. "Ken I hulp yew?" A very tall, thin, androgynous person with chopped black hair and big black glasses peered at her.

Head up. "Yes, Carol Anne Jansen. I have an appointment."

"Follow me." Andro flicked its head, indicating a direction.

CJ was shown to a changing room, where she donned a smock. Then she was ushered to a chair to meet the stylist.

A young woman with pink hair appeared. CJ thought she looked very much like Cyndi Lauper.

"Hi, I'm Alicia. What brings you here today?" the Lauper look-alike inquired.

"Something new. Something fresh. Uh, but not too fresh!"

"Hmmmm . . ." Alicia tilted her head from

one side to another, inspecting CJ's head of hair. "I think a blunt, chin-length cut with some blond and caramel highlights. We may want to do something with the eyebrows. They could use a little shaping. What about makeup? Do you wear any?"

CJ was mortified. Of course she wore makeup! Was it that bad?

"Uh, yes. A little."

"We're not going to make you look like Baby Jane. Just a little perk. Sound okay?" Alicia had seen the type before. Wants a little change. Nothing dramatic but enough that people will notice.

Again, CJ took a big inhale. "Okay. Let's do it!" She made the sign of the cross and laughed, reminding herself again that she wasn't Catholic. But she believed it had worked on getting her car started, so she thought it was important for the makeover, too.

Two and a half hours later, she emerged from the back. Colin stood up. "Holy guacamole! Wow. CJ, you look fantastic! Kinda Uma Thurmanish — but not so blond. Or crazy. At least that's how she is in the movies."

Colin was right. CJ looked great. And she knew it. She felt it, too. Yes, a new CJ was emerging from the chrysalis of the old.

As they headed back to the house, CJ kept pulling down the sun visor to peek at her new look in the mirror. "Wow is right, Colin. I have eyes! And they're pretty!"

Colin was very happy to see that CJ was doing much better than she had over the past few weeks. Heck, past four years. Since the death of her brother, actually.

A few minutes after they arrived, Matt called on the phone at the gate. Colin let him in and walked him to the kitchen. "Wow! You look great!" was the first thing out of Matt's mouth.

"Thank you!" CJ was almost blushing. "But it makes me think I must have been really drab before!"

"Not at all!" Both men realized their over-reaction to her newfound looks might have made her even more self-conscious.

"Okay. So *is* this a new-and-improved version?"

"Absolutely. We just never saw all that beauty you were hiding." Colin gave Matt a "how am I doing?" look. Matt gave him the thumbs-up.

They pulled dishes out of the cabinets, heated up the sides, opened a bottle of Kim Crawford Sauvignon Blanc, and made their way into the great room, taking a seat at the massive dining table. "I don't remember the last time we actually sat at a dinner table." CJ was suddenly sentimental.

"Me either. But this is a day to celebrate the new you. And tomorrow we'll be putting most of this behind us," Colin reassured her.

Clearing his throat, Matt interrupted in a kindly tone. "CJ, this isn't going to be a fast process. It could be months before anything is resolved. I just want you to know I will be sure that whatever measures need to be taken, I will personally oversee them."

CJ didn't want to worry, but she also wanted to be prepared. "What should I expect?"

"How things go tomorrow will determine what the next step will be. I want you to be okay with all of this, which is why I'm telling you. I don't want you to be put off or surprised in any way. We'll know more tomorrow. But in any case, we are here for you."

She grabbed a chicken leg and pointed it at Matt, then at Colin. "I'm holding both of you to Matt's word. So there." She scooped up a big helping of mac and cheese with the spoon in her other hand and plopped it on her plate.

Colin almost did a double take. "You? Mac and cheese?"

"It's the new me." CJ winked and continued gnawing on the bone.

CHAPTER 16

CJ had excused herself after dinner the night before. Another bottle of wine had been tempting, but she knew she was going to need all her faculties on Saturday. She was curious, however, as to how Colin and Matt had spent the evening. It had been a long time since she had been in a relationship. She often wondered if she would ever be in one again. Putting thoughts of her own loneliness out of her mind as she entered the kitchen, she greeted Colin with, "So . . . got anything to report?"

He almost choked on his coffee. "What? No! Absolutely not!"

"But I thought you liked each other," she persisted.

"We do. But now is not the time to take it any further."

"If you say so." She gave him a sly look and poured herself a cup. "So what's the plan for today, Mr. Bodyguard?"

"I'm dropping you at work since you insist on going in on a Saturday. As soon as Matt can pick up the guy, he's going to call and have you come down for a lineup. It may not be today, so we'll continue our usual routine. By the way, you really do look great!"

"Why, thank you, kind sir. I feel pretty good. A sense of renewal." Putting her cup in the dishwasher, she turned to Colin. "Let's get this show on the road. The clock is ticking at work and I have *got* to get through all the mail and start cleaning out my desk. And Snapper's. Jeez. Then there's the memorial service to plan. Everyone has been asking about it."

"Are his ashes back yet?" Colin was trying to be delicate.

"No. I figure I'll wait for the funeral home to let me know, then I'll tackle planning for the service. I'm trying not to get over-whelmed."

Grabbing their belongings, they went out through the front door and walked to the driveway, where Colin had once again parked his car. They drove in a peaceful silence.

"So? Come on. Colin? Something must have transpired between the two of you."

"CJ, I swear you're like a dog with a sock.

And I swear nothing happened. We talked for about an hour and he left. Satisfied?" Colin was trying to put an end to the interrogation.

CJ folded her arms and answered with an emphatic, "No. So there!" Then she stuck out her tongue. They both broke into laughter as Colin shook his head in amusement.

When CJ entered the building, she got a short whistle from Marcus. "I'm sorry, miss, but I need to see some ID. Please." He knew it was CJ, but he was in the mood to tease her a bit.

"Very funny. But thanks for noticing."

"You kinda look like that actress. Just a little younger. You know, the one who was in that *Kill Bill* movie?" Marcus was searching for the name.

"Uma Thurman?"

"Yeah, she's the one! I wouldn't want to get on her bad side!" Marcus chuckled.

"Swell. So now I look like a psycho bitch?" CJ was still smiling at the comparison.

"No! That's not what I meant!" Marcus realized he might have offended her.

"I know! Ha! Gotcha!" She gave a wave with her fingers and sauntered away to her office, noticing the quiet of the building, what with most members of the House gone for the weekend, as usual.

Yes, she was feeling pretty sassy. How refreshing.

She muddled through the reams of paper, sorting the "NIT" (Needs Immediate Attention), "CW" (Can Wait), and "CWF" (Can Wait Forever). That last was one of her favorites. Snapper always relegated the unrealistic requests of his fellow politicians to that pile. She looked in the direction of Snapper's office. "Damn, I miss that guy."

Just around lunchtime, her phone rang. "CJ? It's Agent Mullan."

Matt sounded very official in addition to using his formal title. Something must be up.

"Yes, Agent Mullan?"

Matt cleared his throat, further acknowledging that this was official business.

"Would you be available to come down to the office in an hour?"

CJ was surprised that things were happening so quickly. "Well, of course. Let me check on my chauffeur." She had hoped Matt got the reference.

"We can have someone pick you up if you prefer," Matt continued in his very official voice.

"Hold on a moment. Let me see if I can reach Colin." CJ picked up the landline and dialed. After two rings, Colin answered.

"Hey, Col, I have Agent Mullan on the other line. He wants me to be in their office in an hour."

"I'm on my way." Colin was at the ready to oblige.

CJ turned back to her cell phone. "He's on his way to get me. We'll see you shortly."

CJ's mind started racing at the thought of what was about to happen. She knew that Mr. Crappy Cologne, Leonard Franklin, would not be able to see her, but she also knew that *he* would know she was on the other side of the window. She was certain. And her inner voice affirmed what she was thinking.

She kept repeating to herself out loud, "You're gonna be okay, you're gonna be okay."

Her phone rang fifteen minutes later. It was Colin, announcing his arrival at the curb in front.

Since it was Saturday, traffic was fairly light. He was worried that CJ would be a nervous wreck, although you wouldn't know it by looking at her.

"You okay?"

"Yes. I'm fine. I know this is a big deal, but I feel like we're coming to some kind of crescendo. I want to take this guy down so bad."

"Yeah, but on what counts? They're going to have to come up with some proof. Evidence."

CJ squirmed in the seat. "Are you trying to make me anxious? I know there hasn't been anything tied to this guy. At least nothing *we* know of. But everything I've heard tells me that Matt has something going on. He kept saying he could not reveal any details. So we're going to have to trust him."

"I suppose you're right. And for someone who likes to be in control — as in you, missy — I am surprised you're not freaking out a bit."

"Would you prefer it if I did?"

"No! No. This is fine. Just different. For you, I mean." Colin gave her a quick smile as he pulled into a space just a few feet from the front of the building.

Once inside, they went through the security checkpoint and were ushered down a long hallway with a row of doors on each side. All of them were closed.

A nondescript agent led them into a room that had glass on one side. It gave them a view of another room, one with a chart on the wall. That was where the men would line up.

"Just like in TV," CJ whispered to Colin, nudging him with her elbow.

"Huh. Yeah. Just like it." And Colin didn't like any of it. The enormity of what CJ had been through hit him like a ton of bricks. Snapper. Secret condominium. George. Secret money. Car. Motorcycle. Mr. Crappy Cologne. He was suddenly in awe of her and how she was holding up, confronting the events with grace and stamina. He had another brief thought and smiled. Too bad he played for the other team. If he didn't, he could have easily fallen in love with her. Funny. He had never thought of CJ as a woman before. She had always been Kick's little sister. He resigned himself to finding someone for this extraordinary woman as soon as this mess was over. He thought about what she had said and agreed. One of them should have someone to love.

Colin's reverie was broken when Matt entered the room and a loud sound came from the adjoining room. Several men in uniform and five similar-looking men entered the room.

The hair on the back of CJ's neck began to crawl, and her palms began to sweat. She recognized Franklin in a second. Too bad she couldn't smell him. On second thought, better she couldn't. She might have gagged on her saliva. Although she thought she might gag at any minute anyway.

Colin put his hand on her shoulder. "You okay?"

CJ nodded and pointed to the second man. "That's him. That's the man I saw in the Rayburn Building. Ask one of the guards! He's probably stinking up the room!"

Matt pushed a button. "Thank you, gentlemen. You can all go."

CJ's heart almost stopped. She grabbed Matt's sleeve. "What the hell are you doing? You're letting him go?" She was flabbergasted.

"I'll explain in a minute." Matt turned abruptly, went out to the hallway, then returned just as quickly. "I got a whiff. What is up with that guy? If he thinks he's making himself inconspicuous, he's sadly mistaken." Matt pulled out a handkerchief and absently wiped his nose.

"But you're letting him go!" CJ was trying to keep her voice even. "What the hell is going on?"

Colin was also in a state of shock. "Matt? What the . . . ?"

"I said there were details I could not discuss. We needed to get a positive ID on him so we can put a tail on him. That's all I can say at this time. Please try to understand. This is a very big deal, so we need to be very judicious about it. I wish I could tell you more. And I ask that you keep all of this confidential. I cannot stress that enough."

"But what about my safety? This guy knows where I live!" CJ had gone from calm to horrified in just a few short minutes.

"We have two options," Matt continued. "We can put a security detail on you or put you into Witness Protection for a short time."

"Witness Protection? I have work to finish!" CJ was vacillating between terror and anger. Her head was spinning.

Colin motioned her over to a chair. "Matt? What do you mean Witness Protection?"

"CJ, you would be relocated until after the trial. If there is a trial. These are the things I cannot discuss. But what I can tell you is that we are investigating Leonard Franklin. We need some more evidence before we can make an arrest. In the meantime, we can put someone on you or relocate you. It's up to you."

"I cannot possibly leave town now. I have to finish up in the office and plan a memorial service. It's going to take me weeks!" CJ was still trying to decide if she should panic, or scream, or both.

"Let's do this. Now that you have IDed

him for us — as the man you saw coming from Congressman Dillard's office — we will put on a detail to tail him. You'll have round-the-clock protection as well. So there will be no time when we don't know where the both of you are. It's the best I can do for now other than put you in Witness Protection, which you have declined." Matt was clear and reassuring.

"I think I can handle that." CJ looked up at Colin. "Will you still be my personal bodyguard?"

Colin smiled at CJ. "Of course. I'll work my schedule around yours." Turning to Matt, he said, "Realistically, how long do you think this will take?"

"Hard to say. But I will update you on a regular basis. We hope to wrap this part of it up in a week or two. The rest could take a couple of months, but, CJ, I promise that you will be absolutely safe."

"Fine." CJ was resigned to the latest upheaval. "I'll just keep doing what I do, looking over my shoulder every five seconds."

Agent Mullan walked them out of the viewing room and over to the elevator.

"Seriously, it's going to be okay. We just need a little more time."

During her final weeks in the office CJ continued to have Colin act as her chauffer and bodyguard, muddled through the remaining paperwork, and made the arrangements for Snapper's memorial. She could have gotten the Washington National Cathedral, but she knew Snapper would have been mortified. He hadn't been a religious man, so rather than a ceremony, CJ decided on hosting a dinner. It would be buffet style, allowing people to come and go. Colin would arrange for the catering. She engaged a string quartet to play for two hours, and several of Snapper's close associates would say a few words halfway through the event. She gathered some of his mementos and photos to put on display. Reviewing her list, she was content that this was what Snapper would have wanted. Nothing fancy. Just respectful. It struck her that she would be the closest to family attending. She shrugged her shoulders, and thought, *Who'd have thought I'd be his next of kin? Aside from George, and we know he's not coming. People will come just to be seen. Just like any other DC circus.*

One evening, on the ride home, Colin told

CJ, "I think I know where the money is coming from."

"Wait! What?" CJ was stunned. Colin hadn't mentioned being so close to finding out.

"Yeah. Well, at least one source. It's a stock portfolio. That's where the money that goes into the trust is coming from. I just don't know the source of the portfolio money. There were a number of transactions. All pretty damn good, too. I hate to say it, CJ, but I think the stock money is funny money, and I don't mean 'ha-ha' funny either." Colin was in a pensive mood.

"Hold on. You found a stock portfolio?" CJ was trying to follow the chain.

"Yes. It's an account Snapper had. He traded on the dark Web. Whatever it was, it's all quite mysterious. Could be why he wanted to end it all. And I mean as in 'all.' " Colin was frustrated that he had some but not all the information he had been seeking.

"How strange." CJ recalled Snapper talking about the horse farm soon after he had sold it. "I know he raised a lot of money from selling the farm. But all of that seemed to have gone for George's care. So where else did the money come from? Could he have been a trust-fund baby and never let on?" CJ was trying to put the pieces together.

"Doubtful. Trust-fund money would earn interest, and there would be no reason for any clandestine activity. No. This money was laundered somehow. But how? I don't know that we'll ever figure that out." Colin was clearly frustrated.

"Wow. All these secrets. And I thought I knew Snapper inside and out. He seemed so . . . so . . . normal. And straightforward. I would have *never,* ever thought he would do something unseemly, much less illegal and immoral. Wow." CJ could not wrap her head around the idea that the man she worked for — for twelve years — was hiding such a shadowy secret.

"Yeah. And the thing with Leonard Franklin. I'm going to start calling him by his real name. That could have a role in all of this." Colin was also trying to piece things together.

"It has to. And Dillard. They were all involved in something. Something dangerous."

"Or illegal."

"Or both. If it was illegal, then I suppose it would be dangerous, too. Makes sense. Man oh man oh man. I still don't believe Snapper would take the cowardly way out.

That's just not his style."

"So you thought. I bet you would never have guessed about any of this secret stuff, either," Colin reminded her.

"Very true. Though I may not have known a lot about Snapper's secrets, I do know he was not a wimp. He'd have turned himself in and faced the consequences. Or" — CJ paused — "gotten himself killed, which is the only conclusion I can come up with."

"You saw the tapes, CJ. He put the hose from the exhaust pipe through the window."

"I saw a man in a trench coat put something under the car. I never saw the man's face. Remember?" CJ was not budging on the murder theory. "And my inner self is agreeing with my head."

Colin gave a big sigh, knowing he was not going to win the argument.

The following two weeks were uneventful. There was no word from Matt about Leonard Franklin, but she was satisfied knowing that Agent Becker watched her house at night. The only big thing left on her agenda was the memorial dinner. Otherwise, things were relatively quiet as CJ was wrapping up her work. She packed Snapper's office and had the boxes put into storage. She had no idea what to do with them since she was planning on putting the condos on the market. Her plan was to sell off everything and put the proceeds into the trust fund for George. With any luck the proceeds would cover George for five or more years. If he lived longer, she'd worry about it when the time came. *Poor George.*

She tried to keep the dark Web transactions out of her mind. At least for the time being. She could get around to thinking about them when she had finished her work at the Rayburn Building. As she was marking the cartons to be taken to the storage unit, her phone rang. It was Matt.

"CJ. Agent Mullan here. I wanted to inform you that we arrested Leonard Franklin for securities fraud this morning."

"Fraud? Not murder?" CJ was taken aback.

"No. Not murder, CJ. Unfortunately, we do not have any evidence to substantiate that there even was a murder. Detective Harris went over all of this with you." Matt seemed tense.

"Yes he did. But I thought —"

Matt interrupted with, "I can't go into details —"

She interrupted in return, "With you right now. Yeah. Yeah. I've heard this before. When *can* you go into details?" CJ sounded more annoyed than excited about the arrest.

"CJ, this is a good collar. I'm sorry if you're disappointed, but this is the investigation we've been working on. Thanks to you, we were able to connect him to Dillard. That's all I'm at liberty to say, which is probably too much."

For the first time since she could remember, CJ was speechless.

"Whatever. As long as he stays in jail."

"That's what we're working on. I have to run. I'll call you later with any updates. As long as Franklin is in jail, you should be fine. Agent Becker will stay on one more night. Thanks!" Matt hung up abruptly.

CJ stared at the phone. "What the — ?" And then she dialed Colin. "Col! You are not going to believe this! They arrested Leonard Franklin, but not for murder. Some kind of securities fraud thing. Col? You there?" Colin had hesitated for a moment. This was exactly what he thought Snapper had been involved with. Insider trading. But how? Robotron was the most obvious clue.

"Yes, I'm here. Are you almost ready to leave? I can be there in half an hour. We can talk about this tonight."

"I'll be done shortly. See you in a few."

She hung up the phone, feeling deflated. Half a victory? It sucked.

CHAPTER 17

CJ really hadn't thought about all the acquaintances she had made over the past twelve years. Most recently, with Snapper's untimely death, many had come to offer assistance and say their good-byes before she left the office. She had been moved by their kindness — not the usual paranoia everyone in government seemed to display.

Regardless of everything that had happened since Snapper's death, she still believed that he had not committed suicide but had been murdered. Murdered in order to shut him up. Murdered to protect the other conspirators. Most of whom were lawyers as well as public servants who had gone rogue. How ironic. Those who make the laws break the laws.

Once they had arrested Leonard Franklin, Agent Becker was taken off her security detail, but Colin stuck close by, spending most nights at the house. He was still driving her to and from work every day as well. He felt that doing so would help keep her on an even keel while she wrapped up this chapter of her life. A lot had happened in a short time, including getting a new car. Now the big question for CJ was what to do with the rest of her life. No other member of Congress had offered her a staff position. Maybe they thought it was too soon? She had no significant other. No siblings. No children. She was thirty-four and unemployed. Not a good scenario. And the fact that she was a multimillionaire with a substantial income from the restaurant chain of which she owned half, so had no financial worries, did not keep Colin from being concerned. CJ, he knew, was not the kind of person to look forward to a life of leisure.

"CJ, how about spending some time at the cabin? It might do you some good. Fresh air. The weather is great at this time of year. Whaddya say?" Colin was hoping that a change of scenery would give CJ the boost she needed. Sure, the makeover had helped, but there was an emptiness in her life that was palpable.

"Hmmmm. The cabin? It's over two thousand square feet! Hardly a cabin." CJ always thought referring to the vacation house as a cabin was ludicrous.

"Details. Details. It has a rustic look. Doesn't that count? And it's nestled in the woods, with a view of the water." Colin was only half joking as he defended his favorite spot in the world.

CJ knew what Colin was trying to do, and she actually agreed. A change of scenery would do her some good.

"Okay. Let's do it!" CJ's mood brightened.

"Er . . . well . . . I wasn't planning on going with you." Colin sounded sheepish. "I have a couple of conferences coming up in Canada. One in Toronto, the other in Vancouver."

CJ looked dejected. She had grown accustomed to Colin's company for the past two months.

Trying not to sound disappointed, she chimed in, "Of course. I almost forgot. You have a life!" She mustered a laugh. "Speaking of which. What's happening between you and Matt?"

"You on that again?" Colin shook his head in disbelief — not in disagreement.

"Yes I am. Well?" CJ put both hands on her hips. She wasn't budging this time.

"Okay. Matt is coming with me to Vancouver. We hear the men are really hot!"

"Ha-ha, funny man. I mean are things getting serious?"

"Not just yet. We're feeling our way. Don't go there!"

"Where?" CJ asked innocently.

"You know. We want to spend time together to see if it *will* go anywhere. Look, we're not kids. Relationships need time. We need time to get to know each other. Time when we're not totally distracted with our work."

"But don't you have a conference?" CJ was back to being Nancy Drew.

"Yes, I do. But I am taking an extra five days away, so we can hang out and take in the sights." Colin wasn't sure how CJ would handle the news even though she had been a champion of his pursuing the relationship.

"Colin, I think that's great! As I said, at least one of us should have someone. I'm happy for you. I like Matt. I think he's a good man."

"Me too. On both counts."

"So I'll plan on going to the cabin when you guys are in Vancouver. This way you won't miss me so much!" CJ was starting to embrace a new adventure. "And I'll try not to miss you!"

When the time came, Colin helped CJ pack her SUV. You would have thought she was going away for several months instead of a few weeks. Her stay at the cabin was open-ended. She would remain as long as she wanted. Needed. There were a lot of loose ends as far as indictments and trials, so she might as well enjoy the free time, clear her head, and make a plan for the rest of her life. At least a work in progress.

Just as she was about to leave, Colin took each of her shoulders in his hands and gave her a long stare in the eyes. "CJ, I promise, when I get back, we are going to kick your social life in the butt. Time is precious. Life is short. We should spend the time we have being happy."

"Now who's the philosophical one?" CJ's eyes welled up.

They gave each other big bear hugs, and CJ climbed into her new Ford Escape, waved, opened the sun roof, and cranked up the music. "In the Long Run" by the Eagles was on the radio. "Don Henley is from Texas," she shouted, reminding Colin of their bizarre trip together to California.

It was just under two hours to Colin's place on the eastern shore. He had phoned ahead to Katrina and Eduard, the couple who took care of the house in his absence. He let them know that CJ was coming and that it should be cleaned and the kitchen stocked, including the wine cooler. He gave them a list of CJ's favorite cheeses and vintages. He had house accounts at most places, so the bills would go directly to his office. Not that CJ needed any financial assistance. He simply wanted her to relax completely, without having to do any shopping.

When she pulled into the gravel driveway, a twinge of melancholy hit her as she began to think how much her life had changed in the past two months and how much closer she had gotten to Colin. She really hoped for his happiness.

Katrina welcomed her at the front door. "Welcome, Miss CJ. Happy to see you. Been long time. New hair? Looks beautiful!" Katrina, a tallish woman, maybe five-eight or –nine, with shoulder-length, blue-black hair, brown eyes, freckles, a pug nose, and a beauty mark at the corner of her wide mouth, was originally from Ukraine, and her husband was from Moldova. They had met one summer in Odessa when they were in their late teens. Now they were in their midthirties. Same as CJ. He worked as a nurse's aide, and she was a domestic. Hardworking couple. Married for fourteen years. They kept the house immaculate.

CJ gave Katrina a big hug and took in the fresh, clean air. "It's good to be here!" She started toward the hatch of the car to retrieve her belongings when Eduard, a redhead with green eyes, bushy eyebrows, an aquiline nose, small mouth, and neatly trimmed beard and mustache, came running up the road. "Miss CJ! No. That is job for me!" He was laughing as he playfully reprimanded her.

"My apologies!" CJ bowed her head in respect. "Good to see you both! I'm not sure how long I'll be staying, so I may have overpacked!"

"No worries, Miss CJ. We will take care of everything. You hungry?" Katrina happened to be a very good cook. She had to be. Kick might have been a renowned chef, but he also liked to have good home cooking — as long as someone else did the work.

"I could use a bite to eat." It occurred to CJ that she hadn't had much of an appetite lately. "I'm actually hungry!" That came as a relief to her. Finally. Food started to be appealing again.

"You go change clothes. Make comfortable yourself, and I have food on table in half hour." Katrina still had an accent, but she had worked very hard at the English language. CJ had a lot of respect for the couple. They came here the hard way — in a freight container that was seized by the coast guard. They were lucky to be alive. They were told arrangements were made for them in the United States, and they would have sponsors. It would cost a mere ten thousand dollars . . . each. They worked for four years to amass that kind of money, borrowing from family with the promise that they would send for them once they got established in the US. A very common story. Once they turned over their money, they were herded into a truck with two dozen other immigrant hopefuls, only to realize they were about to become cargo. When they were discovered, they were all suffering from dehydration. They were able to get humanitarian asylum and start their lives over, minus the thousands of dollars they had paid to the smugglers.

It was Snapper who had facilitated their stay in America, and after hearing their story from CJ, Kick and Colin became their sponsors and helped them get on their feet. They were fiercely loyal to Kick, Colin, and CJ. They, too, had been devastated by Kick's death and had vowed to take care of Colin and CJ no matter the time or the day.

CJ went to her usual guest bedroom and stepped out onto the small balcony that overlooked the woods. She was glad it didn't face the water. It was that very river that had taken her brother. Or rather, it was that asshole on the Jet Ski. She often wondered why Colin stayed, but the place, he said, "felt like Kick." It had brought them so much pleasure — from the parties to just chilling out. Leaning on the balcony and breathing in what felt like new air, she agreed it had been a good idea. She needed time to clear her head and attempt to plan the rest of her existence on the planet.

She spent the first few days taking walks, sitting on the deck, flipping through magazines, and feeding the squirrels. But mostly, she stared into space. Before the trip, she thought she had processed all the horrible events until the sound of one lone bird chirping on a branch made her burst into tears. The solitude of her own life smacked her right in the face. She was sobbing uncontrollably. It wasn't until she started hiccupping that she noticed the mucus running down her face, which caused her to laugh out loud. "Get a grip, girl. You're the definition of hysterical." Then she realized she was talking to herself in the third person. "Oh yeah. I'm a red-hot mess."

She pulled her denim shirt out of her jeans and wiped her face with the bottom, then started toward the house, hoping Katrina had whipped up some kind of comfort food.

The hair on the back of her neck started to crawl when she noticed a dark SUV parked a few yards from the house. It had been there all day. Odd. Everyone on the block had long driveways, and the houses were on at least two acres of land. She was about to investigate but thought better of it. "Enough, Nancy Drew. Go get something to eat." Another round of talking to herself. When she reached the kitchen door, she thought she saw something move near the fence. "And you're paranoid, too. Swell."

Giving the heavy screen door a pull, CJ could smell the aroma of Katrina's special chicken stew. "Oh, Miss CJ! I make special meal for you. I know it is most wintertime food, but you look like you need, yes?"

CJ put her arm around the woman. "I need. Yes!"

"Miss CJ, you cry? You okay?"

"I'm okay." This time she used her sleeve to wipe her nose.

"You give me shirt. I wash. You go put on clean shirt, and I make plate for you."

"Deal!" CJ was slowly coming out of her melancholy. Katrina's chicken paprika was always a good antidote for just about anything. She started to climb the steps, glanced out the window, and thought she saw something move in the brush. *Again?*

Gotta stop this.

When she entered her room, she noticed that the window screen was not seated in the sill properly. She thought maybe Eduard had done the windows and hadn't replaced the screen in the track. She yelled down toward the kitchen, "Katrina? Did Eduard wash the screens and windows?"

"Not today. He do last week."

Huh. CJ could have sworn the screen had been in the proper grooves when she opened the window that morning. Her inner voice was sending signals, but her mind was resisting its calls. "Everything is fine," she told herself in a low whisper. "But what if it isn't?" She looked in the mirror and saw another rustling in the bushes out of the corner of her eye. Pulling on a clean sweatshirt, she ran down the steps. "Katrina! Where is Eduard?" She was almost in a panic.

"He go to landscape place to get more soil for herb garden. You say you want herb garden, yes?" Katrina was confused by CJ's sudden agitation. It was different from the sad mood of just a few minutes before.

"Help me lock the doors!" CJ was scrambling to shut and lock all the sliding doors out to the grounds.

"Miss CJ? Miss CJ? What is problem? Is

beautiful outside! Why close and lock doors?"

"Katrina, please call Eduard and tell him to come here now!"

"But what about herb garden?"

"Screw the herb garden. Get him back here, *now*!" CJ pulled out her phone and hit the speed dial for Colin. It went straight to voice mail. Then she tried Matt's. Same thing. Voice mail.

"Damn. Damn. Damn."

"Miss CJ? Please! What is problem?" Katrina was beginning to feel afraid as she watched the woman who was always calm become terror-stricken.

CJ had sent a quick text to Eduard: Come to house. Trouble! He sent a reply: What? and she replied with: Now! Come now!

"Set the alarm!" CJ was shouting orders. "Where is Eduard?" She was close to hyperventilating.

"He come soon! Miss CJ? What I do? What he do?"

"Nothing! It's not you. Not Eduard. I think someone is watching the house."

"Yes, Miss CJ. We watch house for you." Katrina was attempting to console her.

CJ's voice became a whisper. "That's not what I meant. Someone is outside. Looking into the house." CJ went into the pantry and unlocked the cabinet containing the only shotgun in the house. She pulled it out though she did not have a clue how to load it or use it. But if she had to, she would learn in a big hurry.

Katrina clutched her throat in fear. "Who? Who look here?"

"I don't know, but we need to sit still until Eduard gets here."

"We call the police?"

"No. Not yet." CJ was starting to wonder if the person outside had been sent by Leonard Franklin. Realizing she had scared the crap out of Katrina, CJ took several deep breaths and slowed down. "I think there may be someone following me." She saw the horrified look on Katrina's face. "Don't worry. I know someone who can help." *If only he'd answer the damn phone,* she thought to herself. "It's going to be okay." She grabbed Katrina's hand, not sure which of them needed the most comfort at that point.

The minutes seemed like decades until they heard Eduard's truck spin into the gravel driveway. He ran toward the front as CJ disarmed the alarm and let him in.

"What is the problem?" He was almost as frenzied as the two of them.

"Eduard." CJ was feeling less threatened

now that Eduard was back — at least he knew how to use a shotgun. "I think someone may have followed me from Washington."

"But who?" Eduard was confused. He knew very little about the circumstances that had surrounded CJ except that her boss had committed suicide.

"I'm not sure." She then realized that neither had known about the two attempts on her life. "Listen. There are some bad people who have done some very bad things. They think I may have information that can hurt them, but I don't." She knew she was lying, but she didn't want them to freak out.

"Information?" Eduard was familiar with very bad people. "What kind information?"

"It's very complicated, but we are going to be okay. I just need you to stay with me until my friend can tell me what to do. It may mean you both stay here tonight. Can you do that for me?" She was half pleading while trying not to sound desperate.

"Yes. We stay." Eduard took the shotgun from the table. "And *this* stay with me, Miss CJ." He gave her a reassuring smile as he patted the gun.

They had been sitting quietly for several moments when the doorbell rang, practically catapulting all three of them out of their chairs. CJ went to the intercom, pushed the button, and calmly asked, "Who is it?"

A husky voice answered. "Crestview Cable. We got a complaint that this area has no service. We need to check your cable boxes."

"Like hell you do," she muttered. Then, in her normal voice, she responded, "All of our service is fine. Sorry to inconvenience you."

The bell rang again.

"What?" CJ was annoyed now and didn't care if it showed.

"I need you to sign off on it, ma'am. Otherwise, my supervisor will think I didn't come out here."

"Tell him to call me." CJ looked at Katrina and Eduard and rolled her eyes.

"This is private property, mister. If you don't leave immediately, I will call the police, then your supervisor and file a complaint. If you want to keep your job, and not be arrested, I suggest you leave right now. Got it?"

The sound of receding footsteps was followed by the roar of a truck's engine. Eduard made his way to the front window and watched the Crestview Cable truck back out of the driveway. Looking at CJ, he shrugged. "Maybe he was okay, Miss CJ. He come with truck."

"You guys probably think I'm crazy, but I don't want to take any chances. You know that my boss is dead, right? Well, even though it was ruled a suicide, I don't think he killed himself. Everyone else thinks he did, but I don't." She made her way to the wine cooler and pulled out a crisp Sauvignon Blanc. Who cared if it was only lunchtime? Europeans had wine with every meal. She was so anxious, she practically pulled the cork out with her teeth.

"Katrina, what about that stew?"

CJ patted her on the shoulder, knowing she had terrified her two companions. "Colin has a good friend at the FBI. I'm waiting for them to call me. We might as well eat!"

Katrina served up the chicken over buttered noodles as CJ downed almost half the bottle of wine.

The afternoon dragged on as CJ waited to hear back from Colin and Matt. She really did not want to sleep in the house that night, doubting she would actually be able to sleep. Finally, around five o'clock, her cell phone rang.

"CJ? What's going on?" Colin's voice was tense.

"I think someone tried to break into the house. Or did break in."

"What are you talking about?"

"The screen on my bedroom window had been moved, and I saw something . . . someone . . . moving near the fence. Then some guy who said he was from a cable company rang the bell. Col, I'm nervous. I know Leonard Franklin is in jail awaiting trial, but that doesn't mean he doesn't have connections on the outside."

"Are you sure —" Just as Colin was uttering those words, he knew they would set her off.

"Yes, I am freakin' sure," she yelled into the phone. "I thought after identifying Franklin that this would be over!" Her voice was at a fevered pitch.

"Hold on. I am going to put Matt on the phone. Tell him what you just told me."

"CJ? What happened?" Matt was very calm.

"I think someone tried to break into the house. The screen was crooked in the frame. Then a guy rang the bell saying he was from the cable company. I thought this was over!"

"I think we'll have to move you for the time being," Matt continued, speaking slowly.

"Move me? Where? Why?" CJ was back to

a state of agitation.

"We are going to need your testimony again for the trial."

"What? You said it would be over!" She was pissed.

"The judge said we need to have your testimony for when you IDed him."

"And when in the hell were you going to tell me?" CJ was now livid.

"I just found out before we called you back. I was offline and just got the messages."

"Swell. Well, now what the hell are we — *you* going to do?"

"We're going to put you in Witness Protection —"

CJ interrupted. "Witness Protection!"

"CJ, it's going to be okay. You have to trust me." Matt had been through this before and knew how unhinged people could get.

"Someone from the US Marshals Service will accompany you to a safe house. You'll be assigned to a marshal, who will be your contact person. No one will know where you are."

"What about Colin?" CJ was on the verge of hysteria.

"Colin can't know either. It's protocol. We can get messages back and forth but there can be no direct contact. At least not until the trial is over."

"And when might *that* be?" Beads of sweat were forming on her forehead. "And when is this going to take place? And for how long? Months? Years?" She was exasperated.

"We're sending someone over shortly. Pack your clothes in boxes. They will be picked up by what will look like a Salvation Army truck for a donation. Leave your cell phone behind. Have Katrina use it to make a few calls for the next couple of days. We'll get your things to you, but it has to look like you're still at the cabin. At least until you're settled. In an hour, have Eduard drive you to Ruby Tuesday. You will sit with them and order food. You will then go to the restroom. There will be a brown paper bag in the first stall with a jacket, wig, and baseball cap. Put them on and leave through the back door. An FBI agent will be waiting for you in a green Toyota Corolla."

As if Matt sensed that CJ was searching for pen and paper, he added, "And don't write any of this down. It's going to be okay, CJ. I promise. Now repeat the instructions I just gave you."

CJ was shaking but repeated what Matt had said.

"Now get busy. You don't have a lot of time."

"Do you know where I'll be going?"

"I do not. But you will be safe. I am going to put Colin back on the line. Try to stay cool. I realize this is shocking, especially after everything you've been through, but you can do this, CJ. I know you can."

Colin got back on the line. "CJ? It's going to be okay. Think of it as a paid vacation courtesy of the federal government." Colin was trying to calm her nerves with a touch of humor.

"Ha. My tax dollars finally being used to benefit me." CJ's voice cracked, and she choked back a slight sob. "I'm scared, Col. How did all of this happen?"

"I wish I knew."

"What about all the stuff in Snapper's secret condo?" CJ was not ready to get off the phone and face another dark tunnel.

"I'm still working on that."

"Is it all tied in with this catastrofreak?"

"Not sure, but most likely. Listen, you have *got* to get off the phone and get ready. I'll get word to you when I find out more. Meanwhile, take care and try to stay cool. I love you, sweetie."

"Love you too, Col." CJ clicked off the phone and handed it to Katrina. "You have to use this for the next couple of days."

"Why, Miss CJ? I have a phone." Katrina

was still nervous and confused.

"Because I'm asking you to. Will you do that for me?"

"Miss CJ, I do anything for you."

"Okay then! Eduard, please bring some of those banker's boxes up from the basement. We have to move fast." CJ gathered her resolve and proceeded to move on her new mission . . . whatever *that* was. "We are going to pack my clothes in boxes. Tomorrow, you will put them on the front porch with a sign for the Salvation Army. Once we're done packing, we will go to Ruby Tuesday for something to eat —"

"But, Miss CJ, I make dinner for you," Katrina interrupted CJ's instructions.

"I know, and I appreciate that, but we have to do this tonight. As in now."

CJ bolted up the stairs, taking two at a time. Pulling out the clothes from the closet and drawers, she piled them on the bed. Katrina was hot on her heels. "Katrina, we have to leave in an hour, so if I don't finish, you know what to do, yes?"

"Yes, Miss CJ. I pack clothes in boxes and put on porch for Salvation Army."

"Excellent! Now let's get crackin'." CJ threw her arm around Katrina. "I know this is all very sudden and a little frightening, but everything is going to be okay. We're going to Ruby Tuesday together, but I will have to leave by myself. So when I get up to go to the restroom, act like everything is normal. Understood?"

"Yes, Miss CJ. We take you to Ruby Tuesday but not bring you back here."

Having had her own experience of human smuggling, Katrina had an idea of what was about to happen. She had no clue why it was happening, but she was fiercely loyal and would do whatever CJ asked.

CJ pulled together a few personal items such as cosmetics, a few pair of underwear, socks, and a T-shirt. Whatever she could fit in her small tote. Good thing it was reversible. She could turn it inside out in the restroom in which she would put on the clothing and wig awaiting her. She suddenly felt unusually calm, but, avoiding tempting fate, she did not ask herself, *What's next?* She took a deep breath, surveyed what was left for Katrina to pack, threw the tote over her shoulder, and headed down the stairs to a fate unknown.

CHAPTER 18

Katrina and Eduard drove CJ to Ruby Tuesday in silence. CJ didn't know what to say without revealing anything she shouldn't, so she settled for surfing the radio. Once they arrived and were seated, CJ ordered a vodka martini. She needed something to calm her nerves. As the perky waitress with a big smile and bigger eyes returned to take their order, CJ's palms started to sweat. The reality of what was happening was sinking even deeper.

"What can I getcha?" the ponytailed, cherub-cheeked server inquired.

CJ ordered the first thing she saw on the menu. "I'll take the triple play." She stifled a laugh, realizing she had no idea what she had just ordered. Katrina and Eduard gave her an odd look and placed their orders. As soon as the waitress moved toward the kitchen, CJ slid out of her seat. "I'll be right back," she said, and headed to the restroom.

A woman who was coming out as she was going in gave her a slight nod. Just as Matt had explained, a brown bag was in the first stall. CJ didn't know which she should do first, change or throw up. She steadied herself and pulled out the elements of her disguise, a short black wig, a very ugly plaid shirt, and a baseball cap with "John Deere" written on the front. "So glad I went for that makeover," she muttered as she got a glimpse of herself in the mirror. She splashed some cold water on her face, crumpled the bag, put it in the trash, and made her way out the back door. The green Toyota was waiting. The driver nodded for her to get in the front. She was relieved to discover it was the same FBI agent who had been her security detail at home.

"Agent Becker! I cannot tell you how happy I am to see a familiar face!" CJ's eyes welled with tears.

"Hey, Ms. Jansen. Heard you've been through a bit of a rough patch."

"That's an understatement. It's been surreal. I feel like I've been in a bad dream for months." CJ buckled herself in and settled into the seat.

"I'm going to drive you to Pennsylvania, where you will be met by someone from the US Marshals Service. They will transport you to your new location."

"Do you know where I'll be going?" CJ knew the answer but thought she would ask anyway.

"No, I do not. It's all part of the program. No person outside WITSEC knows more than one or two stages. It's for safety reasons."

"I get it. But it does make me anxious." CJ was about to ask Becker if they could stop at a liquor store but decided that wouldn't be appropriate. One brown paper bag a day was enough. She was envisioning herself taking a swig from a pint of cheap vodka and laughed out loud.

"Care to share?" Becker looked over and smiled.

"Just picturing myself, now that I'm homeless . . . drinking a pint of booze out of a brown paper bag."

Becker chuckled. "I know you're worried, but you're not homeless. Just temporarily displaced."

"Can you tell me where you will be dropping me off or are you going to blindfold me?" CJ's spirits were lifting a bit.

"We're going to Lancaster, Pennsylvania. Better than going to Philly. Easier to spot tails. Not that we anticipate any, but back roads are better. Should be there in less than four hours. If you want, I'll pull over so you can hop in the back and take a nap."

"Hmmm . . . don't know if I can sleep, but maybe resting a little would help. I'm a hot mess. And this wig? Creeps me out."

Becker pulled onto the shoulder and waited for an eighteen-wheeler to pass before he let CJ out to get in the backseat. "Get comfy. If you can. Would you like to hear some music?"

"Something mellow if you can find it."

Becker pulled out his Pandora playlist and scrolled to an R and B mix that started with "Let's Stay Together" by Al Green.

CJ took off the hideous flannel shirt she had been given, rolled it up, and propped it under her neck. She was surprised at how comfortable she felt, and, within a few minutes, she nodded off.

Two hours later, Becker woke her and asked if she was hungry.

"I think I can choke down something. I never did get my triple play at Ruby Tuesday!"

"There's a farm market up the road that makes great sandwiches on their fresh-baked bread. They stay open until midnight, so we're in plenty of time."

"Well, it *has* to be better than whatever I ordered. I had no idea what a triple play was, and I was too nervous to read the menu carefully enough to find out. I picked the first thing I saw."

After the rest stop it was only another hour before she would be handed off to a marshal from the US Marshals Service. "How many times have you done this? Accompany a fugitive?"

"You're not a fugitive." Becker laughed. "Many times. You would be surprised at the thousands of people who go through this. Most get to go back to their normal lives after a brief hiatus. It's the ones who committed crimes and are turning state's evidence who have to disappear forever."

"Huh. I never realized it worked that way."

"Yeah. TV. Not always accurate." Becker pulled into a small diner-type café. "Here's where the next part of the relay race begins. Time to put that haute couture shirt back on!" Becker knew CJ would never wear those clothes voluntarily, so he had to get in one last tease.

"Can I hug you?" CJ's fear was starting to mount again.

"You bet!" When Becker gave her a big bear hug, she felt the gun in his holster, which was a bit unnerving. It made her realize that her mind had been on autopilot and that she really hadn't had time to think about much of anything. Just react. And that would probably be her modus operandi for however long this ordeal would take. React.

A woman in her early forties, of middling height, neither fat nor thin, with medium brown hair in a bun and a plain but expressive face approached the two of them and held out her hand. "Becker! How the hell are you?" She had a nice smile and calm demeanor.

"You must be CJ." She turned and extended her hand. "I know this can be overwhelming, but let me assure you that I'm going to take good care of you."

"And she will," Becker chimed in. "CJ, this is US Marshal Donna Napoli. She will be escorting you to your destination and be your key contact."

CJ smiled in return and shook the marshal's hand. "Nice to meet you, and yes, this is a bit harrowing."

"You're gonna be fine. Shall we?" Napoli gestured to a silver SUV. "We have another nine hours ahead, so we'll stop at a motel a few miles up the road for the night."

"Nine hours?" CJ was calculating the four hours she had already spent in the car. "Where the heck are we going? Canada?"

"Pretty close." Napoli smiled, and continued, "I have a change of clothes for you.

Looking at your photo, I figured around a size ten. My apologies if you're smaller. Sometimes it's hard to tell. Got you a nightshirt, leggings, and a lightweight sweater. You did bring underwear, yes?"

CJ chuckled. "Size whatever is fine at this point! I appreciate the change of clothes, and I did bring a spare set of underwear!"

Becker started kicking the gravel around his feet. "Okay, you girls can have your slumber party, but I still have to get back to DC tonight." He threw one arm around CJ. "It's gonna all be fine. You take good care of her," he said, motioning to Napoli.

"You know I will!"

CJ and her new best friend climbed into the SUV and drove a few miles before they pulled into a Homewood Suites. "We have adjoining rooms."

"At this point, I wouldn't care if it was a tent. Okay, maybe not a tent. But a shower and something to sleep on besides the backseat of a car would be divine."

CJ's inner radar was telling her that this woman was in control and she could feel safe with her.

Napoli had checked them in earlier and had the keycards in her pocket. "Follow me." They took the elevator to the second floor, and the marshal opened the doors.

"Need a drink?"

"Boy, do I ever!"

"Good. I brought my own provisions." Napoli pulled out a J. Lohr Hilltop Cabernet and a corkscrew. "Go jump in the shower, and I'll let this breathe and find us real glasses."

"I knew there was something I liked about you! I'll be out in a jiffy."

"Take your time. The wine needs a few minutes to breathe!"

Those words were comforting. If anything else, Marshal Napoli wasn't a stranger to wine.

For years, CJ had followed a fairly strict schedule. Her daily routine rarely fluctuated unless it was work related. Her personal life? Whatever there was of it was rather boring, but the past two months, especially the past two days, were like being at an amusement park on acid. At least that's what CJ thought it was like. Not that she had any LSD experience, but a screwy visual would come to one's mind.

Several minutes later, she emerged from the bathroom with her own hair wrapped in a towel and wearing the fresh nightshirt.

"I have no idea how women can wear these things all day," CJ said, holding the wig as if it were a dirty dish rag.

"I do like the way the real you looks. Kind of Uma Thurmanish."

"Ha. You're not the first to say that. I don't see it, but I went from mousey plain everything to a highlighted blond blunt cut. You can tell that I've led a sheltered life." CJ was being sardonic.

Napoli laughed out loud. "Exactly why you're in WITSEC. Boring life. Needed a change of scenery."

"Speaking of scenery, where am I going?"

"Boothbay Harbor."

"As in Maine?" CJ was dazed. "Another harbor?"

Napoli looked a bit confused at first, but then she remembered reading about CJ's having lost her brother in a boating accident. "Oh right. But I don't think there was any other choice at the moment. Unless you would have preferred Reno?"

CJ threw herself on the bed, almost spilling her wine. "It's not just my brother. My parents were killed on their way home from watching a regatta. Me and the water — not so lucky."

"Maybe this will change your luck. And you won't be there too long."

"And what does 'too long' mean exactly?"

"As long as the trial. Three to six months. It will go by fast. It's the summer, and

Boothbay Harbor is beautiful this time of year."

"If you say so. As long as I don't have to get too close to the water, I guess I'll have to deal with it." CJ sighed with resignation and took a big swig of her wine. Napoli's taste in wine also gave CJ a little more confidence in the woman. Funny. Basing an opinion on someone because of their knowledge of wine. It was, after all, an ancient ritual. CJ smiled to herself.

"You'll be fine. Very nice people. Quaint town. I'll show you around and introduce you to some of the locals."

"And who might I be? Obviously not Carol Anne Jansen, or CJ, witness to Leonard Franklin, aka El Stinko."

Napoli guffawed, thinking about the notes from CJ's file. *Mr. Crappy Cologne, Pepé Le Pew, French Whorehouse.*

"Yeah, tell me about that. Mr. Crappy Cologne?"

"He's the reason I'm here. Leonard Franklin. Wears the most revolting cologne and way too much of it. That's how I made his acquaintance, so to speak. I sniffed him out. No pun intended. But for real." The wine was having a calming effect on CJ as she continued. "I got a whiff of him one night in my boss's office, then in the hallway at the Rayburn House Office Building when he was in with another congressman. By then I was able to pick him out of a lineup — without even being able to smell him." They both laughed and proceeded to finish the Cabernet.

"Okay. Time to hit the sheets. Early start in the morning. Sleep tight." Napoli switched off the light and made her way into her own room.

CJ was exhausted and fell into a coma-like sleep, so when Donna Napoli rapped on the adjoining door the next morning and entered the room, CJ flew out of bed like a projectile.

"Easy girl." Donna had a cup of French roast coffee that she was about to hand CJ but pulled it out of the path of her flailing arms.

"Oh my gosh! You scared the crap out of me!" CJ was part startled, somewhat annoyed, and thoroughly delighted by the aroma of the coffee. "I hope that's for me!"

"Indeed it is. I figured you were a dark roast, light cream kind of girl." Donna handed her the cup.

"Wow. You really did your homework on me."

"Nah. It was the way you polished off that Cabernet. Dark. Deep."

"Excuse me, but I had a little help there, Marshal Napoli." CJ was feeling easy with her new companion and guardian.

"Breakfast? Or are you one of those who waits an hour?"

"Usually a protein shake, but I don't suppose that's on the menu."

"Good thinking. That would be a 'no,' but we'll pick up supplies when we get to our destination, so you can have some sense of normalcy." Napoli put a five-dollar bill on the night table with a note that said "housekeeping," and handed CJ her new clothes for the day. "You should be getting your own stuff in about a week. So we'll pick up some extra things for you when we get there. Move your ass, girl. We have a lot of dirt to cover, and we need to do some shopping."

"Do I have to wear that ratty thing on my head again?" CJ looked dismayed.

"Just until we get on the road a bit. I don't want anyone seeing a person coming out of the hotel with me who didn't go in."

"Gotcha . . . But . . . ick." CJ put on the plaid shirt, stepped into her jeans, and squeamishly affixed the black-haired wig, then covered it with the John Deere cap.

"Lovely. Let's go." Napoli shoved whatever items had been scattered into her duffel . . .

including the empty bottle of wine and the glasses and the contents of the trash. "The less we leave behind, the better."

The nine-hour drive alternated between lovely countrysides, various dilapidated farms, and a few deserted, ramshackle barns. CJ was struck by the contrasts of American life. Washington, DC, seemed like an alien planet when compared to the places where the population of all but the biggest cities lived. No wonder people were disillusioned. The political elite really were clueless about the lives of Americans outside the big cities and, when you got right down to it, even the lives of most of those who lived in those big cities.

The two women made the usual pit stops for food, bathroom breaks, and gas, and each stop reminded CJ what people do to survive and, if they're lucky, thrive.

It was near dinnertime when they finally approached the main area of Boothbay Harbor. CJ tried to keep her anxiety under control as she viewed the surrounding waters. The name of the town could not have been more descriptive.

Sensing her trepidation, Donna reached over and patted her on the knee. "Not to worry. We have a triplex with no view of the water. You will have to look at it at some point . . . hard to get away from it entirely . . . but you won't have to go into it or out on it. There aren't even any bridges to cross."

CJ took in a sigh of relief. "Yeah. This is a bit overwhelming. But lovely. If you like water. Still gives me the heebie-jeebies."

"I'll keep a good watch over you. For your safety and sanity. Deal?"

"If you say so." CJ was craning her neck at the estuaries, which seemed to go on forever.

As they pulled onto Oak Street, CJ was thankful that the triplex wasn't directly on the water. "Is this the place? My new temporary home?"

"It is. Nice couple run it. Retired military. I'll introduce you, then we'll go pick up some supplies and a few clothes. The nice thing about this place is that most of the activities are within walking distance unless you want to venture to the outer perimeter."

"Uh, doubtful." CJ was sure she would not be exploring the surrounding waterways.

"You never know. We'll arrange for a vehicle for you just in case you change your mind. It should be here tomorrow morning. C'mon." Napoli gestured with her arm.

Still scratching her head from having to put on the rat's-nest wig, CJ followed as

Napoli rang the bell.

A neatly dressed man in his late sixties with a big smile on his face answered the door. "Donna! Good to see you."

"Ced, this is Carolyn Johnson." Donna gave CJ an elbow tap as if to say, "Remember your alias" when CJ blinked back in confusion, then realization.

"Carolyn. Very nice to meet you. Come in. Betty? We have a new guest." Ced was calling out to his wife, a short, white-haired woman with a high forehead, brown eyes, bulbous nose, and a slash of a mouth, who was wearing an apron that clearly showed the results of her baking activity.

"Hello, dear. So sorry about the batter. I'm still trying to learn how to use an electric mixer. Never was one for making cookies, but someone signed me up to do so for the festival!" Betty wiped her hands on a damp towel hanging from the belt of the apron.

"Hi. I'm . . . Carolyn. Carolyn Johnson." CJ was trying her new name on for the first time. At least it was close to her real name, something Donna had explained on the way. It made it easier for the person to remember.

"Ced, show Carolyn her apartment, and I'll catch up with Donna."

"Right this way." Cedric, a powerful-looking man who walked with a slight limp, the result of a moped accident a few years ago, motioned toward the door.

They walked around to the side of the building, and he unlocked the door to a spacious one-bedroom apartment. It had an open floor plan, which pleased CJ. She'd had no idea what to expect, and claustrophobia was one of her concerns. It was hard enough being in a strange place, but a cramped one would have driven her up the walls.

"This is lovely." CJ walked along the perimeter of the eight-hundred-square-foot space, taking in the living, dining, and kitchen area. Then she peeked into the bedroom, noticing that the only windows faced the woods. As Donna had promised, there was no view of the water. Thank goodness.

Ced showed her where the thermostat was for the air-conditioning. "Even as far north as we are, we do get some humid weather here." He moved on to the kitchen, pointing out the range, refrigerator "with an ice machine," garbage disposal, and dishwasher. "You got pretty much everything you need. We also have an outdoor grill you're welcome to use. Just let me know, and I'll fire it up for you."

"Thank you so much. I think I'll be very comfortable here." And she meant what she said. Her inner self was telling her that this was probably the best place for her to be at this time. Away from everything. Her distant past, her recent past, and everything in between.

A few minutes later CJ could hear footsteps and Donna's big laugh. "So? Whaddya think? Can you live here for a while?"

"Maybe forever. Except for the water part!" CJ was half laughing.

"Okay, let's go do some shopping. Ced? Did you fill the fridge?"

"Not completely, but I got some cheese, yogurt, fruit, coffee, and cream. You're on your own for the rest. I'll leave you two to get busy." He handed CJ a card with his phone numbers on it. "You need anything, just give a buzz."

"Thanks so much. I appreciate all of it."

The two women walked back to the car. "We'll drive around today, so you can get the lay of the land and pick up what you'll need until your stuff arrives. Work for you?"

"Do I have a choice?" CJ gave Donna a little tap on the arm. She knew she could trust this woman. With her life. Shopping should be a breeze.

As they drove through town, CJ got a big laugh at the Tugboat Inn. It had a real tugboat sitting in the front. The names of some of the places gave her a chuckle as well: Two Salty Dogs Pet Outfitters, and Schooner Lazy Jack Cruises. There was McSeagull's Restaurant, the Topside Inn, and the Wharfside Gallery. "They sure take their nautical theme to the max!" But she also noticed how beautiful and breathtaking Boothbay Harbor was. It was on the water, so she wanted to hate it. She believed that if she could like something or someplace with this much water, she was somehow betraying her brother. Crazy. Bittersweet.

Donna explained that Boothbay Harbor had long been considered by mariners to be the finest deepwater port north of Boston, with many calling it the "Boating Capital of New England." "So, yes it is a harbor, dear."

They pulled in front of Gimbel and Sons Country Store and went inside. "Kind of a throwback." Donna said hello to the clerk and introduced CJ. "Henry, this is Carolyn. She's going to be staying for the summer."

"Nice to meet you, Carolyn," the bespectacled teenager responded. "If you don't see what you need, just let me know, and we'll order it for you. Usually takes one or two days to get here."

"Thanks, Henry. I'll keep that in mind."

CJ picked out a few pairs of shorts and T-shirts and another pair of jeans. As she was looking for her wallet, Donna immediately pulled out a credit card and handed it to the clerk. She gave CJ a look that said, "Don't say a word."

Once they left the store, CJ blurted, "I do have money, you know."

"Yes, but you still have your original ID, and I don't want anyone to see it. When we get back you'll lock your personal items in the safe, and I'll give you your new insurance ID and driver's license."

Through all the chaos, it hadn't occurred to CJ that she would have to take on the new identity so completely, including a complete set of documents. "Ah. Yes, Carolyn Johnson. Do I get a credit card, too?"

"A debit card. Everything should be at the house when we get back."

"So how long do you babysit me?"

"I'll be here for a few days, until you get settled, then I'll be back about once a week."

"But what if I need you?" CJ was trying not to panic.

"Ced and Betty know how to reach me. I spent almost all of my summers here when I was growing up. They'll find me if anything happens. But don't worry. Nothing will.

You're not the first person in Witness Protection that has spent time in Boothbay Harbor."

"So what am I allegedly doing here? Vacationing? Do I have a job?"

"Do you *want* a job?"

"I need to be doing something, or I'll go nuts. Considering that most of everything here has to do with water, there don't seem to be a lot of options."

"I figured you weren't the type to sit around watching game shows and eating bonbons and thought I could hook you up at the Wharfside Gallery. You know about art, right?"

"Yeah, but not nautical art."

"It's not just nautical art. They have stuff from over thirty local artists. They need someone to catalog everything. I think you can handle that."

"Brilliant!" CJ was impressed at Donna's ability to think ahead, or even at a moment's notice. "But how will you convince them to hire me?"

"I already have. I know the owners." Donna gave her a wink. "My brother shows some of his work there."

"Seriously?"

"Yes. As I said, I spent almost every summer here. When you get up the nerve, I suggest you visit the Coastal Maine Botanical Gardens. It is awe-inspiring."

"Yeah. Uh. No. I get a visceral reaction to anything with the word 'coastal.' "

"Like hives?" Donna was poking fun at her.

"Something like that."

"Okay, kiddo. We're going to have to get you past your phobia."

"I hate to disillusion you, but even four years of therapy didn't help."

"Ah, what do those shrinks know anyway?" Donna opened the hatch and tossed the packages inside. "Hey, it's almost seven o'clock. Dinner?"

"Sure. Wine?"

"Would I bring you anywhere else?"

They headed to the Boathouse Bistro Tapas Bar and Restaurant. "Okay, I'm warning you," Donna said. "This place is on the water, but you won't have to go near the railings. We can stay as far inside as you want."

"Give me a martini, and I think I'll be okay." CJ gave her a big smile.

"Attagirl. You're going to be fine."

After the hostess had seated them at an inside table, Donna whispered, "We'll get you out on that deck at some point!"

"Don't bet on it," CJ whispered loudly in return.

CHAPTER 19

CJ had been surprised at how relaxed she was at dinner the night before. Maybe it was the wine. The air. Or maybe just the fact that the past two days of whirlwind activity were finally at an end, and she finally had some clue as to where she would be — at least for the next three or more months. The disturbing events of the past two months — from the alleged suicide, the discovery of the secret condo, the trip to Sun Valley Institute, literally bumping into Leonard Franklin, the accident after her brakes had been tampered with, the attempt by a crazy person on a motorcycle to kill her, and finding that someone was watching her at Colin and Kick's cabin — were enough to send shivers down her spine. Or to have a nervous breakdown. Throw in having had sixty days to finish up Snapper's congressional business after the rest of the staff had vamoosed, clear out her office, and make memorial arrangements for Snapper. And after all that, she had to start thinking about how to dispose of Snapper's condo. Anyone would have flipped out by now. And then there was the secret condo. She still had no idea what to do about that, and Colin insisted she sit on any real-estate transactions until the trial was over. The trial at which she would identify Leonard Franklin as the person who assaulted Snapper in Snapper's office, and who was a frequent visitor to Congressman Dillard. Yep. It was quite a lot to process.

Her body and mind were in the process of taking a needed break from all of that. There wasn't anything she had to do now but wait.

The prior evening, when they had returned to the triplex, Donna and CJ, aka Carolyn, reviewed her cover story. She was Carolyn Johnson from New York. She was working on her master's degree in regional Americana art. CJ would work at the gallery four hours a day three days a week. Her limited exposure to other people would be enough to keep her busy but not enough to raise too many questions. It was the peak of the summer season and many resident and visiting artists used the time to exhibit their work. The gallery was busy with paintings coming in and going out the door in large volumes, and they all needed to be cataloged. The job would keep her in the back room most of the time. Another plus for her.

Her only problem was what to do with the rest of her time. Nothing related to water was in the cards. Ever. Maybe she'd finally catch up on some reading. It had been a while since she'd curled up with a good book.

After a quick breakfast, Donna rapped on CJ's door. "Ready?"

"As much as I ever will be!" It was less than a five-minute drive, but Donna needed her car for the afternoon, and CJ could easily walk back.

"Cute place," she noted, as they entered the small gallery. "Wow. And lots of . . . whales."

"It *is* called Boothbay Harbor. You're gonna see a few whales. And sharks and sailboats. You okay with that? Inanimate versions?"

"Yeah. Yeah. Shut up." CJ poked Donna lightly with her elbow.

"Maggie!" Donna called out to an artist who was delivering a new oil painting of a three-masted schooner. "Very nice!"

"Hey, Donna. Yeah, it was commissioned by a yacht club in Sag Harbor. Need to pack and send."

"Maggie, meet Carolyn Johnson. She's going to be working here part-time for a couple of months. Doing something with a master's degree."

CJ extended her hand, then realized Maggie was balancing the large painting. "Here, let me help you with that. I suppose I'm the one who's going to be packing it for you anyway!"

"Really? That would be great. I have to go pick up the kids from swimming lessons." Maggie pulled out a sealed envelope with the invoice, a packing slip, and a sheet of paper with the address on it and handed them to CJ. "Thanks and welcome! I'll catch you later. Good to see you, Donna!" Maggie left CJ holding the painting and the papers and bolted out the door.

"Wow. My first assignment." CJ looked confused. "What the heck am I supposed to do with this?"

"Set it down, and we'll go find Steve. He'll get you started."

Steve was sitting outside in his usual place — a small bistro table — drinking a cup of what looked like a cappuccino.

"Got some for the whole class?" Donna teased the manager.

"For you? Absolutely!" Steve was a portly

guy in his early fifties with a bit of a gnarly, seafaring look to him. His black hair was long, his eyes green, and his chin jutted out. He stood and thrust his chubby, callused hand at CJ. "You must be my new clerk!"

"I am indeed. Nice to meet you. And thank you for this opportunity. I just met Maggie, and she has a project for me already."

"Yeah, be careful of that one." Steve showed a mischievous grin. "She'll have you doing all sorts of things. Good girl but a little scatterbrained, and a talker. Artists! You know how they can be."

"I heard you were one!" CJ flashed a smile.

"Actually, I build model ships. You've got to follow precise directions. The idea is to get as close to the real thing in miniature. So, not a lot of creativity but a lot of little slices from the Exacto knives if you're not careful."

"If you didn't sniff all that glue, maybe you wouldn't hurt yourself so much." Donna could not resist teasing him.

"That's why I need the cappuccino," Steve roared. "Let me get you two gals some. Sit. I'll be right back."

CJ was taken aback at how friendly everyone was. And relaxed. Things in Boothbay

Harbor were very different from Capitol Hill. "Is everyone always this nice?" she asked Donna, trying not to sound sarcastic.

"Yeah. Funny, eh? Once you get away from the world of politics or the corporate jungle, it's a very different world. That's why I can actually stand my job. I spent six years in the DC office, then in the Chicago branch. I kept putting in for transfers to some of the outer, smaller cities. Took long enough, but now I get to do the work I enjoy in a place that doesn't suck."

"Balance. That's what life is about, isn't it?" CJ was becoming increasingly aware of how different her life had been. And the decision about what to do with it next was beginning to look very different than it had only two or three days ago. She could probably get used to a quieter life somewhere other than Washington or any other big city.

"I think this air will help clear your head," Donna reassured her. "It has a very therapeutic effect."

Steve returned with two frothing cups and a stack of shortbread cookies. As he set the plate down, he made a confession. "I can't resist them. My weakness."

"Oh, Steve, anything that has sugar in it is your weakness. Or salt. Or pepper." Donna enjoyed verbal jousting with her old friend.

Steve patted his girth. "Helps me keep my girlish figure. So, Carolyn, tell me about yourself. How long have you been studying Americana art?"

CJ tried not to fumble her words or her cover. "I only got interested in it lately. I'm a bit of a museum hound and was drawn to the Museum of the City of New York. I love the history, so I took a class that traced the growth through art. That's when it dawned on me that there must be so many places in the US that have their own art, style, and artist colonies, and I decided that I wanted to do something that would perhaps lead to producing an encyclopedia of Americana art. And here I am." CJ stopped talking because she had absolutely no idea where her next sentence would come from. *Not bad for an impromptu reply,* she thought, *but I do not want to press my luck by saying something that would raise more questions.*

"Great!" Steve's big voice boomed again. "Have you studied any other parts of the country yet?"

Now it was getting tricky. "Actually, this is my first, so I guess you could call me a newbie. That's why Donna thought doing cataloging for you would be a great way to get me on track."

"So, how do you two know each other?"

Steve was aware that Donna worked for the government, but he didn't know in what capacity. Probably some sort of desk job, he assumed.

Donna jumped in with, "I was in New York at the Museum of Modern Art when they had the Frank Lloyd Wright exhibit. I met Carolyn at the cocktail party afterward. We struck up a conversation, and here she is!" Donna, too, had not expected a full-blown interrogation.

"Excellent! Well, we're glad to have you, Carolyn. Follow me, and I'll show you your work area." Steve pushed back on the little chair, and CJ and Donna gave each other a side glance as if to say, "Dodged that bullet."

CJ asked where the restroom was, and Steve pointed and said, "Through that door. First one on the right."

"You seem rather fond of her." Steve gave Donna a "what's up?" kind of glance.

"I like her. She's had a rough go. Lost her brother in an accident. Some guy was drunk on a Jet Ski and slammed into his boat while it was tied up at the marina. So she's a little nervous about water. It was a lot of talkin' getting her up here, so go easy on her if water activities arise, as you know they will."

"Not to worry. I'll keep an eye out for

her." Steve gave Donna his biggest heartening grin.

Once CJ returned, Donna excused herself. "I've got to be in Portland this afternoon. I'll see you for dinner, Carolyn. Steve, don't you work her too hard on her first day!" Giving a slight wave, she disappeared through the front door.

Steve led the way to the back of the gallery. "She's a real peach." He nodded in the direction of the front door. "Known her since she was a kid. Got some fancy job with the feds, but you probably know that. Not sure what she does, but she comes up here from time to time."

"She's easy to be with. We became fast friends after we met at the Wright opening. I lost my brother four years ago, and I was trying to be as social and active as possible. When Donna suggested I come up here, I was very apprehensive. Then I thought, 'What's the worst that can happen?' But then I did think about the worst thing that could happen. I almost changed my mind, but as they say, 'Feel the fear and do it anyway.' " CJ realized she had already said more than she should, especially the part about losing her brother. How much background did people know? She made a mental note to herself to ask Donna about that.

The first four hours passed quickly as CJ tagged the paintings and recorded them in a ledger. "Steve, I know we said I'd only work four hours a day but I'd like to stay longer and really get a feel for the place and the art. You don't have to pay me, but if it's okay with you, I'd like to dig in more."

"No problem, Carolyn. Whatever works for you. You can also break up the hours any way you want. But heck, if you want to put in overtime for free, well, you won't hear me doing any complaining!"

"Great. Would you also mind if I tidied up the mailroom?"

"We have a mailroom?" Steve looked surprised.

CJ let out a snort. "Uh, I think that is what the space is for. Shipping stuff?"

"It's kind of our catchall room. I suppose it is a little disorganized, but hell's bells, be my guest."

CJ went back into the catchall room and agreed with his description. Just about anything that passed through the door ended up sitting in the room: empty boxes, balsa wood, several staple guns, bubble wrap, tape guns, tarps. For the first time in a while, CJ felt that she had a purpose, even if it was simply to organize a mailroom.

Around four o'clock, Maggie returned with a kid in tow. "Carolyn, this is Gina, my four-year-old. Gina, say hi to Carolyn."

Gina gave a shy hello and hid behind her mother's skirt. "I have one more. Gerry. He's six. He's playing at his cousin's. You'll get to meet the whole tribe next weekend. It's our Windjammer Days kickoff! Wait until you see the parade of schooners! It's breathtaking! All kinds of activities, food, music! You got here just in time!" Maggie's enthusiasm was delightful. Her face lit up, bringing out the dimples and making her appear younger than her thirty-plus years. She was a tall, large-breasted woman, with brown, windblown hair, green eyes, and a jutting chin. CJ was not thrilled about the parade of schooners. Perhaps she should have gotten a prescription for Valium before she left DC, but then again, she'd had no idea she would be spending her summer harborside!

CJ took in Maggie's animated persona. She figured she was in her early thirties. At least pretty close to her in age. Funny the differences in people even from the same generation. Maggie had a bohemian look with her long maxiskirt and peasant-style blouse, while CJ was conservative with her

318

Talbots wardrobe. Artsy versus political arena. Like night and day.

She didn't know if Maggie was married because there was no ring. She didn't want to ask, either. Could be ugly.

"My husband Randy will be back from a charter fishing trip. He and his brother Derek run a boat business."

CJ stifled an acid-reflux reaction. She thought to herself: *Yeah, this is going to be one helluva voyage. . . . Every stinking day . . . water. Maybe I should go to Reno. I wonder if it's too late to change up. It's the desert. Now, that's what I call balance.*"

"You okay, Carolyn? You got a little green around the gills."

"I'm . . . I'm fine. I'm just a little squeamish when it comes to boating."

"Wow. Really? This isn't exactly the place for landlubbers!" Maggie was still being sweet but looked puzzled.

"I came here for the art," CJ tossed in.

"Gotcha. Still kinda crazy, doncha think? Coming here?" Maggie gave her a vacuous stare. CJ was beginning to think Maggie was a bit of a twit. Then she remembered what Steve had said — scatterbrained.

"Yeah. Crazy." CJ shrugged and gave the ceiling a "what am I doing here?" kind of look.

"Hey, not that it's any of my business, but you married? Boyfriend? Girlfriend?" Maggie was getting very personal for only knowing CJ about four minutes.

"No. No. And, definitely not. 'Not that there's anything wrong with it,' " she added, mimicking a favorite line from *Seinfeld* when referring to relationships among gays.

Maggie cackled at the familiar phrase. "Didn't you just *love* that show? I watch the reruns all the time! Do people really live like that in New York? You're from New York, right?"

CJ's head was spinning. Too many questions. Rapid-fire. "Most shows don't come close to the real thing, but Jerry's apartment was pretty typical of a one-bedroom. *Sex and the City?* Ridiculous. And don't even get me started on *Friends.* CJ laughed at her passion for accurate portrayals. "Sorry. Makes me nuts. I'm sure cops feel the same way. Even fishermen!" CJ was trying to change the subject from her life in the Big Apple before she tripped up. In addition, she wasn't sure how much she was supposed to say about anything.

"Yeah. Boy, after that movie *The Perfect Storm,* Derek and Randy's business tanked for a while. Even though the storm happened in '91 most people hadn't heard about it until that movie came out in 2000. I was still in high school when they made the movie, but we all grew up together. It was tough on them. But then things turned around slowly. Randy and I started dating a couple years later, when he had enough money to buy me a hot dog!" Maggie sure could talk, but that was better than having to answer too many questions.

"Your family is in the fishing business, too?" CJ thought she knew what the answer would be.

"Yep. My daddy was a fisherman."

Of course he was, CJ thought to herself. *Would there be anything they could talk about that was not related to the sea? Probably not.*

CJ was getting antsy and glanced down at her watch when she remembered she needed to get the value of the painting for insurance. "Maggie, I packed up the painting with the envelope but you didn't tell me how much to insure it for." CJ pulled out the pad from the now neatly arranged mailing station.

"Fifteen thousand," Maggie said calmly.

CJ tried not to look surprised, but she suddenly had a new respect for this gabby gal of the gulls. CJ was amused at her own alliteration but wasn't about to share it.

"Got it. It will go out first thing tomorrow." CJ tapped the pen on the paper.

"Wow. That's great! It usually takes me two or three days just to find stuff in this room. Hey . . ." Maggie finally noticed the organized space. "Did you do this? I've been nagging Steve since forever to do something. It was a junkyard war zone in here. I swear, you could never find anything —"

"I'm glad you like it." CJ had to interrupt. Maggie's continuous chatter was making her ears ring. "I'm going to head out. I'll be back here in the morning and send out your painting. Have a good evening." CJ turned to walk out.

"Carolyn? Carolyn?" Maggie called.

CJ stopped suddenly, remembering that was her new name. "Yes? Sorry . . . I got distracted."

"If you want to tag along with us Saturday, that would be swell. It's me, Randy, Derek, and the kids for the parade and some food, then the kids go home with a sitter. It's our *big night* out," Maggie said with a warm, enthusiastic smile.

"Sure. But no water rides, okay? I'll be fine watching from a distance." CJ gave her the "promise me?" stare.

As if she read the clue, Maggie quickly responded with, "Promise."

CJ let Steve know she was leaving for the

day and walked back to the triplex, making sure she stayed on the side of the street farthest from the harbor. She knew she was being ridiculous, but she needed time to adjust. If she ever would. She thought about jogging, but that would also take her every-where around the grand tidal basin. Maybe not a great idea. She heaved a big sigh, knowing that her phobia was getting the better of her.

As she neared her new living quarters, she noticed Donna's car in the driveway and felt a sense of relief. It has been a stressful day but in a different kind of way. Today, instead of dealing with political intrigue and someone's trying to kill her, she was craft-ing her fake identity, acutely aware that she needed to choose her words very carefully. She was also looking forward to seeing what Donna had procured from the wine shop, having given her a list of some of her favorites that wouldn't break the bank. CJ had every intention of paying Donna back for whatever money she spent until Donna had reminded her that there was a modest expense account she could draw from. "Just don't expect a bottle of Joseph Phelps every night!"

CJ took the stairs two at a time. If she wasn't going to run, she could at least get her thighs fired up. "Is that a cork I hear?"

"You bet!" Donna had opened the bottle and began to pour them each a glass. "How was your day?"

"Pretty good. Cleaned up that mess of a back room for Steve. I don't know how anyone could work in that space! Also had a little chat with Maggie, or should I say Maggie had a big chat with me! Wow, she's a rapid-fire mouthful!" CJ wasn't being unkind. Just making an observation.

"Yeah. She's good folks. Nice family. And she's pretty talented. Won a lot of awards but keeps it local. She loves being a mom, so this is the best of both worlds for her."

"And her work isn't cheap either," CJ added. "Fifteen thousand for that painting she brought in!"

"Says the money's for the kids' college, although sometimes I think Randy would like for her to put it into the business. Those guys work really hard, and running a charter boat isn't cheap."

"Yes. She mentioned Randy and his brother Derek. She invited me to go to the Windjammer Days festival with them on Saturday. What do you think?"

"Great idea! You'll get a real feel for the place that way."

CJ was apprehensive about a few things.

"Okay, but . . ."

"Yeah, I know. No water stuff," Donna chimed in. "That will be hard to avoid, but you won't have to go on the water. Just watch. The parade of schooners is worth the anxiety!"

"It's not just that. How much information can I reveal? Obviously *not* the obvious . . . witness protection, somebody tried to kill me, maybe my boss was murdered. You know, the usual." CJ was being playful. "I'm not the best actress, so give me some guidelines, please."

"Keep it simple. You're from New York. You're on an assignment studying local art."

"I think I got that part down already. Maybe throw in I just broke up with my boyfriend?"

"Did you?"

"If I had one, I would have."

"What?"

"I have a list of jerks. That is something I am good at — meeting jerks. So if I had a boyfriend, I most likely would have broken up with him because he would have been a jerk."

"There you go! Backstory!" Donna was egging her on.

"I can do a montage of assholes!" CJ lifted her wineglass and toasted the air. "Brilliant!

I can create the perfect asshole."

"Uh, that might be an oxymoron, no?"

CJ started to giggle. "I'll add a tube of Preparation H to the story line!"

They each finished their second glass and decided to walk to McSeagull's for dinner. As they walked past the many shops, Donna suggested that CJ check out the Art Foundation. It would help to beef up her character's background.

"Good idea. I imagine there are several galleries I should visit. Good to know what the competition is doing." CJ gave Donna a wink.

"It's interesting how much arts-and-crafts stuff there is in this town, and most of it supports itself. Crazy tourists." Donna nodded at a family of five wearing a variety of Boothbay Harbor T-shirts. "They're everywhere."

When they arrived at McSeagull's, CJ fished for more information about Randy, Derek, Maggie, and Steve.

Donna gave her the same info she had heard earlier from Maggie about Randy and Derek's having taken over the family business and *The Perfect Storm*. "It was a perfect crapshoot if you ask me. Strange. A family of fishing-boat and charter-boat captains. Derek and Randy's dad and two uncles.

Derek went to college, graduated, then came back to work on boats. Go figure."

"I guess what they say is true about DNA. It's in your blood." CJ still wasn't sure what was running through her veins. Though she had no talent for cooking, she did have a talent for organization. But she certainly did not get that from her mother. The only thing she had inherited from her mother was her taste for good wine. She supposed that in a pinch she could become a sommelier. But where was the fun in that? You only tasted it. You didn't get to drink enough of it. CJ laughed out loud.

"Care to share?" Donna poked.

"Just wondering what's in my blood besides a nice Cabernet Sauvignon!"

Chapter 20

It had been a week since CJ moved into her triplex, and she was settling in better than she had expected. The town was mellow and the pace was easy, but she was getting antsy about contacting Colin to see how far he had come with the mysterious money transfers. Before she left for the gallery, she and Donna were sharing their morning coffee.

"Donna, when will I be able to speak to Colin?"

"We'll set up a call where we can bounce the signals. I'll get word to him and make the arrangements. We wanted to be sure that no one could trace you to Boothbay Harbor. My contacts say there's been no attempt on Franklin's part to find out where you are. He's in a federal facility and cannot have any contact with the outside except for his lawyer, and his lawyer isn't going to do anything to screw up his career. At least if he's got half a brain."

CJ was relieved. "There are still a lot of things that need to be explained before I can start to settle Snapper's estate."

Donna got a look in her eye that portended something unpleasant about to happen, and said, "CJ, there's something you need to know."

"I don't like the sound of that." CJ didn't think she could deal with any more bad news.

"There is an ongoing investigation into securities fraud and insider trading. That's why Leonard Franklin was arrested, not because of anything he might or might not have done to you. That's why they needed you to identify him as coming and going into the Rayburn House Office Building and whom you saw him with."

"But what does that have to do with —" CJ immediately stopped asking her question, realizing what was coming next. "Snapper?"

"They're pretty sure that he was involved, which is why he committed suicide. The wheels were coming off that bus."

"God Almighty." CJ deflated like a punctured balloon. "I cannot believe Snapper would get involved in something like that. But that would certainly explain the mysterious stock trading on the dark Web." CJ was struck by her own stupidity in letting information about what Colin had learned out of the bag. "Damn it. I mean . . . son of a bitch."

"They know about those stock transactions, CJ. They just couldn't reveal anything while evidence was being collected. Your pal Colin almost blew the whole thing when he started poking around."

"So they also know about the secret condo?" CJ's eyes widened.

"Pretty much." Donna felt sad for CJ. She had admired her boss to such an extent that the idea of Snapper doing anything untoward struck her as impossible.

"I simply cannot believe it," CJ said, her voice a mere whisper.

"As far as they can tell, he was using the money to support his brother. What he was doing was noble in one way even if it was highly illegal. Unfortunately, that sort of behavior can't be swept under the rug."

"I think I might puke." CJ wasn't kidding. She finally understood why Snapper would take his own life. "I guess we can tell Colin he doesn't have to play forensic-accountant detective anymore."

"They already have. Actually, it was Matt who told him. He had to. Colin was about to screw up the entire investigation. Not intentionally, mind you, but they had to stop his snooping. I'm really sorry about all this, CJ."

"Wow. Wow. Wow," was all she could muster, as her eyes began to well with tears.

"Come on. You're going to play hooky today. Grab your sunglasses and a cap."

"Where are we going?" CJ was almost afraid to find out.

"Some place pretty. Let's go."

Donna pulled two bottles of water from the fridge and tossed one to CJ. "I promise this is as close to water as you're going to get."

They climbed into the car and Donna pointed the vehicle in the direction of the Coastal Maine Botanical Gardens. "Most people think of Maine as a very rocky place, which is true to some extent, but the flora here is absolutely spectacular!" Donna's passion for her home state was obvious, and once they arrived, CJ could understand why.

The red celosia and purple alliums scattered among the rich greenery were breathtaking, and the sound of a brook in the distance created a sense of peace and wonder. CJ allowed herself to become immersed in a place of calm and beauty. When she finally let the muscles in her neck relax, she realized just how tense she had been from learning about Snapper's involvement in illegal stock manipulation.

They walked silently along the meandering paths of the rich, lush gardens. "Donna, this place is incredible. Thank you so much for bringing me here." For the second time that day, CJ's eyes welled up with tears.

"The day isn't over yet, my friend. We have one more stop to make."

CJ gave her a suspicious look. "Not to worry. No water involved. Well, maybe a little, but it comes from a tap! Trust me." Donna put her arm around CJ's shoulder and gave her a friendly shove toward the car.

Within a short time, they pulled in front of Whispering Winds, the local spa.

"Thought you could use a facial and a massage."

"Boy could I! You're *the* best!" CJ's day had gone from the gloomy disappointment at learning about Snapper's connection to Franklin, to the calm serenity of walking in the beautiful gardens, to a lovely way of winding down. She was truly grateful for Donna's kindness.

Feeling totally relaxed after two hours at the spa, they went back to the triplex and unwound further with a bottle of Whispering Angel Rosé. They joked about whispering being the theme of the afternoon, and CJ carried on with a hushed conspiratorial query. "So tell me something about the Wellington men. The kids are cute, and so is Maggie. I assume that Randy is, too." CJ was looking forward to something different. Different from all the cloak-and-dagger activity of the past couple of months.

"Oh, the Wellington men are very good-looking. When they shave, that is. You don't want to see them after they've been out a few days. Salty dogs. But they sure clean up real nice!" Donna was enjoying the girl time she was having with CJ. Most of her witnesses were white-collar criminals. Boring men. Having a personable woman to shepherd was a welcome change.

"Really?" CJ was intrigued. "What's Derek's story? Single, I assume, since he's tagging along with his brother and sister-in-law."

"Single indeed. It's a sad story. He was engaged, and she dumped him for some rich old guy who had a bigger boat. Broke his heart. They had started dating about four years ago, then moved in together a couple of years after that. Everyone assumed they would be getting married, but last summer, when Derek and Randy were out for a week, he came home to an empty apartment and a note that had one word — 'Sorry.' "

"Wow. That sucks." CJ winced, remembering something similar happening with one guy in her succession of asshole boyfriends.

"Yeah. Not sure if he's over it yet. He was crushed." Donna swirled her wine in her glass. "The two of you will get along just fine."

"Don't even *think* about going there. He's a *boat* guy. *Not* on my playlist," CJ protested. "I was just curious as to what I was getting myself into for the *evening.*" CJ emphasized "evening." "Nothing more."

"Take it easy, girl. We haven't printed the bridal shower invitations yet. That will have to wait a week." Donna was trying to cool CJ with a bit of wit. "Besides, it was Maggie who invited you, and you won't be here forever." She stood and poured another glass for both of them. "Relax. Just making small talk. They are very nice people. I'm sure they'll show you a good time. It's almost impossible not to enjoy the Windjammer festival even if you hate the water!"

"I know you mean well. It seems like everyone around here does. Hard to get used to. It's nothing like DC."

"See? I told you. Water or no water, it doesn't suck here."

CJ had to admit to herself that her phobia

had gotten worse over the past two months. PTSD? In her case it spelled Political Trauma Sudden Death. It was as if Snapper's death had magnified all her fears. Losing a person as close to her as Snapper was a reminder of all the other people no longer in her life, asshole boyfriends included.

The only person left was Colin, but other than him, she had no one. She felt utterly alone and feared she would remain that way forever.

"You okay?" Donna's voice pulled CJ out of her dark musings.

"Just thinking."

"Sometimes not a good idea." Donna's concern was obvious.

"I guess I have a lot of baggage. I should probably ask for a refund from that therapist." CJ was valiantly pulling herself from the deep pessimism into which she had sunk.

"Therapy can work, but more often than not we need to just 'do the thing and cut the shit.' I heard that from Shakti Gawain. She's a New Age author. Wrote *Creative Visualization* about forty years ago. Maybe more. She did a workshop here one summer. But that was my takeaway from it. We spend so much time talking about things rather than doing something about whatever it is that's getting in our way. Of course, we don't want to completely throw caution to the wind, but think about how many people have been going to shrinks for more than half their lives. Anyhoo . . . enough woo-woo guru stuff. Try to relax while you're here. I know the trial is looming, but that will only take a few days. You won't have to do much. Enjoy this beautiful place and the wonderful people while you can."

A tear rolled down CJ's cheek. She realized she had been close to an emotional breakdown the past couple of days. Heck, probably the past two and half months, but except for the episode at the cabin just before she became aware of being watched, she had not allowed herself to feel, to grieve, to express her profound sadness.

CJ walked over to Donna, wrapped her arms around her, and began to weep in earnest. Heavy sobs emerged from her chest. Small explosions of emotions.

Donna rocked her in her arms as CJ finally surrendered to her pain.

When CJ's body began to relax, Donna walked her over to the sofa and grabbed a hand towel. Tissues were not going to clean up the waterfall.

She handed CJ the towel, and said, "You sure are soaked, girlfriend." Her comment helped to lift CJ's gloom, and CJ finally gave Donna a tiny smile.

"Wow. Who knew I could expel so much water? And other stuff?" CJ was more than surprised at the emotional meltdown she had just gone through.

"You've been holding it in for a long time. Stoicism isn't always healthy."

"I guess that's what they mean when they say 'have a good cry,' but that seems like a big contradiction to me. On the other hand, my mother would always say 'Don't cry. It makes you look ugly.' Not very motherly advice, eh?"

Donna didn't want to pry, but it sure made CJ's mother sound cold.

"Go wash your *pretty* face, and we'll get some dinner. Then we have to decide what you will be wearing to the festival. It's dress-up day!" Donna tried to be as re-assuring as she could be considering she'd had no idea CJ would break down the way she had.

"Oh goodie. Dress-up day. Please don't tell me I have to wear a pirate costume or a mermaid outfit." CJ was being facetious since she had no idea what to expect. Maybe she should Google it and see if there was a YouTube video. She wasn't in the mood for any surprises.

"Ha. No, but you have to wear a sailor suit. Just kidding!" Donna figured she should ease up on overboard attempts at humor. CJ was a bit fragile at the moment.

"Seriously. How dressed up do I need to be? I don't know if I have anything dressier than khakis and a buttondown white shirt!"

"Let's go to Mona's on the way to dinner. She has a boutique of some cool clothes. Nothing nautical!"

"What a relief!"

Mona's proved to have a selection of stylish clothes, and CJ settled on a pair of floral Capri pants with a cobalt-blue tunic. She looked stunning, the shade of her shirt complementing her eyes and hair. "Wow. You clean up real nice, too!" Donna was hit by just how striking CJ looked. "Maybe a new purse? That backpack-tote thing isn't going to do it." Donna handed over a white straw-and-canvas bag. "Perfect." She then looked down at CJ's feet. "New sandals? Please?"

"Okay, fine!" CJ was quite pleased with the image she saw in the store's triple mirror. "Yes. Fine indeed. Who is that person?" She pointed to herself and let out a guffaw. Her makeover part two was in the works.

"Mona, wrap it up for my friend Carolyn. She'll be spending the next month here, and we need to get her in the summer groove ASAP." Donna made the veiled introduction. "She's working at the Wharfside Gallery. School project."

"Welcome to the Boating Capital of New England!" Mona held out her hand to CJ while Donna looked on with trepidation.

"Thank you! Beautiful town. Lovely people." CJ shook Mona's hand and responded in a surprisingly comfortable way. "Lovely store, too! I'm sure I'll be back." Mona handed CJ a colorful shopping bag, and she and Donna proceeded to the bistro.

"See, that was relatively painless, right?" Donna was still paying attention to CJ's mood.

"You're right. I've been too rigid about pretty much everything. Pretty much my whole life. And thanks again for such a lovely day. I feel like I've shed a skin of sorts. That big cry was shocking to me, but I really do feel better. I did have a minimeltdown at the cabin, but this one was much more wrenching, not to say drenching."

"Yeah, that was some kind of downpour!" As both women doubled over in laughter, Donna was relieved that CJ was pulling it together.

For the first time in she couldn't remem-

ber how long, CJ was feeling better about
life.

CHAPTER 21

The day of the parade, CJ was feeling both anxious and excited. Never since the death of her parents had she thought she would be eager to meet new people and try to experience something related to water. Maybe that stroll in the gardens, the massage and facial, and that great big sobfest had shifted her attitude. Perhaps the other thing at work was the thought that she could finally put the idea of a murder conspiracy to rest. Even though she was disturbed about the circumstances surrounding Snapper's death, at least now she knew why he would have committed suicide. That mystery had been solved. Sad. Disappointing. Even shocking. But solved nonetheless. Soon enough, she would be able to settle his estate — unless, of course, the government confiscated his assets. That would create a major problem when it came to continuing George's care.

Then, as if she had been hit by a bolt of lightning, she thought about the money she had inherited from Kick. She was, after all, a multimillionaire with a substantial income apart from what she earned from the investment portfolio Colin managed for her, as he had for Kick. Finally, she decided, she was comfortable about the size of her inheritance since she could see a way to use it other than spending it on frivolous luxuries.

She'd have Colin figure out how to use some of that money for George. That was the least she could do for her former boss, the boss who'd had enough faith in her to give her a job for which she had no experience, a job she had wanted in the worst way, and then seen her abilities and moved her up the ladder until she was the chief of staff to the chairman of the House Ways and Means committee.

An unexpected sense of calm washed over her. She was finally undergoing a real makeover, on the inside as well as on the outside. Exactly what she had hoped for when she stepped into that salon many weeks before was coming to pass. As she looked in the mirror for her final once-over, she also realized she was going to need a touch-up soon. She was hoping Donna could direct her to a hairdresser who could do the same meticulous transformation.

Donna rapped on the door and CJ pulled it open, displaying her new outfit and shoes, and wearing a bit of makeup.

"Holy smoke! And I do mean 'smoke'! You look hot!" Donna was taken aback by how gorgeous CJ looked. And not only that, what she saw was a CJ quite different from the sad, apprehensive young woman she had come to know. "Boy, you *do* clean up real nice! I don't know if the townies can deal with you!"

"Oh stop!" CJ was slightly embarrassed. She had never thought of herself as a beauty. Just normal, even verging on plain. "It feels good, I must admit."

"Well, let's not keep our friends waiting. I'll walk you down to the gallery. That's where you said you'd meet them, right? Derek and Randy always get a good spot for the parade of schooners. They used to take their boat out, but the harbor gets so cluttered with amateurs that it takes too long to get back to the dock to drop the kids off."

"What are you going to be doing today?" It hadn't occurred to CJ until that moment that Donna had never mentioned her own plans.

"I've got to run back to Portland. If I still

want to have a boyfriend, that is. He's working this weekend, so he can't come up, and if I ignore him for another day, I might be the one getting the 'sorry' note."

"That's funny. I mean all this time you never mentioned anyone. I just assumed you were single." CJ looked puzzled.

"Yeah, Kurt and I've been on-again off-again for about three years. He works for the Bureau. That's how we met. Our schedules are never the same, so it's been slow going in getting the show on the road, if you know what I mean."

"I sure do. Working for a congressman means you have no life. But I guess I'm going to have one now if I can actually figure out what it might be."

"You will. Another month or so here, then the trial, and you'll have time to sort things out. Heck, you might actually like cataloging for a gallery!"

"Well, it's been interesting, and as you like to say, 'It doesn't suck!' "

CJ grabbed her new bag and slung it over her shoulder. "I'm a little nervous. Not sure why. Or maybe it's just the excitement of doing something I would never have planned on my own."

"Sometimes that's the best way to approach life. A little Zen will do ya!"

As they rounded the corner to the street of the parade, the crowd was getting deeper. "Wow. This *is* a big deal, isn't it?" CJ hadn't seen so many people in one place since the lighting of the National Christmas Tree.

"You have the disposable phone I gave you, yes? And you know only to call me and no one else if you need anything?"

"Yes, ma'am!" CJ saluted her, acknowledging the rule. Donna had given CJ a burner phone just in case of emergencies, and CJ was not foolish enough to use it for anything else. She would have her call with Colin Monday morning at a secure location, as Donna planned. For today, she was going to let herself be open to whatever the day would bring and leave her worries, concerns, and apprehensions behind.

Donna spotted Maggie and her crew and waved wildly. "Mags! Randy! Derek!" They snaked their way through the throng of people, most of whom were wearing a T-shirt from one of the gift shops. Donna pointed that out to CJ. "See . . . crafts, shirts, tourists. Keeps the town alive!"

When they finally reached the Wellington crew, Donna introduced Carolyn.

"Derek, Randy, Gerry, and you remember Gina? This is my new friend Carolyn."

Derek was a tall, clean-shaven, physically

345

fit man with dirty-blond hair and suntanned cheeks. He had a dazzling smile that was only overshadowed by his emerald-green eyes. His handshake was firm but warm. "Nice to meet you, Carolyn. Welcome to Boothbay's Windjammer Days! This is my mom, Ellie, and dad, Jacob." Everyone else greeted her warmly, and CJ immediately felt welcome. She reminded herself that she was Carolyn now.

Derek was the first to jump in with "Can I get you something to drink? There's just about anything you'd want here, including a special drink made just for the festival. But I have to warn you, it's lethal! It's called a Windjammer Slammer! Made with several kinds of alcohol and lime juice. I think it's the juice that makes it so wicked." He was genuinely warm and friendly.

"Sure! Why not!" If CJ was going to experience this festival, she might as well go all in.

"A girl after my own heart." The words tumbled easily from Derek's mouth. A very fine mouth, CJ noted to herself. Warm red lips. His tanned, handsome face was a nice contrast to what was probably light brown hair bleached dirty blond by the sun. He could have been a California surfer dude but lacked the vacuous look so many of them had. Looking at him, CJ thought, *Like, wow, man.* She started to blush when it occurred to her that she hadn't felt attracted to a man in a very long time. Certainly not since Kick's death. She searched her memory for the time before and came up blank.

"You okay?" Derek shot her a sideways glance.

"Oh yes. I'm fine! I could use something cold to drink." *Boy, can I ever.*

"Come on. I have a few benches reserved for us." Derek led the way to the area where they were serving the somewhat lethal cocktail and handed one to CJ. "Here. This should help." His callused hands reminded her of Kick's.

What surprised her the most were the next few words she uttered. "I had a brother who was an avid sailor. I lost him four years ago to a boating accident. Your hands remind me of his." This soft side to CJ was alien even to herself. What was happening to her? Was it the air? Or was it that her hormones were going wild with the immediate attraction she felt to this stranger. A boat-guy stranger, no less. Cripes.

She took a big gulp of her drink.

"Yes, I heard. Sorry. We boaters take it very hard when a fellow is lost at sea . . . or in port. Anywhere, for that matter." Derek wasn't sure of the details, but he could imagine how painful it must have been for her.

"Well, let's not turn maudlin. I don't know what came over me. I guess being here among all the schooners, sailboats, the smell of the air . . . everything reminded me of him. And, of course, sailor hands!" With that she smiled, pointed to Derek's hand and her empty cup. "How about using them to fetch me another!" Clearly, the first one was having an effect on her. She was feeling quite playful!

"You're a brave woman!" Derek's eyes lit up. "Let's get everyone settled first, then I'll go grab another drink."

They continued for several yards when they came across an area that was cordoned off with bunting and a sign that read: RE-SERVED SEATING.

The entire Wellington family exchanged hellos with everyone they came in contact with. People would lean over to pinch Gina's face, then she would shoo the next person away. Yes, the Wellingtons had been in Boothbay Harbor for a very long time, generations, as had Maggie's family. It was easy to understand why each generation stayed.

The cocktail was easing its way through

CJ's bloodstream, and that same warm sense of calm engulfed her again. She noticed that it came in waves. *No pun intended,* she thought to herself, *ebb and flow.* And "flow" was going to be the operative word from now on. Or at least for the moment.

Derek took charge and motioned for everyone to grab a seat, leaving one for him open next to hers. It was a bit tight, which meant there would be less than a few inches between them. CJ was all atwitter. There was something about this man to which she was strongly attracted. Was it the sailor hands? The atmosphere? The Windjammer Slammer? Or all of the above? For one of the few times in her life, CJ decided that instead of analyzing it, she would just go with it. That too struck her. She supposed it was just another aspect of her makeover, inside and outside. On second thought, it was probably that Windjammer Slammer. But she didn't care. She was feeling a sense of freedom she hadn't felt in . . . well, she couldn't remember that either.

Derek returned with two cups of the dangerous beverage. As he handed one to CJ, his leg brushed up against hers. She thought she was going to faint. "You sure you're all right?" Derek gave her a concerned look.

She reached for the cup, trying to control her trembling hands. "Oh yes. Yes, of course. It's all just . . . well a *lot* to take in. Thank you. That first one went down rather easily."

"And quickly! I guess I am going to have to keep a sharp eye on you!" Derek was teasing, but CJ was hoping he really meant it. She liked the idea, perhaps a bit too much.

"Speaking of you, you look familiar." Derek was now staring at her straight on.

"The Uma Thurman thing? Some people say I look like her, but, frankly, I don't see it." She was trying to be modest.

"Maybe." Derek had a contemplative look on his face. It was something else, he was sure.

The warm afternoon went quickly as the tall, elegant ships passed through the harbor. CJ understood why her brother had loved it so much. There was a peaceful quietude as sailboats of all kind moved gracefully through the water. She could see how Maggie was inspired to paint the majestic schooners. Off to one side of the harbor were dozens of Sunfish boats, the colors of their sails seeming to float against the azure sky and deep blue waters. It was a scene of breathtaking beauty. She was almost brought to tears by the majesty and splendor of it all.

Looking at her again, Derek repeated, "You sure you're okay?"

In a hushed voice, she replied, "It's so . . . so very beautiful." CJ was coming to appreciate some of the little pleasures of life that she had been so indifferent to for so many years. The simplicity of things.

Derek was giving her a blow-by-blow description of the schooners: who were regulars and how long they'd been participating, their ages, and the way in which they were all rigged in traditional fashion. Some schooners, he informed her, provided non-boaters a five-day sail for as many as twenty people. All those on board would participate in the actual sailing of the vessel, sleep on board, and share chores. Many of them on any trip were repeat customers who returned year after year.

It was a lot to take in. The entire week was filled with events and parades. This was just the beginning.

After a couple of hours of sitting idly, enjoying the camaraderie, and listening to Derek's smooth voice giving her some of the history of the town, he suggested they get something to eat. CJ was delighted with that idea; she was feeling the effects of not one, not two, but three of those mind-erasing drinks. She wasn't sure if she could stand up without tumbling into the other spectators. As she began to rise, she felt as if her head was made of fuzz and put her hand on Derek's shoulder to steady herself.

Derek immediately stood and tucked her arm into his. "Looks like those Windjammer Slammers gave you sea legs!" CJ was grateful for the support, but also nervous about the physical nearness of this man. Their arms were linked, and she could feel the heat of his body next to hers. If that drink didn't make her faint, the proximity just might.

She couldn't help but giggle a bit. "I think I might be making a fool of myself," she managed to whisper. When he leaned closer to her mouth to hear what she said, she became flush and, without warning, threw up all over him. "Okay. Now I know I'm making a fool of myself!" CJ was mortified and tried to wipe his shirt with a damp cocktail napkin.

Derek broke out in a thunderous laugh. "You're cut off, missy!"

"Oh my God! Oh my God! This is so embarrassing! I am so sorry!" CJ continued to wipe his shirt, shredding the skimpy napkin mixed with her regurgitated beverage. Her light-headedness evaporated with the hurl, and she was instantly sober. A little shaky, but sober enough to want to run all the way back to the triplex and die.

Derek continued to laugh, as did Gerry and Gina. "Uncle Derek! You've got puke all over you!"

"I think I should go." CJ's humiliation was growing with each passing second. "I am so very sorry." She turned to leave, but Derek pulled her back.

"You think you're leaving me here with your drink and a few unidentifiable tidbits all over my clothes? I think not. Besides you're not the first person to heave on me. Happens all the time on the boat. Sit tight. I'll be back in fifteen minutes." He turned to his family. "And this landlubber is flagged. Randy, can you go grab Carolyn a Coke? I'll be back in a few. Gotta change my shirt!"

CJ didn't know what to say next. Thankfully, blabbermouth Maggie had more than a few words to spare. "Bah. No worries. Kids puke on me all the time. And if you hang out here long enough, by the end of the day there will be a river of vomit!" She grabbed CJ's arm and handed her a damp washcloth she pulled out of her backpack.

"Like I said, kids puke. I always carry a few of these in a plastic bag! Here. Put it on your forehead. Luckily, you have good aim and hit Derek smack-dab in the middle of his chest and got nothing on yourself!" Maggie was lighthearted and kind, and CJ was more than grateful. She must have apologized a half dozen times mixed in with a lot of "thank-yous!"

Randy returned with a huge mug of Coke and handed it to CJ. "Welcome to Windjammer Days! You're now officially initiated! No one gets through their first without a little "give back"! Randy was smiling a grin similar to his older brother's.

"Thanks so much. I feel like such an idiot. Amateur, I guess, would be a better description." She was starting to regain her composure until she thought about what to say to Derek when he returned with a clean shirt. Maybe something funny. But what? She looked over at Maggie, and asked, "Do you happen to have a bib in that bag of yours?"

"I think it's too late for that!" Maggie laughed.

"I know. I want to give it to Derek when he gets back." CJ winked at Maggie, who got the message loud and clear.

"Now, *that's* funny!" Maggie dug through

her sack and pulled out a bib with a sailboat on it.

CJ thought it was some kind of sign. A sailboat. Maybe Kick was watching over her? The thought gave her some comfort, and she let out a big sigh.

In a very short time, Derek returned with a clean shirt and a beaming smile.

"Let's start from the beginning. Except no Slam-Yaws." He held out his hand and introduced himself. "Hello. I'm Derek Wellington. Welcome to the Windjammer Days."

"Nice to meet you, Mr. Wellington. Perhaps you should wear this if you plan on sitting next to me." CJ offered the bib, which brought a roar of laughter from everyone seated around them. Derek's eyes lit up at her sense of humor. It had been a long time since he had been in the company of a woman who could put a smile on his face.

"Do you think you can choke down some food after that display?" Derek was eyeing her carefully.

"Yes, I do. I think there's room for some in there now!" CJ was enjoying the playful back and forth they were engaged in.

"Excellent. Come. Follow me. I promise not to set you adrift among the sea of people." His simile was not lost on her.

"And you're a comedian, too." CJ was very pleased with herself, in spite of that revolting display of her inability to hold her liquor. Although that kind of cocktail was something she hadn't consumed in years. Maybe since her college days.

Derek took her by the elbow and shuffled her through the crowd. "There's a little place a few blocks from here. Should be quieter."

The physical contact with this man who had total control of the situation was comforting, but also alarming. She was amazed at how much at ease she was and how natural it felt to be with him.

As they made their way from the crowd, they came to a little bistro. It quickly became obvious that it was a place where Derek spent a lot of time. A hostess with a long gray braid gave him a hug and showed them to a table on the patio. "Joan, this is Carolyn. She's visiting us for a month or so and working at the Wharfside. Carolyn, this is Joan, the proprietor and chef."

The two exchanged greetings, and Joan rattled off the specials of the day. "Do you need a corkscrew?"

"I didn't bring anything to drink, sorry." He gave CJ a questioning look. "I wasn't sure if you were up for it after your episode."

"I'm fine. Really." CJ was actually feeling fine at that point. Too bad they had gone to a BYOB place. She could have pulled something out of her "wine cellar."

"I do have a nice unoaked Chardonnay in the back. I can *give* it to you if you promise to replace it." Joan gave Derek the "I've got you covered" look.

He looked at CJ with raised eyebrows. "You game?"

"Sure. Just like the shirt you were wearing earlier." CJ could not help herself. She was downright giddy.

"Carolyn had a little accident earlier. She had a run-in with three Windjammer Slammers."

"First-timer?" Joan remarked with a knowing nod. "They go down smooth but can come back to haunt ya. I'll go grab that bottle, and you guys can decide what you'd like for dinner. Derek, you probably know this already. Be right back."

"What do you recommend?" CJ was making small talk to cover her excitement. Had this become a date? Or was Derek simply being kind to a newcomer. A newcomer who had puked on him. She sat back in her chair and looked at him thoughtfully. Handsome. Strong. Kind. Personable. There had to be something wrong with this guy. But at that moment, she was taking in all the fine qualities of the man she had just met. And vomited on. She gave him extra points for being such a good sport about it. Now he was treating her to dinner. Or was it Dutch treat? That thought suddenly made her uncomfortable.

"You okay?" Derek queried. Those two words were becoming a bit repetitious.

"Yes. Please stop asking me. It's been a lot to absorb."

"Obviously, because you couldn't hold all of it in!" He gave her a winning smile and a wink.

"Like I said . . . you're a comedian, too."

"So tell me more about Carolyn Johnson." Derek opened with a prodding question that CJ was not prepared to answer.

"I think I've revealed enough . . . no pun intended. Tell me about you." CJ was relieved that her brain cells were functioning at a normal level.

"I grew up here. My dad and uncle were in the charter-boat business. My mom hated it. She always worried that something was going to happen to them, especially when the seasons with the rough seas arrived."

"I totally get that." CJ nodded in agreement.

"Right. You would know."

"Yes, but it was a freak accident. Some a-hole was drunk, ripped through the marina in a Jet Ski, and slammed into my brother's boat while he was on board. It hadn't even left the dock. So, crazy things can happen no matter what." CJ's mind went to Snapper, too. That was pretty crazy on all counts.

"True. You could be sitting next to someone, and she turns around and throws up on your shirt." Derek didn't want to bring up unpleasant memories and thought one more gag about CJ's drinking accident would keep things light.

"Can we let that go, puh-lease? I will *buy* you a new shirt."

"Not necessary, but I appreciate the offer. So, yeah, the family business was steady but not without a lot of angst. I actually went to college to try to make some other kind of life for myself. But here I am."

"Well, I'm glad you are. You've been a wonderful and forgiving host."

Joan brought the wine to the table and handed the corkscrew to Derek, who proceeded to open and pour. CJ raised her glass in a toast, and said, "Down the hatch! Correct? That's what they say in seafaring lingo, right?"

"Yes they do." Derek was enjoying his newfound company as much as she was enjoying hers.

Joan stood over them with one hand on her hip. "Ready to order?"

CJ looked at Derek for some guidance. "Suggestions?"

"Well, there are Ellie's daily specials. Sure smelled good when I stopped by this morning."

CJ gave Derek a quizzical look.

"Yeah. Ellie's specials. My mom. That's how she managed to overcome her panic with all of her men at sea. She started cooking, and now she makes boxed lunches for our customers and the daily specials for this place. Saved her life." Derek was contemplative.

CJ saw a brief cloud pass through Derek's emerald eyes and brightened her voice. "Well, then, you must tell me your favorite!"

"Pretty much everything! But the seafood chowder is a prizewinner. Start with that."

Derek continued his verbal tour of the area, giving CJ an in-depth view of the coastal waters. It was odd that she felt a sense of peace there with him, a stranger, and within several hundred yards of the biggest estuaries in the Northeast.

More small talk ensued, dinner, then the

walk back to CJ's. She was trying not to panic. Should she invite him in? What if he tried to kiss her? Should she link her arm in his like before? So many questions were racing through her head. She silently admonished herself for feeling like a schoolgirl on her first date.

But Derek took control. Once again, he pulled her arm through his and walked her back to the triplex. He cleared his throat. "Would you like to catch the fireworks on Wednesday?"

"Do they serve a good cocktail? Something with little explosives in it?" CJ was pulling out all the humor she could muster to hide her nervousness.

"Ha. No. And if they did, I wouldn't let you near one! The display starts at nine o'clock. We could grab some dinner beforehand if you'd like." Derek was hoping this lovely, mysterious woman would agree.

"I would like that very much. And I promise to behave." CJ took the initiative and gave him a peck on the cheek. "Thank you again."

She turned quickly, so he wouldn't see her blushing. *What came over me? I cannot believe I was so forward.* But then her face broke into a wry smile. *Yes, this is the new and improved CJ. Carolyn. Whatever.* She was beginning to like the person she was becoming.

"A pleasure. I'll stop by around six thirty. See you Wednesday." Derek turned on his heel, raised his right arm in victory, and somehow resisted the temptation to skip all the way home.

CHAPTER 22

Derek and Randy Wellington had been raised to respect the sea. Their dad had taught them the rules of boating at a very young age, and each of them had gotten his license as a teenager. Their mother encouraged them to study hard in school so they could go to college. She didn't want her boys to have the same kind of life their father and uncle had.

Yes, there were good times and sometimes profits, but danger always hung in the air like a dense fog. According to the US government, fishing was second on the list of "The Ten Most Dangerous Jobs for Men." Why Eleanor "Ellie" Bessler married a fishing-boat captain was not a mystery, though. She had fallen in love with Jacob Wellington when he was the tight end on the high-school football team. It was a typical small-town story. With Boothbay having fewer than three thousand residents year-round, it was very difficult not to know everyone; and with only a couple of hundred students in school at any given time, it was a sure bet that as a student yourself, you'd either be related to or dating one.

Ellie's dad was the local pharmacist, and she helped in the summers, when the vacationers and yachters arrived. She had fond memories of the time in 1956 when a movie crew came into town to do some location filming for the "June Is Bustin' Out All Over" sequence in the movie *Carousel*. She was just five years old, but she could still recall how excited everyone was to have real movie stars in their midst. It was probably one of the only glamorous experiences in her life. Because her father owned the local pharmacy, the production team was in and out of there on a daily basis and gave her family special access to watch the filming of the extravagant dance sequence. It wasn't until two years later that they would actually get to see it on the big screen, and to do that they had to drive over an hour to Portland, which had the only movie theater within one hundred fifty miles.

Ellie was mesmerized by how big Boothbay looked, and exclaimed with delight when she recognized a few neighbors who, on their sailboats, were used as extras during the sequence. She decided at that moment she would be a dancer and go off to be in a musical spectacular just like the one she was watching. But that didn't happen. Not even the dancer part. By the time she was eight, she had lost interest in most things artistic and decided she wanted to be a pharmacist just like her dad. The fact that her parents and other relatives kept drilling into her mind the idea that she would never stand a chance at show business had squashed all her dreams, and she buried her nose in books.

Once she entered high school, the only two options she seemed to have after she graduated were to get married or try for a scholarship to the University of New England. She had been dating Jacob Wellington since her junior year, and that relationship made getting married the logical choice. She knew she'd be lost somewhere else, even if it was only an hour away. It was 1969, and times were tumultuous. Vietnam, civil rights, burning bras and draft cards, and books like *Portnoy's Complaint* and movies like *Easy Rider* were sure signs that there was a cultural shift occurring, and it was not necessarily a good one — at least so it seemed to a small-town girl like Ellie Bessler. There was that horrible murder spree during which Sharon Tate and four other people in Hollywood were killed, and on the opposite side of the country, a half million hippies had descended upon a small town called Woodstock for a rock-and-roll festival. Even though we had managed to put a man on the moon, that didn't mean Ellie was comfortable about leaving the peaceful, calm, and happy life in which she had grown up to enter a world seemingly in turmoil. It was a no-brainer that staying close to home was the safest alternative.

Jacob, on the other hand, was intent on going to college, which created a great deal of conflict between the two of them. But after he left, he kept his word and came home on weekends, and when he couldn't, Ellie would visit him. He had applied to the University of Maine and majored in marine biology. When he graduated in 1973, instead of pursuing an advanced degree and entering the academy as a teacher and researcher, he decided that what he really wanted to do was to own his own boat — a fishing boat. It was something that his brother Adam was very passionate about. So, right after Jacob graduated, he and Adam bought a weathered seventy-foot boat and set their minds to starting a charter fishing business. The path they set out on was the same one many others in their town had followed.

Ellie wasn't bitter about having squandered her opportunity for higher education. She was bitter because she thought she had sacrificed her own future for one that was safe and predictable as a wife. But she loved Jacob, so she was going to follow her heart, no matter how much worry life with him would involve.

The first four years of their marriage were a struggle. Jacob and Adam poured every penny they earned into the cranky vessel, and Ellie continued to run the family pharmacy as the store manager. If she had gotten her degree, she could have been filling prescriptions and making more money, but that wasn't in the cards. Not anymore. They both had to work to keep a roof over their heads and took every precaution to avoid having children. Being parents was not fiscally prudent, but in 1977, Ellie missed her period two months in a row. She was pregnant with Derek.

The additional expense of a child forced Jacob to work more hours, going on long and dangerous trips on commercial fishing boats to supplement their income. Ellie lived in a constant state of anxiety and despair. At first, everyone thought it was postpartum depression, but to Ellie it was

367

"husband-boat-captain" angst. She was never fully comfortable and found it impossible to relax. Even when Jacob and Adam returned from a trip, she knew it was just a matter of days before he would be in harm's way again.

Then, two years later, she found herself pregnant with Randy, and this time postpartum depression hit with a vengeance. And the depression lasted for years. Derek remembered being eight years old when an ambulance had to take his mother to the hospital. She had overdosed on Valium. Though she survived the episode, Derek found it hard not to wonder why she had done it. Didn't she love them? Why would she want to leave them?

After the attempted suicide, Ellie was admitted to a long-term nursing facility for several months until she "felt better." But she never did. At least not for a very long time. Yes, she resumed her wifely and motherly duties, but she was always sad or distant, only going through the motions of everyday life.

After a decade of walking on eggshells around his mother, Derek left for college and majored in political science. He wanted to make a difference and was planning to go into local and state government. Randy still had two years of high school left and spent all his free time helping his father and uncle with the charter-boat business.

During Derek's years at college, Randy had become even more skilled around boats. Derek could have been jealous of his brother's expertise if he hadn't admired his younger brother so much for pursuing something he was fervent about. In addition, since by 1999 politics had become a dirty business, Derek decided to join his family in an enterprise where he could do something that mattered. Mattered to the people he loved. By then, his dad was not in the best physical condition, but Derek knew that as skilled as Randy was, he couldn't run the company — such as it was. Randy had the physical skills but no business sense. Derek, on the other hand, had the business sense. The similarity between the two brothers on the one hand and their father and uncle on the other was uncanny. Two generations of fishermen — despite having been given other opportunities — lured to the dangers that lurked in the depths of the sea.

When Ellie had first heard about Derek's decision to help purchase another boat, she thought she would fall apart. Her husband and now her two sons were challenging the deep every day. When Derek first returned from college, he lived with his folks for a short time. He knew that fairly soon he would have to find his own space. The tension between his parents was too thick to be endured indefinitely. Ellie blamed Jacob for influencing their sons to enter a life of backbreaking and dangerous work. Jacob would respond by telling her that they were grown men who know their own minds. To which Ellie would reply that he had brainwashed them.

It wasn't until after Derek moved out and Jacob had a mild stroke — which Ellie blamed on that awful movie, in which the *Andrea Gail* was lost at sea during a nor'easter — that Ellie decided to start cooking. This helped her to cope with her anxiety, which in turn allowed some kind of harmony between husband and wife. With Jacob out of action, the burden of keeping the business alive fell on the two sons, and that dreadful film was scaring off their regular customers. It took months of rehab before Jacob could function at almost 90 percent. He was still having trouble with his left hand, but he was determined to continue to work at the business.

When Ellie finally accepted that she was fighting a losing battle, she decided it was time to find her own niche, so she decided to become part of what she considered a thoroughly unreasonable way to make a living. She set out to provide meals for their customers at a modest cost. With two boats in the family business, she thought she just might make a few dollars at it and began a small catering company, working out of her own kitchen. It wasn't fancy, just simple food that could be packed and carried and kept fresh on ice and heated in the boat's microwave. There was nothing like hot stew at the end of a very cold day of struggling with game fish.

Jacob spent less and less time at sea and more and more time peeling potatoes, which mollified Ellie to a certain point. Now, with just the two of them living at home, they were able to settle into a peaceful coexistence — at least until the next nor'easter.

Derek moved out when he found a comfortable studio apartment within walking distance of his folks' house and the dock. He'd stop by every morning to check on them and to see what Ellie was cooking and if Jacob was up for some light swabbing of the deck.

The ritual continued until 2013, when Derek met Jennifer Parker during the Harbor Lights Festival. She had been visiting friends just before the holidays, and Derek was smitten. Jennifer had been a beauty queen and lived in New York City with several other aspiring models and actresses. Ten years his junior, she appreciated his very steady, solid, responsible approach to life. They maintained a long-distance relationship for a couple of years, but after too many incidents of sexual harassment on job interviews and photo shoots, she decided a quieter lifestyle might suit her better and suggested she should move to Boothbay Harbor.

"But what about your career?" Derek asked, happily stunned at her suggestion.

"It gets harder as you get older. I'm going to be twenty-eight this year. I'm already considered 'over the hill' at most agencies. Besides, I want to have a family someday." Jennifer sounded convincing.

"Wow. I guess it's time we had 'the talk.' I'm closing in on forty myself, so yeah. Let's make some plans." Derek had been so focused on his family business he really hadn't thought much about starting a family of his own, and now, with this beautiful woman at his side, it seemed like doing so was possible.

"If I move up here, what kind of work would I get? I'm sure I won't be doing any modeling." Jennifer might be skeptical, but she was determined not to let an opportunity for stability slip through her hands. Not this time.

"Well, you're certainly not going to become a fishmonger or a sea rat!" Derek took her hand and kissed it. "We'll figure it out. Maybe you can help my mom with her catering business."

"Derek, you know I don't cook."

"Okay, how about managing one of the boutiques? You certainly have an eye and expertise when it comes to fashion."

"Fashion? In this town?" Jennifer sounded a bit superior.

"Yes. *This* town. It's a yachter's paradise in the summer, and I can tell you that there are a lot of women with big wallets and their hubbies' plastic who have nothing better to do but shop. I'll talk to Mona. She goes to New York several times a year during fashion week. I'm sure she'd appreciate your experience." Derek was pleased with his solution and dialed Mona's number on the spot. Since Mona was very fond of the Wellington family, she promised to hire Jennifer on a small salary-and-commission basis, and yes, Jennifer could accompany her to the city if she paid her own travel expenses.

Within a few months, Jennifer arrived with

her things, and Derek realized they needed a much bigger place to live. The studio would not be suitable, and he knew that Jennifer could be a bit of a snob. She would expect something less of a man cave and more lavish. Fortunately, that summer had proven to be lucrative and he was able to find a beautiful two-bedroom with a view of the harbor to rent. He would do anything to please this woman and assure her comfort and security. But Jennifer never seemed satisfied. Their relationship had been long-distance until they set up a household, which meant that the time they had spent together was minimal — a week at a time at the most.

After the first year of living together, he came to realize just how spoiled she was. Even Mona gingerly mentioned that Jennifer had a bit of an elitist attitude with some of the customers. Derek defended her by saying that she was trying to find her way in a new and different place. But deep down something about the situation didn't feel quite right. Every time he brought up the subject of marriage, she would say she wanted to be sure they could afford a real house — not an apartment, or that she wanted more financial security. The idea of starting a family with her had pretty much disappeared — she had just about become a "friend with benefits," so he was not all that shocked when he came home to a one-word note left on the table. He was embarrassed, but not surprised.

Of course, those who knew him assumed that he was devastated, and he saw no reason to disabuse them. And though after his experience with Jennifer he was wary of getting involved with anyone else, on balance he probably felt more relieved than angry at her abrupt departure.

Derek threw himself into his work and kept up with his hobby of following the political scene — nearby and nationally. Even though he had chosen a different vocation, his interest in government had never waned. He was very active in communicating with his representatives and attending council meetings.

"If you don't tell them what you want or expect, they'll never know. It's up to us to keep them on track! Do something! Send an e-mail! If you spent even one percent of the time you wasted on Facebook and contacted your senators or congressmen, maybe our country wouldn't be as screwed up as it is." That was his battle cry when everyone would bitch and complain — the one thing that could get Derek all riled up.

The Monday afternoon before his fireworks date with Carolyn, he was almost certain that she reminded him of someone he had seen, or seen a picture of, somewhere. Maybe it was the Uma Thurman thing, but he wasn't quite sure. Until he Googled her, Derek couldn't even quite remember what Uma Thurman looked like, so he didn't think that was it. Yes, there was a slight resemblance, especially the hair and the big eyes, but it was something beyond those things that made him think he had seen her before. Unable to figure it out, he shrugged and looked through his closet, picking out his favorite shirt and slacks. He also decided that he would take a plastic parka with him, like those they would hand out to their customers if the weather became inclement. That should set off a laugh or two. He liked her, a lot, but it dawned on him that he knew practically nothing about her. Odd. She said very little at dinner since he had done most of the talking. He shrugged again. Maybe he'd pry more out of her on Wednesday. He was happy to have some companionship during the Windjammer Days. It had been almost exactly a year since Jennifer had given him the heave-ho, and for now, Carolyn would be a nice distraction.

CHAPTER 23

CJ was a mix of emotions that Monday morning. She had spent time with a very nice, charming man two days before. Aside from her gastrointestinal issue, it had been a lovely afternoon that lingered into the early evening. And now she had a second date with him. A date. Even though that was a foreign activity for her, she was rather keen about it. She was also anticipating her first phone call with Colin since she had been in Witness Protection. It seemed like a lifetime to her. She wanted to share what seemed to be her changing feelings about being so close to the water, but knew she could not reveal any information as to her whereabouts.

A light rap on the door broke into CJ's deep thoughts. It was Donna, ready to take her to the Portland location of the US Marshals office, where she could speak freely to Colin on a landline. Cell towers, no matter how secure the server, would show any kind of ping. This would require a highly protected connection.

"So?" Donna peeked her head in the door with a strong vibe of curiosity in her voice. "How was your outing on Saturday?"

"Aside from making a total fool of myself, it was quite nice actually."

"What do you mean, 'fool'?"

"Let's just say I overestimated my ability to consume alcohol. And I owe Derek a new shirt."

"What on earth are you talking about?"

"Those Windjammer Kill-yas or whatever they're called. I deposited mine on Derek's shirt — after I had supposedly digested it."

"You mean you —"

"Yeah. Hurled it right at him. Smack-dab in the middle of his chest." CJ was sounding a bit forlorn. "Nice first impression, eh?"

"And?" Donna's eyes widened, begging to hear more.

"And he was the perfect gentleman. Went home, changed his shirt while Maggie and Randy babysat. I was mortified, but he was very cool about it. He even took me to dinner. Who knew projectile vomit was a turn-on? I'd have used it much sooner in life!" CJ was beginning to appreciate how her disastrous action had led to something really enjoyable.

Donna's eyes widened still further. "Wow. Who knew is right! Were you okay? I mean, did you feel like you were about to take an encore?"

"No, actually. I guess I got rid of all of it in one fell swoop. Promise you will never let me near one of those things again!"

"Promise. But wait. Did you say dinner? He took you to dinner?"

"The Bistro. It was very nice. Apparently, his mom provides the daily specials?" CJ knew this was common knowledge.

"Yeah, Ellie can make some fine comfort food. I think she started it to give *herself* some comfort when the guys were away. It's a tough life, being married to a fisherman, and then to have your sons turn into one of them? I'd be on antianxiety medication if it were me!"

"I know that dread too well. I just never considered medication unless it came from a bottle that had a year and a vintage stamped on it." CJ was thoughtful about her own way of dealing with stress. "Heck, you saw me when I first got here! I'm really surprised how relaxed I've become in less than two weeks."

"It's funny how, when you have little or no control over a situation, you can surrender to it." Donna always had a calming, rational response to things.

"Ha. You don't know my OCD side." CJ smirked.

"I think I got a glimpse of it when I first met you, but I'm glad you're being open to each new day as it comes." Donna had a very philosophical side to her that CJ found endearing and inspiring.

"In retrospect, and considering all the crap I've been through over the past four-plus years, I figure surrender is probably a better option than fretting. I *am* compulsive, you know!"

"Duh. Of course. You just said so. That's what the *C* stands for in OCD: obsessive-compulsive disorder," Donna said.

"I prefer not to call it a disorder. It's almost counterintuitive. If you're compulsive about order, why would you call it a disorder?" CJ laughed at the irony.

"Good point!" Donna replied. "Ready?"

"Yes indeed." CJ grabbed her new bag as they walked toward the door.

"I really like my new outfit. I may go back there and get a few more things."

"Mona's? Yeah. Like I said, she has some pretty cool stuff. Oh . . . you know what? Derek's ex, Jennifer Parker, used to work there. Lasted about five minutes. Well, not really. Had a bad attitude."

"Sounds like she had a bad attitude all around, dumping Derek the way she did." CJ considered how hurtful it must have been. Just spending a few hours with him gave her a sense that he was a decent guy and didn't deserve to be ditched with a one-word note.

Donna gave her the quick rundown of the relationship. "Jennifer. She was pretty enough. Gorgeous, actually. Long legs, narrow waist, your typical model shape. She actually was a model from New York but was getting long in the tooth, like twenty-seven or something, and decided it was time to settle down. Derek was bonkers over her and took it really hard when she left him high and dry. Apparently she found some older tourist with a lot more dinero than Derek would ever have. He hasn't dated anyone since, as far as I know, so I'm glad you guys hung out. It's good for both of you, if you ask me."

"Well, I didn't ask you, but I'm glad you encouraged me to go." CJ could barely contain herself at this point. "And we have a date for the fireworks!" She jumped about two inches into the air.

"Wait! What?" Donna was equally excited. "Like as in a d-a-t-e date?"

"I guess you could call it that. Yeah. I'm a little . . . I don't know . . . a little . . . excited? It's been a long time since I was on a real date with a man! I guess that means another new outfit!"

"C'mon, girlfriend. Phone line is waiting for us." Donna had to snap CJ out of her daze.

When they arrived in Portland, they entered a building that looked like it could be an insurance agency. Donna flashed her ID, nodded to the receptionist, and guided CJ through a hallway and into a small office.

CJ took in her surroundings, noticing the familiar government decor of not-a-whole-lot and a variety of gray walls. The Rayburn Building was teeming with history, as were a number of the structures in DC, but as government grew and grew, most of the agencies were located in bland and sterile office buildings.

The room they entered had a rectangular table about six feet wide by two feet deep, with several electronic devices and a few laptops. Two hard plastic chairs were parked on one side. CJ thought it looked like an interrogation room.

Donna pointed to one of the molded black chairs. "Make yourself comfortable — if that's possible." She gave CJ a quick wink.

"Lavish," CJ responded in a mocking manner.

Donna sat next to CJ, picked up two headsets with microphones, and handed one to CJ. "Accessories."

"But does it match my outfit?" CJ was trying to mask her jitters by cracking wise.

Donna tapped several buttons on a keyboard, and CJ heard a loud *boop-boop* sound that was the ringing of the phone on the other end.

"This is 4735," came over the earphones.

"This is 7392," was Donna's response.

For a moment, CJ felt she was in a scene from a James Bond movie but without a young, handsome Sean Connery or a brooding Daniel Craig.

"We've got her on the line," Donna said into her mic.

"CJ?" Colin's familiar voice brought tears to CJ's eyes as his face appeared on the screen of the laptop.

"Hey! How are you? I miss you." CJ was trying hard to keep her emotions in check. It had been a wild ride over the past two months, and Colin had been her stabilizing force.

"I'm good. And you? How are you dealing with your temporary new life?" Colin jumped right in, knowing they only had a few minutes.

"Actually, it's better than I thought. Donna has been fantastic. She's my new BFF."

"You sound pretty good! And you look good, too!" Colin was relieved to hear CJ so chipper and see that she was maintaining her new coiffed look. "What are you doing with yourself?"

"Well, I got a job working at a local gallery cataloging artwork. Donna took me to some garden, then to a spa, and I've been eating better than I have in months!" CJ was considering her words. She was, indeed, enjoying this adventure. "I even went to" — Donna immediately gave her the "cut" sign under her chin for fear CJ would reveal her whereabouts — "an aquarium!"

"Wow. Some kind of water-related activity? Impressive. You didn't mention how much you've been drinking, though." Colin was half kidding.

"I had a bit of a run-in with some festival thing but it turned out okay, actually." CJ grimaced at the recollection, and Donna broke out in a wide smile.

"Huh." Colin didn't know what to make of CJ's uplifted mood. "Well, you certainly sound a lot better than you did two weeks ago. Are you sure you're not drinking? As in now?" he continued to prod.

"Very funny. Seriously. The people here are so nice, it's pretty, and the air is so clean!" CJ was aware that she needed to tone it down. So she lowered her voice. "So enough about me. What about you? How was your week with Matt?"

"Excellent." Colin paused for a moment, anticipating her next question. "And don't even go there, missy."

"I wouldn't dream of it." CJ gave Donna a "yeah, right" kind of look.

"I saw that!" Colin was about to continue to tease her, but then he suddenly put on his CEO, investment-counselor, chairman-of-the-board voice. "I heard you've been told about Snapper."

CJ took in a big breath, her shoulders slumping. "Yes. I find it so hard to believe, but then again, he was caring for George, and we know how much more that cost than he could possibly have anticipated thirteen years ago. It's just too surreal. All of it. I think I may still be in a state of shock from everything. But speaking of George, I am guessing the government is going to seize Snapper's assets, so I want to set up a fund for George from my inheritance."

"Seriously?" Colin sounded alarmed.

"You realize that's twenty-five thousand dollars a month?"

"Yes, I do. But I haven't gone near any of the money, and given the way you've grown the stock portfolio, there's plenty of money from there alone. And this is something I want to do for Snapper, whatever he did. He was good to me. Besides, you're such an excellent businessman and investor, I expect you'll make that money back in no time," she replied lightheartedly.

"Let me work on it, CJ. I'll pull together a report of all of your assets and see what's feasible. Of course, you have enough coming in from the business to live on quite well, even if up to now you've refused to touch it."

"And why should I do so now? I have a job!" CJ rolled her eyes at Donna.

"You do realize I can see you," Colin chided her.

CJ made a goofy face as she got closer to the camera lens installed on the computer.

Colin gave her a grin but replied sternly, "Yes. I'm sure your minimum wage job is going to let you live in the lap of luxury."

"Okay. Okay. But you know I've always lived modestly. Figure out what I have and how it can be used to fund George's care. Please." She gave him her best puppy-dog look as she peered even closer.

"Of course, CJ. I take it you're going to move back to the house?" Colin was trying to get as much information as possible from this new CJ he was talking to.

"Probably. Maybe. I hadn't given it much thought. I've been trying to be Zen about things."

"Who is this person?" Colin was being facetious. "Are you sure you're not on any kind of drug? When did you get this 'live in the now' thing? Was it after that salon appointment? Maybe it was the dye they put in your hair?" Colin mimicked CJ by getting his face as close as possible to the camera on his end.

"Great. Another comedian. For real, Colin. Just figure it out for me, okay? I have no idea how long I'm going to be here, and I haven't had much time to think about what I want to do with the rest of my life. It's been a long time since I wasn't on a crazy schedule that demanded all my attention every hour of the day every day of the week. I know it seems weird, but in a good way. Kind of a vacation from some bizarre reality in which I had been living. I never had much time to think, either. It was one reaction after another. This is a refreshing change. At least for now."

"So you went from Nancy Drew to a resident of Nirvana? Is that what you're telling me?" Colin reminded her how compulsive she had been.

"Not exactly, but it is like being deposited on an island. You can't get off until someone comes to get you, so you might as well enjoy the warm days, cool evenings, and everything else to be found there. Besides, if I ever do want to open a detective agency, you'll still be my Hardy Boy, right?"

"Donna? You there?" Colin's voice went into both headsets.

"I'm here."

"Is this really CJ on the line with me?"

"I would say she is adapting extremely well. She's made a few friends, bought some clothes, works in a gallery. It's a different kind of life for her. At the very least, the pace is a snail's crawl in comparison to what she was used to." Donna was trying to reassure Colin that CJ was, in fact, doing well and not on the verge of a nervous breakdown.

CJ jumped in. "Maybe if they dragged me to Vegas or Reno or somewhere deep in the heart of Texas, I'd have a different attitude, but so far, life where I am definitely does not suck."

"Ah! Now that's the CJ I know and love."

Colin let out a huge sigh of relief. "I'll get working on the finances. Meanwhile, you keep up that great attitude. Do you know when we can talk again?"

CJ gave Donna a questioning look. "Two weeks," Donna replied.

"Sounds good. I take it I'll be notified in advance?" Colin sounded reassured.

"Yes, you will." Donna made a note on the pad in front of her.

CJ leaned into the camera one more time. "Love you, Col. Take care of yourself and *you* have some fun, too!"

"Love you too," he replied, as the lines clicked off and the monitors went dark.

"You did fine, but you still have to remember no one can know where you are." Donna was trying to be kind but firm.

"I know . . . I know. It was just so good to hear his voice and see his face that I almost forgot the rules. Sorry. I will be more mindful. Speaking of rules. What about my date with Derek on Wednesday? I let him do most of the talking the other night, but I'm going to have to offer some kind of information about me; otherwise, he may think I'm an escaped convict, or a sociopath, or something even worse!" CJ's concern was showing on her face when Donna interrupted her with a dose of reality.

"You do realize he's a sailor, right?"

"I was trying to put that on a shelf and not think about it. He's very nice, and I enjoyed his company. Besides, I won't be here very long, so it's not as if I'm picking out a china pattern or setting up a wedding registry." CJ was trying to convince both of them that she was blasé about Derek.

Donna eyed her carefully. "Interesting. He *is* handsome, and he's a terrific guy, so why not have some fun and companionship while you're here, right? We'll come up with a background story, something you'll be able to remember. We can talk about it over lunch. Okay with you?"

"Food. I wasn't kidding when I told Colin I haven't eaten this much in ages. When I was working, grabbing a bite to eat was the norm, and when I'd get home, it was so late it would be takeout. I'm surprised I haven't gained a hundred pounds!"

"It's been less than two weeks. A hundred pounds takes a few months to pack on!" Donna laughed as she patted her curvy hips.

The ride back from Portland took just under an hour, and they decided to stop on the way for a bite to eat. While they were looking at the menu, they decided to keep to the original background outline of CJ being a master's degree student studying

American art. She grew up in New York, which was true. She could talk about her childhood and mention losing her parents in an accident and having her brother raise her. Pretending her last name was Johnson would make it a little more difficult for a Google search as long as she kept specific details out of the conversation and had a new name for her brother. They decided on Kent. Easy to remember. And instead of the restaurant business, he was an insurance agent. That would be boring enough to end further inquiries. If the question came up about what she had been doing before enrolling in her master's program, she could say she was a teacher. Everyone has stories about school. She could conjure something from her experience as a student and reverse the role.

By the time they returned to Boothbay Harbor, they had enough of an easy-to-remember backstory for CJ to tell and, if necessary, embellish upon.

Later that afternoon, CJ went to the gallery to catalog the latest works of art to arrive. Maggie stopped by to let her know she would be bringing another piece to be shipped at the end of the week.

"I heard you and Derek had a bite at the

Bistro?" Maggie's curiosity was obvious.

"Yes! The food was wonderful. Ellie's handiwork, eh?" CJ wasn't immune to the subtext, so she gave Maggie what she was looking for. "And Derek is such a nice guy. And forgiving! I felt *so* stupid!" She was anticipating the next question, which, true to form for Maggie, came almost immediately.

"So, you're going to the fireworks together, huh?" Maggie leaned on the edge of a table. "It's a pretty spectacular sight." She was trying to sound casual, but her quirky side quickly got the better of her. It was also her protective side since she remembered the emotional beating Derek was supposed to have taken when Jennifer took off.

"I'm looking forward to it." CJ smiled warmly. "Your family has been so very kind and welcoming. I really appreciate it."

"So you know about that bitch Jennifer, who dumped him, right?" Maggie went straight to the point.

"Yes. How awful! But he's probably better off. If that's the kind of person she is, then he would only have gotten hurt worse down the road." CJ was trying to instill Maggie's confidence in her. "Derek deserves someone who can appreciate him the way all of you do. I can tell that by the way you treat each other. Lots of respect."

"Yeah. We're all pretty close." Maggie still had some reservations about this mysterious new woman. "So how long are you going to be here in Boothbay Harbor?"

"It's supposed to be three months max. School won't pay for any more time, and I have to turn the project in at the start of the new term." CJ was getting more comfortable with her backstory.

"Too bad you'll miss the Harbor Lights Festival for the holidays. We have Mr. and Mrs. Claus, elves, moose, lobsters, and tons more, all arriving on boats!" Maggie's voice grew louder as her enthusiasm became more and more evident. "And there are horse-drawn carriage rides, the festival of trees, a craft show, story time, a tree-lighting ceremony, and caroling." She was almost out of breath. "At the end of the day, there's a lighted-boat parade, where local captains deck their hulls with twinkling lights for a festive spin around the harbor! Derek and Randy participated last year, and the kids went crazy!"

"Wow. You should be working for the tourist board. Definitely makes me want to come back!" CJ was actually visualizing how magnificent it must be.

"Well, maybe you can. Just remember,

though, that's when Derek met you-know-who. He's still a little sore on the subject." Maggie had to take a few deep breaths to get back her wind.

"Sore on what? The festival or what's her name? Jessica?" CJ was trying to be laid-back about her query.

"Jennifreak," Maggie mocked. "I'd use the other word, but I try not to curse. I used to have such a potty mouth, but with the kids, well, you gotta be careful."

CJ chuckled. "I get your drift."

"Yeah, but anyway, last year Derek de-cided the best antidote to melancholy was to be proactive, so they decided to join in the festivities. Did him a lot of good. I could just punch her in the face. But you're right. He's better off without her, and besides, I wouldn't want that spoiled brat as a sister-in-law. It would turn the holidays into horror-days!" She laughed out loud at her own joke.

CJ laughed too. "He seems to be adjust-ing well. I mean, you wouldn't know he was a guy who had his heart smashed up. He's pretty upbeat."

"That's Derek. Always the rock, and with a smile. I once painted one with a big grin and gave it to him. I told him he could throw it at something if he wanted to get rid of his frustrations!"

"He doesn't seem the type to throw things, either." CJ was trying to learn anything she could about the man she found so fascinating and was immensely attracted to, but she was trying to be circumspect in the questions she asked.

"Derek? Oh, don't get him mad. I mean, it takes a lot to do that, but he can throw a good punch if he has to. Once in a while, some of their customers would get blotto, and he'd have to manhandle them. He's never started a fight — as far as I can remember — but if he needs to defend himself or someone else, I'd sure want to be on his side, not the other guy's!"

"I'll certainly keep that in mind." CJ told herself to remember that little nugget. "Listen, Maggie, I meant what I said earlier. I really appreciate the kindness everyone has shown me. It's not easy when you're alone."

"Sure thing! You're a pretty good sport. All that vomiting, and you hung in there!"

"I'd say Derek is the good sport here!" CJ uncharacteristically put her arm around Maggie's shoulder and gave her a quick hug. She drew back suddenly, realizing that this, too, was not usual for her, to make displays of affection. It occurred to her that she might be going through a midlife crisis even though she was well short of forty. *Maybe it's just a life-life crisis,* she thought to herself. At least it was a beautiful place to have a meltdown, if one was on the agenda. In retrospect, she considered the possibility that she was over the limit for lifetime meltdowns even though she couldn't recall ever having had one. A real one. The kind where you can't even get out of bed.

"Carolyn? Carolyn? Earth to Carolyn!" Maggie was breaking CJ's trance with her new, almost forgotten name.

"Oh, sorry. Just thinking about my family. Or lack thereof. You guys are lucky to have each other." CJ regained her composure and picked up a yellow pad and started jotting down gibberish to make it look like she was busy.

"Yes we are. And for real, if you're still here for the holidays you're most welcome to join us! Gotta run. We'll probably see you at the fireworks! Ta!"

When Maggie spun around like a whirling dervish and waltzed out the door, CJ leaned against the wall and contemplated her very cloudy future. Taking a deep breath, she decided not to think too hard. "Be Zen," she whispered out loud to herself. "Just think about the next few days and your date." A shiver went up her arms as she visualized the upcoming fireworks. Maybe there would be other fireworks after the fireworks. With that thought, another wave of goose bumps crawled up her arms.

CHAPTER 24

CJ realized she needed to do something physical, not just for the sake of keeping her size ten figure but also to clear her head and think about the future. Even though she'd promised herself she wouldn't dwell on it, she still needed to come up with some kind of plan.

She dialed Donna's number from the apartment's landline. "Hey, Donna! I think I want to start running. Can you recommend a path for me?"

"Sure. If you promise you'll come back!" Donna laughed lightly into the phone.

"Again with the jokes. You guys should do a TV show." CJ was teasing as well.

"There's the Boothbay Harbor route, a short distance as the crow flies, and mostly away from the water. Very scenic, not too difficult. Should take you a little over a half hour. How does that sound?"

"Right up my alley. Is it marked?"

"Should be easy enough for you. There's a map in the kitchen cabinet next to the fridge. Take Townsend to Pear to Union. You'll know where you are. Hard to get lost."

"Sounds good. I'll take the phone just in case. Thanks!"

"Hey, CJ, you *will* call me Thursday with the details, right?" Donna said with a conspiratorial tone to her voice.

"Of course I will! Wish me luck. I'm going to Mona's this afternoon to buy another outfit. A girl can't be caught wearing the same thing too soon!" CJ was pleased with herself and her new attitude.

"You're absolutely right! Enjoy the run, the shopping, and the fireworks . . . all of them!" It was as if Donna had read her mind from the day before.

"Ha!" CJ tried to sound like she was protesting, but she knew she couldn't fool her newfound friend. "Okay. Gotta run! For real! See you Saturday! And yes, I will call you Thursday!"

CJ pulled out the local tourist map to get her bearings. The route was easy enough to remember, and only a short distance near the water. She slipped her hair into a short ponytail, pulled on a pair of shorts, a local T-shirt, and a cap. Fitbit. Check. Secret cell phone. Check.

It had occurred to her that she hadn't gone for a run since her close call with the motorcycle, over a month ago. Even though she never found out who the jerk was, she figured Leonard Franklin must have had something to do with it even if he wasn't the one riding the bike. At least she didn't have to worry about him at the moment. Of course, she didn't know how she was going to react when she finally had to go to court, but she recalled the famous words of Scarlett O'Hara, "I'll think of it tomorrow."

As CJ jogged along the path, a sense of freedom washed over her. It was invigorating and calming at the same time. It occurred to her that she really had no obligations, no particular place to be, no one to answer to, and, fortunately, no financial worries. Her eyes welled with tears. It was bittersweet. She fought back her mood by focusing on her surroundings and fantasizing about her upcoming date.

As she was going down Commerce, she noticed what appeared to be a small stroller on the edge of the dock. It looked like something a child would use to push a doll. She squinted toward the carriage and noticed it was moving precariously toward the edge. She still couldn't quite make out what was in the stroller and ran faster toward the dock. As she drew near, she realized it was a little dog dressed in doll clothes. It was squirming to get out, which was making the buggy move.

For a moment, it seemed as if, when the stroller with the dog tumbled into the water, it did so in slow motion. CJ frantically waved her arms, yelling and pointing, but to no avail. No one could hear her yelling over the din of loud music and voices. Without thinking of her feelings about water, she made a beeline toward the water, dove in, and swam feverishly toward the struggling pup. When she had finally reached the sinking pooch, a busboy from the Dockside Grill noticed her wrestling with the stroller and trying to free the little West Highland White Terrier mix. He immediately disposed of the empty beer glasses, reached over the railing, pulled the big, round, orange life buoy off its hooks, and tossed it in her direction. Gasping for air, she pulled the dog under her arm and half paddled toward the big, round tube attached to a rope. By then, dozens of onlookers were clamoring to help, and the two were pulled to safety to a large round of applause and cheers. Both the dog and CJ were trembling — CJ from fright, and the dog trying hard to shake off the ridiculous-looking wet clothes.

Lots of voices were coming at her. "Are you okay? What happened? Is that your dog?" CJ thought she was going to faint. "Somebody grab her a towel!"

"I'm . . . I'm . . . okay. No, not my dog. Don't know whose." She was stammering. "Saw him go over."

"Wow, lady. You're some kind of hero," the pimply-faced busboy chimed in.

CJ scanned the faces in the crowd. "Whose dog is it?" No one answered. No one came forward. She clenched the dog closer and raised her voice. "Who is the owner of this dog?" Still nothing except a huge sign of appreciation from the little mutt as she licked CJ's face.

The acne-prone kid broke in again with, "Looks like he's yours now!"

The commotion continued as people pulled out their phones and started snapping photos of the heroic rescuer and the dog when she realized she needed to cover her face. She buried her nose in the dog's neck and moved through the crowd as quickly as possible. Someone offered her a chair and a beer, but she politely declined. She knew she had to get out of there pronto.

She held the dog in a manner that would

shield her from further photos as she rummaged through her pocket, hoping the phone would still be there and in working order. She managed to dial Donna's number as she worked her way out to the street.

After two rings, Donna answered. "Don't tell me you're lost!"

"No. Worse. I think I'm now the local hero." CJ's voice was quivering.

"What are you talking about? Are you okay?" Donna could sense CJ's panic.

"I think you need to come up here. I rescued a dog from drowning, and people began taking pictures. I'm a wreck." CJ was trying to sound calm, but it wasn't working. "I have this dog in my arms, and no one seems to know who the owners are. I don't know what to do."

"Okay. I'll leave in a few minutes. Go back to the apartment and take the dog with you. We'll sort it out."

CJ wrapped the dog in the towel someone had handed her and walked briskly home. Another crisis had entered her life.

When she got back to the triplex, CJ peeled off her clothes and ran a shower. As she waited for the water to warm, she also peeled the clothes off the dog. "Who on earth would have dressed you like this? And left you?" The dog began to lick her face again. "You're such a sweet little thing. I don't get it." CJ did her best to wipe the dog down. "And who dressed you in this stupid pirate outfit?" The dog gave a few quick sharp barks as if to say, "The same idiot who left me alone on the dock!"

"You really are cute." CJ shook her head in bewilderment. "What am I supposed to do with you now? Maybe your owners will come forward if someone posts that photo, which would be good for you but very bad for me." She gave the dog a hug, took a big sigh, and stepped into the shower. "Just when I thought I'd have some kind of normalcy in my not-so-normal life."

A little over an hour later, Donna knocked on the door. CJ had already poured herself a glass of wine and handed a second glass to Donna before she was inside the door. "You're gonna need this."

"What the hell happened?" Donna took the wine and swallowed half of it.

"Easy on that. It's one of the good bottles." CJ was trying to stay calm.

"I'll buy you another one. Now, tell me everything."

CJ recalled the event as Donna's eyes widened with every sentence. "So now there are photos of me with this wet dog. I tried to hide my face, but I don't know how recognizable I am."

"Son of a bitch." Donna emptied her glass and handed it to CJ for a refill. "What were you wearing?"

"A local T-shirt, shorts, and a baseball cap that had a butterfly on the brim."

"Okay. All nondescript. We'll be sure to toss those clothes."

"Does this mean I'll have to move? Again?" CJ was forlorn and close to panic. "I don't think I can handle any more upheaval."

"I'll check social media and see if anyone posts anything, which I am sure someone will. It will be a matter of how much exposure you get. Did you give anyone your name?" Donna was sounding like a US marshal.

"No. When no one came forward to claim the dog, I wrapped it in a towel, used her, it, to block my face, and made a beeline out of there."

"I'll also check the local papers to see if there's any coverage. I wonder whom the dog belongs to," Donna said almost absentmindedly. "Although Boothbay Harbor gets an influx of abandoned pets every season. It's horrible. They bring their animals with them on vacation and leave them here. People really suck sometimes."

The dog hopped on the sofa and snuggled next to CJ. "Looks like you've got a new friend." Donna reached over to stroke the damp bundle of fur. "If someone puts an ad in the paper, or notifies the authorities about a missing dog, I'll handle it. I think we have to give it a few days and the old 'wait and see.' Meanwhile, we had better get some chow for this mutt."

Donna grabbed her purse and keys and headed out the door. "I'll be back in a few. You try to relax, and I'll grab another bottle of wine. Don't worry. We'll figure this out."

CJ threw herself against the back of the sofa as her new friend climbed onto her lap. She looked the dog straight in the eye, and said in an earnest manner, "I hope you didn't ruin my date for tomorrow night." The little dog let out a slight whimper and nudged CJ's hand.

Half an hour later, Donna returned with some Blue Buffalo kibble and a bottle of Flowers Sonoma Coast Pinot Noir. As she uncorked the bottle, she turned to CJ, and said, "I called one of my colleagues, and he advised that you lay low for the next few days. Call in sick to work."

"Lay low? As in cancel my date for tomorrow night?" CJ was bordering on hysteria.

"Oh man. I forgot about that. I don't

know if that's a good idea."

"What if I get my hair done tomorrow? Make it blond-blond? It was in a ponytail, so I can wear it down." CJ was almost pleading.

"Well, you will be wearing dry clothes I assume." Donna was trying to keep CJ's spirits up but wasn't sure how things would work out if social media got ahold of the event.

"Oh please, Donna. My life has sucked for a very long time. I was *just* starting to feel like a human being. Please give me this one night. If I have to leave, I promise that I'll have my nervous breakdown afterward, not before. But after the past decade plus, and today, one more lovely evening to remember would be nice."

Donna looked at the dog, then at CJ. She wasn't sure who was begging the most.

"Fine. Just don't let Derek see that dog." With that decided, they clinked glasses and enjoyed the rest of the wine.

CHAPTER 25

Even though Derek Wellington had abandoned his political aspirations, he still took a very strong interest in the goings-on in government — locally, nationally, and internationally. He thought that perhaps one day he would decide to run for office at the state level, but that would only happen when he could afford to walk away from the family business because it was thriving and would continue to without him.

His morning routine included a short workout on his Bowflex Trainer, a shower, and a cup of New England fresh brew and the newspapers at the Java Stop. He'd bring his daily collection back to his place and scroll through the online papers as he drank his grande cup of coffee; then he would flip through the print editions.

As he picked up the *Boothbay Register,* he let out a loud "What the hell?" when he saw a photo of what looked like Carolyn clutching a wet dog. Her face was slightly obscured by the soaked mutt, but he swore he recognized the one big, round eye that was visible. He squinted at the headline: MYSTERY WOMAN SAVES MYSTERY FANCY POOCH.

A brief paragraph followed:

Tuesday afternoon, during a beer-tasting party at the Dockside Grill, a woman was pulled from the basin clutching a dog. Apparently the pooch was in a toy stroller on the deck and accidentally rolled into the water. The unidentified woman had been jogging when she saw the animal tumble into the cove and swam to its rescue. A fast-thinking busboy threw the restaurant's orange life buoy over the railing and pulled both to safety. The woman remains unidentified, and the owner of the dog also remains unknown.

Derek squinted again, trying to make out the woman's facial features.

A few blocks away, CJ was making her morning coffee and speaking to the dog as if she were having a normal conversation with another person. "I hope I don't get attached to you because the way my life is going, I'll fall in love, and someone will claim

409

you. Then I'll have another wonderful date with a really nice guy, and I'll have to move away. See what I mean? I try really hard not to think negative thoughts, but my life is just one horror show after another." Throughout her monologue, the dog sat at attention, eyes on her, tail wagging. "And stop being so damn cute!" As if on cue, the dog lifted his paw to shake hands. "Nice to meet you, but I don't even know your name. I'm CJ, but they call me Carolyn now. Long story. I'll spare you the details." CJ checked her watch. The salon Donna had recommended would be open by now, so she dialed, hoping to get an appointment as soon as possible.

"Bay Cut and Curl. Can I help you?" said the woman who answered with a New England accent.

"Hi, yes. I am in desperate need of a touch-up. Would it be possible to squeeze me in today?" CJ sounded half desperate and half beseeching.

"Well, if you can get here in fifteen minutes, I think we can get it done. How long is your hair and what do you need?" The woman already sounded weary, and it wasn't quite ten o'clock.

"Hair is to my collarbone. It's currently an ombré, from medium brown to medium blond. I'd like to go all blond. Do you think you can accommodate me?" CJ had her fingers on both hands crossed.

"Sure. I may have to remove the color. That will cost a little extra." The woman was all business.

"Whatever it takes! Thank you so much! I'll be over in a jiffy!" Delighted, CJ picked up the dog and gave her a kiss on the head. "You know, maybe you'll be my lucky charm! And you're quite lucky! Aha! That will be your name! At least for now. Or is that more of a boy's name? Whatever . . ."

CJ dialed Donna and told her she was running over to the Cut and Curl and could she come over and walk the dog? Donna was concerned about someone's recognizing the dog, but CJ reminded her that the dog had been wearing a hideous outfit and was soaking wet. Donna agreed and reminded CJ to lay as low as possible. She gave her strict instructions: If the conversation at the salon went to the rescue from the day before, she had to pretend she hadn't heard anything about it. "Act dumb."

"Thanks. You're a pal!"

CJ pulled on a pair of Capri pants, a tunic, a sun hat, and sunglasses and headed out the door.

When she arrived at the salon, she thought

411

she must have stepped into a time warp. Maybe it was supposed to look like a 1950s beauty parlor, or maybe it simply hadn't been redecorated in fifty years. In either case, CJ was relieved that no one seemed to recognize her, and the morning went by without a mention of the previous rescue. Edith, the matronly owner, was quite adept at hair color and produced a new, very blond CJ. She gave Edith a good tip, thanked her profusely for taking her on such short notice, and dashed out the door. Mission accomplished. She then headed to Mona's to pick out a few more items for her wardrobe, hoping she wouldn't have to relocate to the desert.

Earlier that morning, she phoned the gallery and told them she had a conference call with her professor and wouldn't be able to make it in that afternoon. Steve had been so impressed with her accuracy and speed that he had no problem with her missing the few hours she promised to make up at the end of the week.

When she stopped in Mona's, she felt the urge to find out more information about Jennifer, Derek's ex. But how? A new shirt! Mona carried a few items for men, particularly shirts. The male tourist clientele never seemed to pack enough, and they gladly paid full price.

"Hey, Carolyn. Nice to see you again!" Mona walked over briskly and extended her hand. "What are you in the mood for today?"

"Well. I have to share something if you promise not to tell?" CJ was being coy.

Mona leaned in conspiratorially to hear. "Do tell!"

"The other day, at the parade of schooners, I overestimated my safe consumption level. You see, I had one more Windjammer thing than I should have."

"Happens a lot," Mona offered in sympathy.

"Yes, but do the drinks end up on someone's shirt? After they've been ingested?"

CJ kept a straight face.

"Oh my goodness! You mean . . . ?"

"Yes. Projectile. I was mortified."

Mona tried to keep from laughing. "Who was the lucky recipient?"

"Derek Wellington." CJ waited a beat.

"Derek? Oh no! What did he do?"

"Got me a few napkins, went home, changed, and came back," CJ said matter-of-factly.

"How did you meet Derek?" Now Mona was the inquisitive one.

"Maggie. I met her at the gallery, and she

was kind enough to invite me to join her family for the parade. I bet she had second thoughts after my bad behavior."

"Nah. They're a good bunch. Probably the nicest people in town. Really."

"They have been lovely. So, I wanted to make it up to Derek. I certainly hope he tossed the shirt!"

"I have a few button-downs and some polo shirts. What are you interested in?"

CJ thought a moment. "You know him better than I do. What do you recommend?" She was hoping for some kind of gossip.

Mona tilted her head and whispered, "His ex-girlfriend used to work here, you know. She would buy him polo shirts with her employee discount."

"Then maybe I should get him a button-down?" CJ gave Mona a devious smile.

"Good idea. That ex was a nightmare." Mona seemed almost gleeful in her recounting of life with Jennifer. "I think the only reason she showed up to pretend to work was so she could get her discount! I felt bad for Derek, but he is so much better off without her."

"How long ago was this?" CJ pretended she didn't know much about it.

"Last summer. Such. A. Bitch. Good riddance to bad rubbish, I say." Mona gestured for CJ to follow her over to the corner where she kept the menswear. "So how long will you be in town?"

"Only until the end of the summer. That's when the grant funds expire." CJ was beginning to believe her made-up story.

"Oh, too bad. Boothbay Harbor is such a great place the entire year. Most people only think of us as the 'Boating Capital of New England,' but there is so much more to do here."

"Yes. Maggie is a great ambassador. She clued me in about the holidays. Sounds lovely."

"Well, maybe you'll come back and visit." Mona pulled a few Ralph Lauren shirts from the shelf. "I think he's a large, if I remember. Big shoulders."

"He can always exchange it, right?" CJ asked absentmindedly as her mind was engaged in imagining him bare chested.

"Of course. Do you want me to wrap it?"

"Just tissue and a shopping bag. I have to get a few things for myself, so I'm going to browse a little." CJ floated toward the maxi dresses with her head in the clouds.

"Just let me know if you need anything," Mona called out.

CJ found two beautiful pastel dresses and held each one up to her as she gazed into the mirror. Mona sidled up and made her recommendation: "Buy both. I'm not saying that because I want the sale. They're both very pretty and feminine."

"I'm so used to wearing conservative clothes" — CJ immediately caught herself — "working in academia." *That was a close call,* she thought. *Better pay attention and stop daydreaming.*

"These will look great on you. And if you change your mind after you get home, you can bring them back. How's that?" Mona was encouraging without being pushy.

"Deal!" CJ was still in a wistful mood but aware she needed to be cautious. She headed toward the accessory table and picked a pair of earrings and a bracelet to go with her new purchases. She considered another pair of sandals and a handbag, but she wasn't accustomed to spending money on clothes, let alone on herself.

Mona packed the two dresses in one bag and the shirt for Derek in another.

"I think you'll both like your purchases. Hope to see you again soon."

"Thanks, Mona!" CJ gave her a wave and strolled out the door and back to the triplex. She was feeling almost giddy, as if she had "the world on a string," to borrow a line from one of her Frank Sinatra all-time favorites.

When CJ got back to the triplex, Donna was waiting with sandwiches for them and dog biscuits for Lucky.

"Wow! Well, look at you, all blond and everything. Oh, and *two* shopping bags from Mona's! My goodness. Aren't you fancy?"

CJ started to giggle. "I had to see if I could get any more info about Jennifer, so I told Mona about spewing on Derek and wanting to buy him a new shirt. Boy, that woman was not well liked."

"You bought Derek a shirt?" Donna seemed amused.

"Well, yeah. I would imagine he would have thrown out the other one, and besides, I had to dish a little to get a little." CJ was proud of her approach.

"You obviously worked in DC. Your schmoozing skills are highly developed, aren't they?" Donna eyed her warily.

"Don't worry. I emphasized my work in academia. At least one of my skills from working in 'the swamp' is useful." She used air quotes as emphasis.

Donna went on, "I spoke to the home office. The investigation has been going on for almost two years. If the taxpayers knew how much money it was costing them to find out their representatives were profiting through illegal means, we'd be on the verge of a revolution."

"Oh please, don't get me started on government corruption. I swear, I think that learning about it is a good way of dieting. You get so sick to your stomach with stuff you hear that you have no appetite. At least that seems to have worked for me." CJ was recalling the abundance of rumors and gossip, a lot which was the truth.

"You may be out of here sooner than expected." Donna waited for a reaction. CJ was struck at how the news was both good and bad. Her charade would be over soon, but that would mean leaving a lovely place where she was actually enjoying herself. Enjoying herself for the first time in years.

"Oh," was all she could muster as she tossed the bags on the table and slumped into a chair.

"Listen, I know you've been through the mill, and Boothbay Harbor has been a port in a storm, so to speak, but you'll be able to get back to your own life." Donna was throwing all the logic she could at her newfound friend.

"But that's the problem. I had no life. And with Snapper gone, I don't even have working for him to go back to." CJ was clearly stricken. "I was actually enjoying this pretend life. I pretended I was a graduate student. Pretended I had friends. Pretended I had a date. This news sucks."

"Well, you do have friends, real ones, and you do have a date, a real one."

"What's the point? Just more things that will be taken away from me." CJ was on the verge of tears.

"Tell me about Washington. What did you do for a social life?"

"Nothing; I had none. After Kick died, I really threw myself into my work. Twelve-hour days sometimes. Friends? You can't trust anyone inside the Beltway. The only person I hung out with was Colin. As far as men? Another list of people you can't trust. Damn. Damn it all to hell." CJ buried her face in her hands.

"Take it easy." Donna put her hand on CJ's shoulder. "Maybe you can figure out a way to stay through the summer. We can't fund you, but from what I heard you and Colin discuss, I understand you are, essentially, independently wealthy. That means you can still stay here as long as you pay the rent. You could even keep the gallery job. Steve needs the help. And if you find you hate it here, then you can go back to DC. Give it some thought. Meanwhile, let's see what you have in those bags, eat some lunch, and get you ready for your big date."

CJ heaved a sigh. Maybe staying on wasn't a bad idea. She had nowhere else to go and no one to go to. She was sure Colin and Matt would be on their way into a solid relationship, so she couldn't depend on him for her sole entertainment anymore.

"Besides, we haven't heard anything about the pooch, so you have a doggy to think about!" Donna tossed Lucky a treat.

CJ bent over, picked up the dog, and gave her a big hug. "I guess you're my family now, Lucky."

"Attagirl. Let's have some lunch!"

After his morning routine, Derek headed to the small office they kept near the dock. He could see the pub where the dog rescue had occurred yesterday and wondered again what was so familiar about the woman in the photo. He went online to see if he could find any more information about the rescue, but all the photos were similar except for one where the woman's ear was slightly exposed. It had a little peak to it — not quite elfin, but definitely an unusual characteristic. *Where have I seen that before?* He tried to shake his curiosity, but he kept mulling it over in his head when it hit him.

Carolyn? A disturbing feeling came over him. He sat back in his chair and recalled their dinner. She had very little to offer as far as her background. He had done most of the talking. Replaying the evening, he tried to ferret out some detail — some information. He came up empty. *Who is Carolyn Johnson?* He promised himself he would find out. He had been played once, and even though Jennifer's deserting him was the best thing to happen to him since he had gotten involved with her, he wasn't going to let himself be played again.

As the evening drew near, CJ and Donna were all atwitter as CJ was getting ready for her date. Donna poured them each a glass of wine. "To steady your nerves."

CJ replied with, "As if I need a reason!" Both laughed, and Lucky chimed in with a *woof.* "Do you really think I could stay here? At least until the end of the summer? I need time to sort out my life, and this place gives me the space to think."

"We'll figure it out."

"What do I tell Derek?"

"You say you have to go out of town for a few days. Family stuff. Period."

"So am I going to be Carolyn Johnson forever? Will I ever have a backstory?"

"Yes. You'll be able to tell them who you are but not why you were here. We'll blend in your real life with this one. I'll coach you. Stop fretting and put on your prettiest face. You have a date with a very handsome and charming man!"

"But what about Snapper? Will I be able to tell them I worked for him?" CJ wasn't letting it go.

"Yes, but not anything further. Now stop interrogating me and get dressed!"

Donna was half kidding as she gave CJ a slight shove.

"Okay. Okay. You can be *so* bossy. Someone would think you are a US marshal, or something." CJ laughed and began her transformation into the stunning woman she had been hiding beneath the bland clothes. While she was putting on her makeup, CJ recounted the day she had gone to the salon in Washington to start her new look. "I was trying to hit my personal reset button after Snapper died. You know, new hairdo, new attitude. But then some asshole tried to kill me, and here I am."

"Well, as they say, 'You've come a long way, baby.' Even from the first night I met you with that really bad wig! Hard to believe it was just a couple of weeks ago, eh?"

"I feel like I've been on the Wild Mouse

ride at an amusement park. You know the kind, like a roller coaster but with big dips and spins? And when you get off, you puke?"

"At least you got the puking part right." Donna couldn't help herself.

"Very funny. But you know what I mean, right? It's been a crazy ride, and I'm a little dizzy."

"Don't be too dizzy. You have a big night ahead." Donna took another sip, and continued, "Derek really is a good guy. I want you both to enjoy yourselves, so forget about the trial, and forget about tomorrow — at least for tonight. Okay?"

"I will do my utmost, Marshal!" CJ gave Lucky a kiss on the head, grabbed her purse, and walked down to the garden of the triplex. She didn't want Derek to see the dog, so she would head him off before he could knock on the door.

CHAPTER 26

The breezy evening caught the hem of CJ's dress, causing the chiffon to billow and flow. She felt like a princess, a princess about to turn into a pumpkin in a couple of weeks. She silently reprimanded herself for thinking too far ahead. Maybe she would stay for a while. Maybe, just maybe, everything would be okay. She hesitated for a moment, resisting the temptation to go to a dark, negative place. "Be Zen. Go with the flow." She said it out loud.

After a few moments she spotted a tall, well-built figure approaching the patio area. She could barely catch her breath. Derek was ruggedly handsome. His green eyes sparkled against his tanned skin and sun-streaked hair. It's not that she hadn't noticed before, but the first night was filled with booze, vomit, and reticence. She had been on her guard. Tonight was different. She was free to be herself. Well, her Carolyn

Johnson self, anyway.

His stride was confident and smooth. As he grew closer, she thought her legs would buckle under. She could almost smell his masculinity and grabbed onto the picket fence to steady herself. *Easy girl.* She was so nervous she thought she might have said that out loud, and her face turned a bit red.

"Good evening." Derek's baritone sent a tremor down her bones. She thought she was going to faint.

"Good evening to you, sir." She feigned a curtsy, which brought a chuckle from both of them. She was still trying to figure out how to wipe the sweat from her palms without being too obvious. Then she remembered the handkerchief. It wasn't her mother who taught her to always carry one, but her father. And she did. After her parents passed away, she and Kick split their father's collection, and she always had one in her purse.

CJ immediately reached for the cloth before she extended her hand to greet her date. Derek gave her a peck on the cheek, which sent her reeling again. She could not remember the last time a man had this kind of effect on her, and she wasn't sure she was comfortable about it, either.

"You look lovely," Derek offered. "I like

your hair. It gives you a bit of a halo effect."

She was blushing so much that her face was getting redder by the minute. "I promise not to ruin your shirt tonight." *I'm such an idiot,* she thought to herself. *I couldn't come up with a better line?*

"I'll keep an eye on you." Derek's double entendre was lost on her. She had no clue about his suspicions. He was perfectly charming, and his follow-up thought of *whoever you are* was easily hidden amid the playful banter.

"Oh good. I think I need adult supervision." CJ's mood was light in spite of her nerves. She had forgotten the button-down she purchased earlier that day but didn't want to go back to the apartment to get it. She decided she would deliver it sometime over the next few days. That is, if all went well that evening. If not, she would have someone else deliver it.

"I don't know how adult I am, but I am a good supervisor." Derek motioned for her to put her arm through the crook of his, and she gladly obliged. They strolled into town, chatting about the Windjammer Days and all the festivities. CJ was a good audience, but Derek was determined to solve the puzzle of the mystery woman. "So, tell me, how long have you been in the art world?"

Caught a little off guard, CJ tried not to stammer. "I guess I've been in and out since my undergraduate work. But it's hard to find a good job that pays enough, so I began teaching and working on art projects when school is out." She was beginning to get comfortable about embellishing her back-story. "I'm hoping I can do more projects like this one. My goal is to visit different art colonies each summer and get someone else to pay for it!" She said it half jokingly.

"Other people's money. That's always the way to go." Derek knew firsthand about bor-rowing money, especially with the boat busi-ness. It was a constant shell game.

"Yes. But now with the cuts in the NEA and the humanities, I don't know if there will be any funding left." She suddenly re-alized she was talking politics and tried to steer away from the subject.

"Washington, DC, certainly seems discon-nected from the rest of the country. Don't you think?" Derek was quite comfortable with the subject and plodded ahead. "I know everyone says the same thing. 'Drain the swamp.' Interestingly enough, the capital was built on a swamp."

CJ had to hold her tongue and tried to

move away from that conversation.

"It *is* interesting. So, Derek, tell me more about your fishing business. Do you go out year-round?"

"We can, but it's treacherous out there in the winter, so we head south for two months and work with a few other charter companies in Florida and the Caribbean. It's the only way we can stay afloat."

"The Caribbean? That doesn't sound too bad." CJ was imagining herself on a beach with a cocktail in her hand.

"It's not." Derek smiled at her. "It took us a couple of years to figure out we were losing money up here in the winter. Maggie hates that Randy is gone, but he gets home every couple of weeks for an extended weekend."

"It's so beautiful here," she said wistfully. "But it must get pretty cold in the winter."

"Exactly. Only real diehards want to fish off the waters of Maine in the winter."

"So you're not a diehard?" CJ looked up into the pools of emerald.

"Me? No. When I left for college, it wasn't my intention to help run the family business, but after I graduated Dad hadn't been feeling well, and Randy was saddled with everything. I had to step in to help keep the family business alive."

"What were your original plans?" CJ was sincerely interested in learning about this kind, fine-looking man.

"I was planning on getting my master's in political science."

CJ almost missed a step. "Really?" she asked, with almost too much incredulity.

"Yeah. I wanted to be one of those people who wasn't a swamp thing and get into state politics, but then I realized politics was a cesspool at almost every level; and I was really needed here."

CJ was beginning to tremble.

"You okay?" Derek noticed the chill that went through her.

"Yes. Just a little chilly. I guess I should have brought a sweater or something."

"We'll be there in a couple of minutes. A glass of red wine should warm you up."

"Excellent idea. I'll stay away from those Slammers!" CJ was trying to quell her anxiety with another joke about her inability to hold her alcohol.

The patio at the restaurant was comfortably warm from the outdoor fire pits.

"This is charming," she remarked, as Derek pulled her chair out.

As Derek settled into his seat, he glanced at the wine list and ordered a bottle of Flowers Pinot Noir. He then inquired, "So tell me more about Carolyn Johnson. Where did you grow up?"

"New York. So, yes I know of 'the swamp.' Oh, you ordered a bottle of Flowers. Donna and I shared one last night." She was looking for any opportunity to change the subject.

"And how do you know Donna again?" Derek wasn't giving up.

"We met at an art gallery function." She was relieved that she could recall her imaginary backstory so quickly.

"And what made you pick Boothbay Harbor?" Derek was still prodding.

"Donna. She kept raving about what a quaint town it is and how art was a big deal here. So I applied for a grant through Pratt, and here I am." She was hoping that would end what was beginning to sound like an interrogation.

"The Pratt Institute?" Derek was even more engrossed.

"Yep." CJ was wondering how she could move on to something else. "So what's your favorite island in the Caribbean?"

"Hard to say. Barbados is great but a very long flight from here. St. Barts is fantastic, too. Jamaica is still a bit underdeveloped, which is a good thing. The mountains and foliage are breathtaking." Derek realized he was drifting to palm trees and flora. "Where do you like to go for vacation? Or do you spend all your free time working on art projects?" Again, he was trying to steer the conversation back to her.

"Funny. When I was growing up, we spent a lot of summers in the Outer Banks. My parents were killed when I was twelve, and my older brother raised me. He was busy building his business, so we didn't vacation much. He loved to sail, though, so most of the time it was hanging out at marinas." She realized she had probably said too much already.

"So you're familiar with boats?" Derek eyed her carefully.

"Yes and no. I know the difference between port and starboard, but it was my brother who was the skilled sailor."

"Sorry if this is a sore subject." Derek was annoyed with himself for bringing it up even if it was inadvertently.

"That's okay. I do miss him. A lot." CJ picked up her glass and made a toasting gesture. "Here's to sailors everywhere."

"I hope that includes me." Derek was leaning in a bit. CJ was so out of practice when it came to dating that she wasn't sure if he was flirting with her.

"I believe it does." She clinked her glass

against his.

Derek decided there had been enough Q & A for the moment. He liked this woman — mystery or not. She was pretty, bright, funny, and very easy to be with. He, too, had a hard time recalling his last pleasant experience with someone of the opposite sex.

They each ordered surf and turf, polished off the bottle of wine, and shared a dessert. "We have about an hour before the fireworks begin." Derek had glanced at his watch.

CJ was so relaxed and satiated that she had completely forgotten about the fireworks display.

"Oh goody!" She sounded almost childlike.

Derek smiled at this charming woman. "Did Maggie give you the Chamber of Commerce speech about the Harbor Lights Festival? That's another one of our big claims to fame here. And if you can't wait until December, we have Harbor Fest in September."

"Now you're starting to sound like the ambassador!" CJ teased back. "Yes, Maggie gave me the ten-second elevator pitch. Santa arrives on a boat."

"It's another full week of activities. You wonder how anyone gets any work done!"

Derek chuckled. "Oh, and a word of caution. We have a drink called Harbor Fist. One too many can knock you out!"

"I don't doubt it. But I can promise you that I won't go anywhere near one. I've learned my lesson." CJ sipped her espresso pensively. "Otherwise, it sounds fantastic. I just might have to come back for Harbor Fest, sans Fist."

"So tell me, you leave after the summer?" Derek wasn't ready to think about CJ's leaving. He wanted to get to know her better, probably *a lot* better. It wasn't just about satisfying his curiosity about the mystery surrounding this beautiful and charming woman; it was sincerely about getting to know her better.

More idle chatter followed, Derek paid the check, and they headed toward another special place Derek had picked for the fireworks. As they strolled, she resisted the temptation to take his hand but craved some physical contact. She bravely threaded her arm through his as if she needed his guidance along the path. To her delight, he not only did not resist but drew her slightly closer than when they had walked arm in arm earlier. The ease each felt in the other's company was significant. These two strang ers definitely had connected at some basic level.

Before Derek picked her up, he had left a basket with wine, glasses, and a blanket at the spot where they would watch the fireworks. As they approached the grassy area, Derek looked up and saw the Dockside Grill. It was a perfect opportunity to engage in some more detective work.

"Hey, did you hear about that dog rescue yesterday? A dog went into the drink, and a woman jumped in and saved him!"

CJ almost gagged. By the look on her face, Derek knew it was CJ in that photo. He looked her straight in the eye, and asked, "It was you, wasn't it?" He wasn't being so much accusatory but seriously inquisitive.

"Uh. Uh." She didn't know how to respond. Derek had nailed it. "Yes. It was me." She was dejected. Donna would make her leave the next day if she knew Derek had recognized her.

"So why did you bolt with the dog?" Derek was sincerely puzzled.

"It's a long story. Can we just skip it for the time being?" CJ was pleading. "When no one claimed the dog, I took off. I guess it was a bit silly, but I had to get out of there. I promise we can go into it some other time."

"Were you dodging someone? Or did you decide you needed a new pet?" Derek was half serious.

"A little bit of both, I suppose. Cute dog, though. We never had pets when we were growing up. My mother thought they were all mangy, and she didn't want pet hair on her expensive clothing."

"She sounds a bit tough. Mothers can be that way sometimes." Derek was beginning to feel the emptiness CJ had experienced for most of her life.

"Sometimes? That was her modus operandi. She was always tough. Frankly, I don't know how my father put up with her." CJ once again recalled the late-night arguments she had overheard. "But they say you shouldn't speak ill of the dead, so I'll just leave it at that."

Derek instinctively put his arm around her and gave her a tug. "If you want to spill, go ahead. You already puked on my shirt. We're best friends now!"

She leaned into him, finally able to relax against his muscled arm and shoulder. "Thanks. I appreciate that. I think I said this before, so I apologize for being redundant, but you and your family have been very kind."

"It's been a pleasure meeting you, Ms.

Johnson." Derek felt he knew enough about this woman that he needn't pry further. At least not that night.

They sat quietly for a few moments, then the fireworks display began both on the water and between the two of them. Derek gently brushed a wisp of hair from her face and brushed her cheek. He took her face between both his hands and kissed her gently on the mouth. It was a sweet kiss with the underlying urgency of passion.

CJ's legs were trembling. Her mind was exploding with thoughts and fears as quickly as her body desired pleasure. She let his soft lips explore hers as her body became flush. She knew she had to stop, but she didn't know how to slow down without upsetting either one of them. "Derek, I . . ."

He immediately interrupted. "I'm so sorry. I didn't mean to be so forward. But you look so beautiful in this light. I had a Cary Grant–Grace Kelly flashback from *To Catch a Thief.*"

They both broke out in laughter. She and Kick would have movie marathons, and Alfred Hitchcock provided many of their favorites. Quoting Grace Kelly's character, CJ replied with, "Give up, John. Admit who you are." The irony was not lost on her as she realized she was begging the question

— except it was directed at her.

She felt her face cool a bit, and her body was no longer in a state of arousal — at least for now. A relationship with this man was something she hoped she could pursue if she was able to stay in Boothbay Harbor long enough.

Derek pulled open the basket and retrieved the bottle of Moscato he had wrapped in a thermos quilt, two stemmed wineglasses, and a few chocolate truffles for dessert.

"You really know how to impress a girl." The Moscato would make it her third glass of wine that evening. They shared a bottle at the restaurant, and now this delicious after-dinner bubbly. It was dizzying, but in a good way, and she felt unencumbered. She was still aware that she was pretending to be Carolyn Johnson, just maybe not as acutely as Donna would have preferred. "You know something, Mr. Wellington? I do believe I am having an incredible evening."

"My master plan is working." Derek chortled as he leaned back and rested his elbows on the soft blanket.

CJ joined him in the reclining pose, hoping he would make another move. Or maybe not. She was confused, but also in a good way. This kind of confusion was foreign to her, but at the moment she preferred it to all the other confusion she had been experiencing. She muttered softly, "Go with the flow." Derek didn't know if that was an invitation or simply musing on Carolyn's part. Either way, he hoped he could pursue a relationship further; maybe not that night, but on nights to come.

The exploding colors were spectacular, both overhead and as reflected off the water. CJ thought she had never seen anything quite this spectacular in her life. Having Derek by her side could have accounted for a lot of it as well. So far, it had been a perfect night.

As the grand finale vaporized and flickered, Derek packed up the basket and stood. He reached down to help her up, pulling her close to him again. They embraced in a sweet, gentle way. It was comforting, with both of them understanding that they needed to take their time with this sudden attraction. It was intense. It was all the more reason to proceed with caution, especially with the prospect that she would leave though both secretly hoped she would stay.

On the walk back to the triplex, Derek picked up the dog conversation again. "So where's the pooch?"

"The what?" In her fanciful state, CJ had almost forgotten about the dog.

"Oh, my new friend, Lucky?" She broke out in a wide grin.

"Is that his name?"

"Her name. I had a hard time at first because of that hideous pirate outfit she was wearing. Imagine putting a patch over the dog's eye. No wonder she wanted to get outta Dodge!"

"A pirate outfit?" Derek was amused.

"Yes. You'd have thought a sailor suit or something. Even a mermaid if you wanted to go nautical." CJ was rather adamant about the costume.

"You have quite the opinion in dog fashion."

"She is a girl after all. I don't recall any female pirates, ever!"

"Let me disabuse you of that notion." Derek took on a professorial tone. "There was Anne Bonny, who dressed like a female, but her shipmate Mary Read masqueraded as a male. Our claim to fame is Rachel Wall. Rachel Wall was a Beacon Hill maid, and her husband, George, was a Boston fisherman. After stealing a ship at Essex, they began pirating off the Isle of Shoals. Rachel would pretend to be a damsel in distress and stand out at the mast and cry for help.

When the rescuers arrived, George and his men would kill them, rob them of all their valuables, and sink their ship. In 1782, George drowned in a storm, and Rachel was rescued. She went back to Boston and continued to steal, this time from the cabins of ships docked in Boston Harbor. She was accused and convicted of murdering a sailor and was hanged in 1789."

"Holy cow. They sure don't teach that in school! I might have paid more attention in history class if they did."

Derek laughed. "Yes, New Englanders are known for hangings and burnings — not that it's something we should be proud of!"

"Well, no, but it is fascinating."

As they strolled lazily toward the triplex CJ almost panicked, wondering what she should do to end the evening. She couldn't invite him in unless Donna had taken the dog. Now that Derek knew about her rescue accomplishment, she didn't know how she was going to break the news to Donna. She was sure Donna would have her on the first plane to Reno. As they approached the gate, CJ turned to face him. She grabbed the front of his shirt with both hands. "Wait here," she directed him with vigor.

"Yes, ma'am!" Derek gave her a salute.

She ran up the steps and retrieved the

shopping bag with the shirt. No dog was visible. She knocked softly on Donna's door. "Hey! How was your date?"

"Fantastic. Listen, I just wanted to see if you had Lucky. I wasn't sure if I should invite Derek in for a nightcap or not."

Donna nodded toward the couch. "She's snoring up a storm. No worries. I'll keep her for the night."

"Well, I don't know if it will be all night. I don't want to move that fast."

"I hear ya. Just enjoy yourself. Tomorrow is another day, Scarlett." Donna gave her a wink.

"Thanks. You're a pal." CJ turned quickly and headed back to where she had left Derek standing.

"Here. I wanted to repay you for ruining your shirt the other night." She shoved the shopping bag at him.

"What? What is this?" Derek looked skeptically at the bag from Mona's when CJ remembered his ex used to work there.

"An apology."

"For?"

"Ruining your shirt. I hope you threw it away!"

"Well, yes, but you didn't have to do this." Derek was pleased but also slightly embarrassed. It was such a thoughtful gesture, raising his opinion of her even higher.

"Oh, I think I did. At least now I can hold my head high and my booze down!"

He gave her a light kiss on the cheek, brushing his lips toward hers.

She eagerly accepted the sweetness of his mouth but was acutely aware that she had to stop. Right now! She gave him what could have been construed as a sisterly hug, but he recognized what she did — they needed to go slow.

"Thank you for a wonderful evening, Derek. I'd offer to cook for you, but I barely know my way around a microwave."

"Not to worry. This shirt is more than enough of a thank-you." He lifted her chin and gave her another luscious kiss. They looked deeply into each other's eyes. "I'll call you tomorrow if that's okay. I'd like to take you out on the boat."

CJ became alarmed. The boat thing had completely left her mind. What was she to do? "Yes, please call," was all she could muster.

"I will."

CHAPTER 27

CJ had decided not to go back to Donna's the night before, but with the dawn of a new day, she knew she had to let Donna know that Derek had found out about the dog rescue. She wanted to just savor the feelings from her romantic evening, but that wasn't going to happen. She had to tell her. A soft knock on the door made her jump slightly. She took in a deep breath and reminded herself once again of one of her favorite author's advice, "Head up, boobs out, ass in place," and marched toward the door.

Before Donna had the opportunity to say "good morning" CJ was blurting out her dilemma. "Derek knows it was me who rescued the dog. How he recognized me with my drowned-rat-looking hair, and the dog in front of my face is mind-boggling, but recognize me he did! What are we going to do?" She was almost frantic.

"Calm down. Start again." Donna was

exercising her talent at being patient and composed, while Lucky jumped excitedly at CJ.

CJ picked up the pooch and continued, "We were walking over to see the fireworks, and Derek glanced at the Dockside and asked me if I had heard about the dog rescue. Before I could mutter a word, he said, 'It was you, wasn't it?' "

"What did you say?" Donna still remained composed.

"I told him yes. Then he asked me why I bolted the scene, and I told him I really didn't want to talk about it and kind of shrugged it off. I said it was 'a long story' and we'd discuss it another time."

"Was he okay with that? I mean did he press you for more information?"

Now Donna was prodding.

"No, I changed the subject to my petless childhood and selfish mother. It sounded like he had had some issues with his mom in the past, so we moved on from there."

"Yeah, Ellie went through a bit of a bad spell when Derek was a kid but regrouped when she decided to start a business making food. Are you sure nothing else was discussed?"

"I'm sure. Nothing. Donna, it was such a great night, and I'm really torn. I like him, but I feel like I'm deceiving him. The guy already had one bitch in his life, and now I'm feeling like another one." CJ looked utterly forlorn.

"Did you tell Derek not to mention it to anyone?"

"Damn. No, I didn't. Damn. Damn. Damn it to hell." CJ was almost spitting.

"Okay, this is what we're going to do. But wait! How *was* the date?"

"Fantastic. But let's get this anxiety over with. What are we going to do?"

"*You* are going to go to the café and get him a cup of coffee and a croissant, and bring it to their little office as a token of your appreciation for a marvelous evening. Then you ask him if he can please keep quiet about the dog thing for now. You can tell him that you're avoiding an old boyfriend. He should be able to relate to that."

"Good idea! Want to walk with me? Then I can tell you about my incredible night." CJ regained her dreamy-eyed look.

"I cannot wait to hear the details. Leave nothing out, Ms. Johnson." Donna put on her authoritative voice.

"You mean like the way he kissed me?" CJ started to blush.

"Oh. My. God." Donna's delight was obvious.

"Yes, indeed." CJ checked herself in the mirror, dragged a brush through her blond locks, and swiped a dash of gloss on her lips. "Okay, Lucky, you mind the fort. We'll be back in a bit." She lifted the dog and gave her a hug and got a big lick on the cheek in return. "So much for blush."

"I think you have plenty of blush!" Donna could not resist.

As they walked toward the village, CJ gave her account of the evening: dinner, fireworks — both on the water and on the blanket — the wine, and the walk home. "I swear, Donna, I feel like I'm in high school. Not that I ever had a real boyfriend in high school. Or ever, for that matter!"

"Oh stop. You must have had a boyfriend in your life!"

"Boys, yes. Even at age thirtysomething, they're still boys. And, I haven't had anything resembling a relationship in a very long time. There's something about Derek that is so compelling — aside from those dreamy eyes and that magnificent body!"

"Hold on, sister! You didn't . . ."

"*No!* But come on. He doesn't wear sweatshirts and sweatpants. You can tell there's something good going on under those clothes!"

Donna stopped abruptly. "Are you sure

you're the same person I picked up in Harrisburg two weeks ago?"

"Yeah. Funny, isn't it? I mean how you can go from living in a horror show to a romantic date in what seems like five minutes!"

"Kinda like the weather?" Donna said absentmindedly.

"Kinda." CJ gave a girlish giggle.

They had reached the small office of Wellington and Sons Charter Boat Service when Donna asked, "Do you want me to go in with you?"

"I think I can handle this one unless you want to stop in and say hello. You know, like you and I were on our way to the café, and I suggested we bring Derek a cup?"

"Nah. I trust you. But do say hello for me," Donna said, and patted CJ on the arm. "I'll catch you for lunch, okay?"

"Sounds good." CJ nervously tapped on the door, and it swung open.

Derek jumped out of his chair. "Carolyn! So nice to see you! What brings you here? A boat ride?" Before she had a chance to answer, he followed with, "Just kidding. Well, not entirely, but if or when, you let me know!"

"Good morning." CJ ignored the last remark. "I was in the café with Donna and thought you could use a cup of coffee after all the wine we had last night." She handed him the cup. "I couldn't remember how you took your coffee. I must confess, I wasn't paying attention. Blame the wine! It's got a little cream, and I brought some packets of sugar." She reached into her pocket and presented two packets to him.

"This is perfect. Very thoughtful. Thank you. Please have a seat." He motioned to an old wooden chair next to his desk.

"Thanks. Derek, listen, I wanted to talk to you about last night."

He interrupted with, "I apologize if I came on too strong. We can blame the wine for that, too!"

"No. That's not it. You were a perfect host and gentleman. It's about the conversation we had about the dog and me. Could we keep my secret a secret for now?"

"Absolutely! I got the impression you were trying to maintain a low profile, and I don't want to blow your cover." Derek had no idea how close to the truth what he had just said was.

"Thank you. As I said, it's a long story, and I don't want to bore you with the details."

"I don't think anything you could say would be boring." He flashed that winning smile and took her hand. "You have been a delight to spend time with." CJ was waiting for the "but," but it didn't come. Instead he continued with, "I know this seems sudden, but I hope you'll consider coming back to visit in the fall."

"I would love that. Maggie has been singing the praises of Boothbay Harbor and how there's always something exciting and fun going on. I bet it's beautiful that time of year."

"Yes it is." Derek stopped abruptly, not wanting to sound too pushy. What he really wanted to say was that he wished they could spend more time together.

CJ was all atwitter and fought hard to keep herself from squirming. "Well, I should let you get to work. I have some papers to write. Thank you again for last night." She stood and gave him a peck on the cheek.

"Call you later?"

"Please do!" CJ turned and headed out as Derek stood still for a few moments, watching her float through the doorway.

Around noon, Donna returned to CJ's with lunch in hand. "How did it go with Derek?"

"Fine. I asked him to keep it between us for now, and he seemed totally fine with it. Didn't ask any more questions. So I think we're good." CJ was sure Derek would not violate her confidence.

"Excellent. I think you need to stay out of sight for at least one more day. There's been no chatter about the pooch here, so I think that incident is a distant memory for the onlookers, especially since most of them were probably a bit tipsy. Vacationers have no respect for the time of day before they start drinking." Donna was half serious, but then she became totally serious. "We need to discuss your deposition, the trial, the logistics, et cetera."

CJ knew the day was coming but was having a hard time thinking any further ahead than the next day. It was part of her new commitment to living in the present. She was also aware that giving a deposition and testifying at the trial was inevitable and that she needed to prepare. "Okay. Shoot. Bad choice of words."

"We'll drive to Portland and take a flight to DC. You'll probably be gone overnight."

"When is this fun excursion supposed to take place?" CJ's anxiety was returning.

"On Tuesday. Your deposition will be Wednesday."

"Oh. Wow. I didn't realize it was going to be that soon."

"They're trying to get the investigation

over and done with before the upcoming election, and people will start campaigning by the end of the summer." Donna was matter-of-fact.

CJ looked at Lucky, who was sitting comfortably on the sofa. "What about her? Who's going to take care of her while we're gone?"

"My brother can stop by and change the wee-wee pads and feed her. We don't want the dog seen in public. At least not for another week or so. No one has called anywhere — sheriff, vet, groomer — so whoever left her in that ridiculous outfit obviously isn't missing her. Still, we need to keep her out of sight for now. Meanwhile, you lay low today, too."

"Yeah, I told Derek and Steve I was working on a paper."

"Good thinking. So when are you and Derek getting together again?"

"He said he'd call me later. I told him I would offer to cook for him, but I barely know how to use a microwave. And I wasn't sure if having him here was off-limits."

"Tell him to bring some of Ellie's home cooking and you'll watch a movie. He already knows about the dog, so you don't have to hide her."

"I dunno if I should be alone with him."

CJ was considering the possibilities.

"Hmmmm . . . or maybe you *should*!" Donna cackled, and Lucky barked.

"See! She agrees with me!"

"It's a conspiracy!" CJ was feeling more comfortable in spite of all the chaos. "But that just might be a good idea!"

CJ fumbled through the local phone book, looking for Wellington and Sons Charter Boat Service. She put her finger on the number and dialed. Her heart was thumping so loud, she feared Derek would be able to hear it through the phone.

"Wellington," boomed his baritone, "this is Derek."

"Hey, Derek. CJ, I mean Carolyn here." She wanted to kick herself for slipping.

"Well, hello. What can I do for you, CJ?" he asked quizzically, emphasizing the CJ.

"Yeah, that's my nickname. Carolyn Johnson. CJ." She was relieved she was able to quickly recover from her faux pas.

"I like it!" Derek could not have been more charming, and CJ's knees were buckling under her.

"This may sound a little strange — and it's not exactly an invitation — but what if you brought over some of Ellie's fine cooking, I'll set the table, and we can watch a movie?" She was cringing and making a "what-in-the-hell-am-I-doing?" face at Donna.

"It is kind of a backward invitation, but I think I can wrap my head around it. When were you thinking?"

"Almost any night is good for me." CJ was shaking from nerves.

"How about Saturday? We have a charter in the morning, and I promised Randy I'd go out with them. Big spenders. Big jerks. We should be back in time for me to scrape off the smell and take a shower." She could see his winning smile as he spoke.

"Sounds like a plan. Do you have any favorite movie genres?" CJ was regaining her composure.

"A good thriller or mystery. No zombie apocalypse, please."

"No worries there. I'm not much of a horror freak, either." CJ had enough of her own personal horror show, so there was no need to watch more of it on a screen.

"Ellie will be fixing something for the charter, so I'll have her make some extra for us. Sound good?" Derek was pleased that Carolyn, aka CJ, was beginning to relax more with him, and it would be a good opportunity for them to get to know each other better.

"Sounds great! What time is good?"

"Six?"

"Excellent. See you then." CJ hung up the phone and started jumping up and down, Lucky yapping at her heels.

"Now just be careful." Donna began to give her advice.

"Oh, I will. I'm not ready for the . . . you know . . . the *thing*!

"I didn't mean *that*!" Donna laughed. "I meant, be careful what you talk about. Maybe you *should* have a big make-out session, so you can keep your mouth shut. Well, at least you won't be talking!"

CJ clasped her hand over her mouth. "Ha! Jeez, it's been so long since I've been with a man, I'm not sure I'd know what to do!" She was half serious.

"It's like riding a bike," Donna joked.

"I haven't done that in a long time, either, so let's not use it as an example!"

"You'll be fine. Relax. Remember, we're going to DC on Tuesday."

"What about my call with Colin?"

"You can call him when we're there."

"Would I be able to see him?" CJ was almost begging.

"Not sure about that. Let's take care of business first. Once you give your deposition, we'll see how much time we have."

CJ took in a long, deep breath. "I can't

believe this is happening so fast."

"What? The date or the trial?"

"Both, really. Time seems to go by faster and faster."

"It does, indeed."

On Friday, CJ spent the morning running a path that was much closer to the triplex. After lunch, she went to the gallery. It was the height of the season, and the artists were very active. She was happy to be busy, so she wouldn't focus too much on her upcoming dinner with Derek and the dreaded deposition.

On Saturday morning, she fussed about the apartment, trying to make it look a little homier. There wasn't much to work with, so she walked into the village and bought several bunches of flowers at the florist's shop and some toss pillows and candles at the general store. It was going to be her first night of entertaining a man in . . . she couldn't remember when. Maybe five years? Probably more like ten. As the day wore on, she was becoming nervous and excited, checking the clock every ten minutes. It was still early afternoon. She thought she would jump out of her skin soon.

She checked Netflix and found a couple of British mysteries; then she considered popcorn. Maybe not. It gets stuck in your teeth. She decided on cappuccino with some Baileys Irish Cream and cookies. Cookies! Damn. She had to go back out and get cookies. Checking her watch for the eighth or ninth time, she saw it was still only two o'clock. Plenty of time. Too much time.

After her second trip into the village, she began arranging the flowers, pillows, and candles. She didn't want it to look too much like a come-on, but at the very least, she wanted it to look cozy. The scented candles made it warm and inviting as she set the table. Mission accomplished.

She took a long, hot bath to try to relax as her mind spun with possible scenarios, and she argued with herself. *What if he wants to have sex? Nah. He's too polite. Yeah, but he is a man. Men like sex. Men want sex. But he doesn't seem the type that would push very hard. Hard. Now there's something we might not be able to avoid.*

CJ actually giggled at that thought, and said aloud, "Girl, you may need to use some of that soap on your brain!" Lucky gave her a curious look, to which she responded, "You just never mind. You're not old enough to know about that stuff."

The next few hours seemed to last a full decade until a knock on the door almost sent her through the ceiling. It was only five.

Derek was early. But it wasn't Derek. It was Donna.

"What's up?" CJ was curious.

"Change of plans." Donna looked serious.

"What's wrong?"

"A little glitch in the schedule."

CJ was worried that it was going to interfere with her evening with Derek.

"You know they brought Leonard Franklin into custody, right?"

"Yes, and . . . ?" CJ was about to panic.

"Well, somehow word got out in the prison that he was a pedophile."

"A pedophile? Is he really?" CJ was flabbergasted.

"Yes, he had a prior criminal history. The guy had a lot of issues besides greed. Sex offenders are always targets within prisons. When they were moving him to a different cell, he got shanked."

"What are you talking about? Shanked?" CJ's eyes grew bigger.

"Yes. You do know what that means, right?"

"Of course. Stabbed with a makeshift knife. But how? I don't understand."

"No one seems to know all the details except that, as they were moving the prisoners down the hall, someone stumbled, causing a little scuffle, and one of the prisoners stabbed him in the neck. He bled out before the medics could get to him."

"You mean he's dead?" CJ flopped down on a chair.

"Yes," Donna said matter-of-factly.

"So what does that mean?" CJ was getting more apprehensive.

"It means that you still do your deposition because they need to make the connection between Franklin and his accomplices, but afterward, you'll be free to go."

"Are you sure? I mean, we don't know if Franklin was the one who tried to kill me. What if he has others who do his dirty work?"

"The FBI is pretty sure it was Franklin who tried to run you down on the bike, and there were some latent prints on your brake lines. Enough to get a partial match. And from what little I've been told, he was the bully-kingpin of the operation."

CJ's head was spinning. She opened the bottle of the Flowers Pinot Noir she was saving for dinner and poured each of them a glass, her hands shaking.

"I . . . I . . . don't understand." She was also stuttering.

"The Bureau has enough to make the case on those it was investigating. Franklin was the link. Now he's dead, but they still need verification that he was in the Rayburn Building on more than one occasion and was seen with the other suspects."

"Or smelled with." CJ remembered the rank stench like it was in the room.

"So does this mean I don't get to come back here next week?" She was becoming alarmed.

"Only if you want to. As I said, if you want to pay for it, you can stay as long as you want."

Tears were rolling down CJ's cheeks. Too many things were happening at once. She thought she was going to fall apart.

"Don't do that. It'll make your eyes all puffy, and Derek won't see how pretty you are. Not that he hasn't noticed already." Donna gave CJ a wink and pulled her out of the chair. "Now go get ready. You have a new adventure awaiting you! Scoot!"

CJ splashed cold water on her face, blew her nose, and began applying makeup. She yelled in Donna's direction, "What should I wear?"

"Something comfortable but not *too* comfortable if you get my drift." Donna laughed, then suggested the navy-blue terry-cloth Capri pants with the matching hoodie and a lace camisole. Casual, pretty, and not sloppy. "It makes your eyes stand out. And the top has a zipper for easy removal!"

CJ blurted, "Stop! Don't even go there!"

Donna chuckled softly. "Honey, you better get used to the idea of a man's being interested in you that way. As in *all* of you, not just your mind and organizing skills."

CJ stuck her head out through the doorway, and begged, "Please stop. I'm a wreck."

"You'll be just fine. I've gotta run." Donna drank the rest of her wine and left CJ to finish her primping and the last of the wine.

This time when the knock came, CJ was ready. "As ready as I will ever be," she muttered to herself and Lucky.

Derek stood in the doorway with a thermal container, flowers, and a bottle of wine. It looked like he was the clown in a juggling act.

"Oh my goodness. Let me help you with that." CJ took the bouquet, let him in, and placed the bottle of white wine in the refrigerator.

Derek looked around the apartment. "Cozy. Very nice."

"Thanks. It was a bit austere when I first got here."

The sexual tension in the room was almost palpable. They were drawn to each other, and both were skittish.

"So, what movies did you pick out for us?"

Derek asked, breaking the awkward mood.

Trying to maintain her composure, she replied, "*The Interview* and *Exam*. That one is from Australia. Both are thriller/twisters. Is that okay with you?"

"Sounds intriguing." He gave her a smile and a wink.

"What's for dinner?" she tossed back.

"Ellie's Fisherman's Stew, complete with garlic croutons." Suddenly, Derek realized that garlic wasn't exactly the best thing for getting close to someone when CJ chimed in with, "Ooohhhh garlic. How aromatic." She was thinking along the same line.

"It's good for the heart, helps to fight colds, coughs, and also lowers blood pressure." Derek was looking for the upside of the pungent herb.

CJ laughed at his feeble attempt. "What's so funny?" he asked innocently.

"I think I have plenty of gum."

More laughter ensued, and CJ was finally starting to relax. *Focus on the now. Yeah . . . now I'm nervous.* Her mind was still racing from everything that had happened and was about to happen. Donna's news about Leonard Franklin, making a decision about whether or not to stay, and now being alone with Derek. It was unnerving. Her life seemed to be constantly unraveling, or least undergoing constant change.

The smell of the garlic hit them in the face when they walked into the living room, which brought more chuckles. CJ rummaged through a drawer and pulled out a plastic container of Orbit gum and held it up. "Life preservers."

The table had been set earlier and looked lovely, but what she really wanted to do was sit on the floor and have dinner the way she and Kick used to do. "Hey, Derek. Would you mind if we sat on the floor over by the coffee table? It's a ritual my brother and I used to have."

"Whatever floats your boat. I mean . . ." Derek realized his clever remark was probably not appropriate at the time.

"No problem, Captain." CJ was becoming used to the nautical terms and expressions.

Derek unpacked the dinner and began to fix their plates, floating a large, garlicky baguette on top of the savory stew. CJ took the place settings and arranged them on the coffee table. The aroma was indeed intoxicating. Derek retrieved the bottle of Anthony Girard, La Clef du Récit, Sancerre 2015 from the fridge and poured each of them a glass.

"A man after my own heart." She contemplated how much she really meant what she had just said and reminded herself that he had said almost the exact same thing a week earlier.

They dove into their stew like they hadn't seen food in weeks, both expressing their delight with murmurs of pleasure. "Oh my gosh! This is fantastic." CJ finally took a breath and was able to utter her appreciation.

"Yes, my mom does know how to cook. Some kind of revenge!"

"What do you mean, revenge?" CJ looked confused.

"She hated the idea that Dad and my uncle had a charter business. Then, when Randy and I came on board — pun intended — we thought she might spiral down into depression again. We don't know what the turning point was in her head, but one morning she announced she was going to start a catering business for our clientele. At first, we were skeptical, or maybe we thought she was going to poison us." He let out a short laugh. "But she was dead serious and started making boxed lunches. When that went well, she decided she wanted to be in charge of providing the daily specials to the Bistro. It kinda worked out for all of us. Granted, Dad put on a few pounds, and I have to work at keeping them off, but there's nothing like a home-cooked meal at the end of the day. Or a healthy lunch when you're out there wrestling tuna. Or a cranky customer."

The conversation was light as they mopped up their bowls with the extra bread. Derek helped CJ clear the table and do the dishes. She pulled the cookies from the bakery box, opened the Baileys, and brewed a pot of coffee.

They finally settled back to the floor and began to watch the films CJ had chosen for the evening. She marveled to herself at how comfortable it was being with Derek. It wasn't as awkward as she had feared, and she moved closer to him. He casually put his arm around her shoulder as the titles appeared on the screen. She didn't budge. Their closeness seemed quite natural. As the film progressed, they discussed the "whodunit?" plot, each giving their opinion, often with light banter as accompaniment.

At one point, Derek easily pulled her closer, turned her face toward his, and gave her a warm, deep, sensuous kiss. She returned his ardor, despite knowing it could lead to a place where she was afraid to go. *It's like riding a bike,* she thought, reminding herself of Donna's advice. But Derek wasn't quite ready to make another move. He was keenly aware that they were on the brink of deepening their relationship, and he wanted it to be special. He also wanted to be sure they were both ready to take the next step. They had known each other for such a short time, actually only a week, and even though they meshed seamlessly every time they were together, he hesitated and slowed the pace. Plus, her mysterious background was still nagging at him.

CJ felt the energy shift. "Is it my breath?" she asked in a half-joking manner.

"No! Not at all. It's just that I don't want to rush you. Or me, to be completely honest."

"Oh good. I've been thinking the same thing." CJ was also struck by how adult Derek was in his communication. Most men tried to avoid conversations about anything having to do with the emotional side of life. "I've really enjoyed the time we've spent together. But I think I've already said that."

"Yes, you have, and I as well." They each could feel the heat emanating from the other's body. "And, if you don't mind my saying so, you're a darn good kisser."

CJ began to blush the way she had the first time he kissed her. "Thank you. Please be aware that I'm not at all adverse to a good make-out session!" She could not believe she had just uttered those words. She truly was becoming someone else; but she was also beginning to like this new version of herself. She was feeling a sense of freedom that she had never known before.

Derek took that as an invitation, so he brushed the hair from her face and kissed her again, their lips lingering. But he was also very conscious of keeping his hands above her shoulders and being satisfied with the closeness they were developing. It could be the beginning of something extraordinary, and he didn't want to blow it by moving too fast. He had learned his lesson from the last romantic debacle, and he truly liked Carolyn . . . CJ . . . whatever her name was.

CHAPTER 28

CJ and Derek had spent an enjoyable night watching movies, joking, and cuddling — cuddling just enough to be at ease with each other without crossing any lines. It was too risky for both of them. There was a lot to think about. Were they both rebounding from relationships? Derek's seemed obvious to outsiders even though he was actually relieved, if somewhat embarrassed, at Jennifer's betrayal, but CJ's was multilayered. One doesn't have to have lost a romantic partner to rebound. People did it all the time without realizing they were barreling into something simply to avoid pain. It didn't matter if they lost a job, a friend, a family member, or a loved one. People experienced loss all the time, and too often had knee-jerk positive reactions to the first nice person who happened to come along. CJ had been wondering about her reaction to Derek for days. Was she attracted to him simply because he had shown her kindness given all she had lost? Was he just too good to be true? Or was it that, maybe for the first time, she had met a man with whom she could imagine having a true, and possibly lasting, relationship?

She relived every moment of the night before, from Donna's bombshell to the warmth of Derek's kiss good night. They were both flushed but, thankfully, reserved. There were plenty more days ahead to explore this newfound relationship, and CJ didn't want to become another statistic.

The few days ahead of her trip to DC required a lot of concentration and composure. Having decided to stay in Boothbay Harbor for an extended period of time, she had to put funds into a checking account so she could pay for the rental. But how? She was unclear as to whether or not she could use her real name. Donna had only given her a prepaid debit card to cover her expenses. That was temporary, and things were about to get permanent. At least for now. *How ironic,* she thought to herself. Was that even possible? *Her life was a litany of temporaries that had seemed permanent at the time. But isn't that merely a fact of life?*

She made a pot of coffee as she waited for Donna to arrive with her instructions — for next week, possibly the next year, or for however long. She scrolled through the local *Patch* on her tablet to see if there were any further developments on the missing dog. Nothing. She was relieved. She had grown fond of her new family member. They had both been lost — in different ways, to be sure, but lost nonetheless. She reached down and patted Lucky's head where she lay at her feet.

A slight rap on the door sent Lucky's ears up, and CJ answered. Donna had a three-ring binder, a bag of croissants, and two cappuccinos.

"Ah. I made a pot, but this coffeemaker is crap. I'll invest in a Nespresso as soon as this ordeal is over!" She grabbed the bag and the cups. "That looks ominous," she added, pointing to the antiquated-looking book.

"It's your dossier," Donna said plainly.

"My what?" CJ looked stupefied.

"Your history. You know what a dossier is." Donna was mildly serious.

"I do indeed. Snapper had one on me. That blew my mind."

"I'm sure it wasn't a trust issue with him. He always wanted to know every nitty-gritty detail. I don't have to tell you that."

"You're not kidding." CJ opened the lid of

the coffee and took in a deep inhale, and said, referring to the cappuccino, "Leave it to the Italians to invent such an elixir. Did you know it was created by a group of friars? The color of the espresso mixed with the steamed milk was similar to the color of their Capuchin robes. They're part of the Franciscan order of monks. Huh. I just realized St. Francis is also the patron saint of animals. See that, Lucky? St. Francis works in wonderful and mysterious ways!"

"You're chock-full of trivia today. You should go on *Jeopardy!*" Donna cleared a space on the table and plopped the tome on it.

"Not good in front of a camera. As you could see by that photo of me and Lucky."

"You were fine that day." Donna pulled out a pair of reading glasses and began thumbing through the pages.

"This looks serious. Glasses and all." CJ pulled her chair closer. "What's first?"

Donna went over the account CJ had given to the authorities about Leonard Franklin, aka Crappy Cologne. It began with the first time she had smelled and heard him in Snapper's office. CJ stopped her, and asked, "If he's dead, how can I make a clear ID?"

"We have a photo array and your statement when you picked him out of a lineup, and we also have voice recognition."

"So I'll listen to a tape?"

"Yes, they will play several versions of the same sentence. You'll pick out the one that you think is his. That way, we'll have three identifiers: photo, live, and audio."

"Too bad you don't have smell-o-vision," CJ grunted.

They spent the better part of two hours recounting the weeks of turmoil and near misses. When they got to the part about Snapper's secret condominium, CJ stiffened. "What's going to happen with all of that?"

"It's being held as evidence. Obviously, we can't prosecute the congressman now that he's dead, but if we can show a link between him, the insider-trading scam, and the secret accounts, the government will confiscate his estate."

"That doesn't seem right. I mean, he was doing it for his brother."

"But it was illegal, CJ. That's the bottom line."

CJ knew that the law was the law, but having known Snapper for as long as she did, then discovering the situation with George, her heart sank. True, Colin was working on a plan to provide the funding for George's care, so he would not go without, but the entire situation was sad. Snapper would still be alive today had he not been desperate. Some people would look the other way or throw a sibling in George's condition into the system and let the government figure out how to care for them, and pretend they didn't exist. Snapper's aims were noble, whether what he did to achieve them were legal or not.

After the run-through of the previous events, Donna began discussing how CJ could integrate herself into the community. She could retain all of her own documents such as license, voter registration, insurance ID. "No one is going to ask you for identification here. The utilities will be covered in your rent."

"What about Derek? What do I tell him?"

"You tell him nothing. At least until I give you the green light. You can fake it for the summer — just like the original plan."

"Are you sure this will be the end of my involvement? I really don't need another rug pulled out from under me." CJ was anxious to get on with her life — her new one now.

"I don't see any further complications. Lay low, do your job, and spend the time to get to know Derek better. You may end up being a permanent resident of Boothbay Harbor." Donna gave her a little elbow shove.

"I just want to get through the next few days, and then I'll be able to breathe."

Tuesday finally arrived. Donna picked up CJ, and they drove to Portland, where they boarded an Express Jet to Washington National. A car was waiting and brought them to a hotel near the J. Edgar Hoover Building. CJ was to give her deposition at nine o'clock the next morning. "Would it be possible for me to see Colin?" CJ sounded weary. He had been her stabilizing force for the past four years. She could use his support, especially having had to deal with everything surrounding the life and death of Otto "Snapper" Lewis.

"Not a good idea. We don't want anyone to know your whereabouts."

"But I thought you said I was safe now that Franklin is dead." CJ's voice was beginning to rise.

"Yes, but until the paperwork is complete, we need to keep you under wraps. It's protocol." Donna, once again, was being a US marshal.

"Yeah, yeah. Can I at least talk to him? Maybe tomorrow after I give my deposition?"

"I think we can arrange that for you." Donna's attitude softened.

They ordered lunch from room service and went through the details of her testimony one more time. CJ channel-surfed, looking for something to distract her the rest of the afternoon.

The next morning, a black sedan was waiting in the front of the hotel. Donna had given CJ another motley-looking wig for her to wear as she was getting in and out of the car.

"Is this rat's nest really necessary?" CJ gingerly took the headgear between her fingers.

"Please."

"Fine." She slapped it on her head, which made her look like one of the Beatles. "George, John, Paul, or Ringo?" She gave Donna a smirk.

"Paul was always the best-looking. Go with Paul."

They entered the building with plain-clothes security guards on each side of them, headed to the elevator, and went to the conference room where her deposition would be taken.

The questions were tedious and repetitious. CJ's memory was one of her best assets. It was a big reason she and Snapper got along so well. She was as much a stickler for detail as he was, and her recall was sharp. After almost three hours, they broke for lunch. "What about my call with Colin?" CJ was exhausted but still a little edgy.

"Coming right up." Donna led her to a room similar to the one in which she had had her previous conversation with Colin. Same routine — laptops, headsets, secret codes, then Colin's face.

"Hey!" CJ was glowing. "How are you?"

"I'm good! And you? Another new look? Blondie this time?" Colin noticed her hair first thing.

"Long story. You like it?" This time CJ was acutely aware not to reveal details as to her whereabouts and whatabouts. "So, tell me about you! What's happening with Matt?" She could tell by the look on Colin's face that the relationship had progressed a little.

"All good with him, too. Spending more time together and planning a week in St. Kitts in October."

"Ah. Planning ahead? That's promising." CJ was genuinely happy for him. They both needed companionship. She hadn't realized until recently the importance of a relationship. A romantic one, for sure. "I'm glad you guys are moving forward. You deserve it, Col."

"So do you, Nancy Drew. Maybe when all of this is over, you'll be able to find someone who will treat you the way you should be treated." Colin had hoped for a good companion for CJ for a long time — even before Kick had died. She had been married to her job, and she was hitting her midthirties. If she wanted to have a family, the clock was ticking. She deserved someone kind, generous, and smart. Most of the men she had dated were career climbers or just plain assholes.

Suddenly a sheepish grin crossed her face. "What's that smile all about?" Colin knew her too well for that to slip past him.

"Oh nothing." But the grin on her face belied her nonchalance.

"Don't you tell me 'nothing,' missy. I know you too well." Colin peered deeper into the camera lens so only his eyeball was visible.

"Let's just say I've had a couple of dates with a very nice man."

"Wow. Boy do you move fast!" Colin was stunned. CJ had rarely showed any interest in dating, and she had only been gone a few weeks.

"Yep! Remember? It's the new me!" She laughed out loud, and continued, "Let's not get crazy. It's just been a few dates."

"A few? You haven't had 'a few' dates in the past five years. And I'm talkin' cumulatively!" Colin was joking though the interesting observation was dead-on.

"Don't rub it in, buster. I'm making up for lost time. Besides, I think by now I know what I *don't* want, so that eliminates a vast majority of the male population!" Quickly changing the subject and knowing she would have to hang up soon, she continued, "Did you figure out the George thing with my finances?"

Colin smiled. "Yes. You can do it without risking your portfolio at all. I'll set up the trust. You're going to have to sign papers, though."

Donna unmuted her mic. "Give them to Matt. He'll forward them to me."

"Okay. I should have them drawn up in a few days. Thanks."

Donna motioned for her to wrap it up. "Listen, I've gotta go. I'll find out when we can talk again. Love you!"

"Love you too!" Colin signed off, and the screens went dark.

The next two hours felt like like déjà vu. The same questions were asked in a variety of ways, not necessarily to try to trick CJ but to confirm all the details. A total of five hours of what was in essence an interrogation had been grueling.

"Are we heading back tonight?" CJ longed for the calm of Boothbay Harbor and the comfort of her pooch.

Donna looked at her watch. "If the traffic isn't too bad, we can make the five-twenty American flight." She picked up the phone and called for the car. "Let's hustle. We'll still have an hour drive once we land. If all goes well we should be back by eight thirty or so. We might have to settle for prepackaged sandwiches for dinner, though."

"That's fine with me. All I want to do is take a hot bath and climb into my bed."

"Interesting. *Your* bed? Feeling more like home to you?" Donna looked pleased. She was glad CJ had decided to stay on through the summer. They had become good buddies, and Donna could use a girlfriend. In her line of work, it was hard to meet women for companionship. She was surrounded by men. Not that it was a bad thing, but there were a lot of subjects she could never discuss with her colleagues, and her schedule was erratic at best. Having family in Boothbay Harbor was a plus, and for the moment, it looked like she had a new BFF.

They both dozed on the flight back. It had been a whirlwind couple of days. Donna tried to imagine what CJ had been through, recently and over the past few years. She admired CJ for her resolve and her ability to be kind and open considering the dramas in her life. Most people would be cynical, if not absolutely miserable.

The ride home, as the sun started to set, was pleasant. "This is a beautiful part of the country," CJ said wistfully. "I was so caught up in my job that I never even took a vacation. Not in twelve years."

"Seriously?" Donna gave her a quick look.

"Yeah. Oh, I would go to Kick's cabin for a few days, but there was always something going on, even when Congress was in recess." CJ was thinking back over the years. "Snapper had no family. At least not that anyone knew of, so he was a workaholic. Kick was busy with his business — another workaholic. I guess we gravitated to each other. Is there such a thing as Workaholics Anonymous?"

"As a matter of fact there is. Started in 1983," Donna was quick to respond.

"You are a wealth of information yourself! Maybe *you* should try out for *Jeopardy!"* CJ said, throwing Donna's own comment about trivia back at her.

"Ha. Not good on camera, either."

CHAPTER 29

With the deposition behind her, CJ began making arrangements for leasing the apartment until the end of the summer. The couple who managed the triplex told her it would be cheaper if she signed a year's lease, but CJ didn't want to press her luck. What if she decided she didn't want to stay any longer? What if she and Derek ended up hating each other? What if she couldn't find another job? Not that she needed one, but she had to do something with her time. Too many "what-ifs." No, she would pay for the balance of the summer and consider her options in the fall.

The Fourth of July was right around the corner, and in true Boothbay Harbor fashion, there was a lot on the community calendar: spectacular pyrotechnics, concerts, food, and parades. She was most interested in the Horribles Parade — a satire on local politics — which had begun in 1888.

She had only seen Derek once since she got back from DC because he was out on a three-day charter trip. They had gone to dinner and walked through the village. This time, they walked hand in hand. It felt good to have a strong man by her side. It allowed her to relax and get more in touch with her feminine side, her yin energy. He kissed her softly on the lips and bid her good night at her door. She didn't invite him in, and he didn't ask. It was better this way.

As the days turned into weeks, CJ developed a routine. She was confident that she could take Lucky for short walks around the building, and Lucky seemed to be able to tell time. At 6:30 A.M., Lucky would be sitting right in front of the door with a "will you hurry up?" look on her face. After Lucky's jaunt, CJ would go for a short run in the neighborhood. Even though she was becoming more accustomed to the water, she was still a little leery about having people recognize her from the rescue incident. And she was very leery about going out on a boat. She wasn't ready for that just yet, and thankfully Derek didn't push her. Much to her delight, Derek was becoming part of her routine. Depending on his schedule, they would meet twice a week for dinner, a concert, or an exhibit. Occasionally, they would stay in and watch a movie, but the physical contact was limited to what they were comfortable with, both of them. There were a few times that she thought she would go over the edge, but Derek had a knack for knowing when to retreat. It was as if he could read her mind. *Please. Stop. Don't. Stop. Don't stop.* He wasn't being sensible just for her sake. He wanted to be sure for his own as well.

It was now mid-August, and CJ had to decide what she was going to do come end of summer. It was only three weeks away. She was grateful that her landlords hadn't pressed her for a commitment. She knew she had to go back to DC at some point. Kick's estate was just sitting there. And there were the beautiful cars in the garage. It was sinful for them to be hidden away and not driven the way they were meant to be. She knew she had to come to some decision. It had been freeing to "just be" for the last two months, but now, as the summer was drawing to an end and she had no place to be, it was time for decision-making.

Only a few days before, Donna had delivered the news that CJ would not have to return to DC to testify. Prosecutors had decided that her deposition would be enough for them to link Leonard Franklin to the targets of the FBI investigation. "Just think, in a few months, this crazy year will be behind you, Ms. Jansen . . . or Johnson. As expected, the government has confiscated Snapper's assets, so there is nothing for you to do in regard to his estate."

"It's interesting. A few months ago, I could not wait to get my old life back, but then I realized that I didn't really have one — a life. Sure, I had my work, but that's all I had, which really means I didn't have a life. And when Snapper died, there wasn't anything left. Before Kick died, I was a shadow in his life. Don't get me wrong. He didn't treat me like a shadow, but between him and Snapper, there wasn't much of *me*. Being here has been revelatory. And now I have to decide what my next move should be." CJ was somber.

"I hate to disagree with you, my friend. But I think you've already figured it out." Donna went to the cabinet and poured each of them a glass of wine. " 'Life isn't about finding yourself. Life is about creating yourself.' George Bernard Shaw. Here's to your creation!"

The next day, CJ called the property managers and said she wanted to stay on through the end of the year. Provided that things moved forward with Derek, she wanted to be there for the holiday festivities. She was feeling more confident in their burgeoning relationship, but she was still hesitant about feeling too good. That would take time and maybe some therapy, although she was not convinced her previous experience with therapy had brought her any peace of mind. She did admit she was feeling much more comfortable in her own skin now. But whether therapy had had anything to do with that, who knows.

Later that week, she and Derek were planning on having dinner at the Bistro and attending an outdoor concert. She was going to tell him that evening that she planned on staying through the holidays. She had to make a short trip to DC, but would only be gone for about ten days. She was nervous about letting him know of her decision to stay. Would he be elated or feel like she was cornering him? She resigned herself to, *Que sera, sera. I guess I'll find out one way or the other!*

It was a few days before Labor Day weekend and Harbor Fest. All along, CJ and Derek had not discussed her imminent departure. Derek had secretly hoped she would agree to return to Boothbay in the fall, and particularly for the holidays. When he thought about the time with Jennifer, which was infrequently at best, he wondered if he had ever really been in love with her in the first place. He rebuked himself for having been superficial, feeling attracted to her because she was, let's face it, absolutely gorgeous. He supposed he should send her a thank-you note for having left when she did. Had she hung around longer, he might never have met and fallen in love with Carolyn. The note would be just as simple as hers but with two words instead of one — "Thank you." He snickered at the thought.

That night, he was going to ask CJ to come back for the Boothbay Harbor Foliage Festival. It was in early October, so their time away from each other would be no more than a month. How the relationship fared after that would be a good barometer as to how strong their bond was.

He arrived around six and suggested they take his Jeep. He wanted to take her for a ride after dinner. They climbed in and headed to the Bistro.

As soon as they sat down, in unison both blurted what was on their mind. CJ said, "Derek, I'm staying through the end of the year." And Derek said, "Carolyn, please come back for the Fall Foliage Festival." Suddenly, they both stopped.

"You go first," Derek prodded.

"I've decided to stay on through the holidays. Steve said he can still use the help, and I can always finish my graduate work online."

Derek was thrilled beyond belief. "Really?"

CJ wasn't sure if that was a good really or a "you've got to be kidding" really? So she asked him. "What do you think?"

"I think I am over the moon with this development." He put his hands behind his head and leaned back in his chair.

"Oh good! I wasn't sure how you would react." CJ was matter-of-fact, not wanting to give away her insecurity.

"Well, I was going to ask you if you would come back in October for the Fall Foliage Festival, so it looks like we're on the same page." He was grinning from ear to ear.

"It would be a pleasure to accompany you, sir." CJ nodded in ladylike fashion.

In hopeful anticipation of her saying yes, Derek had dropped off a bottle of Veuve Clicquot champagne before he picked her up. The waitress was ready for his nod and brought the French bubbly to the table in an ice bucket.

"What's this?" CJ looked surprised.

"I was hoping you would say you'd come

back. I wanted to be prepared. If you didn't, then the waitress would have had a nice bottle of Veuve for herself and the staff!" Derek was almost blushing. He felt like a high-school kid who had just been told that the most popular girl in school wanted him to take her to the senior prom. One of the things that made being with Carolyn so alluring was the way it made him feel about himself, as someone on the verge of something extraordinary.

"You're quite the planner." CJ was quite impressed with his gallantry and confidence — confidence in their relationship.

"Here's to another season together." Derek looked deeply into her eyes as his glass clinked against hers.

"Indeed." CJ could barely keep her composure. "I do have some unfinished business to attend to, but I'll wait until after Harbor Fest. I'll be gone about ten days, give or take."

"I'll take whatever time you can spare." Derek was letting it all out.

"My, Mr. Wellington, I do declare you make me blush." CJ did her best Scarlett O'Hara impersonation.

"My, Ms. Johnson, you do make me tingle." Derek realized that could have been misconstrued, and added, "In the most delightful way, of course."

CJ thought for a moment about how she would tell Derek everything when the time came, but those thoughts could wait.

CHAPTER 30

A few days after Harbor Fest, CJ headed back to Washington, where she would finally face her past and embrace her future — at least the near future.

Colin had sent the paperwork regarding George's trust to Donna a few weeks before, so that had been sorted out and finalized. Now the big decision was about the house and the cars. She picked up the phone and dialed Colin's number.

"Hey! What are you up to?" Colin was sounding chipper.

"We need to talk about Kick's stuff."

"As in what kind of stuff?" Colin's voice quickly changed to apprehension.

"As in *all* of his stuff. We can't keep the Kick Museum going forever."

CJ was determined.

"Museum?" Colin was on the brink of being offended. "CJ, I never wanted it to be a museum. I thought *you* did. I never said anything because I thought it was what you wanted."

"Col, I'm sorry. I guess I didn't want to let go. But he's gone. It's been over four years now, and it's time for me to move on." CJ was being quite adult about a very emotional tie.

"Sweetie, I agree completely. I loved your brother very much, but you're right. He's gone, and we're still here. I don't think he would want us to be sitting around just looking at his stuff and memorializing him every day."

"So what should we do?" CJ was confused but persistent.

"What do you want to do? The house and the cars are worth a small fortune."

"Can you meet me at the house tomorrow night? We can discuss it over a bottle or two, wine, and cheese. And toast my brother. Okay with you?"

"Very okay with me. What time?" Colin was secretly relieved that CJ was ready to move on. Not that one can put a time line on grief, but those who are still living need to live.

"Six?"

"Sure, see you then. I'll bring the wine." Colin clicked off the phone and let out a big sigh.

CJ did the same. It was time. Time to move on. Time to get on with her life, her new life.

The following evening, Colin arrived with several bottles of wine. "Wow. I didn't think we'd need *that* much, but heck . . . start popping those corks!" CJ was taken aback that Colin had brought a half case of a variety of vintages.

"I wanted to give you options." Colin gave her a peck on the cheek.

"I appreciate it." CJ pecked him back. "You're not going to believe this, but I made dinner!"

Colin stopped in his tracks. "You're kidding, right? The woman who almost blew up the house with the microwave?"

"That would be me. But remember, I am now a different me. I fixed us a stew. Some call it bouillabaisse."

"You can't be serious. You can hardly fix toast!" Colin was mocking her in a brotherly way.

"We'll just see about that." CJ had taken Ellie's recipes with her and, for the first time, used the state-of-the-art, high-tech kitchen. "Easy-peasy."

"I'll be the judge of that." Colin was quite skeptical, but he had to admit that the aroma was enticing. "Sure smells good."

CJ scooped up the shellfish stew, put it into a soup bowl, and topped it with garlic toast.

"Where on earth did you learn how to do this?" Colin was stunned.

"A friend of mine. She caters."

Colin dipped the garlic toast into the luscious mix. "Wow. What a difference a season makes."

"Very true. There is a lot I have to tell you, but let's stick with the task at hand for now. Okay?"

"What do you mean by 'a lot'?" Colin's curiosity was growing by the second.

"Focus, bro, focus. How much is the house worth? The cars? Anything else I should know about?"

"Wow, listen to you, Miss Bossy Pants!"

"Seriously, Colin. I have some thinking and planning to do, and I want to have as much information as possible."

"Who are you?" Colin was only half joking.

"Please, Col. I'm only going to be here for about ten days, so I want to move as quickly as possible."

"Really? What's the hurry?" His interest was peaking at every word coming from CJ.

"Obviously, I have to go back until this investigation is over. But I like where I'm staying. It's a lovely town, the people are kind, and I've made some friends. Yep. Friends. Fancy that."

"And?" Colin knew there was more to this story.

"And . . ." CJ took a dramatic pause. "Well, the couple of dates I mentioned led to a few more dates, and I really like the guy! As in really, really, really like him!"

Colin broke out into the biggest smile CJ had seen from him in years. "Well, fancy that, indeed! Who is he? Details, please!"

"I'm not sure how much detail I can reveal but — are you ready for this — his family owns a charter-boat company. I know . . . I know . . . but I still haven't set foot on one . . . yet. Col, he's *so* nice, handsome, and considerate."

"Sounds too good to be true. And a little quick, don't you think?"

"I'm sure I'll find something wrong with him at some point, but until now, he's been a wonderful companion. Obviously, he doesn't know the real story of my life. And I hope when I do get to tell him, he won't walk away because I lied to him."

"Well, if he's a decent guy, he'll understand, especially if he cares about you. So what's his story? Divorced? Widowed? Never been married?"

"He had a relationship with a model for about three years, but she left him a little more than a year ago for someone with a bigger boat and a lot more money."

"You're kidding, right?"

"Nope. Anyway, we met through his sister-in-law, who is an artist at the gallery where I work. Her husband and he own two boats and seem to have a thriving business."

Colin gave CJ a big bear hug. "Wow. And by your mood, he makes you happy. So when's the big day?" He was trying to tease her but not successfully.

"Shut up. We haven't even done 'it' yet." She was beginning to blush.

"Don't apologize for that. If you remember, Matt and I took our time, too. We've discussed this before. At this point in life, caution is wise."

"Phew. I was hoping you'd have a good reaction to my news. It's a big change for me: a dog, a boyfriend, a calm life."

"Wait. A dog? What's that about? Give!"

"Yes, Lucky is her name. I rescued her from the water. She was in a small doll-type stroller and rolled off the dock."

"Wait. Water?"

"Yes, water. I was jogging and saw her tumble off the dock. No one else was paying attention, so I dove in. They pulled us up with a big orange life buoy, and no one claimed her. She's kind of a Westie mix. Sweetest thing."

"So tell me more. As much as you can. I am mystified."

With a dreamy look in her eyes, CJ began her story of how she had spent her summer vacation, from her first few days of water terror to meeting the gallery owner, puking on her soon-to-be beau, and the dog. Colin marveled at how much of a transformation had taken place over the past four months. Then he realized that he, too, had moved forward with his life. They ate, drank, talked past midnight, and never got to the business at hand. That would have to wait until the next day.

The following morning, Colin greeted CJ with fresh-brewed coffee, an assortment of baked goods, and a whole load of paperwork, neatly set out for her.

"Dining-room table? Must be serious." With a sleepy look on her face, CJ stretched and grabbed a mug.

"It is, actually. Do you want to know the bottom line figure of just the house and cars?"

"Should I be sitting down?" CJ instinctively pulled out a chair.

"The house is worth seven point three

million, and the cars are a little over one million total. So that puts the value around eight and a half million."

"Good God." Her eyes were as wide as saucers now.

Colin sat down next to her. He could see that she was trembling. "This means you can do whatever you want, wherever you want, and with whomever you want, including the boat guy."

CJ blinked for several seconds. "Okay. So if I want to continue to work part-time at the gallery and do some community projects, I can do it without breaking a sweat?"

"Not one bead of sweat, my dear. And remember, you still have a substantial income from your half ownership of KC's Hatchery. What about a place to live?"

"I don't want to get over my head just yet. I think renting is a good option for now. I can keep the place where I'm staying for as long as I want — I just have to give them two months notice."

Discussion continued, and they agreed that Colin would set up the sale of the estate, which he would invest for her, and CJ would receive a monthly deposit into her checking account for twenty-five thousand. That was more than quadruple what she had been making as Snapper's chief of staff and more than enough to live on very comfortably, especially since she knew how to live modestly and had no desire to change her lifestyle in that respect. If she stayed in Boothbay Harbor, she would almost certainly be the richest person there, but she had no intention of showing off her wealth. Even though Kick's house was paid for and the taxes were paid for out of his estate, she had still lived within her means as a government employee.

And Boothbay Harbor had a much lower cost of living, so it should be easy enough for her to live quite comfortably, work part-time at the gallery, and help with fund-raising for many of the local charities. It was a very reasonable plan. CJ's only challenge now was how to explain to Derek that she would be staying on and still keep her true identity a secret until indictments were announced. If they were announced. Everyone assured her that the investigation would end soon, indictments would be handed down, and she could resume her life. But she had no intention to return to her old life. She was intent on moving forward with the new. Sure, change was scary, but living a life of loneliness was much more frightening.

CJ was elated that she could soon begin

her new life and leave her past behind her. It was exhilarating. It would still be a while before she could get out from the shadows and tell Derek the whole story, but she could see light at the end of the tunnel, and for once, it wasn't the headlights of an oncoming train. Finally, she would be free to be her new self without concern about the person she left behind.

With the days getting shorter, the fall months moved quickly. CJ and Derek had settled into a nice routine. Their level of intimacy increased but at a snail's pace. Several times, she wondered if they would ever make love. But Derek was tender and affectionate. Affectionate to the point that she thought she would scream from desire. She wasn't sure how much longer she could hold out before she confronted him about the matter. She didn't want to bring up the subject, but it was, after all, the twenty-first century. Consenting adults did make love. Maybe he had issues? Then again, there was always that little blue pill. But she didn't want to embarrass him by asking. They would sleep in the same bed, cuddled and wrapped around each other like spoons. She could feel him against her. It drove her up the wall.

Little did she know that he wanted her as much as she wanted him, but after the Jennifer debacle he had decided to employ a six-month rule — no sex until six months of courtship. Sure, it was corny, but it avoided a lot of other issues. And a cold shower would take care of the immediate one. He thought he should tell her about his personal rule, and when he explained she was so relieved that she started to cry. "Oh my goodness, Derek. I wasn't sure what to say. There's so much passion between us, and then it's as if the train stops before reaching the station!" Realizing the clumsiness of her metaphor, they both broke out in hysterics.

He held her close and whispered, "We are going to have one serious Christmas package to open!" Again, squeals of laughter rang through the apartment, causing Lucky to bark wildly. "And you mind your own business!" Derek joked at the pooch.

The elections had come and gone without any major political upsets. One morning, during a news broadcast, the bubble-headed blond announcer said, "Today, shake-ups in Washington sent the stock market and Capitol Hill into a tailspin. Indictments were handed down for Senators Maxwell

Reemer and Henry Brigart, and Congressmen Gerard Dillard and Kenneth Freeman for insider trading, money laundering, and violations of the STOCK Act, which prohibits passing laws in order to benefit financially. The STOCK Act was signed into law by President Obama in 2012 and prohibits members of Congress and other government employees from using nonpublic information for private profit. Several months ago, the FBI gained access to the financial records of these politicians, seeking evidence about a ring of individuals engaged in the illegal financial activities for which they were indicted today. There have been rumors of involvement by Congressman Otto Lewis, but owing to his suicide earlier this year, he was not named as either a defendant or an unindicted coconspirator, and this network is unable to verify the rumors. An outside party, Leonard Franklin, was also a target of the investigation. He was killed in prison awaiting trial for breaking and entering, but he was known to many members of the House of Representatives and the Senate. The news has sent the financial market into a steep decline. More on this story later."

CJ almost dropped her coffee mug. She had

known that this day would come but had also thought she would be given a heads-up.

At the same time, Derek was in his apartment watching the same news broadcast. Thinking about Otto Lewis's suicide, he wondered if that was an admission of guilt. He Googled "Otto Lewis" and found several hundred articles about him. And some photos. He almost choked when a very familiar face appeared next to the congressman at a fund-raiser. He tried to enlarge it. It was her. Carolyn Johnson. But the name said Carol Anne Jansen and identified her as Congressman Lewis's chief of staff. *Oh my God. How is this possible?*

Derek's emotions went from shock to devastation to rage. He had known that something was amiss with her in the beginning, but their relationship had grown into something remarkable. Something special. But now? Who was this woman he had fallen in love with? He'd been played for a fool again. His first reaction was to call her, but she would probably have some kind of lie already rehearsed. He began to pace, repeatedly punching his right fist into his left palm. He grabbed his coat and burned rubber charging over to her apartment. He needed to see the look in her eyes.

"Hey! I wasn't expecting you so early!" She moved toward him to give him a kiss, but he put his hands out to block her.

"Who are you?" he demanded.

"What are you talking about?"

"You know exactly what I'm talking about, CJ, Carol Anne, or whatever the hell your name is!"

"Derek, please calm down. Sit. Please. Let me explain." CJ knew this was going to be a very difficult conversation. It was one she had known would come but hadn't quite prepared for. How do you tell the man you've fallen in love with that you've been lying about your life?

"First, let me say that I care for you very much." She tried to take his hand in hers, but he pulled away as if he had touched a hot stove.

"Derek, please. Listen to me. I was in Witness Protection. I could not tell you who I really was." There. Done. Out in the open.

"You were what?" He seemed dubious.

CJ ran through the months that had preceded her move to Maine: Snapper's suicide and how she thought it was murder; her roping Colin, her dead brother's life partner, into being a Hardy Boy to her Nancy Drew; how they uncovered Snapper's secret condo; how they learned about his brother George; and, finally, how there had been two attempts on her life. "And that's how I ended up here." She was exhausted from recalling the events of the two months before she had come to Boothbay Harbor.

"I understand how angry you must be, but I could not tell you anything. When I was away for ten days, I went to Washington because I needed to take care of some personal business, but I came back here to be with you." By now, CJ's eyes had filled with tears and they were streaming down her face, and she began to weep in earnest.

Derek could feel her pain. Her loss. Her reconciliation. CJ kept repeating through her sobs: "I'm so sorry . . . I'm so sorry. I wanted to tell you, but I couldn't. Please forgive me. Please, Derek."

His heart melted, and he drew her into his arms, brushed the tears away, held her tightly, and rocked her in his arms. "This must have been a terrible ordeal for you. I'm so sorry you had to go through all that. It's going to be okay; it's going to be okay. I promise."

He continued to stroke her hair and her face and rock her in his arms. He finally broke the long silence when he looked deeply into her eyes, and said, "So, CJ,

Carolyn, whatever you want me to call you, you know you're going to need a last name. Would Wellington work for you?"

"What?" Her sobs turned to hiccups, and she tried to speak. "What are you saying?"

"Sorry. Didn't mean to scare you! I know it's been fast, but when you feel something in your heart, and it's telling you 'it's right,' you gotta go for it."

CJ's inner self had never failed her in the past, and she wasn't going to question it this time, either. She had known since the moment when she threw up on this man's shirt that he was the kind of man she wanted to be with. Not that she was planning on a lot of vomiting; it was the calmness, kindness, and class under duress that she was looking for.

"I . . . I don't know what to say." She was trying to grasp the words Derek had said. "Marriage? Really?"

"Please say 'yes.' I know we are good together." Derek got down on one knee. "Be Mrs. Derek Wellington. You can pick whatever first name you want." He looked up at her with that alluring smile.

CJ rubbed her eyes and wiped her running nose on her sleeve. "Sorry. That's kind of gross." She tried not to stammer. "I . . . I've been on plenty of adventures this year.

Why not another?" CJ took his face in her hands, leaned over, and kissed him more deeply than ever before. Lucky was sitting nearby, tail wagging and tongue waving, and her paw up, giving them what looked like a high five!

"Wow," Derek said. "I'm *verklemmt, sopraffatto,* and over the moon!" Derek stood, picked her up, and swirled her around, with Lucky yapping at his heels.

"Now, when is this supposed to happen?" CJ asked. She knew this was something real, and her heart felt lighter than it ever had.

"Whenever you want. I don't want to rush into this, but maybe spring? That should give us time to get to know each other even better. That was the original intention of an engagement. Now people use it to register on brides-to-be Web sites!" He gave a nervous laugh.

"Well, one of the things is the three-hundred-pound gorilla in the room. You know . . . the boat thing. You never pushed me, and yet it's your life." CJ was contemplating his response.

"Boating is a vocation, not a life — unless you talk to Ellie. I think it's more of a life for Randy, but it's a business to me. Don't get me wrong. It's one I enjoy immensely. But sport fishing would keep me happy, too.

I just don't know what else I would do to make a living. At least not right now." Derek wanted CJ to know that he planned on making a life with her. Not without her. "And I will keep my promise and never try to force you into it. Whatever works for you, CJ, Carol Anne, Carolyn."

"Derek, I'm afraid that there's one more thing I have to tell you." CJ knew that if she was going to marry this man, she had to lay all her cards on the table.

Derek's face dropped.

Not sure how he would react to her next statement, she shut her eyes tightly, and said in a loud whisper, "My brother. Kick. KC's Hatchery."

"What? What does KC's Hatchery have to do with anything?" Derek was utterly confused.

"When he died, he left me everything, including a half interest in his business and an estate worth millions of dollars." CJ almost sounded apologetic.

"You mean your brother was the *K* in KC's Hatchery?"

"Yep. Derek, I'm so sorry I had to keep all of this from you."

"Is there anything else I should know?" Derek wasn't sure how to respond.

"No. I'm just your secret multimillionaire

fiancée. That is, assuming you still want to marry me."

He stroked her cheek. "Since the day you threw up on my shirt."

They decided a spring wedding would be spectacular at the Coastal Maine Botanical Gardens, when tens of thousands of tulips were in bloom. The ceremony would be followed by a dinner for family and friends, then an open house at one of the bars in town. Derek didn't want anyone to feel slighted.

After the New Year, the wedding plans were well under way. It would be the first week of April amid the glorious blooms in the gardens.

Instead of a maid of honor, she would have a man of honor: Colin. Randy would obviously be the best man. Easy.

The day of the wedding, Donna helped her to get dressed. CJ had splurged on a Vera Wang long-sleeved lace dress. It was simple and elegant and the most expensive thing she had ever bought for herself other than a car. She looked stunning.

"You okay?" Donna kept checking on CJ's state of mind.

"Yes! Why do you keep asking me?"

"It's a big day. Big! Big. Big. Big."

"I don't know who is more nervous, you or me." CJ put both hands on Donna's shoulders. "I'm so okay I don't remember when I was this okay. Okay?"

The string quartet they had engaged began to play. "We've got about ten minutes. I'll go grab Colin."

Colin was at her side in a few minutes. "You look absolutely stunning. I've never seen you glow like this. I can't wait for Matt to see you — I made sure he got a seat right in front!"

As the two of them stood together awaiting their cue, a voice from behind whispered in her ear, "Hello, my dear." Shivers went up CJ's spine, and her knees almost buckled under her. That voice. She knew that voice. She turned abruptly, almost knocking Colin over. Forty pounds lighter, heavily tanned, and sporting a finely groomed beard and mustache, the man was still immediately recognizable.

In a hushed, harsh whisper, she said, "Snapper Lewis? What the hell are you doing here? You're dead. How? Now? Why?" CJ was starting to shake uncontrollably.

"Well, someone has to walk you down the aisle." He took her arm in his, gave her a kiss on the cheek, and said, "I'll explain it all later, but for now, I'm your Uncle Leo."

He winked and guided her to the waiting groom. CJ gave Donna a "what the?" kind of look, but Donna only returned a "get going" motion with her hand.

Colin fell in step behind the two, as confused as everyone else. Derek looked like he had just stepped out of *GQ* magazine, but he also had a very perplexed expression on his face. As CJ and Snapper reached the end of the red carpet, she whispered to Derek, "Explanation to follow."

When the minister asked, "Who gives this woman to be married to this man?" Snapper answered, "I do, her Uncle Leo." CJ had to stifle a laugh.

The ceremony was short and sweet. CJ was trying very hard to concentrate on her vows. "Uncle Leo" had certainly unraveled her sense of calm, but she got through the ceremony, and before she could blink, Derek was kissing her.

As the two moved quickly past the rows of guests, Derek blurted, "Seriously? Who in the hell is Uncle Leo? And why have I never heard you mention him before?" This hardly seemed like a good way to start a marriage.

"Shush. I'll tell you in a minute. Please don't be upset. I'm just as surprised as you are." They plastered smiles on their faces as they shook hands with the exiting guests. As soon as the last one passed them, Derek grabbed CJ and Uncle Leo, dragged them into the adjacent building, and pushed them into a small restroom. The three of them could barely fit. CJ had to grab the hem of her dress and wrap it around her arm.

"What in the hell is going on?" Derek demanded.

"I'd like to know, too, Otto Lewis!" CJ was thrilled to see Snapper but stunned at the same time. "You're supposed to be dead!"

"On paper, yes, I am dead. So we need to be very careful. I turned state's evidence in return for Witness Protection."

There was a rap on the door. "It's me, Donna. Let me in!"

The three of them wiggled in order for Derek to open the door. Donna squeezed herself in with the trio. "I didn't know this was part of the wedding ceremony — spending time in the bathroom with the bride, groom, and her 'Uncle Leo.' "

"Donna, would you please explain," Otto asked calmly.

"You knew?" CJ turned to Donna.

"Well, yeah. I work for WITSEC, remember. Snapper is still in witness protection. He was always inquiring about your well-being. When I told him you were getting married, he asked if there was any way he could be here. We made the arrangements for an overnight, but he has to leave first thing in the morning."

"Reno?" CJ remembered her other option. "You have a tan and it's spring."

"Can't say. Heck, aren't you glad to see me? And that I'm not dead?" Snapper looked hurt.

"Oh, of course! I never believed that story about suicide."

Another knock on the door. This time it was Colin. "Someone is going to have to stand on the toilet if we let him in." Derek was becoming impatient. "Listen, this is supposed to be our wedding. I don't mind the reunion part, but can we take it out of the lavatory, please?" He seemed to have forgotten that it was he who had dragged CJ and "Uncle Leo" into the restroom in the first place.

It finally dawned on all of them at the same time how ridiculous it must look and how glad they were that this scene was not going to be in the photo album.

They piled out in a way that resembled a clown car at a circus. Colin was doubled over in laughter, and while Matt looked on, Colin told him, "This is the family you're getting into, so you've been warned."

Some of the guests had lingered and were very puzzled by this strange ritual of the wedding party convening in a restroom, but it was Boothbay Harbor, after all. Lots of unusual, unexpected, and delightful things happened there.

EPILOGUE

During a rare quiet moment at the reception, Snapper and Donna explained to CJ, Derek, Colin, and Matt how he had faked his own death.

CJ insisted she had combed the security cameras and was certain he had been murdered by Leonard Franklin.

Snapper explained that one night, after too many altercations with Franklin, he decided he was out. Done. He had enough money for several years of care for George stashed away, and he knew he had to stop. When he called a friend at the FBI, he was informed that he was under investigation and if he wanted to turn himself in and tell them what he knew, he could go into WIT-SEC.

The staged suicide was well planned. The cameras had been modified slightly to be able to get only a limited view of the car. Everyone on the Hill wore similar Burberry raincoats. It was, in fact, Snapper who made it look like he had hooked up a hose to the exhaust pipe. He slithered past the car, which accounted for the shadow CJ had spotted. Donna had interjected how concerned the FBI was getting with CJ's nosing around, so they sent someone to the cabin to spook her into WITSEC.

That almost sent her into a tailspin as she remembered how she had had to sneak out of Ruby Tuesday through the back door wearing a black rat's-nest wig. But she realized that they had to make all of it seem real. She would not have gone into WITSEC willingly otherwise.

Snapper gave his deposition to the FBI and was sent to parts unknown — but where he could get some sunshine. Being inside the House Office Building for most of his life had turned him ashen. And the stress was turning him red. Now the only red was from playing a lot of golf.

Shortly after the wedding, when the spring foliage was in full bloom, CJ decided it was time for her to take another big step. For the first time in almost five years, she set foot on Derek's new boat — her wedding present to him — a fifty-foot cabin cruiser christened *Lucky.*

ABOUT THE AUTHOR

Fern Michaels is the *USA Today* and *New York Times* bestselling author of the Sisterhood, Men of the Sisterhood, and Godmothers series, and dozens of other novels and novellas. There are more than ninety-five million copies of her books in print. Fern Michaels has built and funded several large day-care centers in her hometown, and she is a passionate animal lover who has outfitted police dogs across the country with special bulletproof vests. She shares her home in South Carolina with her four dogs and a resident ghost named Mary Margaret. Visit her website at fernmichaels.com.

The employees of Thorndike Press hope you have enjoyed this Large Print book. All our Thorndike, Wheeler, and Kennebec Large Print titles are designed for easy reading, and all our books are made to last. Other Thorndike Press Large Print books are available at your library, through selected bookstores, or directly from us.

For information about titles, please call:
(800) 223-1244

or visit our website at:
gale.com/thorndike

To share your comments, please write:
Publisher
Thorndike Press
10 Water St., Suite 310
Waterville, ME 04901